Dover Thrift Study Edition

Dubliners

JAMES JOYCE

DOVER PUBLICATIONS, INC.
Mineola, New York

GREEN EDITION

At Dover Publications we're committed to producing books in an earth-friendly manner and to helping our customers make greener choices.

Manufacturing books in the United States ensures compliance with strict environmental laws and eliminates the need for international freight shipping, a major contributor to global air pollution. And printing on recycled paper helps minimize our consumption of trees, water and fossil fuels.

The text of this book was printed on paper made with 30% post-consumer waste and the cover was printed on paper made with 10% post-consumer waste. At Dover, we use Environmental Defense's Paper Calculator to measure the benefits of these choices, including: the number of trees saved, gallons of water conserved, as well as air emissions and solid waste eliminated.

Please visit the product page for *Dubliners Thrift Study Edition* at www.doverpublications.com to see a detailed account of the environmental savings we've achieved over the life of this book.

Copyright

Copyright © 2011 by Dover Publications, Inc.
Pages 153–248 copyright © 1996 by Research & Education Association, Inc.
All rights reserved.

Bibliographical Note

This Dover edition, first published in 2011, is an unabridged, republication of the text of the first edition of *Dubliners,* originally published by Grant Richards, London, in 1914, plus literary analysis and perspectives from *MAXnotes® for Dubliners,* published in 1996 by Research & Education Association, Inc., Piscataway, New Jersey.

International Standard Book Number

ISBN-13: 978-0-486-47805-0
ISBN-10: 0-486-47805-X

Manufactured in the United States by Courier Corporation
47805X01
www.doverpublications.com

Publisher's Note

Combining the complete text of a classic novel or drama with a comprehensive study guide, Dover Thrift Study Editions are the most effective way to gain a thorough understanding of the major works of world literature.

The study guide features up-to-date and expert analysis of every chapter or section from the source work. Questions and fully explained answers follow, allowing readers to analyze the material critically. Character lists, author bios, and discussions of the work's historical context are also provided.

Each Dover Thrift Study Edition includes everything a student needs to prepare for homework, discussions, reports, and exams.

Contents

Dubliners

JAMES JOYCE

Contents

Contents

The Sisters

THERE WAS NO hope for him this time: it was the third stroke. Night after night I had passed the house (it was vacation time) and studied the lighted square of window: and night after night I had found it lighted in the same way, faintly and evenly. If he was dead, I thought, I would see the reflection of candles on the darkened blind for I knew that two candles must be set at the head of a corpse. He had often said to me: "I am not long for this world," and I had thought his words idle. Now I knew they were true. Every night as I gazed up at the window I said softly to myself the word paralysis. It had always sounded strangely in my ears, like the word gnomon in the Euclid and the word simony in the Catechism. But now it sounded to me like the name of some maleficent and sinful being. It filled me with fear, and yet I longed to be nearer to it and to look upon its deadly work.

Old Cotter was sitting at the fire, smoking, when I came downstairs to supper. While my aunt was ladling out my stirabout he said, as if returning to some former remark of his:

"No, I wouldn't say he was exactly . . . but there was something queer . . . there was something uncanny about him. I'll tell you my opinion. . . ."

He began to puff at his pipe, no doubt arranging his opinion in his mind. Tiresome old fool! When we knew him first he used to be rather interesting, talking of faints and worms; but I soon grew tired of him and his endless stories about the distillery.

"I have my own theory about it," he said. "I think it was one of those . . . peculiar cases. . . . But it's hard to say. . . ."

He began to puff again at his pipe without giving us his theory. My uncle saw me staring and said to me:

"Well, so your old friend is gone, you'll be sorry to hear."

"Who?" said I.

1

"Father Flynn."

"Is he dead?"

"Mr. Cotter here has just told us. He was passing by the house."

I knew that I was under observation so I continued eating as if the news had not interested me. My uncle explained to old Cotter.

"The youngster and he were great friends. The old chap taught him a great deal, mind you; and they say he had a great wish for him."

"God have mercy on his soul," said my aunt piously.

Old Cotter looked at me for a while. I felt that his little beady black eyes were examining me but I would not satisfy him by looking up from my plate. He returned to his pipe and finally spat rudely into the grate.

"I wouldn't like children of mine," he said, "to have too much to say to a man like that."

"How do you mean, Mr. Cotter?" asked my aunt.

"What I mean is," said old Cotter, "it's bad for children. My idea is: let a young lad run about and play with young lads of his own age and not be . . . Am I right, Jack?"

"That's my principle, too," said my uncle. "Let him learn to box his corner. That's what I'm always saying to that Rosicrucian there: take exercise. Why, when I was a nipper every morning of my life I had a cold bath, winter and summer. And that's what stands to me now. Education is all very fine and large. . . . Mr. Cotter might take a pick of that leg of mutton," he added to my aunt.

"No, no, not for me," said old Cotter.

My aunt brought the dish from the safe and put it on the table.

"But why do you think it's not good for children, Mr. Cotter?" she asked.

"It's bad for children," said old Cotter, "because their minds are so impressionable. When children see things like that, you know, it has an effect. . . ."

I crammed my mouth with stirabout for fear I might give utterance to my anger. Tiresome old red-nosed imbecile!

It was late when I fell asleep. Though I was angry with old Cotter for alluding to me as a child, I puzzled my head to extract meaning from his unfinished sentences. In the dark of my room I imagined that I saw again the heavy grey face of the paralytic. I drew the blankets over my head and tried to think of Christmas. But the grey face still followed me. It murmured; and I understood that it desired to confess something. I felt my soul receding into some pleasant and vicious region; and there again I found it waiting for me. It began to confess to me in a murmuring voice and I wondered why it smiled continually and why the lips were so moist with spittle. But then I remembered that it had died of paralysis and I felt that I too was smiling feebly as if to absolve the simoniac of his sin.

The next morning after breakfast I went down to look at the little house in Great Britain Street. It was an unassuming shop, registered under the vague name of *Drapery.* The drapery consisted mainly of children's bootees and umbrellas; and on ordinary days a notice used to hang in the window, saying: *Umbrellas Re-covered.* No notice was visible now for the shutters were up. A crape bouquet was tied to the door-knocker with ribbon. Two poor women and a telegram boy were reading the card pinned on the crape. I also approached and read:

July 1st, 1895
The Rev. James Flynn (formerly of S. Catherine's Church,
Meath Street), aged sixty-five years.
R. I. P.

The reading of the card persuaded me that he was dead and I was disturbed to find myself at check. Had he not been dead I would have gone into the little dark room behind the shop to find him sitting in his arm-chair by the fire, nearly smothered in his great-coat. Perhaps my aunt would have given me a packet of High Toast for him and this present would have roused him from his stupefied doze. It was always I who emptied the packet into his black snuff-box for his hands trembled too much to allow him to do this without spilling half the snuff about the floor. Even as he raised his large trembling hand to his nose little clouds of smoke dribbled through his fingers over the front of his coat. It may have been these constant showers of snuff which gave his ancient priestly garments their green faded look for the red handkerchief, blackened, as it always was, with the snuff-stains of a week, with which he tried to brush away the fallen grains, was quite inefficacious.

I wished to go in and look at him but I had not the courage to knock. I walked away slowly along the sunny side of the street, reading all the theatrical advertisements in the shop-windows as I went. I found it strange that neither I nor the day seemed in a mourning mood and I felt even annoyed at discovering in myself a sensation of freedom as if I had been freed from something by his death. I wondered at this for, as my uncle had said the night before, he had taught me a great deal. He had studied in the Irish college in Rome and he had taught me to pronounce Latin properly. He had told me stories about the catacombs and about Napoleon Bonaparte, and he had explained to me the meaning of the different ceremonies of the Mass and of the different vestments worn by the priest. Sometimes he had amused himself by putting difficult questions to me, asking me what one should do in certain circumstances or whether such and such sins were mortal or venial or only imperfections. His questions showed me how complex and mysterious were certain institutions of the Church which

I had always regarded as the simplest acts. The duties of the priest towards the Eucharist and towards the secrecy of the confessional seemed so grave to me that I wondered how anybody had ever found in himself the courage to undertake them; and I was not surprised when he told me that the fathers of the Church had written books as thick as the *Post Office Directory* and as closely printed as the law notices in the newspaper, elucidating all these intricate questions. Often when I thought of this I could make no answer or only a very foolish and halting one upon which he used to smile and nod his head twice or thrice. Sometimes he used to put me through the responses of the Mass which he had made me learn by heart; and, as I pattered, he used to smile pensively and nod his head, now and then pushing huge pinches of snuff up each nostril alternately. When he smiled he used to uncover his big discoloured teeth and let his tongue lie upon his lower lip—a habit which had made me feel uneasy in the beginning of our acquaintance before I knew him well.

As I walked along in the sun I remembered old Cotter's words and tried to remember what had happened afterwards in the dream. I remembered that I had noticed long velvet curtains and a swinging lamp of antique fashion. I felt that I had been very far away, in some land where the customs were strange—in Persia, I thought. . . . But I could not remember the end of the dream.

In the evening my aunt took me with her to visit the house of mourning. It was after sunset; but the window-panes of the houses that looked to the west reflected the tawny gold of a great bank of clouds. Nannie received us in the hall; and, as it would have been unseemly to have shouted at her, my aunt shook hands with her for all. The old woman pointed upwards interrogatively and, on my aunt's nodding, proceeded to toil up the narrow staircase before us, her bowed head being scarcely above the level of the banister-rail. At the first landing she stopped and beckoned us forward encouragingly towards the open door of the dead-room. My aunt went in and the old woman, seeing that I hesitated to enter, began to beckon to me again repeatedly with her hand.

I went in on tiptoe. The room through the lace end of the blind was suffused with dusky golden light amid which the candles looked like pale thin flames. He had been coffined. Nannie gave the lead and we three knelt down at the foot of the bed. I pretended to pray but I could not gather my thoughts because the old woman's mutterings distracted me. I noticed how clumsily her skirt was hooked at the back and how the heels of her cloth boots were trodden down all to one side. The fancy came to me that the old priest was smiling as he lay there in his coffin.

But no. When we rose and went up to the head of the bed I saw that he was not smiling. There he lay, solemn and copious, vested as for the altar, his large hands loosely retaining a chalice. His face was very truculent, grey and massive, with black cavernous nostrils and circled by a scanty white fur. There was a heavy odour in the room—the flowers.

We crossed ourselves and came away. In the little room downstairs we found Eliza seated in his arm-chair in state. I groped my way towards my usual chair in the corner while Nannie went to the sideboard and brought out a decanter of sherry and some wine-glasses. She set these on the table and invited us to take a little glass of wine. Then, at her sister's bidding, she filled out the sherry into the glasses and passed them to us. She pressed me to take some cream crackers also but I declined because I thought I would make too much noise eating them. She seemed to be somewhat disappointed at my refusal and went over quietly to the sofa where she sat down behind her sister. No one spoke: we all gazed at the empty fireplace.

My aunt waited until Eliza sighed and then said:

"Ah, well, he's gone to a better world."

Eliza sighed again and bowed her head in assent. My aunt fingered the stem of her wine-glass before sipping a little.

"Did he . . . peacefully?" she asked.

"Oh, quite peacefully, ma'am," said Eliza. "You couldn't tell when the breath went out of him. He had a beautiful death, God be praised."

"And everything . . . ?"

"Father O'Rourke was in with him a Tuesday and anointed him and prepared him and all."

"He knew then?"

"He was quite resigned."

"He looks quite resigned," said my aunt.

"That's what the woman we had in to wash him said. She said he just looked as if he was asleep, he looked that peaceful and resigned. No one would think he'd make such a beautiful corpse."

"Yes, indeed," said my aunt.

She sipped a little more from her glass and said:

"Well, Miss Flynn, at any rate it must be a great comfort for you to know that you did all you could for him. You were both very kind to him, I must say."

Eliza smoothed her dress over her knees.

"Ah, poor James!" she said. "God knows we done all we could, as poor as we are—we wouldn't see him want anything while he was in it."

Nannie had leaned her head against the sofa-pillow and seemed about to fall asleep.

"There's poor Nannie," said Eliza, looking at her, "she's wore out. All the work we had, she and me, getting in the woman to wash him and then laying him out and then the coffin and then arranging about the Mass in the chapel. Only for Father O'Rourke I don't know what we'd done at all. It was him brought us all them flowers and them two candlesticks out of the chapel and wrote out the notice for the *Freeman's General* and took charge of all the papers for the cemetery and poor James's insurance."

"Wasn't that good of him?" said my aunt.

Eliza closed her eyes and shook her head slowly.

"Ah, there's no friends like the old friends," she said, "when all is said and done, no friends that a body can trust."

"Indeed, that's true," said my aunt. "And I'm sure now that he's gone to his eternal reward he won't forget you and all your kindness to him."

"Ah, poor James!" said Eliza. "He was no great trouble to us. You wouldn't hear him in the house any more than now. Still, I know he's gone and all to that. . . ."

"It's when it's all over that you'll miss him," said my aunt.

"I know that," said Eliza. "I won't be bringing him in his cup of beef-tea any more, nor you, ma'am, sending him his snuff. Ah, poor James!"

She stopped, as if she were communing with the past and then said shrewdly:

"Mind you, I noticed there was something queer coming over him latterly. Whenever I'd bring in his soup to him there I'd find him with his breviary fallen to the floor, lying back in the chair and his mouth open."

She laid a finger against her nose and frowned: then she continued:

"But still and all he kept on saying that before the summer was over he'd go out for a drive one fine day just to see the old house again where we were all born down in Irishtown and take me and Nannie with him. If we could only get one of them new-fangled carriages that makes no noise that Father O'Rourke told him about, them with the rheumatic wheels, for the day cheap—he said, at Johnny Rush's over the way there and drive out the three of us together of a Sunday evening. He had his mind set on that. . . . Poor James!"

"The Lord have mercy on his soul!" said my aunt.

Eliza took out her handkerchief and wiped her eyes with it. Then she put it back again in her pocket and gazed into the empty grate for some time without speaking.

"He was too scrupulous always," she said. "The duties of the priesthood was too much for him. And then his life was, you might say, crossed."

"Yes," said my aunt. "He was a disappointed man. You could see that."

A silence took possession of the little room and, under cover of it, I approached the table and tasted my sherry and then returned quietly to my chair in the corner. Eliza seemed to have fallen into a deep revery. We waited respectfully for her to break the silence: and after a long pause she said slowly:

"It was that chalice he broke. . . . That was the beginning of it. Of course, they say it was all right, that it contained nothing, I mean. But still. . . . They say it was the boy's fault. But poor James was so nervous, God be merciful to him!"

"And was that it?" said my aunt. "I heard something. . . ."

Eliza nodded.

"That affected his mind," she said. "After that he began to mope by himself, talking to no one and wandering about by himself. So one night he was wanted for to go on a call and they couldn't find him anywhere. They looked high up and low down; and still they couldn't see a sight of him anywhere. So then the clerk suggested to try the chapel. So then they got the keys and opened the chapel and the clerk and Father O'Rourke and another priest that was there brought in a light for to look for him. . . . And what do you think but there he was, sitting up by himself in the dark in his confession-box, wide-awake and laughing-like softly to himself?"

She stopped suddenly as if to listen. I too listened; but there was no sound in the house: and I knew that the old priest was lying still in his coffin as we had seen him, solemn and truculent in death, an idle chalice on his breast.

Eliza resumed:

"Wide-awake and laughing-like to himself. . . . So then, of course, when they saw that, that made them think that there was something gone wrong with him. . . ."

An Encounter

It was Joe Dillon who introduced the Wild West to us. He had a little library made up of old numbers of *The Union Jack, Pluck* and *The Halfpenny Marvel.* Every evening after school we met in his back garden and arranged Indian battles. He and his fat young brother Leo, the idler, held the loft of the stable while we tried to carry it by storm; or we fought a pitched battle on the grass. But, however well we fought, we never won siege or battle and all our bouts ended with Joe Dillon's war dance of victory. His parents went to eight-o'clock mass every morning in Gardiner Street and the peaceful odour of Mrs. Dillon was prevalent in the hall of the house. But he played too fiercely for us who were younger and more timid. He looked like some kind of an Indian when he capered round the garden, an old tea-cosy on his head, beating a tin with his fist and yelling:

"Ya! yaka, yaka, yaka!"

Everyone was incredulous when it was reported that he had a vocation for the priesthood. Nevertheless it was true.

A spirit of unruliness diffused itself among us and, under its influence, differences of culture and constitution were waived. We banded ourselves together, some boldly, some in jest and some almost in fear: and of the number of these latter, the reluctant Indians who were afraid to seem studious or lacking in robustness, I was one. The adventures related in the literature of the Wild West were remote from my nature but, at least, they opened doors of escape. I liked better some American detective stories which were traversed from time to time by unkempt fierce and beautiful girls. Though there was nothing wrong in these stories and though their intention was sometimes literary they were circulated secretly at school. One day when Father Butler was hearing the four pages of Roman History clumsy Leo Dillon was discovered with a copy of *The Halfpenny Marvel.*

8

"This page or this page? This page? Now, Dillon, up! *'Hardly had the day'* . . . Go on! What day? *'Hardly had the day dawned'* . . . Have you studied it? What have you there in your pocket?"

Everyone's heart palpitated as Leo Dillon handed up the paper and everyone assumed an innocent face. Father Butler turned over the pages, frowning.

"What is this rubbish?" he said. *"The Apache Chief!* Is this what you read instead of studying your Roman History? Let me not find any more of this wretched stuff in this college. The man who wrote it, I suppose, was some wretched fellow who writes these things for a drink. I'm surprised at boys like you, educated, reading such stuff. I could understand it if you were . . . National School boys. Now, Dillon, I advise you strongly, get at your work or . . ."

This rebuke during the sober hours of school paled much of the glory of the Wild West for me and the confused puffy face of Leo Dillon awakened one of my consciences. But when the restraining influence of the school was at a distance I began to hunger again for wild sensations, for the escape which those chronicles of disorder alone seemed to offer me. The mimic warfare of the evening became at last as wearisome to me as the routine of school in the morning because I wanted real adventures to happen to myself. But real adventures, I reflected, do not happen to people who remain at home: they must be sought abroad.

The summer holidays were near at hand when I made up my mind to break out of the weariness of school-life for one day at least. With Leo Dillon and a boy named Mahony I planned a day's miching. Each of us saved up sixpence. We were to meet at ten in the morning on the Canal Bridge. Mahony's big sister was to write an excuse for him and Leo Dillon was to tell his brother to say he was sick. We arranged to go along the Wharf Road until we came to the ships, then to cross in the ferryboat and walk out to see the Pigeon House. Leo Dillon was afraid we might meet Father Butler or someone out of the college; but Mahony asked, very sensibly, what would Father Butler be doing out at the Pigeon House. We were reassured: and I brought the first stage of the plot to an end by collecting sixpence from the other two, at the same time showing them my own sixpence. When we were making the last arrangements on the eve we were all vaguely excited. We shook hands, laughing, and Mahony said:

"Till to-morrow, mates!"

That night I slept badly. In the morning I was first-comer to the bridge as I lived nearest. I hid my books in the long grass near the ashpit at the end of the garden where nobody ever came and hurried along the canal bank. It was a mild sunny morning in the first week of June. I sat up on the coping of the bridge admiring my frail canvas shoes which I had diligently pipeclayed overnight and watching the docile horses pulling a tramload of business people up the hill. All the branches of the tall trees which lined the mall were gay with little light green leaves and the sunlight slanted through them on to the water. The granite stone of the bridge was beginning to be warm and I began to pat it with my hands in time to an air in my head. I was very happy.

When I had been sitting there for five or ten minutes I saw Mahony's grey suit approaching. He came up the hill, smiling, and clambered up beside me on the bridge. While we were waiting he brought out the catapult which bulged from his inner pocket and explained some improvements which he had made in it. I asked him why he had brought it and he told me he had brought it to have some gas with the birds. Mahony used slang freely, and spoke of Father Butler as Old Bunser. We waited on for a quarter of an hour more but still there was no sign of Leo Dillon. Mahony, at last, jumped down and said:

"Come along. I knew Fatty'd funk it."

"And his sixpence . . . ?" I said.

"That's forfeit," said Mahony. "And so much the better for us—a bob and a tanner instead of a bob."

We walked along the North Strand Road till we came to the Vitriol Works and then turned to the right along the Wharf Road. Mahony began to play the Indian as soon as we were out of public sight. He chased a crowd of ragged girls, brandishing his unloaded catapult and, when two ragged boys began, out of chivalry, to fling stones at us, he proposed that we should charge them. I objected that the boys were too small, and so we walked on, the ragged troop screaming after us: "*Swaddlers! Swaddlers!*" thinking that we were Protestants because Mahony, who was dark-complexioned, wore the silver badge of a cricket club in his cap. When we came to the Smoothing Iron we arranged a siege; but it was a failure because you must have at least three. We revenged ourselves on Leo Dillon by saying what a funk he was and guessing how many he would get at three o'clock from Mr. Ryan.

We came then near the river. We spent a long time walking about the noisy streets flanked by high stone walls, watching the working of cranes and engines and often being shouted at for our immobility by the drivers of groaning carts. It was noon when we reached the quays and, as all the labourers seemed to be eating their lunches, we bought two big currant buns and sat down to eat them on some metal piping beside the river. We pleased ourselves with the spectacle of Dublin's commerce—the barges signalled from far away by their curls of woolly smoke, the brown fishing fleet beyond Ringsend, the big white sailing-vessel which was being discharged on the opposite quay. Mahony said it would be right skit to run away to sea on one of those big ships and even I, looking at the high masts, saw, or imagined, the geography which had been scantily dosed to me at school gradually taking substance under my eyes. School and home seemed to recede from us and their influences upon us seemed to wane.

We crossed the Liffey in the ferryboat, paying our toll to be transported in the company of two labourers and a little Jew with a bag. We were serious to the point of solemnity, but once during the short voyage our eyes met and we laughed. When we landed we watched the discharging of the graceful three-master which we had observed from the other quay. Some bystander said that she was a Norwegian vessel. I went to the stern and tried to decipher the legend upon it but, failing to do so, I came back and examined the foreign sailors to see had any of them green eyes for I had some confused notion. . . . The sailors' eyes were blue and grey and even black. The only sailor whose eyes could have been called green was a tall man who amused the crowd on the quay by calling out cheerfully every time the planks fell:

"All right! All right!"

When we were tired of this sight we wandered slowly into Ringsend. The day had grown sultry, and in the windows of the grocers' shops musty biscuits lay bleaching. We bought some biscuits and chocolate which we ate sedulously as we wandered through the squalid streets where the families of the fishermen live. We could find no dairy and so we went into a huckster's shop and bought a bottle of raspberry lemonade each. Refreshed by this, Mahony chased a cat down a lane, but the cat escaped into a wide field. We both felt rather tired and when we reached the field we made at once for a sloping bank over the ridge of which we could see the Dodder.

It was too late and we were too tired to carry out our project of visiting the Pigeon House. We had to be home before four o'clock lest our adventure should be discovered. Mahony looked regretfully at his catapult and I had to suggest going home by train before he regained any cheerfulness. The sun went in behind some clouds and left us to our jaded thoughts and the crumbs of our provisions.

There was nobody but ourselves in the field. When we had lain on the bank for some time without speaking I saw a man approaching from the far end of the field. I watched him lazily as I chewed one of those green stems on which girls tell fortunes. He came along by the bank slowly. He walked with one hand upon his hip and in the other hand he held a stick with which he tapped the turf lightly. He was shabbily dressed in a suit of greenish-black and wore what we used to call a jerry hat with a high crown. He seemed to be fairly old for his moustache was ashen-grey. When he passed at our feet he glanced up at us quickly and then continued his way. We followed him with our eyes and saw that when he had gone on for perhaps fifty paces he turned about and began to retrace his steps. He walked towards us very slowly, always tapping the ground with his stick, so slowly that I thought he was looking for something in the grass.

He stopped when he came level with us and bade us good-day. We answered him and he sat down beside us on the slope slowly and with great care. He began to talk of the weather, saying that it would be a very hot summer and adding that the seasons had changed greatly since he was a boy—a long time ago. He said that the happiest time of one's life was undoubtedly one's schoolboy days and that he would give anything to be young again. While he expressed these sentiments which bored us a little we kept silent. Then he began to talk of school and of books. He asked us whether we had read the poetry of Thomas Moore or the works of Sir Walter Scott and Lord Lytton. I pretended that I had read every book he mentioned so that in the end he said:

"Ah, I can see you are a bookworm like myself. Now," he added, pointing to Mahony who was regarding us with open eyes, "he is different; he goes in for games."

He said he had all Sir Walter Scott's works and all Lord Lytton's works at home and never tired of reading them. "Of course," he said, "there were some of Lord Lytton's works which boys couldn't read." Mahony asked why couldn't boys read them—a question which agitated and pained me because I was afraid the man would think I was as stupid as Mahony. The man, however, only smiled. I saw that he had great gaps in his mouth between his yellow teeth. Then he asked us which of us had the most sweethearts. Mahony mentioned lightly that he had three totties. The man asked me how many I had. I answered that I had none. He did not believe me and said he was sure I must have one. I was silent.

"Tell us," said Mahony pertly to the man, "how many have you yourself?"

The man smiled as before and said that when he was our age he had lots of sweethearts.

"Every boy," he said, "has a little sweetheart."

His attitude on this point struck me as strangely liberal in a man of his age. In my heart I thought that what he said about boys and sweethearts was reasonable. But I disliked the words in his mouth and I wondered why he shivered once or twice as if he feared something or felt a sudden chill. As he proceeded I noticed that his accent was good. He began to speak to us about girls, saying what nice soft hair they had and how soft their hands were and how all girls were not so good as they seemed to be if one only knew. There was nothing he liked, he said, so much as looking at a nice young girl, at her nice white hands and her beautiful soft hair. He gave me the impression that he was repeating something which he had learned by heart or that, magnetised by some words of his own speech, his mind was slowly circling round and round in the same orbit. At times he spoke as if he were simply alluding to some fact that everybody knew, and at times he lowered his voice and spoke mysteriously as if he were telling us something secret which he did not wish others to overhear. He repeated his phrases over and over again, varying them and surrounding them with his monotonous voice. I continued to gaze towards the foot of the slope, listening to him.

After a long while his monologue paused. He stood up slowly, saying that he had to leave us for a minute or so, a few minutes, and, without changing the direction of my gaze, I saw him walking slowly away from us towards the near end of the field. We remained silent when he had gone. After a silence of a few minutes I heard Mahony exclaim:

"I say! Look what he's doing!"

As I neither answered nor raised my eyes Mahony exclaimed again:

"I say . . . He's a queer old josser!"

"In case he asks us for our names," I said, "let you be Murphy and I'll be Smith."

We said nothing further to each other. I was still considering whether I would go away or not when the man came back and sat down beside us again. Hardly had he sat down when Mahony, catching sight of the cat which had escaped him, sprang up and pursued her across the field. The man and I watched the chase. The cat escaped once more and Mahony began to throw stones at the wall she had escaladed. Desisting from this, he began to wander about the far end of the field, aimlessly.

After an interval the man spoke to me. He said that my friend was a very rough boy and asked did he get whipped often at school. I was going to reply indignantly that we were not National School boys to be whipped, as he called it; but I remained silent. He began to speak on the subject of chastising boys. His mind, as if magnetised again by his speech, seemed to circle slowly round and round its new centre. He said that when boys were that kind they ought to be whipped and well whipped. When a boy was rough and unruly there was nothing would do him any good but a good sound whipping. A slap on the hand or a box on the ear was no good: what he wanted was to get a nice warm whipping. I was surprised at this sentiment and involuntarily glanced up at his face. As I did so I met the gaze of a pair of bottle-green eyes peering at me from under a twitching forehead. I turned my eyes away again.

The man continued his monologue. He seemed to have forgotten his recent liberalism. He said that if ever he found a boy talking to girls or having a girl for a sweetheart he would whip him and whip him; and that would teach him not to be talking to girls. And if a boy had a girl for a sweetheart and told lies about it then he would give him such a whipping as no boy ever got in this world. He said that there was nothing in this world he would like so well as that. He described to me how he would whip such a boy as if he were unfolding some elaborate mystery. He would love that, he said, better than anything in this world; and his voice, as he led me monotonously through the mystery, grew almost affectionate and seemed to plead with me that I should understand him.

I waited till his monologue paused again. Then I stood up abruptly. Lest I should betray my agitation I delayed a few moments pretending to fix my shoe properly and then, saying that I was obliged to go, I bade him good-day. I went up the slope calmly but my heart was beating quickly with fear that he would seize me by the ankles. When I reached the top of the slope I turned round and, without looking at him, called loudly across the field:

"Murphy!"

My voice had an accent of forced bravery in it and I was ashamed of my paltry stratagem. I had to call the name again before Mahony saw me and hallooed in answer. How my heart beat as he came running across the field to me! He ran as if to bring me aid. And I was penitent; for in my heart I had always despised him a little.

Araby

NORTH RICHMOND STREET, being blind, was a quiet street except at the hour when the Christian Brothers' School set the boys free. An uninhabited house of two storeys stood at the blind end, detached from its neighbours in a square ground. The other houses of the street, conscious of decent lives within them, gazed at one another with brown imperturbable faces.

The former tenant of our house, a priest, had died in the back drawing-room. Air, musty from having been long enclosed, hung in all the rooms, and the waste room behind the kitchen was littered with old useless papers. Among these I found a few paper-covered books, the pages of which were curled and damp: *The Abbot*, by Walter Scott, *The Devout Communicant* and *The Memoirs of Vidocq*. I liked the last best because its leaves were yellow. The wild garden behind the house contained a central apple-tree and a few straggling bushes under one of which I found the late tenant's rusty bicycle-pump. He had been a very charitable priest; in his will he had left all his money to institutions and the furniture of his house to his sister.

When the short days of winter came dusk fell before we had well eaten our dinners. When we met in the street the houses had grown sombre. The space of sky above us was the colour of ever-changing violet and towards it the lamps of the street lifted their feeble lanterns. The cold air stung us and we played till our bodies glowed. Our shouts echoed in the silent street. The career of our play brought us through the dark muddy lanes behind the houses where we ran the gauntlet of the rough tribes from the cottages, to the back doors of the dark dripping gardens where odours arose from the ashpits, to the dark odorous stables where a coachman smoothed and combed the horse or shook music from the buckled harness. When we returned to the street light from the kitchen windows had filled the areas. If my uncle was seen turning the corner we hid in the shadow until we had seen him safely housed. Or if Mangan's sister came out on the doorstep to call her brother in to his tea we watched her from our shadow peer up and down the street. We waited to see whether she would remain or go in and, if she remained, we left our shadow and walked up to Mangan's steps resignedly. She was waiting for us, her figure defined by the light from the half-opened door. Her brother always teased her before he obeyed and I stood by the railings looking at her. Her dress swung as she moved her body and the soft rope of her hair tossed from side to side.

Every morning I lay on the floor in the front parlour watching her door. The blind was pulled down to within an inch of the sash so that I could not be seen. When she came out on the doorstep my heart leaped. I ran to the hall, seized my books and followed her. I kept her brown figure always in my eye and, when we came near the point at which our ways diverged, I quickened my pace and passed her. This happened morning after morning. I had never spoken to her, except for a few casual words, and yet her name was like a summons to all my foolish blood.

Her image accompanied me even in places the most hostile to romance. On Saturday evenings when my aunt went marketing I had to go to carry some of the parcels. We walked through the flaring streets, jostled by drunken men and bargaining women, amid the curses of labourers, the shrill litanies of shop-boys who stood on guard by the barrels of pigs' cheeks, the nasal chanting of street-singers, who sang a *come-all-you* about O'Donovan Rossa, or a ballad about the troubles in our native land. These noises converged in a single sensation of life for me: I imagined that I bore my chalice safely through a throng of foes. Her name sprang to my lips at moments in strange prayers and praises which I myself did not understand. My eyes were often full of tears (I could not tell why) and at times a flood from my heart seemed to pour itself out into my bosom. I thought little of the future. I did not know whether I would ever speak to her or not or, if I spoke to her, how I could tell her of my confused adoration. But my body was like a harp and her words and gestures were like fingers running upon the wires.

One evening I went into the back drawing-room in which the priest had died. It was a dark rainy evening and there was no sound in the house. Through one of the broken panes I heard the rain impinge upon the earth, the fine incessant needles of water playing in the sodden beds. Some distant lamp or lighted window gleamed below me. I was thankful that I could see so little. All my senses seemed to desire to veil themselves and, feeling that I was about to slip from them, I pressed the palms of my hands together until they trembled, murmuring: *"O love! O love!"* many times.

At last she spoke to me. When she addressed the first words to me I was so confused that I did not know what to answer. She asked me was I going to *Araby.* I forgot whether I answered yes or no. It would be a splendid bazaar, she said she would love to go.

"And why can't you?" I asked.

While she spoke she turned a silver bracelet round and round her wrist. She could not go, she said, because there would be a retreat that week in her convent. Her brother and two other boys were fighting for their caps and I was alone at the railings. She held one of the spikes, bowing her head towards me. The light from the lamp opposite our door caught the white curve of her neck, lit up her hair that rested there and, falling, lit up the hand upon the railing. It fell over one side of her dress and caught the white border of a petticoat, just visible as she stood at ease.

"It's well for you," she said.

"If I go," I said, "I will bring you something."

What innumerable follies laid waste my waking and sleeping thoughts after that evening! I wished to annihilate the tedious intervening days. I chafed against the work of school. At night in my bedroom and by day in the classroom her image came between me and the page I strove to read. The syllables of the word *Araby* were called to me through the silence in which my soul luxuriated and cast an Eastern enchantment over me. I asked for leave to go to the bazaar on Saturday night. My aunt was surprised and hoped it was not some Freemason affair. I answered few questions in class. I watched my master's face pass from amiability to sternness; he hoped I was not beginning to idle. I could not call my wandering thoughts together. I had hardly any patience with the serious work of life which, now that it stood between me and my desire, seemed to me child's play, ugly monotonous child's play.

On Saturday morning I reminded my uncle that I wished to go to the bazaar in the evening. He was fussing at the hallstand, looking for the hat-brush, and answered me curtly:

"Yes, boy, I know."

As he was in the hall I could not go into the front parlour and lie at the window. I left the house in bad humour and walked slowly towards the school. The air was pitilessly raw and already my heart misgave me.

When I came home to dinner my uncle had not yet been home. Still it was early. I sat staring at the clock for some time and, when its ticking began to irritate me, I left the room. I mounted the staircase and gained the upper part of the house. The high cold empty gloomy rooms liberated me and I went from room to room singing. From the front window I saw my companions playing below in the street. Their cries reached me weakened and indistinct and, leaning my forehead against the cool glass, I looked over at the dark house where she lived. I may have stood there for an hour, seeing nothing but the brown-clad figure cast by my imagination, touched discreetly by the lamplight at the curved neck, at the hand upon the railings and at the border below the dress.

When I came downstairs again I found Mrs. Mercer sitting at the fire. She was an old garrulous woman, a pawnbroker's widow, who collected used stamps for some pious purpose. I had to endure the gossip of the tea-table. The meal was prolonged beyond an hour and still my uncle did not come. Mrs. Mercer stood up to go: she was sorry she couldn't wait any longer, but it was after eight o'clock and she did not like to be out late, as the night air was bad for her. When she had gone I began to walk up and down the room, clenching my fists. My aunt said:

"I'm afraid you may put off your bazaar for this night of Our Lord."

At nine o'clock I heard my uncle's latchkey in the hall-door. I heard him talking to himself and heard the hallstand rocking when it had received the weight of his overcoat. I could interpret these signs. When he was midway through his dinner I asked him to give me the money to go to the bazaar. He had forgotten.

"The people are in bed and after their first sleep now," he said.

I did not smile. My aunt said to him energetically:

"Can't you give him the money and let him go? You've kept him late enough as it is."

My uncle said he was very sorry he had forgotten. He said he believed in the old saying: "All work and no play makes Jack a dull boy." He asked me where I was going and, when I had told him a second time he asked me did I know *The Arab's Farewell to his Steed*. When I left the kitchen he was about to recite the opening lines of the piece to my aunt.

I held a florin tightly in my hand as I strode down Buckingham Street towards the station. The sight of the streets thronged with buyers and glaring with gas recalled to me the purpose of my journey. I took my seat in a third-class carriage of a deserted train. After an intolerable delay the train moved out of the station slowly. It crept onward among ruinous houses and over the twinkling river. At Westland Row Station a crowd of people pressed to the carriage doors; but the porters moved them back, saying that it was a special train for the bazaar. I remained alone in the bare carriage. In a few minutes the train drew up beside an improvised wooden platform. I passed out on to the road and saw by the lighted dial of a clock that it was ten minutes to ten. In front of me was a large building which displayed the magical name.

I could not find any sixpenny entrance and, fearing that the bazaar would be closed, I passed in quickly through a turnstile, handing a shilling to a weary-looking man. I found myself in a big hall girdled at half its height by a gallery. Nearly all the stalls were closed and the greater part of the hall was in darkness. I recognised a silence like that which pervades a church after a service. I walked into the centre of the bazaar timidly. A few people were gathered about the stalls which were still open. Before a curtain, over which the words *Café Chantant* were written in coloured lamps, two men were counting money on a salver. I listened to the fall of the coins.

Remembering with difficulty why I had come I went over to one of the stalls and examined porcelain vases and flowered tea-sets. At the door of the stall a young lady was talking and laughing with two young gentlemen. I remarked their English accents and listened vaguely to their conversation.

"O, I never said such a thing!"

"O, but you did!"

"O, but I didn't!"

"Didn't she say that?"

"Yes. I heard her."

"O, there's a . . . fib!"

Observing me the young lady came over and asked me did I wish to buy anything. The tone of her voice was not encouraging; she seemed to have spoken to me out of a sense of duty. I looked humbly at the great jars that stood like eastern guards at either side of the dark entrance to the stall and murmured:

"No, thank you."

The young lady changed the position of one of the vases and went back to the two young men. They began to talk of the same subject. Once or twice the young lady glanced at me over her shoulder.

I lingered before her stall, though I knew my stay was useless, to make my interest in her wares seem the more real. Then I turned away slowly and walked down the middle of the bazaar. I allowed the two pennies to fall against the sixpence in my pocket. I heard a voice call from one end of the gallery that the light was out. The upper part of the hall was now completely dark.

Gazing up into the darkness I saw myself as a creature driven and derided by vanity; and my eyes burned with anguish and anger.

Eveline

SHE SAT AT the window watching the evening invade the avenue. Her head was leaned against the window curtains and in her nostrils was the odour of dusty cretonne. She was tired.

Few people passed. The man out of the last house passed on his way home; she heard his footsteps clacking along the concrete pavement and afterwards crunching on the cinder path before the new red houses. One time there used to be a field there in which they used to play every evening with other people's children. Then a man from Belfast bought the field and built houses in it—not like their little brown houses but bright brick houses with shining roofs. The children of the avenue used to play together in that field—the Devines, the Waters, the Dunns, little Keogh the cripple, she and her brothers and sisters. Ernest, however, never played: he was too grown up. Her father used often to hunt them in out of the field with his blackthorn stick; but usually little Keogh used to keep *nix* and call out when he saw her father coming. Still they seemed to have been rather happy then. Her father was not so bad then; and besides, her mother was alive. That was a long time ago; she and her brothers and sisters were all grown up; her mother was dead. Tizzie Dunn was dead, too, and the Waters had gone back to England. Everything changes. Now she was going to go away like the others, to leave her home.

Home! She looked round the room, reviewing all its familiar objects which she had dusted once a week for so many years, wondering where on earth all the dust came from. Perhaps she would never see again those familiar objects from which she had never dreamed of being divided. And yet during all those years she had never found out the name of the priest whose yellowing photograph hung on the wall above the broken harmonium beside the coloured print of the promises made to Blessed Margaret Mary Alacoque. He had been a school friend of her father. Whenever he showed the photograph to a visitor her father used to pass it with a casual word:

"He is in Melbourne now."

She had consented to go away, to leave her home. Was that wise? She tried to weigh each side of the question. In her home anyway she had shelter and food; she had those whom she had known all her life about her. Of course she had to work hard, both in the house and at business. What would they say of her in the Stores when they found out that she had run away with a fellow? Say she was a fool, perhaps; and her place would be filled up by advertisement. Miss Gavan would be glad. She had always had an edge on her, especially whenever there were people listening.

"Miss Hill, don't you see these ladies are waiting?"

"Look lively, Miss Hill, please."

She would not cry many tears at leaving the Stores.

But in her new home, in a distant unknown country, it would not be like that. Then she would be married—she, Eveline. People would treat her with respect then. She would not be treated as her mother had been. Even now, though she was over nineteen, she sometimes felt herself in danger of her father's violence. She knew it was that that had given her the palpitations. When they were growing up he had never gone for her, like he used to go for Harry and Ernest, because she was a girl; but latterly he had begun to threaten her and say what he would do to her only for her dead mother's sake. And now she had nobody to protect her. Ernest was dead and Harry, who was in the church decorating business, was nearly always down somewhere in the country. Besides, the invariable squabble for money on Saturday nights had begun to weary her unspeakably. She always gave her entire wages—seven shillings—and Harry always sent up what he could but the trouble was to get any money from her father. He said she used to squander the money, that she had no head, that he wasn't going to give her his hard-earned money to throw about the streets, and much more, for he was usually fairly bad on Saturday night. In the end he would give her the money and ask her had she any intention of buying Sunday's dinner. Then she had to rush out as quickly as she could and do her marketing, holding her black leather purse tightly in her hand as she elbowed her way through the crowds and returning home late under her load of provisions. She had hard work to keep the house together and to see that the two young children who had been left to her charge went to school regularly and got their meals regularly. It was hard work—a hard life—but now that she was about to leave it she did not find it a wholly undesirable life.

She was about to explore another life with Frank. Frank was very kind, manly, open-hearted. She was to go away with him by the night-boat to be his wife and to live with him in Buenos Ayres where he had a home waiting for her. How well she remembered the first time she had seen him; he was lodging in a house on the main road where she used to visit. It seemed a few weeks ago. He was standing at the gate, his peaked cap pushed back on his head and his hair tumbled forward over a face of bronze. Then they had come to know each other. He used to meet her outside the Stores every evening and see her home. He took her to see *The Bohemian Girl* and she felt elated as she sat in an unaccustomed part of the theatre with him. He was awfully fond of music and sang a little. People knew that they were courting and, when he sang about the lass that loves a sailor, she always felt pleasantly confused. He used to call her Poppens out of fun. First of all it had been an excitement for her to have a fellow and then she had begun to like him. He had tales of distant countries. He had started as a deck boy at a pound a month on a ship of the Allan Line going out to Canada. He told her the names of the ships he had been on and the names of the different services. He had sailed through the Straits of Magellan and he told her stories of the terrible Patagonians. He had fallen on his feet in Buenos Ayres, he said, and had come over to the old country just for a holiday. Of course, her father had found out the affair and had forbidden her to have anything to say to him.

"I know these sailor chaps," he said.

One day he had quarrelled with Frank and after that she had to meet her lover secretly.

The evening deepened in the avenue. The white of two letters in her lap grew indistinct. One was to Harry; the other was to her father. Ernest had been her favourite but she liked Harry too. Her father was becoming old lately, she noticed; he would miss her. Sometimes he could be very nice. Not long before, when she had been laid up for a day, he had read her out a ghost story and made toast for her at the fire. Another day, when their mother was alive, they had all gone for a picnic to the Hill of Howth. She remembered her father putting on her mother's bonnet to make the children laugh.

Her time was running out but she continued to sit by the window, leaning her head against the window curtain, inhaling the odour of dusty cretonne. Down far in the avenue she could hear a street organ playing. She knew the air. Strange that it should come that very night to remind her of the promise to her mother, her promise to keep the home together as long as she could. She remembered the last night of her mother's illness; she was again in the close dark room at the other side of the hall and outside she heard a melancholy air of Italy. The organ-player had been ordered to go away and given sixpence. She remembered her father strutting back into the sickroom saying:

"Damned Italians! coming over here!"

As she mused the pitiful vision of her mother's life laid its spell on the very quick of her being—that life of commonplace sacrifices closing in final craziness. She trembled as she heard again her mother's voice saying constantly with foolish insistence:

"Derevaun Seraun! Derevaun Seraun!"

She stood up in a sudden impulse of terror. Escape! She must escape! Frank would save her. He would give her life, perhaps love, too. But she wanted to live. Why should she be unhappy? She had a right to happiness. Frank would take her in his arms, fold her in his arms. He would save her.

. . . .

She stood among the swaying crowd in the station at the North Wall. He held her hand and she knew that he was speaking to her, saying something about the passage over and over again. The station was full of soldiers with brown baggages. Through the wide doors of the sheds she caught a glimpse of the black mass of the boat, lying in beside the quay wall, with illumined portholes. She answered nothing. She felt her cheek pale and cold and, out of a maze of distress, she prayed to God to direct her, to show her what was her duty. The boat blew a long mournful whistle into the mist. If she went, to-morrow she would be on the sea with Frank, steaming towards Buenos Ayres. Their passage had been booked. Could she still draw back after all he had done for her? Her distress awoke a nausea in her body and she kept moving her lips in silent fervent prayer.

A bell clanged upon her heart. She felt him seize her hand:

"Come!"

All the seas of the world tumbled about her heart. He was drawing her into them: he would drown her. She gripped with both hands at the iron railing.

"Come!"

No! No! No! It was impossible. Her hands clutched the iron in frenzy. Amid the seas she sent a cry of anguish!

"Eveline! Evvy!"

He rushed beyond the barrier and called to her to follow. He was shouted at to go on but he still called to her. She set her white face to him, passive, like a helpless animal. Her eyes gave him no sign of love or farewell or recognition.

After the Race

THE CARS CAME scudding in towards Dublin, running evenly like pellets in the groove of the Naas Road. At the crest of the hill at Inchicore sightseers had gathered in clumps to watch the cars careering homeward and through this channel of poverty and inaction the Continent sped its wealth and industry. Now and again the clumps of people raised the cheer of the gratefully oppressed. Their sympathy, however, was for the blue cars—the cars of their friends, the French.

The French, moreover, were virtual victors. Their team had finished solidly; they had been placed second and third and the driver of the winning German car was reported a Belgian. Each blue car, therefore, received a double measure of welcome as it topped the crest of the hill and each cheer of welcome was acknowledged with smiles and nods by those in the car. In one of these trimly built cars was a party of four young men whose spirits seemed to be at present well above the level of successful Gallicism: in fact, these four young men were almost hilarious. They were Charles Ségouin, the owner of the car; André Rivière, a young electrician of Canadian birth; a huge Hungarian named Villona and a neatly groomed young man named Doyle. Ségouin was in good humour because he had unexpectedly received some orders in advance (he was about to start a motor establishment in Paris) and Rivière was in good humour because he was to be appointed manager of the establishment; these two young men (who were cousins) were also in good humour because of the success of the French cars. Villona was in good humour because he had had a very satisfactory luncheon; and besides he was an optimist by nature. The fourth member of the party, however, was too excited to be genuinely happy.

He was about twenty-six years of age, with a soft, light brown moustache and rather innocent-looking grey eyes. His father, who had begun life as an advanced Nationalist, had modified his views early. He had made his money as a butcher in Kingstown and by opening shops in Dublin and in the suburbs he had made his money many times over. He had also been fortunate enough to secure some of the police contracts and in the end he had become rich enough to be alluded to in the Dublin newspapers as a merchant prince. He had sent his son to England to be educated in a big Catholic college and had afterwards sent him to Dublin University to study law. Jimmy did not study very earnestly and took to bad courses for a while. He had money and he was popular; and he divided his time curiously between musical and motoring circles. Then he had been sent for a term to Cambridge to see a little life. His father, remonstrative, but covertly proud of the excess, had paid his bills and brought him home. It was at Cambridge that he had met Ségouin. They were not much more than acquaintances as yet but Jimmy found great pleasure in the society of one who had seen so much of the world and was reputed to own some of the biggest hotels in France. Such a person (as his father agreed) was well worth knowing, even if he had not been the charming companion he was. Villona was entertaining also—a brilliant pianist—but, unfortunately, very poor.

The car ran on merrily with its cargo of hilarious youth. The two cousins sat on the front seat; Jimmy and his Hungarian friend sat behind. Decidedly Villona was in excellent spirits; he kept up a deep bass hum of melody for miles of the road. The Frenchmen flung their laughter and light words over their shoulders and often Jimmy had to strain forward to catch the quick phrase. This was not altogether pleasant for him, as he had nearly always to make a deft guess at the meaning and shout back a suitable answer in the face of a high wind. Besides Villona's humming would confuse anybody; the noise of the car, too.

Rapid motion through space elates one; so does notoriety; so does the possession of money. These were three good reasons for Jimmy's excitement. He had been seen by many of his friends that day in the company of these Continentals. At the control Ségouin had presented him to one of the French competitors and, in answer to his confused murmur of compliment, the swarthy face of the driver had disclosed a line of shining white teeth. It was pleasant after that honour to return to the profane world of spectators amid nudges and significant looks. Then as to money—he really had a great sum under his control. Ségouin, perhaps, would not think it a great sum but Jimmy who, in spite of temporary errors, was at heart the inheritor of solid instincts knew well with what difficulty it had been got together. This knowledge had previously kept his bills within the limits of reasonable recklessness and, if he had been so conscious of the labour latent in money when there had been question merely of some freak of the higher intelligence, how much more so now when he was about to stake the greater part of his substance! It was a serious thing for him.

Of course, the investment was a good one and Ségouin had managed to give the impression that it was by a favour of friendship the mite of Irish money was to be included in the capital of the concern. Jimmy had a respect for his father's shrewdness in business matters and in this case it had been his father who had first suggested the investment; money to be made in the motor business, pots of money. Moreover Ségouin had the unmistakable air of wealth. Jimmy set out to translate into days' work that lordly car in which he sat. How smoothly it ran. In what style they had come careering along the country roads! The journey laid a magical finger on the genuine pulse of life and gallantly the machinery of human nerves strove to answer the bounding courses of the swift blue animal.

They drove down Dame Street. The street was busy with unusual traffic, loud with the horns of motorists and the gongs of impatient tram-drivers. Near the Bank Ségouin drew up and Jimmy and his friend alighted. A little knot of people collected on the footpath to pay homage to the snorting motor. The party was to dine together that evening in Ségouin's hotel and, meanwhile, Jimmy and his friend, who was staying with him, were to go home to dress. The car steered out slowly for Grafton Street while the two young men pushed their way through the knot of gazers. They walked northward with a curious feeling of disappointment in the exercise, while the city hung its pale globes of light above them in a haze of summer evening.

In Jimmy's house this dinner had been pronounced an occasion. A certain pride mingled with his parents' trepidation, a certain eagerness, also, to play fast and loose for the names of great foreign cities have at least this virtue. Jimmy, too, looked very well when he was dressed and, as he stood in the hall giving a last equation to the bows of his dress tie, his father may have felt even commercially satisfied at having secured for his son qualities often unpurchaseable. His father, therefore, was unusually friendly with Villona and his manner expressed a real respect for foreign accomplishments; but this subtlety of his host was probably lost upon the Hungarian, who was beginning to have a sharp desire for his dinner.

The dinner was excellent, exquisite. Ségouin, Jimmy decided, had a very refined taste. The party was increased by a young Englishman named Routh whom Jimmy had seen with Ségouin at Cambridge. The young men supped in a snug room lit by electric candle lamps. They talked volubly and with little reserve. Jimmy, whose imagination was kindling, conceived the lively youth of the Frenchmen twined elegantly upon the firm framework of the Englishman's manner. A graceful image of his, he thought, and a just one. He admired the dexterity with which their host directed the conversation. The five young men had various tastes and their tongues had been loosened. Villona, with immense respect, began to discover to the mildly surprised Englishman the beauties of the English madrigal, deploring the loss of old instruments. Rivière, not wholly ingenuously, undertook to explain to Jimmy the triumph of the French mechanicians. The resonant voice of the Hungarian was about to prevail in ridicule of the spurious lutes of the romantic painters when Ségouin shepherded his party into politics. Here was congenial ground for all. Jimmy, under generous influences, felt the buried zeal of his father wake to life within him: he aroused the torpid Routh at last. The room grew doubly hot and Ségouin's task grew harder each moment: there was even danger of personal spite. The alert host at an opportunity lifted his glass to Humanity and, when the toast had been drunk, he threw open a window significantly.

That night the city wore the mask of a capital. The five young men strolled along Stephen's Green in a faint cloud of aromatic smoke. They talked loudly and gaily and their cloaks dangled from their shoulders. The people made way for them. At the corner of Grafton Street a short fat man was putting two handsome ladies on a car in charge of another fat man. The car drove off and the short fat man caught sight of the party.

"André."

"It's Farley!"

A torrent of talk followed. Farley was an American. No one knew very well what the talk was about. Villona and Rivière were the noisiest, but all the men were excited. They got up on a car, squeezing themselves together amid much laughter. They drove by the crowd, blended now into soft colours, to a music of merry bells. They took the train at Westland Row and in a few seconds, as it seemed to Jimmy, they were walking out of Kingstown Station. The ticket-collector saluted Jimmy; he was an old man:

"Fine night, sir!"

It was a serene summer night; the harbour lay like a darkened mirror at their feet. They proceeded towards it with linked arms, singing *Cadet Roussel* in chorus, stamping their feet at every:

"*Ho! Ho! Hohé, vraiment!*"

They got into a rowboat at the slip and made out for the American's yacht. There was to be supper, music, cards. Villona said with conviction:

"It is delightful!"

There was a yacht piano in the cabin. Villona played a waltz for Farley and Rivière, Farley acting as cavalier and Rivière as lady. Then an impromptu square dance, the men devising original figures. What merriment! Jimmy took his part with a will; this was seeing life, at least. Then Farley got out of breath and cried "*Stop!*" A man brought in a light supper, and the young men sat down to it for form's sake. They drank, however: it was Bohemian. They drank Ireland, England, France, Hungary, the United States of America. Jimmy made a speech, a long speech, Villona saying: "*Hear! hear!*" whenever there was a pause. There was a great clapping of hands when he sat down. It must have been a good speech.

Farley clapped him on the back and laughed loudly. What jovial fellows! What good company they were!

Cards! cards! The table was cleared. Villona returned quietly to his piano and played voluntaries for them. The other men played game after game, flinging themselves boldly into the adventure. They drank the health of the Queen of Hearts and of the Queen of Diamonds. Jimmy felt obscurely the lack of an audience: the wit was flashing. Play ran very high and paper began to pass. Jimmy did not know exactly who was winning but he knew that he was losing. But it was his own fault for he frequently mistook his cards and the other men had to calculate his I.O.U.'s for him. They were devils of fellows but he wished they would stop: it was getting late. Someone gave the toast of the yacht *The Belle of Newport* and then someone proposed one great game for a finish.

The piano had stopped; Villona must have gone up on deck. It was a terrible game. They stopped just before the end of it to drink for luck. Jimmy understood that the game lay between Routh and Ségouin. What excitement! Jimmy was excited too; he would lose, of course. How much had he written away? The men rose to their feet to play the last tricks, talking and gesticulating. Routh won. The cabin shook with the young men's cheering and the cards were bundled together. They began then to gather in what they had won. Farley and Jimmy were the heaviest losers.

He knew that he would regret in the morning but at present he was glad of the rest, glad of the dark stupor that would cover up his folly. He leaned his elbows on the table and rested his head between his hands, counting the beats of his temples. The cabin door opened and he saw the Hungarian standing in a shaft of grey light:

"Daybreak, gentlemen!"

Two Gallants

THE GREY WARM evening of August had descended upon the city and a mild warm air, a memory of summer, circulated in the streets. The streets, shuttered for the repose of Sunday, swarmed with a gaily coloured crowd. Like illumined pearls the lamps shone from the summits of their tall poles upon the living texture below which, changing shape and hue unceasingly, sent up into the warm grey evening air an unchanging, unceasing murmur.

Two young men came down the hill of Rutland Square. One of them was just bringing a long monologue to a close. The other, who walked on the verge of the path and was at times obliged to step on to the road, owing to his companion's rudeness, wore an amused listening face. He was squat and ruddy. A yachting cap was shoved far back from his forehead and the narrative to which he listened made constant waves of expression break forth over his face from the corners of his nose and eyes and mouth. Little jets of wheezing laughter followed one another out of his convulsed body. His eyes, twinkling with cunning enjoyment, glanced at every moment towards his companion's face. Once or twice he rearranged the light waterproof which he had slung over one shoulder in toreador fashion. His breeches, his white rubber shoes and his jauntily slung waterproof expressed youth. But his figure fell into rotundity at the waist, his hair was scant and grey and his face, when the waves of expression had passed over it, had a ravaged look.

When he was quite sure that the narrative had ended he laughed noiselessly for fully half a minute. Then he said:

"Well! . . . . That takes the biscuit!"

His voice seemed winnowed of vigour; and to enforce his words he added with humour:

"That takes the solitary, unique, and, if I may so call it, *recherché* biscuit!"

He became serious and silent when he had said this. His tongue was tired for he had been talking all the afternoon in a public-house in Dorset Street. Most people considered Lenehan a leech but, in spite of this reputation, his adroitness and eloquence had always prevented his friends from forming any general policy against him. He had a brave manner of coming up to a party of them in a bar and of holding himself nimbly at the borders of the company until he was included in a round. He was a sporting vagrant armed with a vast stock of stories, limericks and riddles. He was insensitive to all kinds of discourtesy. No one knew how he achieved the stern task of living, but his name was vaguely associated with racing tissues.

"And where did you pick her up, Corley?" he asked.

Corley ran his tongue swiftly along his upper lip.

"One night, man," he said, "I was going along Dame Street and I spotted a fine tart under Waterhouse's clock and said good-night, you know. So we went for a walk round by the canal and she told me she was a slavey in a house in Baggot Street. I put my arm round her and squeezed her a bit that night. Then next Sunday, man, I met her by appointment. We went out to Donnybrook and I brought her into a field there. She told me she used to go with a dairyman. . . . It was fine, man. Cigarettes every night she'd bring me and paying the tram out and back. And one night she brought me two bloody fine cigars—O, the real cheese, you know, that the old fellow used to smoke. . . . I was afraid, man, she'd get in the family way. But she's up to the dodge."

"Maybe she thinks you'll marry her," said Lenehan.

"I told her I was out of a job," said Corley. "I told her I was in Pim's. She doesn't know my name. I was too hairy to tell her that. But she thinks I'm a bit of class, you know."

Lenehan laughed again, noiselessly.

"Of all the good ones ever I heard," he said, "that emphatically takes the biscuit."

Corley's stride acknowledged the compliment. The swing of his burly body made his friend execute a few light skips from the path to the roadway and back again. Corley was the son of an inspector of police and he had inherited his father's frame and gait. He walked with his hands by his sides, holding himself erect and swaying his head from side to side. His head was large, globular and oily; it sweated in all weathers; and his large round hat, set upon it sideways, looked like a bulb which had grown out of another. He always stared straight before him as if he were on parade and, when he wished to gaze after someone in the street, it was necessary for him to move his body from the hips. At present he was about town. Whenever any job was vacant a friend was always ready to give him the hard word. He was often to be seen walking with policemen in plain clothes, talking earnestly. He knew the inner side of all affairs and was fond of delivering final judgments. He spoke without listening to the speech of his companions. His conversation was mainly about himself: what he had said to such a person and what such a person had said to him and what he had said to settle the matter. When he reported these dialogues he aspirated the first letter of his name after the manner of Florentines.

Lenehan offered his friend a cigarette. As the two young men walked on through the crowd Corley occasionally turned to smile at some of the passing girls but Lenehan's gaze was fixed on the large faint moon circled with a double halo. He watched earnestly the passing of the grey web of twilight across its face. At length he said:

"Well . . . tell me, Corley, I suppose you'll be able to pull it off all right, eh?"

Corley closed one eye expressively as an answer.

"Is she game for that?" asked Lenehan dubiously. "You can never know women."

"She's all right," said Corley. "I know the way to get around her, man. She's a bit gone on me."

"You're what I call a gay Lothario," said Lenehan. "And the proper kind of a Lothario, too!"

A shade of mockery relieved the servility of his manner. To save himself he had the habit of leaving his flattery open to the interpretation of raillery. But Corley had not a subtle mind.

"There's nothing to touch a good slavey," he affirmed. "Take my tip for it."

"By one who has tried them all," said Lenehan.

"First I used to go with girls, you know," said Corley, unbosoming; "girls off the South Circular. I used to take them out, man, on the tram somewhere and pay the tram or take them to a band or a play at the theatre or buy them chocolate and sweets or something that way. I used to spend money on them right enough," he added, in a convincing tone, as if he was conscious of being disbelieved.

But Lenehan could well believe it; he nodded gravely.

"I know that game," he said, "and it's a mug's game."

"And damn the thing I ever got out of it," said Corley.

"Ditto here," said Lenehan.

"Only off of one of them," said Corley.

He moistened his upper lip by running his tongue along it. The recollection brightened his eyes. He too gazed at the pale disc of the moon, now nearly veiled, and seemed to meditate.

"She was . . . a bit of all right," he said regretfully.

He was silent again. Then he added:

"She's on the turf now. I saw her driving down Earl Street one night with two fellows with her on a car."

"I suppose that's your doing," said Lenehan.

"There was others at her before me," said Corley philosophically.

This time Lenehan was inclined to disbelieve. He shook his head to and fro and smiled.

"You know you can't kid me, Corley," he said.

"Honest to God!" said Corley. "Didn't she tell me herself?"

Lenehan made a tragic gesture.

"Base betrayer!" he said.

As they passed along the railings of Trinity College, Lenehan skipped out into the road and peered up at the clock.

"Twenty after," he said.

"Time enough," said Corley. "She'll be there all right. I always let her wait a bit."

Lenehan laughed quietly.

"Ecod! Corley, you know how to take them," he said.

"I'm up to all their little tricks," Corley confessed.

"But tell me," said Lenehan again, "are you sure you can bring it off all right? You know it's a ticklish job. They're damn close on that point. Eh? . . . What?"

His bright, small eyes searched his companion's face for reassurance. Corley swung his head to and fro as if to toss aside an insistent insect, and his brows gathered.

"I'll pull it off," he said. "Leave it to me, can't you?"

Lenehan said no more. He did not wish to ruffle his friend's temper, to be sent to the devil and told that his advice was not wanted. A little tact was necessary. But Corley's brow was soon smooth again. His thoughts were running another way.

"She's a fine decent tart," he said, with appreciation; "that's what she is."

They walked along Nassau Street and then turned into Kildare Street. Not far from the porch of the club a harpist stood in the roadway, playing to a little ring of listeners. He plucked at the wires heedlessly, glancing quickly from time to time at the face of each new-comer and from time to time, wearily also, at the sky. His harp, too, heedless that her coverings had fallen about her knees, seemed weary alike of the eyes of strangers and of her master's hands. One hand played in the bass the melody of *Silent, O Moyle*, while the other hand careered in the treble after each group of notes. The notes of the air sounded deep and full.

The two young men walked up the street without speaking, the mournful music following them. When they reached Stephen's Green they crossed the road. Here the noise of trams, the lights and the crowd released them from their silence.

"There she is!" said Corley.

At the corner of Hume Street a young woman was standing. She wore a blue dress and a white sailor hat. She stood on the curbstone, swinging a sunshade in one hand. Lenehan grew lively.

"Let's have a look at her, Corley," he said.

Corley glanced sideways at his friend and an unpleasant grin appeared on his face.

"Are you trying to get inside me?" he asked.

"Damn it!" said Lenehan boldly, "I don't want an introduction. All I want is to have a look at her. I'm not going to eat her."

"O . . . A look at her?" said Corley, more amiably. "Well . . . I'll tell you what. I'll go over and talk to her and you can pass by."

"Right!" said Lenehan.

Corley had already thrown one leg over the chains when Lenehan called out:

"And after? Where will we meet?"

"Half ten," answered Corley, bringing over his other leg.

"Where?"

"Corner of Merrion Street. We'll be coming back."

"Work it all right now," said Lenehan in farewell.

Corley did not answer. He sauntered across the road swaying his head from side to side. His bulk, his easy pace, and the solid sound of his boots had something of the conqueror in them. He approached the young woman and, without saluting, began at once to converse with her. She swung her umbrella more quickly and executed half turns on her heels. Once or twice when he spoke to her at close quarters she laughed and bent her head.

Lenehan observed them for a few minutes. Then he walked rapidly along beside the chains at some distance and crossed the road obliquely. As he approached Hume Street corner he found the air heavily scented and his eyes made a swift anxious scrutiny of the young woman's appearance. She had her Sunday finery on. Her blue serge skirt was held at the waist by a belt of black leather. The great silver buckle of her belt seemed to depress the centre of her body, catching the light stuff of her white blouse like a clip. She wore a short black jacket with mother-of-pearl buttons and a ragged black boa. The ends of her tulle collarette had been carefully disordered and a big bunch of red flowers was pinned in her bosom stems upwards. Lenehan's eyes noted approvingly her stout short muscular body. Frank rude health glowed in her face, on her fat red cheeks and in her unabashed blue eyes. Her features were blunt. She had broad nostrils, a straggling mouth which lay open in a contented leer, and two projecting front teeth. As he passed Lenehan took off his cap and, after about ten seconds, Corley returned a salute to the air. This he did by raising his hand vaguely and pensively changing the angle of position of his hat.

Lenehan walked as far as the Shelbourne Hotel where he halted and waited. After waiting for a little time he saw them coming towards him and, when they turned to the right, he followed them, stepping lightly in his white shoes, down one side of Merrion Square. As he walked on slowly, timing his pace to theirs, he watched Corley's head which turned at every moment towards the young woman's face like a big ball revolving on a pivot. He kept the pair in view until he had seen them climbing the stairs of the Donnybrook tram; then he turned about and went back the way he had come.

Now that he was alone his face looked older. His gaiety seemed to forsake him and, as he came by the railings of the Duke's Lawn, he allowed his hand to run along them. The air which the harpist had played began to control his movements. His softly padded feet played the melody while his fingers swept a scale of variations idly along the railings after each group of notes.

He walked listlessly round Stephen's Green and then down Grafton Street. Though his eyes took note of many elements of the crowd through which he passed they did so morosely. He found trivial all that was meant to charm him and did not answer the glances which invited him to be bold. He knew that he would have to speak a great deal, to invent and to amuse, and his brain and throat were too dry for such a task. The problem of how he could pass the hours till he met Corley again troubled him a little. He could think of no way of passing them but to keep on walking. He turned to the left when he came to the corner of Rutland Square and felt more at ease in the dark quiet street, the sombre look of which suited his mood. He paused at last before the window of a poor-looking shop over which the words *Refreshment Bar* were printed in white letters. On the glass of the window were two flying inscriptions: *Ginger Beer* and *Ginger Ale*. A cut ham was exposed on a great blue dish while near it on a plate lay a segment of very light plum-pudding. He eyed this food earnestly for some time and then, after glancing warily up and down the street, went into the shop quickly.

He was hungry for, except some biscuits which he had asked two grudging curates to bring him, he had eaten nothing since breakfast-time. He sat down at an uncovered wooden table opposite two work-girls and a mechanic. A slatternly girl waited on him.

"How much is a plate of peas?" he asked.

"Three halfpence, sir," said the girl.

"Bring me a plate of peas," he said, "and a bottle of ginger beer."

He spoke roughly in order to belie his air of gentility for his entry had been followed by a pause of talk. His face was heated. To appear natural he pushed his cap back on his head and planted his elbows on the table. The mechanic and the two work-girls examined him point by point before resuming their conversation in a subdued voice. The girl brought him a plate of grocer's hot peas, seasoned with pepper and vinegar, a fork and his ginger beer. He ate his food greedily and found it so good that he made a note of the shop mentally. When he had eaten all the peas he sipped his ginger beer and sat for some time thinking of Corley's adventure. In his imagination he beheld the pair of lovers walking along some dark road; he heard Corley's voice in deep energetic gallantries and saw again the leer of the young woman's mouth. This vision made him feel keenly his own poverty of purse and spirit. He was tired of knocking about, of pulling the devil by the tail, of shifts and intrigues. He would be thirty-one in November. Would he never get a good job? Would he never have a home of his own? He thought how pleasant it would be to have a warm fire to sit by and a good dinner to sit down to. He had walked the streets long enough with friends and with girls. He knew what those friends were worth: he knew the girls too. Experience had embittered his heart against the world. But all hope had not left him. He felt better after having eaten than he had felt before, less weary of his life, less vanquished in spirit. He might yet be able to settle down in some snug corner and live happily if he could only come across some good simple-minded girl with a little of the ready.

He paid twopence halfpenny to the slatternly girl and went out of the shop to begin his wandering again. He went into Capel Street and walked along towards the City Hall. Then he turned into Dame Street. At the corner of George's Street he met two friends of his and stopped to converse with them. He was glad that he could rest from all his walking. His friends asked him had he seen Corley and what was the latest. He replied that he had spent the day with Corley. His friends talked very little. They looked vacantly after some figures in the crowd and sometimes made a critical remark. One said that he had seen Mac an hour before in Westmoreland Street. At this Lenehan said that he had been with Mac the night before in Egan's. The young man who had seen Mac in Westmoreland Street asked was it true that Mac had won a bit over a billiard match. Lenehan did not know: he said that Holohan had stood them drinks in Egan's.

He left his friends at a quarter to ten and went up George's Street. He turned to the left at the City Markets and walked on into Grafton Street.

The crowd of girls and young men had thinned and on his way up the street he heard many groups and couples bidding one another good-night. He went as far as the clock of the College of Surgeons: it was on the stroke of ten. He set off briskly along the northern side of the Green hurrying for fear Corley should return too soon. When he reached the corner of Merrion Street he took his stand in the shadow of a lamp and brought out one of the cigarettes which he had reserved and lit it. He leaned against the lamp-post and kept his gaze fixed on the part from which he expected to see Corley and the young woman return.

His mind became active again. He wondered had Corley managed it successfully. He wondered if he had asked her yet or if he would leave it to the last. He suffered all the pangs and thrills of his friend's situation as well as those of his own. But the memory of Corley's slowly revolving head calmed him somewhat: he was sure Corley would pull it off all right. All at once the idea struck him that perhaps Corley had seen her home by another way and given him the slip. His eyes searched the street: there was no sign of them. Yet it was surely half-an-hour since he had seen the clock of the College of Surgeons. Would Corley do a thing like that? He lit his last cigarette and began to smoke it nervously. He strained his eyes as each tram stopped at the far corner of the square. They must have gone home by another way. The paper of his cigarette broke and he flung it into the road with a curse.

Suddenly he saw them coming towards him. He started with delight and keeping close to his lamp-post tried to read the result in their walk. They were walking quickly, the young woman taking quick short steps, while Corley kept beside her with his long stride. They did not seem to be speaking. An intimation of the result pricked him like the point of a sharp instrument. He knew Corley would fail; he knew it was no go.

They turned down Baggot Street and he followed them at once, taking the other footpath. When they stopped he stopped too. They talked for a few moments and then the young woman went down the steps into the area of a house. Corley remained standing at the edge of the path, a little distance from the front steps. Some minutes passed. Then the hall-door was opened slowly and cautiously. A woman came running down the front steps and coughed. Corley turned and went towards her. His broad figure hid hers from view for a few seconds and then she reappeared running up the steps. The door closed on her and Corley began to walk swiftly towards Stephen's Green.

Lenehan hurried on in the same direction. Some drops of light rain fell. He took them as a warning and, glancing back towards the house which the young woman had entered to see that he was not observed, he ran eagerly across the road. Anxiety and his swift run made him pant. He called out:

"Hallo, Corley!"

Corley turned his head to see who had called him, and then continued walking as before. Lenehan ran after him, settling the waterproof on his shoulders with one hand.

"Hallo, Corley!" he cried again.

He came level with his friend and looked keenly in his face. He could see nothing there.

"Well?" he said. "Did it come off?"

They had reached the corner of Ely Place. Still without answering Corley swerved to the left and went up the side street. His features were composed in stern calm. Lenehan kept up with his friend, breathing uneasily. He was baffled and a note of menace pierced through his voice.

"Can't you tell us?" he said. "Did you try her?"

Corley halted at the first lamp and stared grimly before him. Then with a grave gesture he extended a hand towards the light and, smiling, opened it slowly to the gaze of his disciple. A small gold coin shone in the palm.

The Boarding House

MRS. MOONEY WAS a butcher's daughter. She was a woman who was quite able to keep things to herself: a determined woman. She had married her father's foreman and opened a butcher's shop near Spring Gardens. But as soon as his father-in-law was dead Mr. Mooney began to go to the devil. He drank, plundered the till, ran headlong into debt. It was no use making him take the pledge: he was sure to break out again a few days after. By fighting his wife in the presence of customers and by buying bad meat he ruined his business. One night he went for his wife with the cleaver and she had to sleep in a neighbour's house.

After that they lived apart. She went to the priest and got a separation from him with care of the children. She would give him neither money nor food nor house-room; and so he was obliged to enlist himself as a sheriff's man. He was a shabby stooped little drunkard with a white face and a white moustache and white eyebrows, pencilled above his little eyes, which were pink-veined and raw; and all day long he sat in the bailiff's room, waiting to be put on a job. Mrs. Mooney, who had taken what remained of her money out of the butcher business and set up a boarding house in Hardwicke Street, was a big imposing woman. Her house had a floating population made up of tourists from Liverpool and the Isle of Man and, occasionally, *artistes* from the music halls. Its resident population was made up of clerks from the city. She governed the house cunningly and firmly, knew when to give credit, when to be stern and when to let things pass. All the resident young men spoke of her as *The Madam*.

Mrs. Mooney's young men paid fifteen shillings a week for board and lodgings (beer or stout at dinner excluded). They shared in common tastes and occupations and for this reason they were very chummy with one another. They discussed with one another the chances of favourites and outsiders. Jack Mooney, the Madam's son, who was clerk to a commission agent in Fleet Street, had the reputation of being a hard case. He was fond

38

of using soldiers' obscenities: usually he came home in the small hours. When he met his friends he had always a good one to tell them and he was always sure to be on to a good thing—that is to say, a likely horse or a likely *artiste*. He was also handy with the mits and sang comic songs. On Sunday nights there would often be a reunion in Mrs. Mooney's front drawing-room. The music-hall *artistes* would oblige; and Sheridan played waltzes and polkas and vamped accompaniments. Polly Mooney, the Madam's daughter, would also sing. She sang:

> *"I'm a . . . naughty girl*
> *You needn't sham:*
> *You know I am."*

Polly was a slim girl of nineteen; she had light soft hair and a small full mouth. Her eyes, which were grey with a shade of green through them, had a habit of glancing upwards when she spoke with anyone, which made her look like a little perverse madonna. Mrs. Mooney had first sent her daughter to be a typist in a corn-factor's office but, as a disreputable sheriff's man used to come every other day to the office, asking to be allowed to say a word to his daughter, she had taken her daughter home again and set her to do housework. As Polly was very lively the intention was to give her the run of the young men. Besides, young men like to feel that there is a young woman not very far away. Polly, of course, flirted with the young men but Mrs. Mooney, who was a shrewd judge, knew that the young men were only passing the time away: none of them meant business. Things went on so for a long time and Mrs. Mooney began to think of sending Polly back to typewriting when she noticed that something was going on between Polly and one of the young men. She watched the pair and kept her own counsel.

Polly knew that she was being watched, but still her mother's persistent silence could not be misunderstood. There had been no open complicity between mother and daughter, no open understanding but, though people in the house began to talk of the affair, still Mrs. Mooney did not intervene. Polly began to grow a little strange in her manner and the young man was evidently perturbed. At last, when she judged it to be the right moment, Mrs. Mooney intervened. She dealt with moral problems as a cleaver deals with meat: and in this case she had made up her mind.

It was a bright Sunday morning of early summer, promising heat, but with a fresh breeze blowing. All the windows of the boarding house were open and the lace curtains ballooned gently towards the street beneath the raised sashes. The belfry of George's Church sent out constant peals and worshippers, singly or in groups, traversed the little circus before the church, revealing their purpose by their self-contained demeanour no less than by the little volumes in their gloved hands. Breakfast was over in the boarding house and the table of the breakfast-room was covered with plates on which lay yellow streaks of eggs with morsels of bacon-fat and bacon-rind. Mrs. Mooney sat in the straw arm-chair and watched the servant Mary remove the breakfast things. She made Mary collect the crusts and pieces of broken bread to help to make Tuesday's bread-pudding. When the table was cleared, the broken bread collected, the sugar and butter safe under lock and key, she began to reconstruct the interview which she had had the night before with Polly. Things were as she had suspected: she had been frank in her questions and Polly had been frank in her answers. Both had been somewhat awkward, of course. She had been made awkward by her not wishing to receive the news in too cavalier a fashion or to seem to have connived and Polly had been made awkward not merely because allusions of that kind always made her awkward but also because she did not wish it to be thought that in her wise innocence she had divined the intention behind her mother's tolerance.

Mrs. Mooney glanced instinctively at the little gilt clock on the mantelpiece as soon as she had become aware through her revery that the bells of George's Church had stopped ringing. It was seventeen minutes past eleven: she would have lots of time to have the matter out with Mr. Doran and then catch short twelve at Marlborough Street. She was sure she would win. To begin with she had all the weight of social opinion on her side: she was an outraged mother. She had allowed him to live beneath her roof, assuming that he was a man of honour, and he had simply abused her hospitality. He was thirty-four or thirty-five years of age, so that youth could not be pleaded as his excuse; nor could ignorance be his excuse since he was a man who had seen something of the world. He had simply taken advantage of Polly's youth and inexperience: that was evident. The question was: What reparation would he make?

There must be reparation made in such cases. It is all very well for the man: he can go his ways as if nothing had happened, having had his moment of pleasure, but the girl has to bear the brunt. Some mothers would be content to patch up such an affair for a sum of money; she had known cases of it. But she would not do so. For her only one reparation could make up for the loss of her daughter's honour: marriage.

She counted all her cards again before sending Mary up to Mr. Doran's room to say that she wished to speak with him. She felt sure she would win. He was a serious young man, not rakish or loud-voiced like the others. If it had been Mr. Sheridan or Mr. Meade or Bantam Lyons her task would have been much harder. She did not think he would face publicity. All the lodgers in the house knew something of the affair; details had been invented by some. Besides, he had been employed for thirteen years in a great Catholic wine-merchant's office and publicity would mean for him, perhaps, the loss of his job. Whereas if he agreed all might be well. She knew he had a good screw for one thing and she suspected he had a bit of stuff put by.

Nearly the half-hour! She stood up and surveyed herself in the pier-glass. The decisive expression of her great florid face satisfied her and she thought of some mothers she knew who could not get their daughters off their hands.

Mr. Doran was very anxious indeed this Sunday morning. He had made two attempts to shave but his hand had been so unsteady that he had been obliged to desist. Three days' reddish beard fringed his jaws and every two or three minutes a mist gathered on his glasses so that he had to take them off and polish them with his pocket-handkerchief. The recollection of his confession of the night before was a cause of acute pain to him; the priest had drawn out every ridiculous detail of the affair and in the end had so magnified his sin that he was almost thankful at being afforded a loophole of reparation. The harm was done. What could he do now but marry her or run away? He could not brazen it out. The affair would be sure to be talked of and his employer would be certain to hear of it. Dublin is such a small city: everyone knows everyone else's business. He felt his heart leap warmly in his throat as he heard in his excited imagination old Mr. Leonard calling out in his rasping voice: "Send Mr. Doran here, please."

All his long years of service gone for nothing! All his industry and diligence thrown away! As a young man he had sown his wild oats, of course; he had boasted of his free-thinking and denied the existence of God to his companions in public-houses. But that was all passed and done with . . . nearly. He still bought a copy of *Reynold's Newspaper* every week but he attended to his religious duties and for nine-tenths of the year lived a regular life. He had money enough to settle down on; it was not that. But the family would look down on her. First of all there was her disreputable father and then her mother's boarding house was beginning to get a certain fame. He had a notion that he was being had. He could imagine his friends talking of the affair and laughing. She *was* a little vulgar; sometimes she said "I seen" and "If I had've known." But what would grammar matter if he really loved her? He could not make up his mind whether to like her or despise her for what she had done. Of course he had done it too. His instinct urged him to remain free, not to marry. Once you are married you are done for, it said.

While he was sitting helplessly on the side of the bed in shirt and trousers she tapped lightly at his door and entered. She told him all, that she had made a clean breast of it to her mother and that her mother would speak with him that morning. She cried and threw her arms round his neck, saying:

"O Bob! Bob! What am I to do? What am I to do at all?"

She would put an end to herself, she said.

He comforted her feebly, telling her not to cry, that it would be all right, never fear. He felt against his shirt the agitation of her bosom.

It was not altogether his fault that it had happened. He remembered well, with the curious patient memory of the celibate, the first casual caresses her dress, her breath, her fingers had given him. Then late one night as he was undressing for bed she had tapped at his door, timidly. She wanted to relight her candle at his for hers had been blown out by a gust. It was her bath night. She wore a loose open combing-jacket of printed flannel. Her white instep shone in the opening of her furry slippers and the blood glowed warmly behind her perfumed skin. From her hands and wrists too as she lit and steadied her candle a faint perfume arose.

On nights when he came in very late it was she who warmed up his dinner. He scarcely knew what he was eating feeling her beside him alone, at night, in the sleeping house. And her thoughtfulness! If the night was anyway cold or wet or windy there was sure to be a little tumbler of punch ready for him. Perhaps they could be happy together. . . .

They used to go upstairs together on tiptoe, each with a candle, and on the third landing exchange reluctant good-nights. They used to kiss. He remembered well her eyes, the touch of her hand and his delirium. . . .

But delirium passes. He echoed her phrase, applying it to himself: "*What am I to do?*" The instinct of the celibate warned him to hold back. But the sin was there; even his sense of honour told him that reparation must be made for such a sin.

While he was sitting with her on the side of the bed Mary came to the door and said that the missus wanted to see him in the parlour. He stood up to put on his coat and waistcoat, more helpless than ever. When he was dressed he went over to her to comfort her. It would be all right, never fear. He left her crying on the bed and moaning softly: "*O my God!*"

Going down the stairs his glasses became so dimmed with moisture that he had to take them off and polish them. He longed to ascend through the roof and fly away to another country where he would never hear again of his trouble, and yet a force pushed him downstairs step by step. The implacable faces of his employer and of the Madam stared upon his discomfiture. On the last flight of stairs he passed Jack Mooney who was coming up from the pantry nursing two bottles of *Bass*. They saluted coldly; and the lover's eyes rested for a second or two on a thick bulldog face and a pair of thick short arms. When he reached the foot of the staircase he glanced up and saw Jack regarding him from the door of the return-room.

Suddenly he remembered the night when one of the music-hall *artistes*, a little blond Londoner, had made a rather free allusion to Polly. The reunion had been almost broken up on account of Jack's violence. Everyone tried to quiet him. The music-hall *artiste*, a little paler than usual, kept smiling and saying that there was no harm meant: but Jack kept shouting at him that if any fellow tried that sort of a game on with his sister he'd bloody well put his teeth down his throat, so he would.

.   .   .   .

Polly sat for a little time on the side of the bed, crying. Then she dried her eyes and went over to the looking-glass. She dipped the end of the towel in the water-jug and refreshed her eyes with the cool water. She looked at herself in profile and readjusted a hairpin above her ear. Then she went back to the bed again and sat at the foot. She regarded the pillows for a long time and the sight of them awakened in her mind secret, amiable memories. She rested the nape of her neck against the cool iron bed-rail and fell into a revery. There was no longer any perturbation visible on her face.

She waited on patiently, almost cheerfully, without alarm, her memories gradually giving place to hopes and visions of the future. Her hopes and visions were so intricate that she no longer saw the white pillows on which her gaze was fixed or remembered that she was waiting for anything.

At last she heard her mother calling. She started to her feet and ran to the banisters.

"Polly! Polly!"

"Yes, mamma?"

"Come down, dear. Mr. Doran wants to speak to you."

Then she remembered what she had been waiting for.

A Little Cloud

EIGHT YEARS BEFORE he had seen his friend off at the North Wall and wished him godspeed. Gallaher had got on. You could tell that at once by his travelled air, his well-cut tweed suit, and fearless accent. Few fellows had talents like his and fewer still could remain unspoiled by such success. Gallaher's heart was in the right place and he had deserved to win. It was something to have a friend like that.

Little Chandler's thoughts ever since lunch-time had been of his meeting with Gallaher, of Gallaher's invitation and of the great city London where Gallaher lived. He was called Little Chandler because, though he was but slightly under the average stature, he gave one the idea of being a little man. His hands were white and small, his frame was fragile, his voice was quiet and his manners were refined. He took the greatest care of his fair silken hair and moustache and used perfume discreetly on his handkerchief. The half-moons of his nails were perfect and when he smiled you caught a glimpse of a row of childish white teeth.

As he sat at his desk in the King's Inns he thought what changes those eight years had brought. The friend whom he had known under a shabby and necessitous guise had become a brilliant figure on the London Press. He turned often from his tiresome writing to gaze out of the office window. The glow of a late autumn sunset covered the grass plots and walks. It cast a shower of kindly golden dust on the untidy nurses and decrepit old men who drowsed on the benches; it flickered upon all the moving figures—on the children who ran screaming along the gravel paths and on everyone who passed through the gardens. He watched the scene and thought of life; and (as always happened when he thought of life) he became sad. A gentle melancholy took possession of him. He felt how useless it was to struggle against fortune, this being the burden of wisdom which the ages had bequeathed to him.

He remembered the books of poetry upon his shelves at home. He had bought them in his bachelor days and many an evening, as he sat in the little room off the hall, he had been tempted to take one down from the bookshelf and read out something to his wife. But shyness had always held him back; and so the books had remained on their shelves. At times he repeated lines to himself and this consoled him.

When his hour had struck he stood up and took leave of his desk and of his fellow-clerks punctiliously. He emerged from under the feudal arch of the King's Inns, a neat modest figure, and walked swiftly down Henrietta Street. The golden sunset was waning and the air had grown sharp. A horde of grimy children populated the street. They stood or ran in the roadway or crawled up the steps before the gaping doors or squatted like mice upon the thresholds. Little Chandler gave them no thought. He picked his way deftly through all that minute vermin-like life and under the shadow of the gaunt spectral mansions in which the old nobility of Dublin had roystered. No memory of the past touched him, for his mind was full of a present joy.

He had never been in Corless's but he knew the value of the name. He knew that people went there after the theatre to eat oysters and drink liqueurs; and he had heard that the waiters there spoke French and German. Walking swiftly by at night he had seen cabs drawn up before the door and richly dressed ladies, escorted by cavaliers, alight and enter quickly. They wore noisy dresses and many wraps. Their faces were powdered and they caught up their dresses, when they touched earth, like alarmed Atalantas. He had always passed without turning his head to look. It was his habit to walk swiftly in the street even by day and whenever he found himself in the city late at night he hurried on his way apprehensively and excitedly. Sometimes, however, he courted the causes of his fear. He chose the darkest and narrowest streets and, as he walked boldly forward, the silence that was spread about his footsteps troubled him, the wandering, silent figures troubled him; and at times a sound of low fugitive laughter made him tremble like a leaf.

He turned to the right towards Capel Street. Ignatius Gallaher on the London Press! Who would have thought it possible eight years before? Still, now that he reviewed the past, Little Chandler could remember many signs of future greatness in his friend. People used to say that Ignatius Gallaher was wild. Of course, he did mix with a rakish set of fellows at that time, drank freely and borrowed money on all sides. In the end he had got mixed up in some shady affair, some money transaction: at least, that was one version of his flight. But nobody denied him talent. There was always a certain . . . something in Ignatius Gallaher that impressed you in spite of yourself. Even when he was out at elbows and at his wits' end for money he kept up a bold face. Little Chandler remembered (and the remembrance brought a slight flush of pride to his cheek) one of Ignatius Gallaher's sayings when he was in a tight corner:

"Half time now, boys," he used to say light-heartedly. "Where's my considering cap?"

That was Ignatius Gallaher all out; and, damn it, you couldn't but admire him for it.

Little Chandler quickened his pace. For the first time in his life he felt himself superior to the people he passed. For the first time his soul revolted against the dull inelegance of Capel Street. There was no doubt about it: if you wanted to succeed you had to go away. You could do nothing in Dublin. As he crossed Grattan Bridge he looked down the river towards the lower quays and pitied the poor stunted houses. They seemed to him a band of tramps, huddled together along the river-banks, their old coats covered with dust and soot, stupefied by the panorama of sunset and waiting for the first chill of night to bid them arise, shake themselves and begone. He wondered whether he could write a poem to express his idea. Perhaps Gallaher might be able to get it into some London paper for him. Could he write something original? He was not sure what idea he wished to express but the thought that a poetic moment had touched him took life within him like an infant hope. He stepped onward bravely.

Every step brought him nearer to London, farther from his own sober inartistic life. A light began to tremble on the horizon of his mind. He was not so old—thirty-two. His temperament might be said to be just at the point of maturity. There were so many different moods and impressions that he wished to express in verse. He felt them within him. He tried to weigh his soul to see if it was a poet's soul. Melancholy was the dominant note of his temperament, he thought, but it was a melancholy tempered by recurrences of faith and resignation and simple joy. If he could give expression to it in a book of poems perhaps men would listen. He would never be popular: he saw that. He could not sway the crowd but he might appeal to a little circle of kindred minds. The English critics, perhaps, would recognise him as one of the Celtic school by reason of the melancholy tone of his poems; besides that, he would put in allusions. He began to invent sentences and phrases from the notice which his book would get. *"Mr. Chandler has the gift of easy and graceful verse."* . . . *"A wistful sadness pervades these poems."* . . . *"The Celtic note."* It was a pity his name was not more Irish-looking. Perhaps it would be better to insert his mother's name before the surname: Thomas Malone Chandler, or better still: T. Malone Chandler. He would speak to Gallaher about it.

He pursued his revery so ardently that he passed his street and had to turn back. As he came near Corless's his former agitation began to overmaster him and he halted before the door in indecision. Finally he opened the door and entered.

The light and noise of the bar held him at the doorway for a few moments. He looked about him, but his sight was confused by the shining of many red and green wine-glasses. The bar seemed to him to be full of people and he felt that the people were observing him curiously. He glanced quickly to right and left (frowning slightly to make his errand appear serious), but when his sight cleared a little he saw that nobody had turned to look at him: and there, sure enough, was Ignatius Gallaher leaning with his back against the counter and his feet planted far apart.

"Hallo, Tommy, old hero, here you are! What is it to be? What will you have? I'm taking whisky: better stuff than we get across the water. Soda? Lithia? No mineral? I'm the same. Spoils the flavour. . . . Here, *garçon*, bring us two halves of malt whisky, like a good fellow. . . . Well, and how have you been pulling along since I saw you last? Dear God, how old we're getting! Do you see any signs of aging in me—eh, what? A little grey and thin on the top—what?"

Ignatius Gallaher took off his hat and displayed a large closely cropped head. His face was heavy, pale and clean-shaven. His eyes, which were of bluish slate-colour, relieved his unhealthy pallor and shone out plainly above the vivid orange tie he wore. Between these rival features the lips appeared very long and shapeless and colourless. He bent his head and felt with two sympathetic fingers the thin hair at the crown. Little Chandler shook his head as a denial. Ignatius Gallaher put on his hat again.

"It pulls you down," he said, "Press life. Always hurry and scurry, looking for copy and sometimes not finding it: and then, always to have something new in your stuff. Damn proofs and printers, I say, for a few days. I'm deuced glad, I can tell you, to get back to the old country. Does a fellow good, a bit of a holiday. I feel a ton better since I landed again in dear dirty Dublin. . . . Here you are, Tommy. Water? Say when."

Little Chandler allowed his whisky to be very much diluted.

"You don't know what's good for you, my boy," said Ignatius Gallaher. "I drink mine neat."

"I drink very little as a rule," said Little Chandler modestly. "An odd half-one or so when I meet any of the old crowd: that's all."

"Ah, well," said Ignatius Gallaher, cheerfully, "here's to us and to old times and old acquaintance."

They clinked glasses and drank the toast.

"I met some of the old gang to-day," said Ignatius Gallaher. "O'Hara seems to be in a bad way. What's he doing?"

"Nothing," said Little Chandler. "He's gone to the dogs."

"But Hogan has a good sit, hasn't he?"

"Yes; he's in the Land Commission."

"I met him one night in London and he seemed to be very flush. . . . Poor O'Hara! Boose, I suppose?"

"Other things, too," said Little Chandler shortly.

Ignatius Gallaher laughed.

"Tommy," he said, "I see you haven't changed an atom. You're the very same serious person that used to lecture me on Sunday mornings when I had a sore head and a fur on my tongue. You'd want to knock about a bit in the world. Have you never been anywhere even for a trip?"

"I've been to the Isle of Man," said Little Chandler.

Ignatius Gallaher laughed.

"The Isle of Man!" he said. "Go to London or Paris: Paris, for choice. That'd do you good."

"Have you seen Paris?"

"I should think I have! I've knocked about there a little."

"And is it really so beautiful as they say?" asked Little Chandler.

He sipped a little of his drink while Ignatius Gallaher finished his boldly.

"Beautiful?" said Ignatius Gallaher, pausing on the word and on the flavour of his drink. "It's not so beautiful, you know. Of course, it is beautiful. . . . But it's the life of Paris; that's the thing. Ah, there's no city like Paris for gaiety, movement, excitement. . . ."

Little Chandler finished his whisky and, after some trouble, succeeded in catching the barman's eye. He ordered the same again.

"I've been to the Moulin Rouge," Ignatius Gallaher continued when the barman had removed their glasses, "and I've been to all the Bohemian cafés. Hot stuff! Not for a pious chap like you, Tommy."

Little Chandler said nothing until the barman returned with two glasses: then he touched his friend's glass lightly and reciprocated the former toast. He was beginning to feel somewhat disillusioned. Gallaher's accent and way of expressing himself did not please him. There was something vulgar in his friend which he had not observed before. But perhaps it was only the result of living in London amid the bustle and competition of the Press. The old personal charm was still there under this new gaudy manner. And, after all, Gallaher had lived, he had seen the world. Little Chandler looked at his friend enviously.

"Everything in Paris is gay," said Ignatius Gallaher. "They believe in enjoying life—and don't you think they're right? If you want to enjoy yourself properly you must go to Paris. And, mind you, they've a great feeling for the Irish there. When they heard I was from Ireland they were ready to eat me, man."

Little Chandler took four or five sips from his glass.

"Tell me," he said, "is it true that Paris is so . . . immoral as they say?"

Ignatius Gallaher made a catholic gesture with his right arm.

"Every place is immoral," he said. "Of course you do find spicy bits in Paris. Go to one of the students' balls, for instance. That's lively, if you like, when the *cocottes* begin to let themselves loose. You know what they are, I suppose?"

"I've heard of them," said Little Chandler.

Ignatius Gallaher drank off his whisky and shook his head.

"Ah," he said, "you may say what you like. There's no woman like the Parisienne—for style, for go."

"Then it is an immoral city," said Little Chandler, with timid insistence—"I mean, compared with London or Dublin?"

"London!" said Ignatius Gallaher. "It's six of one and half-a-dozen of the other. You ask Hogan, my boy. I showed him a bit about London when he was over there. He'd open your eye. . . . I say, Tommy, don't make punch of that whisky: liquor up."

"No, really. . . ."

"O, come on, another one won't do you any harm. What is it? The same again, I suppose?"

"Well . . . all right."

"*François*, the same again. . . . Will you smoke, Tommy?"

Ignatius Gallaher produced his cigar-case. The two friends lit their cigars and puffed at them in silence until their drinks were served.

"I'll tell you my opinion," said Ignatius Gallaher, emerging after some time from the clouds of smoke in which he had taken refuge, "it's a rum world. Talk of immorality! I've heard of cases—what am I saying?—I've known them: cases of . . . immorality. . . ."

Ignatius Gallaher puffed thoughtfully at his cigar and then, in a calm historian's tone, he proceeded to sketch for his friend some pictures of the corruption which was rife abroad. He summarised the vices of many capitals and seemed inclined to award the palm to Berlin. Some things he could not vouch for (his friends had told him), but of others he had had personal experience. He spared neither rank nor caste. He revealed many of the secrets of religious houses on the Continent and described some of the practices which were fashionable in high society and ended by telling, with details, a story about an English duchess—a story which he knew to be true. Little Chandler was astonished.

"Ah, well," said Ignatius Gallaher, "here we are in old jog-along Dublin where nothing is known of such things."

"How dull you must find it," said Little Chandler, "after all the other places you've seen!"

"Well," said Ignatius Gallaher, "it's a relaxation to come over here, you know. And, after all, it's the old country, as they say, isn't it? You can't help having a certain feeling for it. That's human nature. . . . But tell me something about yourself. Hogan told me you had . . . tasted the joys of connubial bliss. Two years ago, wasn't it?"

Little Chandler blushed and smiled.

"Yes," he said. "I was married last May twelve months."

"I hope it's not too late in the day to offer my best wishes," said Ignatius Gallaher. "I didn't know your address or I'd have done so at the time."

He extended his hand, which Little Chandler took.

"Well, Tommy," he said, "I wish you and yours every joy in life, old chap, and tons of money, and may you never die till I shoot you. And that's the wish of a sincere friend, an old friend. You know that?"

"I know that," said Little Chandler.

"Any youngsters?" said Ignatius Gallaher.

Little Chandler blushed again.

"We have one child," he said.

"Son or daughter?"

"A little boy."

Ignatius Gallaher slapped his friend sonorously on the back.

"Bravo," he said, "I wouldn't doubt you, Tommy."

Little Chandler smiled, looked confusedly at his glass and bit his lower lip with three childishly white front teeth.

"I hope you'll spend an evening with us," he said, "before you go back. My wife will be delighted to meet you. We can have a little music and——"

"Thanks awfully, old chap," said Ignatius Gallaher, "I'm sorry we didn't meet earlier. But I must leave to-morrow night."

"To-night, perhaps . . . ?"

"I'm awfully sorry, old man. You see I'm over here with another fellow, clever young chap he is too, and we arranged to go to a little card-party. Only for that . . ."

"O, in that case. . . ."

"But who knows?" said Ignatius Gallaher considerately. "Next year I may take a little skip over here now that I've broken the ice. It's only a pleasure deferred."

"Very well," said Little Chandler, "the next time you come we must have an evening together. That's agreed now, isn't it?"

"Yes, that's agreed," said Ignatius Gallaher. "Next year if I come, *parole d'honneur*."

"And to clinch the bargain," said Little Chandler, "we'll just have one more now."

Ignatius Gallaher took out a large gold watch and looked at it.

"Is it to be the last?" he said. "Because you know, I have an a.p."

"O, yes, positively," said Little Chandler.

"Very well, then," said Ignatius Gallaher, "let us have another one as a *deoc an doruis*—that's good vernacular for a small whisky, I believe."

Little Chandler ordered the drinks. The blush which had risen to his face a few moments before was establishing itself. A trifle made him blush at any time: and now he felt warm and excited. Three small whiskies had gone to his head and Gallaher's strong cigar had confused his mind, for he was a delicate and abstinent person. The adventure of meeting Gallaher after eight years, of finding himself with Gallaher in Corless's surrounded by lights and noise, of listening to Gallaher's stories and of sharing for a brief space Gallaher's vagrant and triumphant life, upset the equipoise of his sensitive nature. He felt acutely the contrast between his own life and his friend's, and it seemed to him unjust. Gallaher was his inferior in birth and education. He was sure that he could do something better than his friend had ever done, or could ever do, something higher than mere tawdry journalism if he only got the chance. What was it that stood in his way? His unfortunate timidity! He wished to vindicate himself in some way, to assert his manhood. He saw behind Gallaher's refusal of his invitation. Gallaher was only patronising him by his friendliness just as he was patronising Ireland by his visit.

The barman brought their drinks. Little Chandler pushed one glass towards his friend and took up the other boldly.

"Who knows?" he said, as they lifted their glasses. "When you come next year I may have the pleasure of wishing long life and happiness to Mr. and Mrs. Ignatius Gallaher."

Ignatius Gallaher in the act of drinking closed one eye expressively over the rim of his glass. When he had drunk he smacked his lips decisively, set down his glass and said:

"No blooming fear of that, my boy. I'm going to have my fling first and see a bit of life and the world before I put my head in the sack—if I ever do."

"Some day you will," said Little Chandler calmly.

Ignatius Gallaher turned his orange tie and slate-blue eyes full upon his friend.

"You think so?" he said.

"You'll put your head in the sack," repeated Little Chandler stoutly, "like everyone else if you can find the girl."

He had slightly emphasised his tone and he was aware that he had betrayed himself; but, though the colour had heightened in his cheek, he did not flinch from his friend's gaze. Ignatius Gallaher watched him for a few moments and then said:

"If ever it occurs, you may bet your bottom dollar there'll be no mooning and spooning about it. I mean to marry money. She'll have a good fat account at the bank or she won't do for me."

Little Chandler shook his head.

"Why, man alive," said Ignatius Gallaher, vehemently, "do you know what it is? I've only to say the word and to-morrow I can have the woman and the cash. You don't believe it? Well, I know it. There are hundreds— what am I saying?—thousands of rich Germans and Jews, rotten with money, that'd only be too glad. . . . . You wait a while, my boy. See if I don't play my cards properly. When I go about a thing I mean business, I tell you. You just wait."

He tossed his glass to his mouth, finished his drink and laughed loudly. Then he looked thoughtfully before him and said in a calmer tone:

"But I'm in no hurry. They can wait. I don't fancy tying myself up to one woman, you know."

He imitated with his mouth the act of tasting and made a wry face.

"Must get a bit stale, I should think," he said.

. . . .

Little Chandler sat in the room off the hall, holding a child in his arms. To save money they kept no servant but Annie's young sister Monica came for an hour or so in the morning and an hour or so in the evening to help. But Monica had gone home long ago. It was a quarter to nine. Little Chandler had come home late for tea and, moreover, he had forgotten to bring Annie home the parcel of coffee from Bewley's. Of course she was in a bad humour and gave him short answers. She said she would do without any tea but when it came near the time at which the shop at the corner closed she decided to go out herself for a quarter of a pound of tea and two pounds of sugar. She put the sleeping child deftly in his arms and said:

"Here. Don't waken him."

A little lamp with a white china shade stood upon the table and its light fell over a photograph which was enclosed in a frame of crumpled horn. It was Annie's photograph. Little Chandler looked at it, pausing at the thin tight lips. She wore the pale blue summer blouse which he had brought her home as a present one Saturday. It had cost him ten and elevenpence; but what an agony of nervousness it had cost him! How he had suffered that day, waiting at the shop door until the shop was empty, standing at the counter and trying to appear at his ease while the girl piled ladies' blouses before him, paying at the desk and forgetting to take up the odd penny of his change, being called back by the cashier, and finally, striving to hide his blushes as he left the shop by examining the parcel to see if it was securely tied. When he brought the blouse home Annie kissed him and said it was very pretty and stylish; but when she heard the price she threw the blouse on the table and said it was a regular swindle to charge ten and elevenpence for it. At first she wanted to take it back but when she tried it on she was delighted with it, especially with the make of the sleeves, and kissed him and said he was very good to think of her.

Hm! . . .

He looked coldly into the eyes of the photograph and they answered coldly. Certainly they were pretty and the face itself was pretty. But he found something mean in it. Why was it so unconscious and ladylike? The composure of the eyes irritated him. They repelled him and defied him: there was no passion in them, no rapture. He thought of what Gallaher had said about rich Jewesses. Those dark Oriental eyes, he thought, how full they are of passion, of voluptuous longing! . . . Why had he married the eyes in the photograph?

He caught himself up at the question and glanced nervously round the room. He found something mean in the pretty furniture which he had bought for his house on the hire system. Annie had chosen it herself and it reminded him of her. It too was prim and pretty. A dull resentment against his life awoke within him. Could he not escape from his little house? Was it too late for him to try to live bravely like Gallaher? Could he go to London? There was the furniture still to be paid for. If he could only write a book and get it published, that might open the way for him.

A volume of Byron's poems lay before him on the table. He opened it cautiously with his left hand lest he should waken the child and began to read the first poem in the book:

> *"Hushed are the winds and still the evening gloom,*
> *Not e'en a Zephyr wanders through the grove,*
> *Whilst I return to view my Margaret's tomb*
> *And scatter flowers on the dust I love."*

He paused. He felt the rhythm of the verse about him in the room. How melancholy it was! Could he, too, write like that, express the melancholy of his soul in verse? There were so many things he wanted to describe: his sensation of a few hours before on Grattan Bridge, for example. If he could get back again into that mood. . . .

The child awoke and began to cry. He turned from the page and tried to hush it: but it would not be hushed. He began to rock it to and fro in his arms but its wailing cry grew keener. He rocked it faster while his eyes began to read the second stanza:

> *"Within this narrow cell reclines her clay,*
> *That clay where once . . ."*

It was useless. He couldn't read. He couldn't do anything. The wailing of the child pierced the drum of his ear. It was useless, useless! He was a prisoner for life. His arms trembled with anger and suddenly bending to the child's face he shouted:

"Stop!"

The child stopped for an instant, had a spasm of fright and began to scream. He jumped up from his chair and walked hastily up and down the room with the child in his arms. It began to sob piteously, losing its breath for four or five seconds, and then bursting out anew. The thin walls of the room echoed the sound. He tried to soothe it but it sobbed more convulsively. He looked at the contracted and quivering face of the child and began to be alarmed. He counted seven sobs without a break between them and caught the child to his breast in fright. If it died! . . .

The door was burst open and a young woman ran in, panting.

"What is it? What is it?" she cried.

The child, hearing its mother's voice, broke out into a paroxysm of sobbing.

"It's nothing, Annie . . . it's nothing. . . . He began to cry . . ."

She flung her parcels on the floor and snatched the child from him.

"What have you done to him?" she cried, glaring into his face.

Little Chandler sustained for one moment the gaze of her eyes and his heart closed together as he met the hatred in them. He began to stammer:

"It's nothing. . . . He . . . he began to cry. . . . I couldn't . . . I didn't do anything. . . . What?"

Giving no heed to him she began to walk up and down the room, clasping the child tightly in her arms and murmuring:

"My little man! My little mannie! Was 'ou frightened, love? . . . There now, love! There now! . . . Lambabaun! Mamma's little lamb of the world! . . . There now!"

Little Chandler felt his cheeks suffused with shame and he stood back out of the lamplight. He listened while the paroxysm of the child's sobbing grew less and less; and tears of remorse started to his eyes.

Counterparts

THE BELL RANG furiously and, when Miss Parker went to the tube, a furious voice called out in a piercing North of Ireland accent:

"Send Farrington here!"

Miss Parker returned to her machine, saying to a man who was writing at a desk:

"Mr. Alleyne wants you upstairs."

The man muttered "*Blast* him!" under his breath and pushed back his chair to stand up. When he stood up he was tall and of great bulk. He had a hanging face, dark wine-coloured, with fair eyebrows and moustache: his eyes bulged forward slightly and the whites of them were dirty. He lifted up the counter and, passing by the clients, went out of the office with a heavy step.

He went heavily upstairs until he came to the second landing, where a door bore a brass plate with the inscription *Mr. Alleyne*. Here he halted, puffing with labour and vexation, and knocked. The shrill voice cried:

"Come in!"

The man entered Mr. Alleyne's room. Simultaneously Mr. Alleyne, a little man wearing gold-rimmed glasses on a clean-shaven face, shot his head up over a pile of documents. The head itself was so pink and hairless it seemed like a large egg reposing on the papers. Mr. Alleyne did not lose a moment:

"Farrington? What is the meaning of this? Why have I always to complain of you? May I ask you why you haven't made a copy of that contract between Bodley and Kirwan? I told you it must be ready by four o'clock."

"But Mr. Shelley said, sir——"

"*Mr. Shelley said, sir.* . . . Kindly attend to what I say and not to what *Mr. Shelley says, sir*. You have always some excuse or another for shirking work. Let me tell you that if the contract is not copied before this evening I'll lay the matter before Mr. Crosbie. . . . Do you hear me now?"

"Yes, sir."

"Do you hear me now? . . . Ay and another little matter! I might as well be talking to the wall as talking to you. Understand once for all that you get a half an hour for your lunch and not an hour and a half. How many courses do you want, I'd like to know. . . . Do you mind me now?"

"Yes, sir."

Mr. Alleyne bent his head again upon his pile of papers. The man stared fixedly at the polished skull which directed the affairs of Crosbie & Alleyne, gauging its fragility. A spasm of rage gripped his throat for a few moments and then passed, leaving after it a sharp sensation of thirst. The man recognised the sensation and felt that he must have a good night's drinking. The middle of the month was passed and, if he could get the copy done in time, Mr. Alleyne might give him an order on the cashier. He stood still, gazing fixedly at the head upon the pile of papers. Suddenly Mr. Alleyne began to upset all the papers, searching for something. Then, as if he had been unaware of the man's presence till that moment, he shot up his head again, saying:

"Eh? Are you going to stand there all day? Upon my word, Farrington, you take things easy!"

"I was waiting to see . . ."

"Very good, you needn't wait to see. Go downstairs and do your work."

The man walked heavily towards the door and, as he went out of the room, he heard Mr. Alleyne cry after him that if the contract was not copied by evening Mr. Crosbie would hear of the matter.

He returned to his desk in the lower office and counted the sheets which remained to be copied. He took up his pen and dipped it in the ink but he continued to stare stupidly at the last words he had written: *In no case shall the said Bernard Bodley be* . . . The evening was falling and in a few minutes they would be lighting the gas: then he could write. He felt that he must slake the thirst in his throat. He stood up from his desk and, lifting the counter as before, passed out of the office. As he was passing out the chief clerk looked at him inquiringly.

"It's all right, Mr. Shelley," said the man, pointing with his finger to indicate the objective of his journey.

The chief clerk glanced at the hat-rack, but, seeing the row complete, offered no remark. As soon as he was on the landing the man pulled a shepherd's plaid cap out of his pocket, put it on his head and ran quickly down the rickety stairs. From the street door he walked on furtively on the inner side of the path towards the corner and all at once dived into a doorway. He was now safe in the dark snug of O'Neill's shop, and, filling up the little window that looked into the bar with his inflamed face, the colour of dark wine or dark meat, he called out:

"Here, Pat, give us a g.p., like a good fellow."

The curate brought him a glass of plain porter. The man drank it at a gulp and asked for a caraway seed. He put his penny on the counter and, leaving the curate to grope for it in the gloom, retreated out of the snug as furtively as he had entered it.

Darkness, accompanied by a thick fog, was gaining upon the dusk of February and the lamps in Eustace Street had been lit. The man went up by the houses until he reached the door of the office, wondering whether he could finish his copy in time. On the stairs a moist pungent odour of perfumes saluted his nose: evidently Miss Delacour had come while he was out in O'Neill's. He crammed his cap back again into his pocket and re-entered the office, assuming an air of absent-mindedness.

"Mr. Alleyne has been calling for you," said the chief clerk severely. "Where were you?"

The man glanced at the two clients who were standing at the counter as if to intimate that their presence prevented him from answering. As the clients were both male the chief clerk allowed himself a laugh.

"I know that game," he said. "Five times in one day is a little bit. . . . Well, you better look sharp and get a copy of our correspondence in the Delacour case for Mr. Alleyne."

This address in the presence of the public, his run upstairs and the porter he had gulped down so hastily confused the man and, as he sat down at his desk to get what was required, he realised how hopeless was the task of finishing his copy of the contract before half past five. The dark damp night was coming and he longed to spend it in the bars, drinking with his friends amid the glare of gas and the clatter of glasses. He got out the Delacour correspondence and passed out of the office. He hoped Mr. Alleyne would not discover that the last two letters were missing.

The moist pungent perfume lay all the way up to Mr. Alleyne's room. Miss Delacour was a middle-aged woman of Jewish appearance. Mr. Alleyne was said to be sweet on her or on her money. She came to the office often and stayed a long time when she came. She was sitting beside his desk now in an aroma of perfumes, smoothing the handle of her umbrella and nodding the great black feather in her hat. Mr. Alleyne had swivelled his chair round to face her and thrown his right foot jauntily upon his left knee. The man put the correspondence on the desk and bowed respectfully but neither Mr. Alleyne nor Miss Delacour took any notice of his bow. Mr. Alleyne tapped a finger on the correspondence and then flicked it towards him as if to say: "That's all right: you can go."

The man returned to the lower office and sat down again at his desk. He stared intently at the incomplete phrase: *In no case shall the said Bernard Bodley be* . . . and thought how strange it was that the last three words began with the same letter. The chief clerk began to hurry Miss Parker, saying she would never have the letters typed in time for post. The man listened to the clicking of the machine for a few minutes and then set to work to finish his copy. But his head was not clear and his mind wandered away to the glare and rattle of the public-house. It was a night for hot punches. He struggled on with his copy, but when the clock struck five he had still fourteen pages to write. Blast it! He couldn't finish it in time. He longed to execrate aloud, to bring his fist down on something violently. He was so enraged that he wrote *Bernard Bernard* instead of *Bernard Bodley* and had to begin again on a clean sheet.

He felt strong enough to clear out the whole office single-handed. His body ached to do something, to rush out and revel in violence. All the indignities of his life enraged him. . . . Could he ask the cashier privately for an advance? No, the cashier was no good, no damn good: he wouldn't give an advance. . . . He knew where he would meet the boys: Leonard and O'Halloran and Nosey Flynn. The barometer of his emotional nature was set for a spell of riot.

His imagination had so abstracted him that his name was called twice before he answered. Mr. Alleyne and Miss Delacour were standing outside the counter and all the clerks had turned round in anticipation of something. The man got up from his desk. Mr. Alleyne began a tirade of abuse, saying that two letters were missing. The man answered that he knew nothing about them, that he had made a faithful copy. The tirade continued: it was so bitter and violent that the man could hardly restrain his fist from descending upon the head of the manikin before him:

"I know nothing about any other two letters," he said stupidly.

"*You—know—nothing.* Of course you know nothing," said Mr. Alleyne. "Tell me," he added, glancing first for approval to the lady beside him, "do you take me for a fool? Do you think me an utter fool?"

The man glanced from the lady's face to the little egg-shaped head and back again; and, almost before he was aware of it, his tongue had found a felicitous moment:

"I don't think, sir," he said, "that that's a fair question to put to me."

There was a pause in the very breathing of the clerks. Everyone was astounded (the author of the witticism no less than his neighbours) and Miss Delacour, who was a stout amiable person, began to smile broadly. Mr. Alleyne flushed to the hue of a wild rose and his mouth twitched with a dwarf's passion. He shook his fist in the man's face till it seemed to vibrate like the knob of some electric machine:

"You impertinent ruffian! You impertinent ruffian! I'll make short work of you! Wait till you see! You'll apologise to me for your impertinence or you'll quit the office instanter! You'll quit this, I'm telling you, or you'll apologise to me!"

.   .   .   .

He stood in a doorway opposite the office watching to see if the cashier would come out alone. All the clerks passed out and finally the cashier came out with the chief clerk. It was no use trying to say a word to him when he was with the chief clerk. The man felt that his position was bad enough. He had been obliged to offer an abject apology to Mr. Alleyne for his impertinence but he knew what a hornet's nest the office would be for him. He could remember the way in which Mr. Alleyne had hounded little Peake out of the office in order to make room for his own nephew. He felt savage and thirsty and revengeful, annoyed with himself and with everyone else. Mr. Alleyne would never give him an hour's rest; his life would be a hell to him. He had made a proper fool of himself this time. Could he not keep his tongue in his cheek? But they had never pulled together from the first, he and Mr. Alleyne, ever since the day Mr. Alleyne had overheard him mimicking his North of Ireland accent to amuse Higgins and Miss Parker: that had been the beginning of it. He might have tried Higgins for the money, but sure Higgins never had anything for himself. A man with two establishments to keep up, of course he couldn't. . . .

He felt his great body again aching for the comfort of the public-house. The fog had begun to chill him and he wondered could he touch Pat in O'Neill's. He could not touch him for more than a bob—and a bob was no use. Yet he must get money somewhere or other: he had spent his last penny for the g.p. and soon it would be too late for getting money anywhere. Suddenly, as he was fingering his watch-chain, he thought of Terry Kelly's pawn-office in Fleet Street. That was the dart! Why didn't he think of it sooner?

He went through the narrow alley of Temple Bar quickly, muttering to himself that they could all go to hell because he was going to have a good night of it. The clerk in Terry Kelly's said *A crown!* but the consignor held out for six shillings; and in the end the six shillings was allowed him literally. He came out of the pawn-office joyfully, making a little cylinder of the coins between his thumb and fingers. In Westmoreland Street the footpaths were crowded with young men and women returning from business and ragged urchins ran here and there yelling out the names of the evening editions. The man passed through the crowd, looking on the spectacle generally with proud satisfaction and staring masterfully at the office-girls. His head was full of the noises of tram-gongs and swishing trolleys and his nose already sniffed the curling fumes of punch. As he walked on he preconsidered the terms in which he would narrate the incident to the boys:

"So, I just looked at him—coolly, you know, and looked at her. Then I looked back at him again—taking my time, you know. 'I don't think that that's a fair question to put to me,' says I."

Nosey Flynn was sitting up in his usual corner of Davy Byrne's and, when he heard the story, he stood Farrington a half-one, saying it was as smart a thing as ever he heard. Farrington stood a drink in his turn. After a while O'Halloran and Paddy Leonard came in and the story was repeated to them. O'Halloran stood tailors of malt, hot, all round and told the story of the retort he had made to the chief clerk when he was in Callan's of Fownes's Street; but, as the retort was after the manner of the liberal shepherds in the eclogues, he had to admit that it was not as clever as Farrington's retort. At this Farrington told the boys to polish off that and have another.

Just as they were naming their poisons who should come in but Higgins! Of course he had to join in with the others. The men asked him to give his version of it, and he did so with great vivacity for the sight of five small hot whiskies was very exhilarating. Everyone roared laughing when he showed the way in which Mr. Alleyne shook his fist in Farrington's face. Then he imitated Farrington, saying, *"And here was my nabs, as cool as you please,"* while Farrington looked at the company out of his heavy dirty eyes, smiling and at times drawing forth stray drops of liquor from his moustache with the aid of his lower lip.

When that round was over there was a pause. O'Halloran had money but neither of the other two seemed to have any; so the whole party left the shop somewhat regretfully. At the corner of Duke Street Higgins and Nosey Flynn bevelled off to the left while the other three turned back towards the city. Rain was drizzling down on the cold streets and, when they reached the Ballast Office, Farrington suggested the Scotch House. The bar was full of men and loud with the noise of tongues and glasses. The three men pushed past the whining match-sellers at the door and formed a little party at the corner of the counter. They began to exchange stories. Leonard introduced them to a young fellow named Weathers who was performing at the Tivoli as an acrobat and knockabout *artiste*. Farrington stood a drink all round. Weathers said he would take a small Irish and Apollinaris. Farrington, who had definite notions of what was what, asked the boys would they have an Apollinaris too; but the boys told Tim to make theirs hot. The talk became theatrical. O'Halloran stood a round and then Farrington stood another round, Weathers protesting that the hospitality was too Irish. He promised to get them in behind the scenes and introduce them to some nice girls. O'Halloran said that he and Leonard would go, but that Farrington wouldn't go because he was a married man; and Farrington's heavy dirty eyes leered at the company in token that he understood he was being chaffed. Weathers made them all have just one little tincture at his expense and promised to meet them later on at Mulligan's in Poolbeg Street.

When the Scotch House closed they went round to Mulligan's. They went into the parlour at the back and O'Halloran ordered small hot specials all round. They were all beginning to feel mellow. Farrington was just standing another round when Weathers came back. Much to Farrington's relief he drank a glass of bitter this time. Funds were getting low but they had enough to keep them going. Presently two young women with big hats and a young man in a check suit came in and sat at a table close by. Weathers saluted them and told the company that they were out of the Tivoli. Farrington's eyes wandered at every moment in the direction of one of the young women. There was something striking in her appearance. An immense scarf of peacock-blue muslin was wound round her hat and knotted in a great bow under her chin; and she wore bright yellow gloves, reaching to the elbow. Farrington gazed admiringly at the plump arm which she moved very often and with much grace; and when, after a little time, she answered his gaze he admired still more her large dark brown eyes. The oblique staring expression in them fascinated him. She glanced at him once or twice and, when the party was leaving the room, she brushed against his chair and said *"O, pardon!"* in a London accent. He watched her leave the room in the hope that she would look back at him, but he was disappointed. He cursed his want of money and cursed all the rounds he had stood, particularly all the whiskies and Apollinaris which he had stood to Weathers. If there was one thing that he hated it was a sponge. He was so angry that he lost count of the conversation of his friends.

When Paddy Leonard called him he found that they were talking about feats of strength. Weathers was showing his biceps muscle to the company and boasting so much that the other two had called on Farrington to uphold the national honour. Farrington pulled up his sleeve accordingly and showed his biceps muscle to the company. The two arms were examined and compared and finally it was agreed to have a trial of strength. The table was cleared and the two men rested their elbows on it, clasping hands. When Paddy Leonard said *"Go!"* each was to try to bring down the other's hand on to the table. Farrington looked very serious and determined.

The trial began. After about thirty seconds Weathers brought his opponent's hand slowly down on to the table. Farrington's dark wine-coloured face flushed darker still with anger and humiliation at having been defeated by such a stripling.

"You're not to put the weight of your body behind it. Play fair," he said.

"Who's not playing fair?" said the other.

"Come on again. The two best out of three."

The trial began again. The veins stood out on Farrington's forehead, and the pallor of Weathers' complexion changed to peony. Their hands and arms trembled under the stress. After a long struggle Weathers again brought his opponent's hand slowly on to the table. There was a murmur of applause from the spectators. The curate, who was standing beside the table, nodded his red head towards the victor and said with stupid familiarity:

"Ah! that's the knack!"

"What the hell do you know about it?" said Farrington fiercely, turning on the man. "What do you put in your gab for?"

"Sh, sh!" said O'Halloran, observing the violent expression of Farrington's face. "Pony up, boys. We'll have just one little smahan more and then we'll be off."

A very sullen-faced man stood at the corner of O'Connell Bridge waiting for the little Sandymount tram to take him home. He was full of smouldering anger and revengefulness. He felt humiliated and discontented; he did not even feel drunk; and he had only twopence in his pocket. He cursed everything. He had done for himself in the office, pawned his watch, spent all his money; and he had not even got drunk. He began to feel thirsty again and he longed to be back again in the hot reeking public-house. He had lost his reputation as a strong man, having been defeated twice by a mere boy. His heart swelled with fury and, when he thought of the woman in the big hat who had brushed against him and said *Pardon!* his fury nearly choked him.

His tram let him down at Shelbourne Road and he steered his great body along in the shadow of the wall of the barracks. He loathed returning to his home. When he went in by the side-door he found the kitchen empty and the kitchen fire nearly out. He bawled upstairs:

"Ada! Ada!"

His wife was a little sharp-faced woman who bullied her husband when he was sober and was bullied by him when he was drunk. They had five children. A little boy came running down the stairs.

"Who is that?" said the man, peering through the darkness.

"Me, pa."

"Who are you? Charlie?"

"No, pa. Tom."

"Where's your mother?"

"She's out at the chapel."

"That's right. . . . Did she think of leaving any dinner for me?"

"Yes, pa. I——"

"Light the lamp. What do you mean by having the place in darkness? Are the other children in bed?"

The man sat down heavily on one of the chairs while the little boy lit the lamp. He began to mimic his son's flat accent, saying half to himself: *"At the chapel. At the chapel, if you please!"* When the lamp was lit he banged his fist on the table and shouted:

"What's for my dinner?"

"I'm going . . . to cook it, pa," said the little boy.

The man jumped up furiously and pointed to the fire.

"On that fire! You let the fire out! By God, I'll teach you to do that again!"

He took a step to the door and seized the walking-stick which was standing behind it.

"I'll teach you to let the fire out!" he said, rolling up his sleeve in order to give his arm free play.

The little boy cried, *"O, pa!"* and ran whimpering round the table, but the man followed him and caught him by the coat. The little boy looked about him wildly but, seeing no way of escape, fell upon his knees.

"Now, you'll let the fire out the next time!" said the man, striking at him vigorously with the stick. "Take that, you little whelp!"

The boy uttered a squeal of pain as the stick cut his thigh. He clasped his hands together in the air and his voice shook with fright.

"O, pa!" he cried. "Don't beat me, pa! And I'll . . . I'll say a *Hail Mary* for you. . . . I'll say a *Hail Mary* for you, pa, if you don't beat me. . . . I'll say a *Hail Mary*. . . ."

Clay

THE MATRON HAD given her leave to go out as soon as the women's tea was over and Maria looked forward to her evening out. The kitchen was spick and span: the cook said you could see yourself in the big copper boilers. The fire was nice and bright and on one of the side-tables were four very big barmbracks. These barmbracks seemed uncut; but if you went closer you would see that they had been cut into long thick even slices and were ready to be handed round at tea. Maria had cut them herself.

Maria was a very, very small person indeed but she had a very long nose and a very long chin. She talked a little through her nose, always soothingly: "Yes, *my dear,*" and "No, *my dear.*" She was always sent for when the women quarrelled over their tubs and always succeeded in making peace. One day the matron had said to her:

"Maria, you are a veritable peace-maker!"

And the sub-matron and two of the Board ladies had heard the compliment. And Ginger Mooney was always saying what she wouldn't do to the dummy who had charge of the irons if it wasn't for Maria. Everyone was so fond of Maria.

The women would have their tea at six o'clock and she would be able to get away before seven. From Ballsbridge to the Pillar, twenty minutes; from the Pillar to Drumcondra, twenty minutes; and twenty minutes to buy the things. She would be there before eight. She took out her purse with the silver clasps and read again the words *A Present from Belfast.* She was very fond of that purse because Joe had brought it to her five years before when he and Alphy had gone to Belfast on a Whit-Monday trip. In the purse were two half-crowns and some coppers. She would have five shillings clear after paying tram fare. What a nice evening they would have, all the children singing! Only she hoped that Joe wouldn't come in drunk. He was so different when he took any drink.

Often he had wanted her to go and live with them; but she would have felt herself in the way (though Joe's wife was ever so nice with her) and she had become accustomed to the life of the laundry. Joe was a good fellow. She had nursed him and Alphy too; and Joe used often say:

"Mamma is mamma but Maria is my proper mother."

After the break-up at home the boys had got her that position in the *Dublin by Lamplight* laundry, and she liked it. She used to have such a bad opinion of Protestants but now she thought they were very nice people, a little quiet and serious, but still very nice people to live with. Then she had her plants in the conservatory and she liked looking after them. She had lovely ferns and wax-plants and, whenever anyone came to visit her, she always gave the visitor one or two slips from her conservatory. There was one thing she didn't like and that was the tracts on the walls; but the matron was such a nice person to deal with, so genteel.

When the cook told her everything was ready she went into the women's room and began to pull the big bell. In a few minutes the women began to come in by twos and threes, wiping their steaming hands in their petticoats and pulling down the sleeves of their blouses over their red steaming arms. They settled down before their huge mugs which the cook and the dummy filled up with hot tea, already mixed with milk and sugar in huge tin cans. Maria superintended the distribution of the barmbrack and saw that every woman got her four slices. There was a great deal of laughing and joking during the meal. Lizzie Fleming said Maria was sure to get the ring and, though Fleming had said that for so many Hallow Eves, Maria had to laugh and say she didn't want any ring or man either; and when she laughed her grey-green eyes sparkled with disappointed shyness and the tip of her nose nearly met the tip of her chin. Then Ginger Mooney lifted up her mug of tea and proposed Maria's health while all the other women clattered with their mugs on the table, and said she was sorry she hadn't a sup of porter to drink it in. And Maria laughed again till the tip of her nose nearly met the tip of her chin and till her minute body nearly shook itself asunder because she knew that Mooney meant well though, of course, she had the notions of a common woman.

But wasn't Maria glad when the women had finished their tea and the cook and the dummy had begun to clear away the tea-things! She went into her little bedroom and, remembering that the next morning was a mass morning, changed the hand of the alarm from seven to six. Then she took off her working skirt and her house-boots and laid her best skirt out on the bed and her tiny dress-boots beside the foot of the bed. She changed her blouse too and, as she stood before the mirror, she thought of how she used to dress for mass on Sunday morning when she was a young girl; and she looked with quaint affection at the diminutive body which she had so often adorned. In spite of its years she found it a nice tidy little body.

When she got outside the streets were shining with rain and she was glad of her old brown waterproof. The tram was full and she had to sit on the little stool at the end of the car, facing all the people, with her toes barely touching the floor. She arranged in her mind all she was going to do and thought how much better it was to be independent and to have your own money in your pocket. She hoped they would have a nice evening. She was sure they would but she could not help thinking what a pity it was Alphy and Joe were not speaking. They were always falling out now but when they were boys together they used to be the best of friends: but such was life.

She got out of her tram at the Pillar and ferreted her way quickly among the crowds. She went into Downes's cake-shop but the shop was so full of people that it was a long time before she could get herself attended to. She bought a dozen of mixed penny cakes, and at last came out of the shop laden with a big bag. Then she thought what else would she buy: she wanted to buy something really nice. They would be sure to have plenty of apples and nuts. It was hard to know what to buy and all she could think of was cake. She decided to buy some plumcake but Downes's plumcake had not enough almond icing on top of it so she went over to a shop in Henry Street. Here she was a long time in suiting herself and the stylish young lady behind the counter, who was evidently a little annoyed by her, asked her was it wedding-cake she wanted to buy. That made Maria blush and smile at the young lady; but the young lady took it all very seriously and finally cut a thick slice of plumcake, parcelled it up and said:

"Two-and-four, please."

She thought she would have to stand in the Drumcondra tram because none of the young men seemed to notice her but an elderly gentleman made room for her. He was a stout gentleman and he wore a brown hard hat; he had a square red face and a greyish moustache. Maria thought he was a colonel-looking gentleman and she reflected how much more polite he was than the young men who simply stared straight before them. The gentleman began to chat with her about Hallow Eve and the rainy weather. He supposed the bag was full of good things for the little ones and said it was only right that the youngsters should enjoy themselves while they were young. Maria agreed with him and favoured him with demure nods and hems. He was very nice with her, and when she was getting out at the Canal Bridge she thanked him and bowed, and he bowed to her and raised his hat and smiled agreeably; and while she was going up along the terrace, bending her tiny head under the rain, she thought how easy it was to know a gentleman even when he has a drop taken.

Everybody said: "*O, here's Maria!*" when she came to Joe's house. Joe was there, having come home from business, and all the children had their Sunday dresses on. There were two big girls in from next door and games were going on. Maria gave the bag of cakes to the eldest boy, Alphy, to divide and Mrs. Donnelly said it was too good of her to bring such a big bag of cakes and made all the children say:

"Thanks, Maria."

But Maria said she had brought something special for papa and mamma, something they would be sure to like, and she began to look for her plumcake. She tried in Downes's bag and then in the pockets of her waterproof and then on the hallstand but nowhere could she find it. Then she asked all the children had any of them eaten it—by mistake, of course—but the children all said no and looked as if they did not like to eat cakes if they were to be accused of stealing. Everybody had a solution for the mystery and Mrs. Donnelly said it was plain that Maria had left it behind her in the tram. Maria, remembering how confused the gentleman with the greyish moustache had made her, coloured with shame and vexation and disappointment. At the thought of the failure of her little surprise and of the two and fourpence she had thrown away for nothing she nearly cried outright.

But Joe said it didn't matter and made her sit down by the fire. He was very nice with her. He told her all that went on in his office, repeating for her a smart answer which he had made to the manager. Maria did not understand why Joe laughed so much over the answer he had made but she said that the manager must have been a very overbearing person to deal with. Joe said he wasn't so bad when you knew how to take him, that he was a decent sort so long as you didn't rub him the wrong way. Mrs. Donnelly played the piano for the children and they danced and sang. Then the two next-door girls handed round the nuts. Nobody could find the nutcrackers and Joe was nearly getting cross over it and asked how did they expect Maria to crack nuts without a nutcracker. But Maria said she didn't like nuts and that they weren't to bother about her. Then Joe asked would she take a bottle of stout and Mrs. Donnelly said there was port wine too in the house if she would prefer that. Maria said she would rather they didn't ask her to take anything: but Joe insisted.

So Maria let him have his way and they sat by the fire talking over old times and Maria thought she would put in a good word for Alphy. But Joe cried that God might strike him stone dead if ever he spoke a word to his brother again and Maria said she was sorry she had mentioned the matter. Mrs. Donnelly told her husband it was a great shame for him to speak that way of his own flesh and blood but Joe said that Alphy was no brother of his and there was nearly being a row on the head of it. But Joe said he would not lose his temper on account of the night it was and asked his wife to open some more stout. The two next-door girls had arranged some Hallow Eve games and soon everything was merry again. Maria was delighted to see the children so merry and Joe and his wife in such good spirits. The next-door girls put some saucers on the table and then led the children up to the table, blindfold. One got the prayer-book and the other three got the water; and when one of the next-door girls got the ring Mrs. Donnelly shook her finger at the blushing girl as much as to say: *O, I know all about it!* They insisted then on blindfolding Maria and leading her up to the table to see what she would get; and, while they were putting on the bandage, Maria laughed and laughed again till the tip of her nose nearly met the tip of her chin.

They led her up to the table amid laughing and joking and she put her hand out in the air as she was told to do. She moved her hand about here and there in the air and descended on one of the saucers. She felt a soft wet substance with her fingers and was surprised that nobody spoke or took off her bandage. There was a pause for a few seconds; and then a great deal of scuffling and whispering. Somebody said something about the garden, and at last Mrs. Donnelly said something very cross to one of the next-door girls and told her to throw it out at once: that was no play. Maria understood that it was wrong that time and so she had to do it over again: and this time she got the prayer-book.

After that Mrs. Donnelly played Miss McCloud's Reel for the children and Joe made Maria take a glass of wine. Soon they were all quite merry again and Mrs. Donnelly said Maria would enter a convent before the year was out because she had got the prayer-book. Maria had never seen Joe so nice to her as he was that night, so full of pleasant talk and reminiscences. She said they were all very good to her.

At last the children grew tired and sleepy and Joe asked Maria would she not sing some little song before she went, one of the old songs. Mrs. Donnelly said *"Do, please, Maria!"* and so Maria had to get up and stand beside the piano. Mrs. Donnelly bade the children be quiet and listen to Maria's song. Then she played the prelude and said *"Now, Maria!"* and Maria, blushing very much, began to sing in a tiny quavering voice. She sang *I Dreamt that I Dwelt*, and when she came to the second verse she sang again:

> *"I dreamt that I dwelt in marble halls*
> *With vassals and serfs at my side*
> *And of all who assembled within those walls*
> *That I was the hope and the pride.*

> *"I had riches too great to count, could boast*
> *Of a high ancestral name,*
> *But I also dreamt, which pleased me most,*
> *That you loved me still the same."*

But no one tried to show her her mistake; and when she had ended her song Joe was very much moved. He said that there was no time like the long ago and no music for him like poor old Balfe, whatever other people might say; and his eyes filled up so much with tears that he could not find what he was looking for and in the end he had to ask his wife to tell him where the corkscrew was.

A Painful Case

MR. JAMES DUFFY lived in Chapelizod because he wished to live as far as possible from the city of which he was a citizen and because he found all the other suburbs of Dublin mean, modern and pretentious. He lived in an old sombre house and from his windows he could look into the disused distillery or upwards along the shallow river on which Dublin is built. The lofty walls of his uncarpeted room were free from pictures. He had himself bought every article of furniture in the room: a black iron bedstead, an iron washstand, four cane chairs, a clothes-rack, a coal-scuttle, a fender and irons and a square table on which lay a double desk. A bookcase had been made in an alcove by means of shelves of white wood. The bed was clothed with white bed-clothes and a black and scarlet rug covered the foot. A little hand-mirror hung above the washstand and during the day a white-shaded lamp stood as the sole ornament of the mantelpiece. The books on the white wooden shelves were arranged from below upwards according to bulk. A complete Wordsworth stood at one end of the lowest shelf and a copy of the *Maynooth Catechism*, sewn into the cloth cover of a notebook, stood at one end of the top shelf. Writing materials were always on the desk. In the desk lay a manuscript translation of Hauptmann's *Michael Kramer*, the stage directions of which were written in purple ink, and a little sheaf of papers held together by a brass pin. In these sheets a sentence was inscribed from time to time and, in an ironical moment, the headline of an advertisement for *Bile Beans* had been pasted on to the first sheet. On lifting the lid of the desk a faint fragrance escaped—the fragrance of new cedarwood pencils or of a bottle of gum or of an overripe apple which might have been left there and forgotten.

Mr. Duffy abhorred anything which betokened physical or mental disorder. A mediaeval doctor would have called him saturnine. His face, which carried the entire tale of his years, was of the brown tint of Dublin streets. On his long and rather large head grew dry black hair and a tawny moustache did not quite cover an unamiable mouth. His cheekbones also gave his face a harsh character; but there was no harshness in the eyes which, looking at the world from under their tawny eyebrows, gave the impression of a man ever alert to greet a redeeming instinct in others but often disappointed. He lived at a little distance from his body, regarding his own acts with doubtful side-glances. He had an odd autobiographical habit which led him to compose in his mind from time to time a short sentence about himself containing a subject in the third person and a predicate in the past tense. He never gave alms to beggars and walked firmly, carrying a stout hazel.

He had been for many years cashier of a private bank in Baggot Street. Every morning he came in from Chapelizod by tram. At midday he went to Dan Burke's and took his lunch—a bottle of lager beer and a small trayful of arrowroot biscuits. At four o'clock he was set free. He dined in an eating-house in George's Street where he felt himself safe from the society of Dublin's gilded youth and where there was a certain plain honesty in the bill of fare. His evenings were spent either before his landlady's piano or roaming about the outskirts of the city. His liking for Mozart's music brought him sometimes to an opera or a concert: these were the only dissipations of his life.

He had neither companions nor friends, church nor creed. He lived his spiritual life without any communion with others, visiting his relatives at Christmas and escorting them to the cemetery when they died. He performed these two social duties for old dignity's sake but conceded nothing further to the conventions which regulate the civic life. He allowed himself to think that in certain circumstances he would rob his bank but, as these circumstances never arose, his life rolled out evenly—an adventureless tale.

One evening he found himself sitting beside two ladies in the Rotunda. The house, thinly peopled and silent, gave distressing prophecy of failure. The lady who sat next him looked round at the deserted house once or twice and then said:

"What a pity there is such a poor house to-night! It's so hard on people to have to sing to empty benches."

He took the remark as an invitation to talk. He was surprised that she seemed so little awkward. While they talked he tried to fix her permanently in his memory. When he learned that the young girl beside her was her daughter he judged her to be a year or so younger than himself. Her face, which must have been handsome, had remained intelligent. It was an oval face with strongly marked features. The eyes were very dark blue and steady. Their gaze began with a defiant note but was confused by what seemed a deliberate swoon of the pupil into the iris, revealing for an instant a temperament of great sensibility. The pupil reasserted itself quickly, this half-disclosed nature fell again under the reign of prudence, and her astrakhan jacket, moulding a bosom of a certain fulness, struck the note of defiance more definitely.

He met her again a few weeks afterwards at a concert in Earlsfort Terrace and seized the moments when her daughter's attention was diverted to become intimate. She alluded once or twice to her husband but her tone was not such as to make the allusion a warning. Her name was Mrs. Sinico. Her husband's great-great-grandfather had come from Leghorn. Her husband was captain of a mercantile boat plying between Dublin and Holland; and they had one child.

Meeting her a third time by accident he found courage to make an appointment. She came. This was the first of many meetings; they met always in the evening and chose the most quiet quarters for their walks together. Mr. Duffy, however, had a distaste for underhand ways and, finding that they were compelled to meet stealthily, he forced her to ask him to her house. Captain Sinico encouraged his visits, thinking that his daughter's hand was in question. He had dismissed his wife so sincerely from his gallery of pleasures that he did not suspect that anyone else would take an interest in her. As the husband was often away and the daughter out giving music lessons Mr. Duffy had many opportunities of enjoying the lady's society. Neither he nor she had had any such adventure before and neither was conscious of any incongruity. Little by little he entangled his thoughts with hers. He lent her books, provided her with ideas, shared his intellectual life with her. She listened to all.

Sometimes in return for his theories she gave out some fact of her own life. With almost maternal solicitude she urged him to let his nature open to the full: she became his confessor. He told her that for some time he had assisted at the meetings of an Irish Socialist Party where he had felt himself a unique figure amidst a score of sober workmen in a garret lit by an inefficient oil-lamp. When the party had divided into three sections, each under its own leader and in its own garret, he had discontinued his attendances. The workmen's discussions, he said, were too timorous; the interest they took in the question of wages was inordinate. He felt that they were hard-featured realists and that they resented an exactitude which was the produce of a leisure not within their reach. No social revolution, he told her, would be likely to strike Dublin for some centuries.

She asked him why did he not write out his thoughts. For what, he asked her, with careful scorn. To compete with phrasemongers, incapable of thinking consecutively for sixty seconds? To submit himself to the criticisms of an obtuse middle class which entrusted its morality to policemen and its fine arts to impresarios?

He went often to her little cottage outside Dublin; often they spent their evenings alone. Little by little, as their thoughts entangled, they spoke of subjects less remote. Her companionship was like a warm soil about an exotic. Many times she allowed the dark to fall upon them, refraining from lighting the lamp. The dark discreet room, their isolation, the music that still vibrated in their ears united them. This union exalted him, wore away the rough edges of his character, emotionalised his mental life. Sometimes he caught himself listening to the sound of his own voice. He thought that in her eyes he would ascend to an angelical stature; and, as he attached the fervent nature of his companion more and more closely to him, he heard the strange impersonal voice which he recognised as his own, insisting on the soul's incurable loneliness. We cannot give ourselves, it said: we are our own. The end of these discourses was that one night during which she had shown every sign of unusual excitement, Mrs. Sinico caught up his hand passionately and pressed it to her cheek.

Mr. Duffy was very much surprised. Her interpretation of his words disillusioned him. He did not visit her for a week; then he wrote to her asking her to meet him. As he did not wish their last interview to be troubled by the influence of their ruined confessional they met in a little cake-shop near the Parkgate. It was cold autumn weather but in spite of the cold they wandered up and down the roads of the Park for nearly three hours. They agreed to break off their intercourse: every bond, he said, is a bond to sorrow. When they came out of the Park they walked in silence towards the tram; but here she began to tremble so violently that, fearing another collapse on her part, he bade her good-bye quickly and left her. A few days later he received a parcel containing his books and music.

Four years passed. Mr. Duffy returned to his even way of life. His room still bore witness of the orderliness of his mind. Some new pieces of music encumbered the music-stand in the lower room and on his shelves stood two volumes by Nietzsche: *Thus Spake Zarathustra* and *The Gay Science*. He wrote seldom in the sheaf of papers which lay in his desk. One of his sentences, written two months after his last interview with Mrs. Sinico, read: Love between man and man is impossible because there must not be sexual intercourse and friendship between man and woman is impossible because there must be sexual intercourse. He kept away from concerts lest he should meet her. His father died; the junior partner of the bank retired. And still every morning he went into the city by tram and every evening walked home from the city after having dined moderately in George's Street and read the evening paper for dessert.

One evening as he was about to put a morsel of corned beef and cabbage into his mouth his hand stopped. His eyes fixed themselves on a paragraph in the evening paper which he had propped against the water-carafe. He replaced the morsel of food on his plate and read the paragraph attentively. Then he drank a glass of water, pushed his plate to one side, doubled the paper down before him between his elbows and read the paragraph over and over again. The cabbage began to deposit a cold white grease on his plate. The girl came over to him to ask was his dinner not properly cooked. He said it was very good and ate a few mouthfuls of it with difficulty. Then he paid his bill and went out.

He walked along quickly through the November twilight, his stout hazel stick striking the ground regularly, the fringe of the buff *Mail* peeping out of a side-pocket of his tight reefer overcoat. On the lonely road which leads from the Parkgate to Chapelizod he slackened his pace. His stick struck the ground less emphatically and his breath, issuing irregularly, almost with a sighing sound, condensed in the wintry air. When he reached his house he went up at once to his bedroom and, taking the paper from his pocket, read the paragraph again by the failing light of the window. He read it not aloud, but moving his lips as a priest does when he reads the prayers *Secreto*. This was the paragraph:

DEATH OF A LADY AT SYDNEY PARADE

A Painful Case

To-day at the City of Dublin Hospital the Deputy Coroner (in the absence of Mr. Leverett) held an inquest on the body of Mrs. Emily Sinico, aged forty-three years, who was killed at Sydney Parade Station yesterday evening. The evidence showed that the deceased lady, while attempting to cross the line, was knocked down by the engine of the ten o'clock slow train from Kingstown, thereby sustaining injuries of the head and right side which led to her death.

James Lennon, driver of the engine, stated that he had been in the employment of the railway company for fifteen years. On hearing the guard's whistle he set the train in motion and a second or two afterwards brought it to rest in response to loud cries. The train was going slowly.

P. Dunne, railway porter, stated that as the train was about to start he observed a woman attempting to cross the lines. He ran towards her and shouted, but, before he could reach her, she was caught by the buffer of the engine and fell to the ground.

A juror. "You saw the lady fall?"

Witness. "Yes."

Police Sergeant Croly deposed that when he arrived he found the deceased lying on the platform apparently dead. He had the body taken to the waiting-room pending the arrival of the ambulance.

Constable 57E corroborated.

Dr. Halpin, assistant house surgeon of the City of Dublin Hospital, stated that the deceased had two lower ribs fractured and had sustained severe contusions of the right shoulder. The right side of the head had been injured in the fall. The injuries were not sufficient to have caused death in a normal person. Death, in his opinion, had been probably due to shock and sudden failure of the heart's action.

Mr. H. B. Patterson Finlay, on behalf of the railway company, expressed his deep regret at the accident. The company had always taken every precaution to prevent people crossing the lines except by the bridges, both by placing notices in every station and by the use of patent spring gates at level crossings. The deceased had been in the habit of crossing the lines late at night from platform to platform and, in view of certain other circumstances of the case, he did not think the railway officials were to blame.

Captain Sinico, of Leoville, Sydney Parade, husband of the deceased, also gave evidence. He stated that the deceased was his wife. He was not in Dublin at the time of the accident as he had arrived only that morning from Rotterdam. They had been married for twenty-two years and had lived happily until about two years ago when his wife began to be rather intemperate in her habits.

Miss Mary Sinico said that of late her mother had been in the habit of going out at night to buy spirits. She, witness, had often tried to reason with her mother and had induced her to join a League. She was not at home until an hour after the accident.

The jury returned a verdict in accordance with the medical evidence and exonerated Lennon from all blame.

The Deputy Coroner said it was a most painful case, and expressed great sympathy with Captain Sinico and his daughter. He urged on the railway company to take strong measures to prevent the possibility of similar accidents in the future. No blame attached to anyone.

Mr. Duffy raised his eyes from the paper and gazed out of his window on the cheerless evening landscape. The river lay quiet beside the empty distillery and from time to time a light appeared in some house on the Lucan road. What an end! The whole narrative of her death revolted him and it revolted him to think that he had ever spoken to her of what he held sacred. The threadbare phrases, the inane expressions of sympathy, the cautious words of a reporter won over to conceal the details of a common-place vulgar death attacked his stomach. Not merely had she degraded herself; she had degraded him. He saw the squalid tract of her vice, miserable and malodorous. His soul's companion! He thought of the hobbling wretches whom he had seen carrying cans and bottles to be filled by the barman. Just God, what an end! Evidently she had been unfit to live, without any strength of purpose, an easy prey to habits, one of the wrecks on which civilisation has been reared. But that she could have sunk so low! Was it possible he had deceived himself so utterly about her? He remembered her outburst of that night and interpreted it in a harsher sense than he had ever done. He had no difficulty now in approving of the course he had taken.

As the light failed and his memory began to wander he thought her hand touched his. The shock which had first attacked his stomach was now attacking his nerves. He put on his overcoat and hat quickly and went out. The cold air met him on the threshold; it crept into the sleeves of his coat. When he came to the public-house at Chapelizod Bridge he went in and ordered a hot punch.

The proprietor served him obsequiously but did not venture to talk. There were five or six working-men in the shop discussing the value of a gentleman's estate in County Kildare. They drank at intervals from their huge pint tumblers and smoked, spitting often on the floor and sometimes dragging the sawdust over their spits with their heavy boots. Mr. Duffy sat on his stool and gazed at them, without seeing or hearing them. After a while they went out and he called for another punch. He sat a long time over it. The shop was very quiet. The proprietor sprawled on the counter reading the *Herald* and yawning. Now and again a tram was heard swishing along the lonely road outside.

As he sat there, living over his life with her and evoking alternately the two images in which he now conceived her, he realised that she was dead, that she had ceased to exist, that she had become a memory. He began to feel ill at ease. He asked himself what else could he have done. He could not have carried on a comedy of deception with her; he could not have lived with her openly. He had done what seemed to him best. How was he to blame? Now that she was gone he understood how lonely her life must have been, sitting night after night alone in that room. His life would be lonely too until he, too, died, ceased to exist, became a memory—if anyone remembered him.

It was after nine o'clock when he left the shop. The night was cold and gloomy. He entered the Park by the first gate and walked along under the gaunt trees. He walked through the bleak alleys where they had walked four years before. She seemed to be near him in the darkness. At moments he seemed to feel her voice touch his ear, her hand touch his. He stood still to listen. Why had he withheld life from her? Why had he sentenced her to death? He felt his moral nature falling to pieces.

When he gained the crest of the Magazine Hill he halted and looked along the river towards Dublin, the lights of which burned redly and hospitably in the cold night. He looked down the slope and, at the base, in the shadow of the wall of the Park, he saw some human figures lying. Those venal and furtive loves filled him with despair. He gnawed the rectitude of his life; he felt that he had been outcast from life's feast. One human being had seemed to love him and he had denied her life and happiness: he had sentenced her to ignominy, a death of shame. He knew that the prostrate creatures down by the wall were watching him and wished him gone. No one wanted him; he was outcast from life's feast. He turned his eyes to the grey gleaming river, winding along towards Dublin. Beyond the river he saw a goods train winding out of Kingsbridge Station, like a worm with a fiery head winding through the darkness, obstinately and laboriously. It passed slowly out of sight; but still he heard in his ears the laborious drone of the engine reiterating the syllables of her name.

He turned back the way he had come, the rhythm of the engine pounding in his ears. He began to doubt the reality of what memory told him. He halted under a tree and allowed the rhythm to die away. He could not feel her near him in the darkness nor her voice touch his ear. He waited for some minutes listening. He could hear nothing: the night was perfectly silent. He listened again: perfectly silent. He felt that he was alone.

Ivy Day in the Committee Room

OLD JACK RAKED the cinders together with a piece of cardboard and spread them judiciously over the whitening dome of coals. When the dome was thinly covered his face lapsed into darkness but, as he set himself to fan the fire again, his crouching shadow ascended the opposite wall and his face slowly re-emerged into light. It was an old man's face, very bony and hairy. The moist blue eyes blinked at the fire and the moist mouth fell open at times, munching once or twice mechanically when it closed. When the cinders had caught he laid the piece of cardboard against the wall, sighed and said:

"That's better now, Mr. O'Connor."

Mr. O'Connor, a grey-haired young man, whose face was disfigured by many blotches and pimples, had just brought the tobacco for a cigarette into a shapely cylinder but when spoken to he undid his handiwork meditatively. Then he began to roll the tobacco again meditatively and after a moment's thought decided to lick the paper.

"Did Mr. Tierney say when he'd be back?" he asked in a husky falsetto.

"He didn't say."

Mr. O'Connor put his cigarette into his mouth and began to search his pockets. He took out a pack of thin pasteboard cards.

"I'll get you a match," said the old man.

"Never mind, this'll do," said Mr. O'Connor.

He selected one of the cards and read what was printed on it:

MUNICIPAL ELECTIONS

ROYAL EXCHANGE WARD

Mr. Richard J. Tierney, P.L.G., respectfully solicits the favour of your vote and influence at the coming election in the Royal Exchange Ward.

Mr. O'Connor had been engaged by Tierney's agent to canvass one part of the ward but, as the weather was inclement and his boots let in the wet, he spent a great part of the day sitting by the fire in the Committee Room in Wicklow Street with Jack, the old caretaker. They had been sitting thus since the short day had grown dark. It was the sixth of October, dismal and cold out of doors.

Mr. O'Connor tore a strip off the card and, lighting it, lit his cigarette. As he did so the flame lit up a leaf of dark glossy ivy in the lapel of his coat. The old man watched him attentively and then, taking up the piece of cardboard again, began to fan the fire slowly while his companion smoked.

"Ah, yes," he said, continuing, "it's hard to know what way to bring up children. Now who'd think he'd turn out like that! I sent him to the Christian Brothers and I done what I could for him, and there he goes boosing about. I tried to make him someway decent."

He replaced the cardboard wearily.

"Only I'm an old man now I'd change his tune for him. I'd take the stick to his back and beat him while I could stand over him—as I done many a time before. The mother, you know, she cocks him up with this and that. . . ."

"That's what ruins children," said Mr. O'Connor.

"To be sure it is," said the old man. "And little thanks you get for it, only impudence. He takes th'upper hand of me whenever he sees I've a sup taken. What's the world coming to when sons speaks that way to their fathers?"

"What age is he?" said Mr. O'Connor.

"Nineteen," said the old man.

"Why don't you put him to something?"

"Sure, amn't I never done at the drunken bowsy ever since he left school? 'I won't keep you,' I says. 'You must get a job for yourself.' But, sure, it's worse whenever he gets a job; he drinks it all."

Mr. O'Connor shook his head in sympathy, and the old man fell silent, gazing into the fire. Someone opened the door of the room and called out:

"Hello! Is this a Freemason's meeting?"

"Who's that?" said the old man.

"What are you doing in the dark?" asked a voice.

"Is that you, Hynes?" asked Mr. O'Connor.

"Yes. What are you doing in the dark?" said Mr. Hynes, advancing into the light of the fire.

He was a tall, slender young man with a light brown moustache. Imminent little drops of rain hung at the brim of his hat and the collar of his jacket-coat was turned up.

"Well, Mat," he said to Mr. O'Connor, "how goes it?"

Mr. O'Connor shook his head. The old man left the hearth, and after stumbling about the room returned with two candlesticks which he thrust one after the other into the fire and carried to the table. A denuded room came into view and the fire lost all its cheerful colour. The walls of the room were bare except for a copy of an election address. In the middle of the room was a small table on which papers were heaped.

Mr. Hynes leaned against the mantelpiece and asked:

"Has he paid you yet?"

"Not yet," said Mr. O'Connor. "I hope to God he'll not leave us in the lurch to-night."

Mr. Hynes laughed.

"O, he'll pay you. Never fear," he said.

"I hope he'll look smart about it if he means business," said Mr. O'Connor.

"What do you think, Jack?" said Mr. Hynes satirically to the old man.

The old man returned to his seat by the fire, saying:

"It isn't but he has it, anyway. Not like the other tinker."

"What other tinker?" said Mr. Hynes.

"Colgan," said the old man scornfully.

"Is it because Colgan's a working-man you say that? What's the difference between a good honest bricklayer and a publican—eh? Hasn't the working-man as good a right to be in the Corporation as anyone else—ay, and a better right than those shoneens that are always hat in hand before any fellow with a handle to his name? Isn't that so, Mat?" said Mr. Hynes, addressing Mr. O'Connor.

"I think you're right," said Mr. O'Connor.

"One man is a plain honest man with no hunker-sliding about him. He goes in to represent the labour classes. This fellow you're working for only wants to get some job or other."

"Of course, the working-classes should be represented," said the old man.

"The working-man," said Mr. Hynes, "gets all kicks and no halfpence. But it's labour produces everything. The working-man is not looking for fat jobs for his sons and nephews and cousins. The working-man is not going to drag the honour of Dublin in the mud to please a German monarch."

"How's that?" said the old man.

"Don't you know they want to present an address of welcome to Edward Rex if he comes here next year? What do we want kowtowing to a foreign king?"

"Our man won't vote for the address," said Mr. O'Connor. "He goes in on the Nationalist ticket."

"Won't he?" said Mr. Hynes. "Wait till you see whether he will or not. I know him. Is it Tricky Dicky Tierney?"

"By God! perhaps you're right, Joe," said Mr. O'Connor. "Anyway, I wish he'd turn up with the spondulics."

The three men fell silent. The old man began to rake more cinders together. Mr. Hynes took off his hat, shook it and then turned down the collar of his coat, displaying, as he did so, an ivy leaf in the lapel.

"If this man was alive," he said, pointing to the leaf, "we'd have no talk of an address of welcome."

"That's true," said Mr. O'Connor.

"Musha, God be with them times!" said the old man. "There was some life in it then."

The room was silent again. Then a bustling little man with a snuffling nose and very cold ears pushed in the door. He walked over quickly to the fire, rubbing his hands as if he intended to produce a spark from them.

"No money, boys," he said.

"Sit down here, Mr. Henchy," said the old man, offering him his chair.

"O, don't stir, Jack, don't stir," said Mr. Henchy.

He nodded curtly to Mr. Hynes and sat down on the chair which the old man vacated.

"Did you serve Aungier Street?" he asked Mr. O'Connor.

"Yes," said Mr. O'Connor, beginning to search his pockets for memoranda.

"Did you call on Grimes?"

"I did."

"Well? How does he stand?"

"He wouldn't promise. He said: 'I won't tell anyone what way I'm going to vote.' But I think he'll be all right."

"Why so?"

"He asked me who the nominators were; and I told him. I mentioned Father Burke's name. I think it'll be all right."

Mr. Henchy began to snuffle and to rub his hands over the fire at a terrific speed. Then he said:

"For the love of God, Jack, bring us a bit of coal. There must be some left."

The old man went out of the room.

"It's no go," said Mr. Henchy, shaking his head. "I asked the little shoeboy, but he said: 'O, now, Mr. Henchy, when I see the work going on properly I won't forget you, you may be sure.' Mean little tinker! 'Usha, how could he be anything else?"

"What did I tell you, Mat?" said Mr. Hynes. "Tricky Dicky Tierney."

"O, he's as tricky as they make 'em," said Mr. Henchy. "He hasn't got those little pigs' eyes for nothing. Blast his soul! Couldn't he pay up like a man instead of: 'O, now, Mr. Henchy, I must speak to Mr. Fanning. . . . I've spent a lot of money'? Mean little schoolboy of hell! I suppose he forgets the time his little old father kept the hand-me-down shop in Mary's Lane."

"But is that a fact?" asked Mr. O'Connor.

"God, yes," said Mr. Henchy. "Did you never hear that? And the men used to go in on Sunday morning before the houses were open to buy a waistcoat or a trousers—moya! But Tricky Dicky's little old father always had a tricky little black bottle up in a corner. Do you mind now? That's that. That's where he first saw the light."

The old man returned with a few lumps of coal which he placed here and there on the fire.

"That's a nice how-do-you-do," said Mr. O'Connor. "How does he expect us to work for him if he won't stump up?"

"I can't help it," said Mr. Henchy. "I expect to find the bailiffs in the hall when I go home."

Mr. Hynes laughed and, shoving himself away from the mantelpiece with the aid of his shoulders, made ready to leave.

"It'll be all right when King Eddie comes," he said. "Well, boys, I'm off for the present. See you later. 'Bye, 'bye."

He went out of the room slowly. Neither Mr. Henchy nor the old man said anything, but, just as the door was closing, Mr. O'Connor, who had been staring moodily into the fire, called out suddenly:

" 'Bye, Joe."

Mr. Henchy waited a few moments and then nodded in the direction of the door.

"Tell me," he said across the fire, "what brings our friend in here? What does he want?"

" 'Usha, poor Joe!" said Mr. O'Connor, throwing the end of his cigarette into the fire, "he's hard up, like the rest of us."

Mr. Henchy snuffled vigorously and spat so copiously that he nearly put out the fire, which uttered a hissing protest.

"To tell you my private and candid opinion," he said, "I think he's a man from the other camp. He's a spy of Colgan's, if you ask me. Just go round and try and find out how they're getting on. They won't suspect you. Do you twig?"

"Ah, poor Joe is a decent skin," said Mr. O'Connor.

"His father was a decent, respectable man," Mr. Henchy admitted. "Poor old Larry Hynes! Many a good turn he did in his day! But I'm greatly afraid our friend is not nineteen carat. Damn it, I can understand a fellow being hard up, but what I can't understand is a fellow sponging. Couldn't he have some spark of manhood about him?"

"He doesn't get a warm welcome from me when he comes," said the old man. "Let him work for his own side and not come spying around here."

"I don't know," said Mr. O'Connor dubiously, as he took out cigarette-papers and tobacco. "I think Joe Hynes is a straight man. He's a clever chap, too, with the pen. Do you remember that thing he wrote . . . ?"

"Some of these hillsiders and fenians are a bit too clever if you ask me," said Mr. Henchy. "Do you know what my private and candid opinion is about some of those little jokers? I believe half of them are in the pay of the Castle."

"There's no knowing," said the old man.

"O, but I know it for a fact," said Mr. Henchy. "They're Castle hacks. . . . I don't say Hynes. . . . No, damn it, I think he's a stroke above that. . . . But there's a certain little nobleman with a cock-eye—you know the patriot I'm alluding to?"

Mr. O'Connor nodded.

"There's a lineal descendant of Major Sirr for you if you like! O, the heart's blood of a patriot! That's a fellow now that'd sell his country for fourpence—ay—and go down on his bended knees and thank the Almighty Christ he had a country to sell."

There was a knock at the door.

"Come in!" said Mr. Henchy.

A person resembling a poor clergyman or a poor actor appeared in the doorway. His black clothes were tightly buttoned on his short body and it was impossible to say whether he wore a clergyman's collar or a layman's, because the collar of his shabby frock-coat, the uncovered buttons of which reflected the candlelight, was turned up about his neck. He wore a round hat of hard black felt. His face, shining with raindrops, had the appearance of damp yellow cheese save where two rosy spots indicated the cheekbones. He opened his very long mouth suddenly to express disappointment and at the same time opened wide his very bright blue eyes to express pleasure and surprise.

"O Father Keon!" said Mr. Henchy, jumping up from his chair. "Is that you? Come in!"

"O, no, no, no!" said Father Keon quickly, pursing his lips as if he were addressing a child.

"Won't you come in and sit down?"

"No, no, no!" said Father Keon, speaking in a discreet, indulgent, velvety voice. "Don't let me disturb you now! I'm just looking for Mr. Fanning. . . ."

"He's round at the *Black Eagle*," said Mr. Henchy. "But won't you come in and sit down a minute?"

"No, no, thank you. It was just a little business matter," said Father Keon. "Thank you, indeed."

He retreated from the doorway and Mr. Henchy, seizing one of the candlesticks, went to the door to light him downstairs.

"O, don't trouble, I beg!"

"No, but the stairs is so dark."

"No, no, I can see. . . . Thank you, indeed."

"Are you right now?"

"All right, thanks. . . . Thanks."

Mr. Henchy returned with the candlestick and put it on the table. He sat down again at the fire. There was silence for a few moments.

"Tell me, John," said Mr. O'Connor, lighting his cigarette with another pasteboard card.

"Hm?"

"What he is exactly?"

"Ask me an easier one," said Mr. Henchy.

"Fanning and himself seem to me very thick. They're often in Kavanagh's together. Is he a priest at all?"

" 'Mmmyes, I believe so. . . . I think he's what you call a black sheep. We haven't many of them, thank God! but we have a few. . . . He's an unfortunate man of some kind. . . ."

"And how does he knock it out?" asked Mr. O'Connor.

"That's another mystery."

"Is he attached to any chapel or church or institution or——"

"No," said Mr. Henchy, "I think he's travelling on his own account. . . . God forgive me," he added, "I thought he was the dozen of stout."

"Is there any chance of a drink itself?" asked Mr. O'Connor.

"I'm dry too," said the old man.

"I asked that little shoeboy three times," said Mr. Henchy, "would he send up a dozen of stout. I asked him again now, but he was leaning on the counter in his shirt-sleeves having a deep goster with Alderman Cowley."

"Why didn't you remind him?" said Mr. O'Connor.

"Well, I couldn't go over while he was talking to Alderman Cowley. I just waited till I caught his eye, and said: 'About that little matter I was speaking to you about. . . .' 'That'll be all right, Mr. H.,' he said. Yerra, sure the little hop-o'-my-thumb has forgotten all about it."

"There's some deal on in that quarter," said Mr. O'Connor thoughtfully. "I saw the three of them hard at it yesterday at Suffolk Street corner."

"I think I know the little game they're at," said Mr. Henchy. "You must owe the City Fathers money nowadays if you want to be made Lord Mayor. Then they'll make you Lord Mayor. By God! I'm thinking seriously of becoming a City Father myself. What do you think? Would I do for the job?"

Mr. O'Connor laughed.

"So far as owing money goes. . . ."

"Driving out of the Mansion House," said Mr. Henchy, "in all my vermin, with Jack here standing up behind me in a powdered wig—eh?"

"And make me your private secretary, John."

"Yes. And I'll make Father Keon my private chaplain. We'll have a family party."

"Faith, Mr. Henchy," said the old man, "you'd keep up better style than some of them. I was talking one day to old Keegan, the porter. 'And how do you like your new master, Pat?' says I to him. 'You haven't much entertaining now,' says I. 'Entertaining!' says he. 'He'd live on the smell of an oil-rag.' And do you know what he told me? Now, I declare to God, I didn't believe him."

"What?" said Mr. Henchy and Mr. O'Connor.

"He told me: 'What do you think of a Lord Mayor of Dublin sending out for a pound of chops for his dinner? How's that for high living?' says he. 'Wisha! wisha,' says I. 'A pound of chops,' says he, 'coming into the Mansion House.' 'Wisha!' says I, 'what kind of people is going at all now?' "

At this point there was a knock at the door, and a boy put in his head.

"What is it?" said the old man.

"From the *Black Eagle*," said the boy, walking in sideways and depositing a basket on the floor with a noise of shaken bottles.

The old man helped the boy to transfer the bottles from the basket to the table and counted the full tally. After the transfer the boy put his basket on his arm and asked:

"Any bottles?"

"What bottles?" said the old man.

"Won't you let us drink them first?" said Mr. Henchy.

"I was told to ask for bottles."

"Come back to-morrow," said the old man.

"Here, boy!" said Mr. Henchy, "will you run over to O'Farrell's and ask him to lend us a corkscrew—for Mr. Henchy, say. Tell him we won't keep it a minute. Leave the basket there."

The boy went out and Mr. Henchy began to rub his hands cheerfully, saying:

"Ah, well, he's not so bad after all. He's as good as his word, anyhow."

"There's no tumblers," said the old man.

"O, don't let that trouble you, Jack," said Mr. Henchy. "Many's the good man before now drank out of the bottle."

"Anyway, it's better than nothing," said Mr. O'Connor.

"He's not a bad sort," said Mr. Henchy, "only Fanning has such a loan of him. He means well, you know, in his own tinpot way."

The boy came back with the corkscrew. The old man opened three bottles and was handing back the corkscrew when Mr. Henchy said to the boy:

"Would you like a drink, boy?"

"If you please, sir," said the boy.

The old man opened another bottle grudgingly, and handed it to the boy.

"What age are you?" he asked.

"Seventeen," said the boy.

As the old man said nothing further, the boy took the bottle, said: "Here's my best respects, sir, to Mr. Henchy," drank the contents, put the bottle back on the table and wiped his mouth with his sleeve. Then he took up the corkscrew and went out of the door sideways, muttering some form of salutation.

"That's the way it begins," said the old man.

"The thin edge of the wedge," said Mr. Henchy.

The old man distributed the three bottles which he had opened and the men drank from them simultaneously. After having drunk each placed his bottle on the mantelpiece within hand's reach and drew in a long breath of satisfaction.

"Well, I did a good day's work to-day," said Mr. Henchy, after a pause.

"That so, John?"

"Yes. I got him one or two sure things in Dawson Street, Crofton and myself. Between ourselves, you know, Crofton (he's a decent chap, of course), but he's not worth a damn as a canvasser. He hasn't a word to throw to a dog. He stands and looks at the people while I do the talking."

Here two men entered the room. One of them was a very fat man, whose blue serge clothes seemed to be in danger of falling from his sloping figure. He had a big face which resembled a young ox's face in expression, staring blue eyes and a grizzled moustache. The other man, who was much younger and frailer, had a thin, clean-shaven face. He wore a very high double collar and a wide-brimmed bowler hat.

"Hello, Crofton!" said Mr. Henchy to the fat man. "Talk of the devil . . ."

"Where did the boose come from?" asked the young man. "Did the cow calve?"

"O, of course, Lyons spots the drink first thing!" said Mr. O'Connor, laughing.

"Is that the way you chaps canvass," said Mr. Lyons, "and Crofton and I out in the cold and rain looking for votes?"

"Why, blast your soul," said Mr. Henchy, "I'd get more votes in five minutes than you two'd get in a week."

"Open two bottles of stout, Jack," said Mr. O'Connor.

"How can I?" said the old man, "when there's no corkscrew?"

"Wait now, wait now!" said Mr. Henchy, getting up quickly. "Did you ever see this little trick?"

He took two bottles from the table and, carrying them to the fire, put them on the hob. Then he sat down again by the fire and took another drink from his bottle. Mr. Lyons sat on the edge of the table, pushed his hat towards the nape of his neck and began to swing his legs.

"Which is my bottle?" he asked.

"This, lad," said Mr. Henchy.

Mr. Crofton sat down on a box and looked fixedly at the other bottle on the hob. He was silent for two reasons. The first reason, sufficient in itself, was that he had nothing to say; the second reason was that he considered his companions beneath him. He had been a canvasser for Wilkins, the Conservative, but when the Conservatives had withdrawn their man and, choosing the lesser of two evils, given their support to the Nationalist candidate, he had been engaged to work for Mr. Tierney.

In a few minutes an apologetic "Pok!" was heard as the cork flew out of Mr. Lyons' bottle. Mr. Lyons jumped off the table, went to the fire, took his bottle and carried it back to the table.

"I was just telling them, Crofton," said Mr. Henchy, "that we got a good few votes to-day."

"Who did you get?" asked Mr. Lyons.

"Well, I got Parkes for one, and I got Atkinson for two, and I got Ward of Dawson Street. Fine old chap he is, too—regular old toff, old Conservative! 'But isn't your candidate a Nationalist?' said he. 'He's a respectable man,' said I. 'He's in favour of whatever will benefit this country. He's a big ratepayer,' I said. 'He has extensive house property in the city and three places of business and isn't it to his own advantage to keep down the rates? He's a prominent and respected citizen,' said I, 'and a Poor Law Guardian, and he doesn't belong to any party, good, bad, or indifferent.' That's the way to talk to 'em."

"And what about the address to the King?" said Mr. Lyons, after drinking and smacking his lips.

"Listen to me," said Mr. Henchy. "What we want in this country, as I said to old Ward, is capital. The King's coming here will mean an influx of money into this country. The citizens of Dublin will benefit by it. Look at all the factories down by the quays there, idle! Look at all the money there is in the country if we only worked the old industries, the mills, the ship-building yards and factories. It's capital we want."

"But look here, John," said Mr. O'Connor. "Why should we welcome the King of England? Didn't Parnell himself . . ."

"Parnell," said Mr. Henchy, "is dead. Now, here's the way I look at it. Here's this chap come to the throne after his old mother keeping him out of it till the man was grey. He's a man of the world, and he means well by us. He's a jolly fine decent fellow, if you ask me, and no damn nonsense about him. He just says to himself: 'The old one never went to see these wild

Irish. By Christ, I'll go myself and see what they're like.' And are we going to insult the man when he comes over here on a friendly visit? Eh? Isn't that right, Crofton?"

Mr. Crofton nodded his head.

"But after all now," said Mr. Lyons argumentatively, "King Edward's life, you know, is not the very . . ."

"Let bygones be bygones," said Mr. Henchy. "I admire the man personally. He's just an ordinary knockabout like you and me. He's fond of his glass of grog and he's a bit of a rake, perhaps, and he's a good sportsman. Damn it, can't we Irish play fair?"

"That's all very fine," said Mr. Lyons. "But look at the case of Parnell now."

"In the name of God," said Mr. Henchy, "where's the analogy between the two cases?"

"What I mean," said Mr. Lyons, "is we have our ideals. Why, now, would we welcome a man like that? Do you think now after what he did Parnell was a fit man to lead us? And why, then, would we do it for Edward the Seventh?"

"This is Parnell's anniversary," said Mr. O'Connor, "and don't let us stir up any bad blood. We all respect him now that he's dead and gone—even the Conservatives," he added, turning to Mr. Crofton.

Pok! The tardy cork flew out of Mr. Crofton's bottle. Mr. Crofton got up from his box and went to the fire. As he returned with his capture he said in a deep voice:

"Our side of the house respects him, because he was a gentleman."

"Right you are, Crofton!" said Mr. Henchy fiercely. "He was the only man that could keep that bag of cats in order. 'Down, ye dogs! Lie down, ye curs!' That's the way he treated them. Come in, Joe! Come in!" he called out, catching sight of Mr. Hynes in the doorway.

Mr. Hynes came in slowly.

"Open another bottle of stout, Jack," said Mr. Henchy. "O, I forgot there's no corkscrew! Here, show me one here and I'll put it at the fire."

The old man handed him another bottle and he placed it on the hob.

"Sit down, Joe," said Mr. O'Connor, "we're just talking about the Chief."

"Ay, ay!" said Mr. Henchy.

Mr. Hynes sat on the side of the table near Mr. Lyons but said nothing.

"There's one of them, anyhow," said Mr. Henchy, "that didn't renege him. By God, I'll say for you, Joe! No, by God, you stuck to him like a man!"

"O, Joe," said Mr. O'Connor suddenly. "Give us that thing you wrote— do you remember? Have you got it on you?"

"O, ay!" said Mr. Henchy. "Give us that. Did you ever hear that, Crofton? Listen to this now: splendid thing."

"Go on," said Mr. O'Connor. "Fire away, Joe."

Mr. Hynes did not seem to remember at once the piece to which they were alluding, but, after reflecting a while, he said:

"O, that thing is it. . . . Sure, that's old now."

"Out with it, man!" said Mr. O'Connor.

" 'Sh, 'sh," said Mr. Henchy. "Now, Joe!"

Mr. Hynes hesitated a little longer. Then amid the silence he took off his hat, laid it on the table and stood up. He seemed to be rehearsing the piece in his mind. After a rather long pause he announced:

THE DEATH OF PARNELL

6th October, 1891

He cleared his throat once or twice and then began to recite:

> He is dead. Our Uncrowned King is dead.
>   O, Erin, mourn with grief and woe
> For he lies dead whom the fell gang
>   Of modern hypocrites laid low.
>
> He lies slain by the coward hounds
>   He raised to glory from the mire;
> And Erin's hopes and Erin's dreams
>   Perish upon her monarch's pyre.
>
> In palace, cabin or in cot
>   The Irish heart where'er it be
> Is bowed with woe—for he is gone
>   Who would have wrought her destiny.
>
> He would have had his Erin famed,
>   The green flag gloriously unfurled,
> Her statesmen, bards and warriors raised
>   Before the nations of the World.
>
> He dreamed (alas, 'twas but a dream!)
>   Of Liberty: but as he strove
> To clutch that idol, treachery
>   Sundered him from the thing he loved.
>
> Shame on the coward, caitiff hands
>   That smote their Lord or with a kiss
> Betrayed him to the rabble-rout
>   Of fawning priests—no friends of his.

May everlasting shame consume
 The memory of those who tried
To befoul and smear the exalted name
 Of one who spurned them in his pride.

He fell as fall the mighty ones,
 Nobly undaunted to the last,
And death has now united him
 With Erin's heroes of the past.

No sound of strife disturb his sleep!
 Calmly he rests: no human pain
Or high ambition spurs him now
 The peaks of glory to attain.

They had their way: they laid him low.
 But Erin, list, his spirit may
Rise, like the Phoenix from the flames,
 When breaks the dawning of the day,

The day that brings us Freedom's reign.
 And on that day may Erin well
Pledge in the cup she lifts to Joy
 One grief—the memory of Parnell.

Mr. Hynes sat down again on the table. When he had finished his recitation there was a silence and then a burst of clapping: even Mr. Lyons clapped. The applause continued for a little time. When it had ceased all the auditors drank from their bottles in silence.

Pok! The cork flew out of Mr. Hynes' bottle, but Mr. Hynes remained sitting flushed and bareheaded on the table. He did not seem to have heard the invitation.

"Good man, Joe!" said Mr. O'Connor, taking out his cigarette papers and pouch the better to hide his emotion.

"What do you think of that, Crofton?" cried Mr. Henchy. "Isn't that fine? What?"

Mr. Crofton said that it was a very fine piece of writing.

A Mother

MR. HOLOHAN, ASSISTANT secretary of the *Eire Abu* Society, had been walking up and down Dublin for nearly a month, with his hands and pockets full of dirty pieces of paper, arranging about the series of concerts. He had a game leg and for this his friends called him Hoppy Holohan. He walked up and down constantly, stood by the hour at street corners arguing the point and made notes; but in the end it was Mrs. Kearney who arranged everything.

Miss Devlin had become Mrs. Kearney out of spite. She had been educated in a high-class convent, where she had learned French and music. As she was naturally pale and unbending in manner she made few friends at school. When she came to the age of marriage she was sent out to many houses, where her playing and ivory manners were much admired. She sat amid the chilly circle of her accomplishments, waiting for some suitor to brave it and offer her a brilliant life. But the young men whom she met were ordinary and she gave them no encouragement, trying to console her romantic desires by eating a great deal of Turkish Delight in secret. However, when she drew near the limit and her friends began to loosen their tongues about her, she silenced them by marrying Mr. Kearney, who was a bootmaker on Ormond Quay.

He was much older than she. His conversation, which was serious, took place at intervals in his great brown beard. After the first year of married life, Mrs. Kearney perceived that such a man would wear better than a romantic person, but she never put her own romantic ideas away. He was sober, thrifty and pious; he went to the altar every first Friday, sometimes with her, oftener by himself. But she never weakened in her religion and was a good wife to him. At some party in a strange house when she lifted her eyebrow ever so slightly he stood up to take his leave and, when his cough troubled him, she put the eider-down quilt over his feet and made a strong rum punch. For his part, he was a model father. By paying a small

91

sum every week into a society, he ensured for both his daughters a dowry of one hundred pounds each when they came to the age of twenty-four. He sent the older daughter, Kathleen, to a good convent, where she learned French and music, and afterward paid her fees at the Academy. Every year in the month of July Mrs. Kearney found occasion to say to some friend:

"My good man is packing us off to Skerries for a few weeks."

If it was not Skerries it was Howth or Greystones.

When the Irish Revival began to be appreciable Mrs. Kearney determined to take advantage of her daughter's name and brought an Irish teacher to the house. Kathleen and her sister sent Irish picture postcards to their friends and these friends sent back other Irish picture postcards. On special Sundays, when Mr. Kearney went with his family to the pro-cathedral, a little crowd of people would assemble after mass at the corner of Cathedral Street. They were all friends of the Kearneys—musical friends or Nationalist friends; and, when they had played every little counter of gossip, they shook hands with one another all together, laughing at the crossing of so many hands, and said good-bye to one another in Irish. Soon the name of Miss Kathleen Kearney began to be heard often on people's lips. People said that she was very clever at music and a very nice girl and, moreover, that she was a believer in the language movement. Mrs. Kearney was well content at this. Therefore she was not surprised when one day Mr. Holohan came to her and proposed that her daughter should be the accompanist at a series of four grand concerts which his Society was going to give in the Antient Concert Rooms. She brought him into the drawing-room, made him sit down and brought out the decanter and the silver biscuit-barrel. She entered heart and soul into the details of the enterprise, advised and dissuaded: and finally a contract was drawn up by which Kathleen was to receive eight guineas for her services as accompanist at the four grand concerts.

As Mr. Holohan was a novice in such delicate matters as the wording of bills and the disposing of items for a programme, Mrs. Kearney helped him. She had tact. She knew what *artistes* should go into capitals and what *artistes* should go into small type. She knew that the first tenor would not like to come on after Mr. Meade's comic turn. To keep the audience continually diverted she slipped the doubtful items in between the old favourites. Mr. Holohan called to see her every day to have her advice on some point. She was invariably friendly and advising—homely, in fact. She pushed the decanter towards him, saying:

"Now, help yourself, Mr. Holohan!"

And while he was helping himself she said:

"Don't be afraid! Don't be afraid of it!"

Everything went on smoothly. Mrs. Kearney bought some lovely blush-pink charmeuse in Brown Thomas's to let into the front of Kathleen's dress. It cost a pretty penny; but there are occasions when a little expense is justifiable. She took a dozen of two-shilling tickets for the final concert and sent them to those friends who could not be trusted to come otherwise. She forgot nothing, and, thanks to her, everything that was to be done was done.

The concerts were to be on Wednesday, Thursday, Friday and Saturday. When Mrs. Kearney arrived with her daughter at the Antient Concert Rooms on Wednesday night she did not like the look of things. A few young men, wearing bright blue badges in their coats, stood idle in the vestibule; none of them wore evening dress. She passed by with her daughter and a quick glance through the open door of the hall showed her the cause of the stewards' idleness. At first she wondered had she mistaken the hour. No, it was twenty minutes to eight.

In the dressing-room behind the stage she was introduced to the secretary of the Society, Mr. Fitzpatrick. She smiled and shook his hand. He was a little man, with a white, vacant face. She noticed that he wore his soft brown hat carelessly on the side of his head and that his accent was flat. He held a programme in his hand, and, while he was talking to her, he chewed one end of it into a moist pulp. He seemed to bear disappointments lightly. Mr. Holohan came into the dressing-room every few minutes with reports from the box-office. The *artistes* talked among themselves nervously, glanced from time to time at the mirror and rolled and unrolled their music. When it was nearly half-past eight, the few people in the hall began to express their desire to be entertained. Mr. Fitzpatrick came in, smiled vacantly at the room, and said:

"Well now, ladies and gentlemen. I suppose we'd better open the ball."

Mrs. Kearney rewarded his very flat final syllable with a quick stare of contempt, and then said to her daughter encouragingly:

"Are you ready, dear?"

When she had an opportunity, she called Mr. Holohan aside and asked him to tell her what it meant. Mr. Holohan did not know what it meant. He said that the committee had made a mistake in arranging for four concerts: four was too many.

"And the *artistes!*" said Mrs. Kearney. "Of course they are doing their best, but really they are not good."

Mr. Holohan admitted that the *artistes* were no good but the committee, he said, had decided to let the first three concerts go as they pleased and reserve all the talent for Saturday night. Mrs. Kearney said nothing, but, as the mediocre items followed one another on the platform and the few people in the hall grew fewer and fewer, she began to regret that she had put herself to any expense for such a concert. There was something she didn't like in the look of things and Mr. Fitzpatrick's vacant smile irritated her very

much. However, she said nothing and waited to see how it would end. The
concert expired shortly before ten, and everyone went home quickly.

The concert on Thursday night was better attended, but Mrs. Kearney
saw at once that the house was filled with paper. The audience behaved
indecorously, as if the concert were an informal dress rehearsal. Mr.
Fitzpatrick seemed to enjoy himself; he was quite unconscious that Mrs.
Kearney was taking angry note of his conduct. He stood at the edge of the
screen, from time to time jutting out his head and exchanging a laugh with
two friends in the corner of the balcony. In the course of the evening, Mrs.
Kearney learned that the Friday concert was to be abandoned and that the
committee was going to move heaven and earth to secure a bumper house
on Saturday night. When she heard this, she sought out Mr. Holohan. She
buttonholed him as he was limping out quickly with a glass of lemonade for
a young lady and asked him was it true. Yes, it was true.

"But, of course, that doesn't alter the contract," she said. "The contract
was for four concerts."

Mr. Holohan seemed to be in a hurry; he advised her to speak to Mr.
Fitzpatrick. Mrs. Kearney was now beginning to be alarmed. She called Mr.
Fitzpatrick away from his screen and told him that her daughter had signed
for four concerts and that, of course, according to the terms of the contract,
she should receive the sum originally stipulated for, whether the society
gave the four concerts or not. Mr. Fitzpatrick, who did not catch the point at
issue very quickly, seemed unable to resolve the difficulty and said that he
would bring the matter before the committee. Mrs. Kearney's anger began to
flutter in her cheek and she had all she could do to keep from asking:

"And who is the *Cometty* pray?"

But she knew that it would not be ladylike to do that: so she was silent.

Little boys were sent out into the principal streets of Dublin early on
Friday morning with bundles of handbills. Special puffs appeared in all
the evening papers, reminding the music-loving public of the treat which
was in store for it on the following evening. Mrs. Kearney was somewhat
reassured, but she thought well to tell her husband part of her suspicions.
He listened carefully and said that perhaps it would be better if he went
with her on Saturday night. She agreed. She respected her husband in the
same way as she respected the General Post Office, as something large,
secure and fixed; and though she knew the small number of his talents she
appreciated his abstract value as a male. She was glad that he had
suggested coming with her. She thought her plans over.

The night of the grand concert came. Mrs. Kearney, with her husband
and daughter, arrived at the Antient Concert Rooms three-quarters of an
hour before the time at which the concert was to begin. By ill luck it was a
rainy evening. Mrs. Kearney placed her daughter's clothes and music in

charge of her husband and went all over the building looking for Mr. Holohan or Mr. Fitzpatrick. She could find neither. She asked the stewards was any member of the committee in the hall and, after a great deal of trouble, a steward brought out a little woman named Miss Beirne to whom Mrs. Kearney explained that she wanted to see one of the secretaries. Miss Beirne expected them any minute and asked could she do anything. Mrs. Kearney looked searchingly at the oldish face which was screwed into an expression of trustfulness and enthusiasm and answered:

"No, thank you!"

The little woman hoped they would have a good house. She looked out at the rain until the melancholy of the wet street effaced all the trustfulness and enthusiasm from her twisted features. Then she gave a little sigh and said:

"Ah, well! We did our best, the dear knows."

Mrs. Kearney had to go back to the dressing-room.

The *artistes* were arriving. The bass and the second tenor had already come. The bass, Mr. Duggan, was a slender young man with a scattered black moustache. He was the son of a hall porter in an office in the city and, as a boy, he had sung prolonged bass notes in the resounding hall. From this humble state he had raised himself until he had become a first-rate *artiste*. He had appeared in grand opera. One night, when an operatic *artiste* had fallen ill, he had undertaken the part of the king in the opera of *Maritana* at the Queen's Theatre. He sang his music with great feeling and volume and was warmly welcomed by the gallery; but, unfortunately, he marred the good impression by wiping his nose in his gloved hand once or twice out of thoughtlessness. He was unassuming and spoke little. He said *yous* so softly that it passed unnoticed and he never drank anything stronger than milk for his voice's sake. Mr. Bell, the second tenor, was a fair-haired little man who competed every year for prizes at the Feis Ceoil. On his fourth trial he had been awarded a bronze medal. He was extremely nervous and extremely jealous of other tenors and he covered his nervous jealousy with an ebullient friendliness. It was his humour to have people know what an ordeal a concert was to him. Therefore when he saw Mr. Duggan he went over to him and asked:

"Are you in it too?"

"Yes," said Mr. Duggan.

Mr. Bell laughed at his fellow-sufferer, held out his hand and said: "Shake!"

Mrs. Kearney passed by these two young men and went to the edge of the screen to view the house. The seats were being filled up rapidly and a pleasant noise circulated in the auditorium. She came back and spoke to her husband privately. Their conversation was evidently about Kathleen for they both glanced at her often as she stood chatting to one of her Nationalist friends, Miss Healy, the contralto. An unknown solitary woman with a pale face walked through the room. The women followed with keen eyes the faded blue dress which was stretched upon a meagre body. Someone said that she was Madam Glynn, the soprano.

"I wonder where did they dig her up," said Kathleen to Miss Healy. "I'm sure I never heard of her."

Miss Healy had to smile. Mr. Holohan limped into the dressing-room at that moment and the two young ladies asked him who was the unknown woman. Mr. Holohan said that she was Madam Glynn from London. Madam Glynn took her stand in a corner of the room, holding a roll of music stiffly before her and from time to time changing the direction of her startled gaze. The shadow took her faded dress into shelter but fell revengefully into the little cup behind her collar-bone. The noise of the hall became more audible. The first tenor and the baritone arrived together. They were both well dressed, stout and complacent and they brought a breath of opulence among the company.

Mrs. Kearney brought her daughter over to them, and talked to them amiably. She wanted to be on good terms with them but, while she strove to be polite, her eyes followed Mr. Holohan in his limping and devious courses. As soon as she could she excused herself and went out after him.

"Mr. Holohan, I want to speak to you for a moment," she said.

They went down to a discreet part of the corridor. Mrs. Kearney asked him when was her daughter going to be paid. Mr. Holohan said that Mr. Fitzpatrick had charge of that. Mrs. Kearney said that she didn't know anything about Mr. Fitzpatrick. Her daughter had signed a contract for eight guineas and she would have to be paid. Mr. Holohan said that it wasn't his business.

"Why isn't it your business?" asked Mrs. Kearney. "Didn't you yourself bring her the contract? Anyway, if it's not your business it's my business and I mean to see to it."

"You'd better speak to Mr. Fitzpatrick," said Mr. Holohan distantly.

"I don't know anything about Mr. Fitzpatrick," repeated Mrs. Kearney. "I have my contract, and I intend to see that it is carried out."

When she came back to the dressing-room her cheeks were slightly suffused. The room was lively. Two men in outdoor dress had taken possession of the fireplace and were chatting familiarly with Miss Healy and the baritone. They were the *Freeman* man and Mr. O'Madden Burke. The *Freeman* man had come in to say that he could not wait for the concert as he had to report the lecture which an American priest was giving in the Mansion House. He said they were to leave the report for him at the

Freeman office and he would see that it went in. He was a grey-haired man, with a plausible voice and careful manners. He held an extinguished cigar in his hand and the aroma of cigar smoke floated near him. He had not intended to stay a moment because concerts and *artistes* bored him considerably but he remained leaning against the mantelpiece. Miss Healy stood in front of him, talking and laughing. He was old enough to suspect one reason for her politeness but young enough in spirit to turn the moment to account. The warmth, fragrance and colour of her body appealed to his senses. He was pleasantly conscious that the bosom which he saw rise and fall slowly beneath him rose and fell at that moment for him, that the laughter and fragrance and wilful glances were his tribute. When he could stay no longer he took leave of her regretfully.

"O'Madden Burke will write the notice," he explained to Mr. Holohan, "and I'll see it in."

"Thank you very much, Mr. Hendrick," said Mr. Holohan. "You'll see it in, I know. Now, won't you have a little something before you go?"

"I don't mind," said Mr. Hendrick.

The two men went along some tortuous passages and up a dark staircase and came to a secluded room where one of the stewards was uncorking bottles for a few gentlemen. One of these gentlemen was Mr. O'Madden Burke, who had found out the room by instinct. He was a suave, elderly man who balanced his imposing body, when at rest, upon a large silk umbrella. His magniloquent western name was the moral umbrella upon which he balanced the fine problem of his finances. He was widely respected.

While Mr. Holohan was entertaining the *Freeman* man Mrs. Kearney was speaking so animatedly to her husband that he had to ask her to lower her voice. The conversation of the others in the dressing-room had become strained. Mr. Bell, the first item, stood ready with his music but the accompanist made no sign. Evidently something was wrong. Mr. Kearney looked straight before him, stroking his beard, while Mrs. Kearney spoke into Kathleen's ear with subdued emphasis. From the hall came sounds of encouragement, clapping and stamping of feet. The first tenor and the baritone and Miss Healy stood together, waiting tranquilly, but Mr. Bell's nerves were greatly agitated because he was afraid the audience would think that he had come late.

Mr. Holohan and Mr. O'Madden Burke came into the room. In a moment Mr. Holohan perceived the hush. He went over to Mrs. Kearney and spoke with her earnestly. While they were speaking the noise in the hall grew louder. Mr. Holohan became very red and excited. He spoke volubly, but Mrs. Kearney said curtly at intervals:

"She won't go on. She must get her eight guineas."

Mr. Holohan pointed desperately towards the hall where the audience was clapping and stamping. He appealed to Mr. Kearney and to Kathleen. But Mr. Kearney continued to stroke his beard and Kathleen looked down, moving the point of her new shoe: it was not her fault. Mrs. Kearney repeated:

"She won't go on without her money."

After a swift struggle of tongues Mr. Holohan hobbled out in haste. The room was silent. When the strain of the silence had become somewhat painful Miss Healy said to the baritone:

"Have you seen Mrs. Pat Campbell this week?"

The baritone had not seen her but he had been told that she was very fine. The conversation went no further. The first tenor bent his head and began to count the links of the gold chain which was extended across his waist, smiling and humming random notes to observe the effect on the frontal sinus. From time to time everyone glanced at Mrs. Kearney.

The noise in the auditorium had risen to a clamour when Mr. Fitzpatrick burst into the room, followed by Mr. Holohan, who was panting. The clapping and stamping in the hall were punctuated by whistling. Mr. Fitzpatrick held a few bank-notes in his hand. He counted out four into Mrs. Kearney's hand and said she would get the other half at the interval. Mrs. Kearney said:

"This is four shillings short."

But Kathleen gathered in her skirt and said: "*Now, Mr. Bell*," to the first item, who was shaking like an aspen. The singer and the accompanist went out together. The noise in the hall died away. There was a pause of a few seconds: and then the piano was heard.

The first part of the concert was very successful except for Madam Glynn's item. The poor lady sang *Killarney* in a bodiless gasping voice, with all the old-fashioned mannerisms of intonation and pronunciation which she believed lent elegance to her singing. She looked as if she had been resurrected from an old stage-wardrobe and the cheaper parts of the hall made fun of her high wailing notes. The first tenor and the contralto, however, brought down the house. Kathleen played a selection of Irish airs which was generously applauded. The first part closed with a stirring patriotic recitation delivered by a young lady who arranged amateur theatricals. It was deservedly applauded; and, when it was ended, the men went out for the interval, content.

All this time the dressing-room was a hive of excitement. In one corner were Mr. Holohan, Mr. Fitzpatrick, Miss Beirne, two of the stewards, the baritone, the bass, and Mr. O'Madden Burke. Mr. O'Madden Burke said it was the most scandalous exhibition he had ever witnessed. Miss Kathleen Kearney's musical career was ended in Dublin after that, he said. The baritone was asked what did he think of Mrs. Kearney's conduct. He did not like to say anything. He had been paid his money and wished to be at peace with men. However, he said that Mrs. Kearney might have taken the *artistes* into consideration. The stewards and the secretaries debated hotly as to what should be done when the interval came.

"I agree with Miss Beirne," said Mr. O'Madden Burke. "Pay her nothing."

In another corner of the room were Mrs. Kearney and her husband, Mr. Bell, Miss Healy and the young lady who had to recite the patriotic piece. Mrs. Kearney said that the committee had treated her scandalously. She had spared neither trouble nor expense and this was how she was repaid.

They thought they had only a girl to deal with and that, therefore, they could ride roughshod over her. But she would show them their mistake. They wouldn't have dared to have treated her like that if she had been a man. But she would see that her daughter got her rights: she wouldn't be fooled. If they didn't pay her to the last farthing she would make Dublin ring. Of course she was sorry for the sake of the *artistes*. But what else could she do? She appealed to the second tenor, who said he thought she had not been well treated. Then she appealed to Miss Healy. Miss Healy wanted to join the other group but she did not like to do so because she was a great friend of Kathleen's and the Kearneys had often invited her to their house.

As soon as the first part was ended Mr. Fitzpatrick and Mr. Holohan went over to Mrs. Kearney and told her that the other four guineas would be paid after the committee meeting on the following Tuesday and that, in case her daughter did not play for the second part, the committee would consider the contract broken and would pay nothing.

"I haven't seen any committee," said Mrs. Kearney angrily. "My daughter has her contract. She will get four pounds eight into her hand or a foot she won't put on that platform."

"I'm surprised at you, Mrs. Kearney," said Mr. Holohan. "I never thought you would treat us this way."

"And what way did you treat me?" asked Mrs. Kearney.

Her face was inundated with an angry colour and she looked as if she would attack someone with her hands.

"I'm asking for my rights," she said.

"You might have some sense of decency," said Mr. Holohan.

"Might I, indeed? . . . And when I ask when my daughter is going to be paid I can't get a civil answer."

She tossed her head and assumed a haughty voice:

"You must speak to the secretary. It's not my business. I'm a great fellow fol-the-diddle-I-do."

"I thought you were a lady," said Mr. Holohan, walking away from her abruptly.

After that Mrs. Kearney's conduct was condemned on all hands: everyone approved of what the committee had done. She stood at the door, haggard with rage, arguing with her husband and daughter, gesticulating with them. She waited until it was time for the second part to begin in the hope that the secretaries would approach her. But Miss Healy had kindly consented to play one or two accompaniments. Mrs. Kearney had to stand aside to allow the baritone and his accompanist to pass up to the platform. She stood still for an instant like an angry stone image and, when the first notes of the song struck her ear, she caught up her daughter's cloak and said to her husband:

"Get a cab!"

He went out at once. Mrs. Kearney wrapped the cloak round her daughter and followed him. As she passed through the doorway she stopped and glared into Mr. Holohan's face.

"I'm not done with you yet," she said.

"But I'm done with you," said Mr. Holohan.

Kathleen followed her mother meekly. Mr. Holohan began to pace up and down the room, in order to cool himself for he felt his skin on fire.

"That's a nice lady!" he said. "O, she's a nice lady!"

"You did the proper thing, Holohan," said Mr. O'Madden Burke, poised upon his umbrella in approval.

Grace

TWO GENTLEMEN WHO were in the lavatory at the time tried to lift him up: but he was quite helpless. He lay curled up at the foot of the stairs down which he had fallen. They succeeded in turning him over. His hat had rolled a few yards away and his clothes were smeared with the filth and ooze of the floor on which he had lain, face downwards. His eyes were closed and he breathed with a grunting noise. A thin stream of blood trickled from the corner of his mouth.

These two gentlemen and one of the curates carried him up the stairs and laid him down again on the floor of the bar. In two minutes he was surrounded by a ring of men. The manager of the bar asked everyone who he was and who was with him. No one knew who he was but one of the curates said he had served the gentleman with a small rum.

"Was he by himself?" asked the manager.

"No, sir. There was two gentlemen with him."

"And where are they?"

No one knew; a voice said:

"Give him air. He's fainted."

The ring of onlookers distended and closed again elastically. A dark medal of blood had formed itself near the man's head on the tessellated floor. The manager, alarmed by the grey pallor of the man's face, sent for a policeman.

His collar was unfastened and his necktie undone. He opened his eyes for an instant, sighed and closed them again. One of the gentlemen who had carried him upstairs held a dinged silk hat in his hand. The manager asked repeatedly did no one know who the injured man was or where had his friends gone. The door of the bar opened and an immense constable entered. A crowd which had followed him down the laneway collected outside the door, struggling to look in through the glass panels.

The manager at once began to narrate what he knew. The constable, a young man with thick immobile features, listened. He moved his head slowly to right and left and from the manager to the person on the floor, as if he feared to be the victim of some delusion. Then he drew off his glove, produced a small book from his waist, licked the lead of his pencil and made ready to indite. He asked in a suspicious provincial accent:

"Who is the man? What's his name and address?"

A young man in a cycling-suit cleared his way through the ring of bystanders. He knelt down promptly beside the injured man and called for water. The constable knelt down also to help. The young man washed the blood from the injured man's mouth and then called for some brandy. The constable repeated the order in an authoritative voice until a curate came running with the glass. The brandy was forced down the man's throat. In a few seconds he opened his eyes and looked about him. He looked at the circle of faces and then, understanding, strove to rise to his feet.

"You're all right now?" asked the young man in the cycling-suit.

"Sha, 's nothing," said the injured man, trying to stand up.

He was helped to his feet. The manager said something about a hospital and some of the bystanders gave advice. The battered silk hat was placed on the man's head. The constable asked:

"Where do you live?"

The man, without answering, began to twirl the ends of his moustache. He made light of his accident. It was nothing, he said: only a little accident. He spoke very thickly.

"Where do you live?" repeated the constable.

The man said they were to get a cab for him. While the point was being debated a tall agile gentleman of fair complexion, wearing a long yellow ulster, came from the far end of the bar. Seeing the spectacle, he called out:

"Hallo, Tom, old man! What's the trouble?"

"Sha, 's nothing," said the man.

The new-comer surveyed the deplorable figure before him and then turned to the constable, saying:

"It's all right, constable. I'll see him home."

The constable touched his helmet and answered:

"All right, Mr. Power!"

"Come now, Tom," said Mr. Power, taking his friend by the arm. "No bones broken. What? Can you walk?"

The young man in the cycling-suit took the man by the other arm and the crowd divided.

"How did you get yourself into this mess?" asked Mr. Power.

"The gentleman fell down the stairs," said the young man.

"I' 'ery 'uch o'liged to you, sir," said the injured man.

"Not at all."

" 'an't we have a little . . . ?"

"Not now. Not now."

The three men left the bar and the crowd sifted through the doors in to the laneway. The manager brought the constable to the stairs to inspect the scene of the accident. They agreed that the gentleman must have missed his footing. The customers returned to the counter and a curate set about removing the traces of blood from the floor.

When they came out into Grafton Street, Mr. Power whistled for an outsider. The injured man said again as well as he could:

"I' 'ery 'uch o'liged to you, sir. I hope we'll 'eet again. 'y na'e is Kernan."

The shock and the incipient pain had partly sobered him.

"Don't mention it," said the young man.

They shook hands. Mr. Kernan was hoisted on to the car and, while Mr. Power was giving directions to the carman, he expressed his gratitude to the young man and regretted that they could not have a little drink together.

"Another time," said the young man.

The car drove off towards Westmoreland Street. As it passed the Ballast Office the clock showed half-past nine. A keen east wind hit them, blowing from the mouth of the river. Mr. Kernan was huddled together with cold. His friend asked him to tell how the accident had happened.

"I 'an't 'an," he answered, " 'y 'ongue is hurt."

"Show."

The other leaned over the well of the car and peered into Mr. Kernan's mouth but he could not see. He struck a match and, sheltering it in the shell of his hands, peered again into the mouth which Mr. Kernan opened obediently. The swaying movement of the car brought the match to and from the opened mouth. The lower teeth and gums were covered with clotted blood and a minute piece of the tongue seemed to have been bitten off. The match was blown out.

"That's ugly," said Mr. Power.

"Sha, 's nothing," said Mr. Kernan, closing his mouth and pulling the collar of his filthy coat across his neck.

Mr. Kernan was a commercial traveller of the old school which believed in the dignity of its calling. He had never been seen in the city without a silk hat of some decency and a pair of gaiters. By grace of these two articles of clothing, he said, a man could always pass muster. He carried on the tradition of his Napoleon, the great Blackwhite, whose memory he evoked at times by legend and mimicry. Modern business methods had spared him only so far as to allow him a little office in Crowe Street, on the window blind of which was written the name of his firm with the address— London, E.C. On the mantelpiece of this little office a little leaden battalion of canisters was drawn up and on the table before the window stood four or five china bowls which were usually half full of a black liquid. From these bowls Mr. Kernan tasted tea. He took a mouthful, drew it up, saturated his palate with it and then spat it forth into the grate. Then he paused to judge.

Mr. Power, a much younger man, was employed in the Royal Irish Constabulary Office in Dublin Castle. The arc of his social rise intersected the arc of his friend's decline, but Mr. Kernan's decline was mitigated by the fact that certain of those friends who had known him at his highest point of success still esteemed him as a character. Mr. Power was one of these friends. His inexplicable debts were a byword in his circle; he was a debonair young man.

The car halted before a small house on the Glasnevin road and Mr. Kernan was helped into the house. His wife put him to bed, while Mr. Power sat downstairs in the kitchen asking the children where they went to school and what book they were in. The children—two girls and a boy, conscious of their father's helplessness and of their mother's absence, began some horseplay with him. He was surprised at their manners and at their accents, and his brow grew thoughtful. After a while Mrs. Kernan entered the kitchen, exclaiming:

"Such a sight! O, he'll do for himself one day and that's the holy alls of it. He's been drinking since Friday."

Mr. Power was careful to explain to her that he was not responsible, that he had come on the scene by the merest accident. Mrs. Kernan, remembering Mr. Power's good offices during domestic quarrels, as well as many small, but opportune loans, said:

"O, you needn't tell me that, Mr. Power. I know you're a friend of his, not like some of the others he does be with. They're all right so long as he has money in his pocket to keep him out from his wife and family. Nice friends! Who was he with to-night, I'd like to know?"

Mr. Power shook his head but said nothing.

"I'm so sorry," she continued, "that I've nothing in the house to offer you. But if you wait a minute I'll send round to Fogarty's, at the corner."

Mr. Power stood up.

"We were waiting for him to come home with the money. He never seems to think he has a home at all."

"O, now, Mrs. Kernan," said Mr. Power, "we'll make him turn over a new leaf. I'll talk to Martin. He's the man. We'll come here one of these nights and talk it over."

She saw him to the door. The carman was stamping up and down the footpath, and swinging his arms to warm himself.

"It's very kind of you to bring him home," she said.

"Not at all," said Mr. Power.

He got up on the car. As it drove off he raised his hat to her gaily.

"We'll make a new man of him," he said. "Good-night, Mrs. Kernan."

．　　　．　　　．　　　．　　　．　　　．

Mrs. Kernan's puzzled eyes watched the car till it was out of sight. Then she withdrew them, went into the house and emptied her husband's pockets.

She was an active, practical woman of middle age. Not long before she had celebrated her silver wedding and renewed her intimacy with her husband by waltzing with him to Mr. Power's accompaniment. In her days of courtship, Mr. Kernan had seemed to her a not ungallant figure: and she still hurried to the chapel door whenever a wedding was reported and, seeing the bridal pair, recalled with vivid pleasure how she had passed out of the Star of the Sea Church in Sandymount, leaning on the arm of a jovial well-fed man, who was dressed smartly in a frock-coat and lavender trousers and carried a silk hat gracefully balanced upon his other arm. After three weeks she had found a wife's life irksome and, later on, when she was beginning to find it unbearable, she had become a mother. The part of mother presented to her no insuperable difficulties and for twenty-five years she had kept house shrewdly for her husband. Her two eldest sons were launched. One was in a draper's shop in Glasgow and the other was clerk to a tea-merchant in Belfast. They were good sons, wrote regularly and sometimes sent home money. The other children were still at school.

Mr. Kernan sent a letter to his office next day and remained in bed. She made beef-tea for him and scolded him roundly. She accepted his frequent intemperance as part of the climate, healed him dutifully whenever he was sick and always tried to make him eat a breakfast. There were worse husbands. He had never been violent since the boys had grown up, and she knew that he would walk to the end of Thomas Street and back again to book even a small order.

Two nights after, his friends came to see him. She brought them up to his bedroom, the air of which was impregnated with a personal odour, and gave them chairs at the fire. Mr. Kernan's tongue, the occasional stinging pain of which had made him somewhat irritable during the day, became more polite. He sat propped up in the bed by pillows and the little colour in his puffy cheeks made them resemble warm cinders. He apologised to his guests for the disorder of the room, but at the same time looked at them a little proudly, with a veteran's pride.

He was quite unconscious that he was the victim of a plot which his friends, Mr. Cunningham, Mr. M'Coy and Mr. Power had disclosed to Mrs.

Kernan in the parlour. The idea had been Mr. Power's, but its development was entrusted to Mr. Cunningham. Mr. Kernan came of Protestant stock and, though he had been converted to the Catholic faith at the time of his marriage, he had not been in the pale of the Church for twenty years. He was fond, moreover, of giving side-thrusts at Catholicism.

Mr. Cunningham was the very man for such a case. He was an elder colleague of Mr. Power. His own domestic life was not very happy. People had great sympathy with him, for it was known that he had married an unpresentable woman who was an incurable drunkard. He had set up house for her six times; and each time she had pawned the furniture on him.

Everyone had respect for poor Martin Cunningham. He was a thoroughly sensible man, influential and intelligent. His blade of human knowledge, natural astuteness particularised by long association with cases in the police courts, had been tempered by brief immersions in the waters of general philosophy. He was well informed. His friends bowed to his opinions and considered that his face was like Shakespeare's.

When the plot had been disclosed to her, Mrs. Kernan had said:

"I leave it all in your hands, Mr. Cunningham."

After a quarter of a century of married life, she had very few illusions left. Religion for her was a habit, and she suspected that a man of her husband's age would not change greatly before death. She was tempted to see a curious appropriateness in his accident and, but that she did not wish to seem bloody-minded, she would have told the gentlemen that Mr. Kernan's tongue would not suffer by being shortened. However, Mr. Cunningham was a capable man; and religion was religion. The scheme might do good and, at least, it could do no harm. Her beliefs were not extravagant. She believed steadily in the Sacred Heart as the most generally useful of all Catholic devotions and approved of the sacraments. Her faith was bounded by her kitchen, but, if she was put to it, she could believe also in the banshee and in the Holy Ghost.

The gentlemen began to talk of the accident. Mr. Cunningham said that he had once known a similar case. A man of seventy had bitten off a piece of his tongue during an epileptic fit and the tongue had filled in again, so that no one could see a trace of the bite.

"Well, I'm not seventy," said the invalid.

"God forbid," said Mr. Cunningham.

"It doesn't pain you now?" asked Mr. M'Coy.

Mr. M'Coy had been at one time a tenor of some reputation. His wife, who had been a soprano, still taught young children to play the piano at low terms. His line of life had not been the shortest distance between two points and for short periods he had been driven to live by his wits. He had been a clerk in the Midland Railway, a canvasser for advertisements for *The Irish Times* and for *The Freeman's Journal*, a town traveller for a coal firm on commission, a private inquiry agent, a clerk in the office of the Sub-Sheriff, and he had recently become secretary to the City Coroner. His new office made him professionally interested in Mr. Kernan's case.

"Pain? Not much," answered Mr. Kernan. "But it's so sickening. I feel as if I wanted to retch off."

"That's the boose," said Mr. Cunningham firmly.

"No," said Mr. Kernan. "I think I caught cold on the car. There's something keeps coming into my throat, phlegm or——"

"Mucus," said Mr. M'Coy.

"It keeps coming like from down in my throat; sickening thing."

"Yes, yes," said Mr. M'Coy, "that's the thorax."

He looked at Mr. Cunningham and Mr. Power at the same time with an air of challenge. Mr. Cunningham nodded his head rapidly and Mr. Power said:

"Ah, well, all's well that ends well."

"I'm very much obliged to you, old man," said the invalid.

Mr. Power waved his hand.

"Those other two fellows I was with——"

"Who were you with?" asked Mr. Cunningham.

"A chap. I don't know his name. Damn it now, what's his name? Little chap with sandy hair. . . ."

"And who else?"

"Harford."

"Hm," said Mr. Cunningham.

When Mr. Cunningham made that remark, people were silent. It was known that the speaker had secret sources of information. In this case the monosyllable had a moral intention. Mr. Harford sometimes formed one of a little detachment which left the city shortly after noon on Sunday with the purpose of arriving as soon as possible at some public-house on the outskirts of the city where its members duly qualified themselves as *bona-fide* travellers. But his fellow-travellers had never consented to overlook his origin. He had begun life as an obscure financier by lending small sums of money to workmen at usurious interest. Later on he had become the partner of a very fat, short gentleman, Mr. Goldberg, in the Liffey Loan Bank. Though he had never embraced more than the Jewish ethical code, his fellow-Catholics, whenever they had smarted in person or by proxy under his exactions, spoke of him bitterly as an Irish Jew and an illiterate, and saw divine disapproval of usury made manifest through the person of his idiot son. At other times they remembered his good points.

"I wonder where did he go to," said Mr. Kernan.

He wished the details of the incident to remain vague. He wished his friends to think there had been some mistake, that Mr. Harford and he had missed each other. His friends, who knew quite well Mr. Harford's manners in drinking were silent. Mr. Power said again:

"All's well that ends well."

Mr. Kernan changed the subject at once.

"That was a decent young chap, that medical fellow," he said. "Only for him——"

"O, only for him," said Mr. Power, "it might have been a case of seven days, without the option of a fine."

"Yes, yes," said Mr. Kernan, trying to remember. "I remember now there was a policeman. Decent young fellow, he seemed. How did it happen at all?"

"It happened that you were peloothered, Tom," said Mr. Cunningham gravely.

"True bill," said Mr. Kernan, equally gravely.

"I suppose you squared the constable, Jack," said Mr. M'Coy.

Mr. Power did not relish the use of his Christian name. He was not straight-laced, but he could not forget that Mr. M'Coy had recently made a crusade in search of valises and portmanteaus to enable Mrs. M'Coy to fulfil imaginary engagements in the country. More than he resented the fact that he had been victimised he resented such low playing of the game. He answered the question, therefore, as if Mr. Kernan had asked it.

The narrative made Mr. Kernan indignant. He was keenly conscious of his citizenship, wished to live with his city on terms mutually honourable and resented any affront put upon him by those whom he called country bumpkins.

"Is this what we pay rates for?" he asked. "To feed and clothe these ignorant bostooms . . . and they're nothing else."

Mr. Cunningham laughed. He was a Castle official only during office hours.

"How could they be anything else, Tom?" he said.

He assumed a thick, provincial accent and said in a tone of command: "65, catch your cabbage!"

Everyone laughed. Mr. M'Coy, who wanted to enter the conversation by any door, pretended that he had never heard the story. Mr. Cunningham said:

"It is supposed—they say, you know—to take place in the depot where they get these thundering big country fellows, omadhauns, you know, to drill. The sergeant makes them stand in a row against the wall and hold up their plates."

He illustrated the story by grotesque gestures.

"At dinner, you know. Then he has a bloody big bowl of cabbage before him on the table and a bloody big spoon like a shovel. He takes up a wad of cabbage on the spoon and pegs it across the room and the poor devils have to try and catch it on their plates: *65, catch your cabbage.*"

Everyone laughed again: but Mr. Kernan was somewhat indignant still. He talked of writing a letter to the papers.

"These yahoos coming up here," he said, "think they can boss the people. I needn't tell you, Martin, what kind of men they are."

Mr. Cunningham gave a qualified assent.

"It's like everything else in this world," he said. "You get some bad ones and you get some good ones."

"O yes, you get some good ones, I admit," said Mr. Kernan, satisfied.

"It's better to have nothing to say to them," said Mr. M'Coy. "That's my opinion!"

Mrs. Kernan entered the room and, placing a tray on the table, said: "Help yourselves, gentlemen."

Mr. Power stood up to officiate, offering her his chair. She declined it, saying she was ironing downstairs, and, after having exchanged a nod with Mr. Cunningham behind Mr. Power's back, prepared to leave the room. Her husband called out to her:

"And have you nothing for me, duckie?"

"O, you! The back of my hand to you!" said Mrs. Kernan tartly.

Her husband called after her:

"Nothing for poor little hubby!"

He assumed such a comical face and voice that the distribution of the bottles of stout took place amid general merriment.

The gentlemen drank from their glasses, set the glasses again on the table and paused. Then Mr. Cunningham turned towards Mr. Power and said casually:

"On Thursday night, you said, Jack?"

"Thursday, yes," said Mr. Power.

"Righto!" said Mr. Cunningham promptly.

"We can meet in M'Auley's," said Mr. M'Coy. "That'll be the most convenient place."

"But we mustn't be late," said Mr. Power earnestly, "because it is sure to be crammed to the doors."

"We can meet at half-seven," said Mr. M'Coy.

"Righto!" said Mr. Cunningham.

"Half-seven at M'Auley's be it!"

There was a short silence. Mr. Kernan waited to see whether he would be taken into his friends' confidence. Then he asked:

"What's in the wind?"

"O, it's nothing," said Mr. Cunningham. "It's only a little matter that we're arranging about for Thursday."

"The opera, is it?" said Mr. Kernan.

"No, no," said Mr. Cunningham in an evasive tone, "it's just a little . . . spiritual matter."

"O," said Mr. Kernan.

There was silence again. Then Mr. Power said, point blank:

"To tell you the truth, Tom, we're going to make a retreat."

"Yes, that's it," said Mr. Cunningham, "Jack and I and M'Coy here—we're all going to wash the pot."

He uttered the metaphor with a certain homely energy and, encouraged by his own voice, proceeded:

"You see, we may as well all admit we're a nice collection of scoundrels, one and all. I say, one and all," he added with gruff charity and turning to Mr. Power. "Own up now!"

"I own up," said Mr. Power.

"And I own up," said Mr. M'Coy.

"So we're going to wash the pot together," said Mr. Cunningham.

A thought seemed to strike him. He turned suddenly to the invalid and said:

"D'ye know what, Tom, has just occurred to me? You might join in and we'd have a four-handed reel."

"Good idea," said Mr. Power. "The four of us together."

Mr. Kernan was silent. The proposal conveyed very little meaning to his mind, but, understanding that some spiritual agencies were about to concern themselves on his behalf, he thought he owed it to his dignity to show a stiff neck. He took no part in the conversation for a long while, but listened, with an air of calm enmity, while his friends discussed the Jesuits.

"I haven't such a bad opinion of the Jesuits," he said, intervening at length. "They're an educated order. I believe they mean well, too."

"They're the grandest order in the Church, Tom," said Mr. Cunningham, with enthusiasm. "The General of the Jesuits stands next to the Pope."

"There's no mistake about it," said Mr. M'Coy, "if you want a thing well done and no flies about, you go to a Jesuit. They're the boyos have influence. I'll tell you a case in point. . . ."

"The Jesuits are a fine body of men," said Mr. Power.

"It's a curious thing," said Mr. Cunningham, "about the Jesuit Order. Every other order of the Church had to be reformed at some time or other but the Jesuit Order was never once reformed. It never fell away."

"Is that so?" asked Mr. M'Coy.

"That's a fact," said Mr. Cunningham. "That's history."

"Look at their church, too," said Mr. Power. "Look at the congregation they have."

"The Jesuits cater for the upper classes," said Mr. M'Coy.

"Of course," said Mr. Power.

"Yes," said Mr. Kernan. "That's why I have a feeling for them. It's some of those secular priests, ignorant, bumptious——"

"They're all good men," said Mr. Cunningham, "each in his own way. The Irish priesthood is honoured all the world over."

"O yes," said Mr. Power.

"Not like some of the other priesthoods on the continent," said Mr. M'Coy, "unworthy of the name."

"Perhaps you're right," said Mr. Kernan, relenting.

"Of course I'm right," said Mr. Cunningham. "I haven't been in the world all this time and seen most sides of it without being a judge of character."

The gentlemen drank again, one following another's example. Mr. Kernan seemed to be weighing something in his mind. He was impressed. He had a high opinion of Mr. Cunningham as a judge of character and as a reader of faces. He asked for particulars.

"O, it's just a retreat, you know," said Mr. Cunningham. "Father Purdon is giving it. It's for business men, you know."

"He won't be too hard on us, Tom," said Mr. Power persuasively.

"Father Purdon? Father Purdon?" said the invalid.

"O, you must know him, Tom," said Mr. Cunningham stoutly. "Fine, jolly fellow! He's a man of the world like ourselves."

"Ah, . . . yes. I think I know him. Rather red face; tall."

"That's the man."

"And tell me, Martin. . . . Is he a good preacher?"

"Munno. . . . It's not exactly a sermon, you know. It's just a kind of a friendly talk, you know, in a common-sense way."

Mr. Kernan deliberated. Mr. M'Coy said:

"Father Tom Burke, that was the boy!"

"O, Father Tom Burke," said Mr. Cunningham, "that was a born orator. Did you ever hear him, Tom?"

"Did I ever hear him!" said the invalid, nettled. "Rather! I heard him. . . ."

"And yet they say he wasn't much of a theologian," said Mr. Cunningham.

"Is that so?" said Mr. M'Coy.

"O, of course, nothing wrong, you know. Only sometimes, they say, he didn't preach what was quite orthodox."

"Ah! . . . he was a splendid man," said Mr. M'Coy.

"I heard him once," Mr. Kernan continued. "I forget the subject of his discourse now. Crofton and I were in the back of the . . . pit, you know . . . the——"

"The body," said Mr. Cunningham.

"Yes, in the back near the door. I forget now what. . . . O yes, it was on the Pope, the late Pope. I remember it well. Upon my word it was magnificent, the style of the oratory. And his voice! God! hadn't he a voice! *The Prisoner of the Vatican*, he called him. I remember Crofton saying to me when we came out——"

"But he's an Orangeman, Crofton, isn't he?" said Mr. Power.

" 'Course he is," said Mr. Kernan, "and a damned decent Orangeman, too. We went into Butler's in Moore Street—faith, I was genuinely moved, tell you the God's truth—and I remember well his very words. *Kernan*, he said, *we worship at different altars*, he said, *but our belief is the same*. Struck me as very well put."

"There's a good deal in that," said Mr. Power. "There used always be crowds of Protestants in the chapel when Father Tom was preaching."

"There's not much difference between us," said Mr. M'Coy. "We both believe in——"

He hesitated for a moment.

". . . in the Redeemer. Only they don't believe in the Pope and in the mother of God."

"But, of course," said Mr. Cunningham quietly and effectively, "our religion is *the* religion, the old, original faith."

"Not a doubt of it," said Mr. Kernan warmly.

Mrs. Kernan came to the door of the bedroom and announced:

"Here's a visitor for you!"

"Who is it?"

"Mr. Fogarty."

"O, come in! come in!"

A pale, oval face came forward into the light. The arch of its fair trailing moustache was repeated in the fair eyebrows looped above pleasantly astonished eyes. Mr. Fogarty was a modest grocer. He had failed in business in a licensed house in the city because his financial condition had constrained him to tie himself to second-class distillers and brewers. He had opened a small shop on Glasnevin Road where, he flattered himself, his manners would ingratiate him with the housewives of the district. He bore himself with a certain grace, complimented little children and spoke with a neat enunciation. He was not without culture.

Mr. Fogarty brought a gift with him, a half-pint of special whisky. He inquired politely for Mr. Kernan, placed his gift on the table and sat down with the company on equal terms. Mr. Kernan appreciated the gift all the more since he was aware that there was a small account for groceries unsettled between him and Mr. Fogarty. He said:

"I wouldn't doubt you, old man. Open that, Jack, will you?"

Mr. Power again officiated. Glasses were rinsed and five small measures of whisky were poured out. This new influence enlivened the conversation. Mr. Fogarty, sitting on a small area of the chair, was specially interested.

"Pope Leo XIII.," said Mr. Cunningham, "was one of the lights of the age. His great idea, you know, was the union of the Latin and Greek Churches. That was the aim of his life."

"I often heard he was one of the most intellectual men in Europe," said Mr. Power. "I mean, apart from his being Pope."

"So he was," said Mr. Cunningham, "if not *the* most so. His motto, you know, as Pope, was *Lux upon Lux—Light upon Light*."

"No, no," said Mr. Fogarty eagerly. "I think you're wrong there. It was *Lux in Tenebris*, I think—*Light in Darkness*."

"O yes," said Mr. M'Coy, "*Tenebrae*."

"Allow me," said Mr. Cunningham positively, "it was *Lux upon Lux*. And Pius IX. his predecessor's motto was *Crux upon Crux*—that is, *Cross upon Cross*—to show the difference between their two pontificates."

The inference was allowed. Mr. Cunningham continued.

"Pope Leo, you know, was a great scholar and a poet."

"He had a strong face," said Mr. Kernan.

"Yes," said Mr. Cunningham. "He wrote Latin poetry."

"Is that so?" said Mr. Fogarty.

Mr. M'Coy tasted his whisky contentedly and shook his head with a double intention, saying:

"That's no joke, I can tell you."

"We didn't learn that, Tom," said Mr. Power, following Mr. M'Coy's example, "when we went to the penny-a-week school."

"There was many a good man went to the penny-a-week school with a sod of turf under his oxter," said Mr. Kernan sententiously. "The old system was the best: plain honest education. None of your modern trumpery. . . ."

"Quite right," said Mr. Power.

"No superfluities," said Mr. Fogarty.

He enunciated the word and then drank gravely.

"I remember reading," said Mr. Cunningham, "that one of Pope Leo's poems was on the invention of the photograph—in Latin, of course."

"On the photograph!" exclaimed Mr. Kernan.

"Yes," said Mr. Cunningham.

He also drank from his glass.

"Well, you know," said Mr. M'Coy, "isn't the photograph wonderful when you come to think of it?"

"O, of course," said Mr. Power, "great minds can see things."

"As the poet says: *Great minds are very near to madness*," said Mr. Fogarty.

Mr. Kernan seemed to be troubled in mind. He made an effort to recall the Protestant theology on some thorny points and in the end addressed Mr. Cunningham.

"Tell me, Martin," he said. "Weren't some of the popes—of course, not our present man, or his predecessor, but some of the old popes—not exactly . . . you know . . . up to the knocker?"

There was a silence. Mr. Cunningham said:

"O, of course, there were some bad lots. . . . But the astonishing thing is this. Not one of them, not the biggest drunkard, not the most . . . out-and-out ruffian, not one of them ever preached *ex cathedra* a word of false doctrine. Now isn't that an astonishing thing?"

"That is," said Mr. Kernan.

"Yes, because when the Pope speaks *ex cathedra*," Mr. Fogarty explained, "he is infallible."

"Yes," said Mr. Cunningham.

"O, I know about the infallibility of the Pope. I remember I was younger then. . . . Or was it that——?"

Mr. Fogarty interrupted. He took up the bottle and helped the others to a little more. Mr. M'Coy, seeing that there was not enough to go round, pleaded that he had not finished his first measure. The others accepted under protest. The light music of whisky falling into glasses made an agreeable interlude.

"What's that you were saying, Tom?" asked Mr. M'Coy.

"Papal infallibility," said Mr. Cunningham, "that was the greatest scene in the whole history of the Church."

"How was that, Martin?" asked Mr. Power.

Mr. Cunningham held up two thick fingers.

"In the sacred college, you know, of cardinals and archbishops and bishops there were two men who held out against it while the others were all for it. The whole conclave except these two was unanimous. No! They wouldn't have it!"

"Ha!" said Mr. M'Coy.

"And they were a German cardinal by the name of Dolling . . . or Dowling . . . or——"

"Dowling was no German, and that's a sure five," said Mr. Power, laughing.

"Well, this great German cardinal, whatever his name was, was one; and the other was John MacHale."

"What?" cried Mr. Kernan. "Is it John of Tuam?"

"Are you sure of that now?" asked Mr. Fogarty dubiously. "I thought it was some Italian or American."

"John of Tuam," repeated Mr. Cunningham, "was the man."

He drank and the other gentlemen followed his lead. Then he resumed:

"There they were at it, all the cardinals and bishops and archbishops from all the ends of the earth and these two fighting dog and devil until at last the Pope himself stood up and declared infallibility a dogma of the Church *ex cathedra*. On the very moment John MacHale, who had been arguing and arguing against it, stood up and shouted out with the voice of a lion: '*Credo!*' "

"*I believe!*" said Mr. Fogarty.

"*Credo!*" said Mr. Cunningham. "That showed the faith he had. He submitted the moment the Pope spoke."

"And what about Dowling?" asked Mr. M'Coy.

"The German cardinal wouldn't submit. He left the church."

Mr. Cunningham's words had built up the vast image of the church in the minds of his hearers. His deep, raucous voice had thrilled them as it uttered the word of belief and submission. When Mrs. Kernan came into the room, drying her hands, she came into a solemn company. She did not disturb the silence, but leaned over the rail at the foot of the bed.

"I once saw John MacHale," said Mr. Kernan, "and I'll never forget it as long as I live."

He turned towards his wife to be confirmed.

"I often told you that?"

Mrs. Kernan nodded.

"It was at the unveiling of Sir John Gray's statue. Edmund Dwyer Gray was speaking, blathering away, and here was this old fellow, crabbed-looking old chap, looking at him from under his bushy eyebrows."

Mr. Kernan knitted his brows and, lowering his head like an angry bull, glared at his wife.

"God!" he exclaimed, resuming his natural face, "I never saw such an eye in a man's head. It was as much as to say: *I have you properly taped, my lad.* He had an eye like a hawk."

"None of the Grays was any good," said Mr. Power.

There was a pause again. Mr. Power turned to Mrs. Kernan and said with abrupt joviality:

"Well, Mrs. Kernan, we're going to make your man here a good holy pious and God-fearing Roman Catholic."

He swept his arm round the company inclusively.

"We're all going to make a retreat together and confess our sins—and God knows we want it badly."

"I don't mind," said Mr. Kernan, smiling a little nervously.

Mrs. Kernan thought it would be wiser to conceal her satisfaction. So she said:

"I pity the poor priest that has to listen to your tale."

Mr. Kernan's expression changed.

"If he doesn't like it," he said bluntly, "he can . . . do the other thing. I'll just tell him my little tale of woe. I'm not such a bad fellow——"

Mr. Cunningham intervened promptly.

"We'll all renounce the devil," he said, "together, not forgetting his works and pomps."

"Get behind me, Satan!" said Mr. Fogarty, laughing and looking at the others.

Mr. Power said nothing. He felt completely out-generalled. But a pleased expression flickered across his face.

"All we have to do," said Mr. Cunningham, "is to stand up with lighted candles in our hands and renew our baptismal vows."

"O, don't forget the candle, Tom," said Mr. M'Coy, "whatever you do."

"What?" said Mr. Kernan. "Must I have a candle?"

"O yes," said Mr. Cunningham.

"No, damn it all," said Mr. Kernan sensibly, "I draw the line there. I'll do the job right enough. I'll do the retreat business and confession, and . . . all that business. But . . . no candles! No, damn it all, I bar the candles!"

He shook his head with farcical gravity.

"Listen to that!" said his wife.

"I bar the candles," said Mr. Kernan, conscious of having created an effect on his audience and continuing to shake his head to and fro. "I bar the magic-lantern business."

Everyone laughed heartily.

"There's a nice Catholic for you!" said his wife.

"No candles!" repeated Mr. Kernan obdurately. "That's off!"

. . . .

The transept of the Jesuit Church in Gardiner Street was almost full; and still at every moment gentlemen entered from the side door and, directed by the lay-brother, walked on tiptoe along the aisles until they found seating accommodation. The gentlemen were all well dressed and orderly. The light of the lamps of the church fell upon an assembly of black clothes and white collars, relieved here and there by tweeds, on dark mottled pillars of green marble and on lugubrious canvases. The gentlemen sat in the benches, having hitched their trousers slightly above their knees and laid their hats in security. They sat well back and gazed formally at the distant speck of red light which was suspended before the high altar.

In one of the benches near the pulpit sat Mr. Cunningham and Mr. Kernan. In the bench behind sat Mr. M'Coy alone: and in the bench behind him sat Mr. Power and Mr. Fogarty. Mr. M'Coy had tried unsuccessfully to find a place in the bench with the others, and, when the party had settled down in the form of a quincunx, he had tried unsuccessfully to make comic remarks. As these had not been well received, he had desisted. Even he was sensible of the decorous atmosphere and even he began to respond to the religious stimulus. In a whisper, Mr. Cunningham drew Mr. Kernan's attention to Mr. Harford, the moneylender, who sat some distance off, and to Mr. Fanning, the registration agent and mayor maker of the city, who was sitting immediately under the pulpit beside one of the newly elected councillors of the ward. To the right sat old Michael Grimes, the owner of three pawnbroker's shops, and Dan Hogan's nephew, who was up for the job in the Town Clerk's office. Farther in front sat Mr. Hendrick, the chief reporter of *The Freeman's Journal*, and poor O'Carroll, an old friend of Mr. Kernan's, who had been at one time a considerable commercial figure. Gradually, as he recognised familiar faces, Mr. Kernan began to feel more at home. His hat, which had been rehabilitated by his wife, rested upon his knees. Once or twice he pulled down his cuffs with one hand while he held the brim of his hat lightly, but firmly, with the other hand.

A powerful-looking figure, the upper part of which was draped with a white surplice, was observed to be struggling up into the pulpit. Simultaneously the congregation unsettled, produced handkerchiefs and knelt upon them with care. Mr. Kernan followed the general example. The priest's figure now stood upright in the pulpit, two-thirds of its bulk, crowned by a massive red face, appearing above the balustrade.

Father Purdon knelt down, turned towards the red speck of light and, covering his face with his hands, prayed. After an interval, he uncovered his face and rose. The congregation rose also and settled again on its benches. Mr. Kernan restored his hat to its original position on his knee and presented an attentive face to the preacher. The preacher turned back each wide sleeve of his surplice with an elaborate large gesture and slowly surveyed the array of faces. Then he said:

"For the children of this world are wiser in their generation than the children of light. Wherefore make unto yourselves friends out of the mammon of iniquity so that when you die they may receive you into everlasting dwellings."

Father Purdon developed the text with resonant assurance. It was one of the most difficult texts in all the Scriptures, he said, to interpret properly. It was a text which might seem to the casual observer at variance with the lofty morality elsewhere preached by Jesus Christ. But, he told his hearers, the text had seemed to him specially adapted for the guidance of those whose lot it was to lead the life of the world and who yet wished to lead that life not in the manner of worldlings. It was a text for business men and professional men. Jesus Christ, with His divine understanding of every cranny of our human nature, understood that all men were not called to the religious life, that by far the vast majority were forced to live in the world, and, to a certain extent, for the world: and in this sentence He designed to give them a word of counsel, setting before them as exemplars in the religious life those very worshippers of Mammon who were of all men the least solicitous in matters religious.

He told his hearers that he was there that evening for no terrifying, no extravagant purpose; but as a man of the world speaking to his fellow-men. He came to speak to business men and he would speak to them in a businesslike way. If he might use the metaphor, he said, he was their spiritual accountant; and he wished each and every one of his hearers to open his books, the books of his spiritual life, and see if they tallied accurately with conscience.

Jesus Christ was not a hard taskmaster. He understood our little failings, understood the weakness of our poor fallen nature, understood the temptations of this life. We might have had, we all had from time to time, our temptations: we might have, we all had, our failings. But one thing only, he said, he would ask of his hearers. And that was: to be straight and manly with God. If their accounts tallied in every point to say:

"Well, I have verified my accounts. I find all well."

But if, as might happen, there were some discrepancies, to admit the truth, to be frank and say like a man:

"Well, I have looked into my accounts. I find this wrong and this wrong. But, with God's grace, I will rectify this and this. I will set right my accounts."

The Dead

LILY, THE CARETAKER'S daughter, was literally run off her feet. Hardly had she brought one gentleman into the little pantry behind the office on the ground floor and helped him off with his overcoat than the wheezy hall-door bell clanged again and she had to scamper along the bare hallway to let in another guest. It was well for her she had not to attend to the ladies also. But Miss Kate and Miss Julia had thought of that and had converted the bathroom upstairs into a ladies' dressing-room. Miss Kate and Miss Julia were there, gossiping and laughing and fussing, walking after each other to the head of the stairs, peering down over the banisters and calling down to Lily to ask her who had come.

It was always a great affair, the Misses Morkan's annual dance. Everybody who knew them came to it, members of the family, old friends of the family, the members of Julia's choir, any of Kate's pupils that were grown up enough, and even some of Mary Jane's pupils too. Never once had it fallen flat. For years and years it had gone off in splendid style, as long as anyone could remember; ever since Kate and Julia, after the death of their brother Pat, had left the house in Stoney Batter and taken Mary Jane, their only niece, to live with them in the dark, gaunt house on Usher's Island, the upper part of which they had rented from Mr. Fulham, the corn-factor on the ground floor. That was a good thirty years ago if it was a day. Mary Jane, who was then a little girl in short clothes, was now the main prop of the household, for she had the organ in Haddington Road. She had been through the Academy and gave a pupils' concert every year in the upper room of the Antient Concert Rooms. Many of her pupils belonged to the better-class families on the Kingstown and Dalkey line. Old as they were, her aunts also did their share. Julia, though she was quite grey, was still the leading soprano in Adam and Eve's, and Kate, being too feeble to go about much, gave music lessons to beginners on the old square piano in the back room. Lily, the caretaker's daughter, did housemaid's work for

119

them. Though their life was modest, they believed in eating well; the best of everything: diamond-bone sirloins, three-shilling tea and the best bottled stout. But Lily seldom made a mistake in the orders, so that she got on well with her three mistresses. They were fussy, that was all. But the only thing they would not stand was back answers.

Of course, they had good reason to be fussy on such a night. And then it was long after ten o'clock and yet there was no sign of Gabriel and his wife. Besides they were dreadfully afraid that Freddy Malins might turn up screwed. They would not wish for worlds that any of Mary Jane's pupils should see him under the influence; and when he was like that it was sometimes very hard to manage him. Freddy Malins always came late, but they wondered what could be keeping Gabriel: and that was what brought them every two minutes to the banisters to ask Lily had Gabriel or Freddy come.

"O, Mr. Conroy," said Lily to Gabriel when she opened the door for him, "Miss Kate and Miss Julia thought you were never coming. Good-night, Mrs. Conroy."

"I'll engage they did," said Gabriel, "but they forget that my wife here takes three mortal hours to dress herself."

He stood on the mat, scraping the snow from his goloshes, while Lily led his wife to the foot of the stairs and called out:

"Miss Kate, here's Mrs. Conroy."

Kate and Julia came toddling down the dark stairs at once. Both of them kissed Gabriel's wife, said she must be perished alive, and asked was Gabriel with her.

"Here I am as right as the mail, Aunt Kate! Go on up. I'll follow," called out Gabriel from the dark.

He continued scraping his feet vigorously while the three women went upstairs, laughing, to the ladies' dressing-room. A light fringe of snow lay like a cape on the shoulders of his overcoat and like toecaps on the toes of his goloshes; and, as the buttons of his overcoat slipped with a squeaking noise through the snow-stiffened frieze, a cold, fragrant air from out-of-doors escaped from crevices and folds.

"Is it snowing again, Mr. Conroy?" asked Lily.

She had preceded him into the pantry to help him off with his overcoat. Gabriel smiled at the three syllables she had given his surname and glanced at her. She was a slim, growing girl, pale in complexion and with hay-coloured hair. The gas in the pantry made her look still paler. Gabriel had known her when she was a child and used to sit on the lowest step nursing a rag doll.

"Yes, Lily," he answered, "and I think we're in for a night of it."

He looked up at the pantry ceiling, which was shaking with the stamping and shuffling of feet on the floor above, listened for a moment to the piano and then glanced at the girl, who was folding his overcoat carefully at the end of a shelf.

"Tell me, Lily," he said in a friendly tone, "do you still go to school?"

"O no, sir," she answered. "I'm done schooling this year and more."

"O, then," said Gabriel gaily, "I suppose we'll be going to your wedding one of these fine days with your young man, eh?"

The girl glanced back at him over her shoulder and said with great bitterness:

"The men that is now is only all palaver and what they can get out of you."

Gabriel coloured, as if he felt he had made a mistake and, without looking at her, kicked off his goloshes and flicked actively with his muffler at his patent-leather shoes.

He was a stout, tallish young man. The high colour of his cheeks pushed upwards even to his forehead, where it scattered itself in a few formless patches of pale red; and on his hairless face there scintillated restlessly the polished lenses and the bright gilt rims of the glasses which screened his delicate and restless eyes. His glossy black hair was parted in the middle and brushed in a long curve behind his ears where it curled slightly beneath the groove left by his hat.

When he had flicked lustre into his shoes he stood up and pulled his waistcoat down more tightly on his plump body. Then he took a coin rapidly from his pocket.

"O Lily," he said, thrusting it into her hands, "it's Christmas-time, isn't it? Just . . . here's a little. . . ."

He walked rapidly towards the door.

"O no, sir!" cried the girl, following him. "Really, sir, I wouldn't take it."

"Christmas-time! Christmas-time!" said Gabriel, almost trotting to the stairs and waving his hand to her in deprecation.

The girl, seeing that he had gained the stairs, called out after him:

"Well, thank you, sir."

He waited outside the drawing-room door until the waltz should finish, listening to the skirts that swept against it and to the shuffling of feet. He was still discomposed by the girl's bitter and sudden retort. It had cast a gloom over him which he tried to dispel by arranging his cuffs and the bows of his tie. He then took from his waistcoat pocket a little paper and glanced at the headings he had made for his speech. He was undecided about the lines from Robert Browning, for he feared they would be above the heads of his hearers. Some quotation that they would recognise from Shakespeare or from the Melodies would be better. The indelicate clacking of the men's heels and the shuffling of their soles reminded him that their grade of culture differed from his. He would only make himself ridiculous by quoting poetry to them which they could not understand. They would think that he was airing his superior education. He would fail with them just as he had failed with the girl in the pantry. He had taken up a wrong tone. His whole speech was a mistake from first to last, an utter failure.

Just then his aunts and his wife came out of the ladies' dressing-room. His aunts were two small, plainly dressed old women. Aunt Julia was an inch or so the taller. Her hair, drawn low over the tops of her ears, was grey; and grey also, with darker shadows, was her large flaccid face. Though she was stout in build and stood erect, her slow eyes and parted lips gave her the appearance of a woman who did not know where she was or where she was going. Aunt Kate was more vivacious. Her face, healthier than her sister's, was all puckers and creases, like a shrivelled red apple, and her hair, braided in the same old-fashioned way, had not lost its ripe nut colour.

They both kissed Gabriel frankly. He was their favourite nephew, the son of their dead elder sister, Ellen, who had married T. J. Conroy of the Port and Docks.

"Gretta tells me you're not going to take a cab back to Monkstown to-night, Gabriel," said Aunt Kate.

"No," said Gabriel, turning to his wife, "we had quite enough of that last year, hadn't we? Don't you remember, Aunt Kate, what a cold Gretta got out of it? Cab windows rattling all the way, and the east wind blowing in after we passed Merrion. Very jolly it was. Gretta caught a dreadful cold."

Aunt Kate frowned severely and nodded her head at every word.

"Quite right, Gabriel, quite right," she said. "You can't be too careful."

"But as for Gretta there," said Gabriel, "she'd walk home in the snow if she were let."

Mrs. Conroy laughed.

"Don't mind him, Aunt Kate," she said. "He's really an awful bother, what with green shades for Tom's eyes at night and making him do the dumb-bells, and forcing Eva to eat the stirabout. The poor child! And she simply hates the sight of it! . . . O, but you'll never guess what he makes me wear now!"

She broke out into a peal of laughter and glanced at her husband, whose admiring and happy eyes had been wandering from her dress to her face and hair. The two aunts laughed heartily, too, for Gabriel's solicitude was a standing joke with them.

"Goloshes!" said Mrs. Conroy. "That's the latest. Whenever it's wet underfoot I must put on my goloshes. To-night even, he wanted me to put them on, but I wouldn't. The next thing he'll buy me will be a diving suit."

Gabriel laughed nervously and patted his tie reassuringly, while Aunt Kate nearly doubled herself, so heartily did she enjoy the joke. The smile soon faded from Aunt Julia's face and her mirthless eyes were directed towards her nephew's face. After a pause she asked:

"And what are goloshes, Gabriel?"

"Goloshes, Julia!" exclaimed her sister. "Goodness me, don't you know what goloshes are? You wear them over your . . . over your boots, Gretta, isn't it?"

"Yes," said Mrs. Conroy. "Guttapercha things. We both have a pair now. Gabriel says everyone wears them on the continent."

"O, on the continent," murmured Aunt Julia, nodding her head slowly.

Gabriel knitted his brows and said, as if he were slightly angered:

"It's nothing very wonderful, but Gretta thinks it very funny because she says the word reminds her of Christy Minstrels."

"But tell me, Gabriel," said Aunt Kate, with brisk tact. "Of course, you've seen about the room. Gretta was saying . . ."

"O, the room is all right," replied Gabriel. "I've taken one in the Gresham."

"To be sure," said Aunt Kate, "by far the best thing to do. And the children, Gretta, you're not anxious about them?"

"O, for one night," said Mrs. Conroy. "Besides, Bessie will look after them."

"To be sure," said Aunt Kate again. "What a comfort it is to have a girl like that, one you can depend on! There's that Lily, I'm sure I don't know what has come over her lately. She's not the girl she was at all."

Gabriel was about to ask his aunt some questions on this point, but she broke off suddenly to gaze after her sister, who had wandered down the stairs and was craning her neck over the banisters.

"Now, I ask you," she said almost testily, "where is Julia going? Julia! Julia! Where are you going?"

Julia, who had gone halfway down one flight, came back and announced blandly:

"Here's Freddy."

At the same moment a clapping of hands and a final flourish of the pianist told that the waltz had ended. The drawing-room door was opened from within and some couples came out. Aunt Kate drew Gabriel aside hurriedly and whispered into his ear:

"Slip down, Gabriel, like a good fellow and see if he's all right, and don't let him up if he's screwed. I'm sure he's screwed. I'm sure he is."

Gabriel went to the stairs and listened over the banisters. He could hear two persons talking in the pantry. Then he recognised Freddy Malins' laugh. He went down the stairs noisily.

"It's such a relief," said Aunt Kate to Mrs. Conroy, "that Gabriel is here. I always feel easier in my mind when he's here. . . . Julia, there's Miss Daly and Miss Power will take some refreshment. Thanks for your beautiful waltz, Miss Daly. It made lovely time."

A tall wizen-faced man, with a stiff grizzled moustache and swarthy skin, who was passing out with his partner, said:

"And may we have some refreshment, too, Miss Morkan?"

"Julia," said Aunt Kate summarily, "and here's Mr. Browne and Miss Furlong. Take them in, Julia, with Miss Daly and Miss Power."

"I'm the man for the ladies," said Mr. Browne, pursing his lips until his moustache bristled and smiling in all his wrinkles. "You know, Miss Morkan, the reason they are so fond of me is——"

He did not finish his sentence, but, seeing that Aunt Kate was out of earshot, at once led the three young ladies into the back room. The middle of the room was occupied by two square tables placed end to end, and on these Aunt Julia and the caretaker were straightening and smoothing a large cloth. On the sideboard were arrayed dishes and plates, and glasses and bundles of knives and forks and spoons. The top of the closed square piano served also as a sideboard for viands and sweets. At a smaller sideboard in one corner two young men were standing, drinking hop-bitters.

Mr. Browne led his charges thither and invited them all, in jest, to some ladies' punch, hot, strong and sweet. As they said they never took anything strong, he opened three bottles of lemonade for them. Then he asked one of the young men to move aside, and, taking hold of the decanter, filled out for himself a goodly measure of whisky. The young men eyed him respectfully while he took a trial sip.

"God help me," he said, smiling, "it's the doctor's orders."

His wizened face broke into a broader smile, and the three young ladies laughed in musical echo to his pleasantry, swaying their bodies to and fro, with nervous jerks of their shoulders. The boldest said:

"O, now, Mr. Browne, I'm sure the doctor never ordered anything of the kind."

Mr. Browne took another sip of his whisky and said, with sidling mimicry:

"Well, you see, I'm like the famous Mrs. Cassidy, who is reported to have said: 'Now, Mary Grimes, if I don't take it, make me take it, for I feel I want it.'"

His hot face had leaned forward a little too confidentially and he had assumed a very low Dublin accent so that the young ladies, with one instinct, received his speech in silence. Miss Furlong, who was one of Mary Jane's pupils, asked Miss Daly what was the name of the pretty waltz she had played; and Mr. Browne, seeing that he was ignored, turned promptly to the two young men who were more appreciative.

A red-faced young woman, dressed in pansy, came into the room, excitedly clapping her hands and crying:

"Quadrilles! Quadrilles!"

Close on her heels came Aunt Kate, crying:

"Two gentlemen and three ladies, Mary Jane!"

"O, here's Mr. Bergin and Mr. Kerrigan," said Mary Jane. "Mr. Kerrigan, will you take Miss Power? Miss Furlong, may I get you a partner, Mr. Bergin. O, that'll just do now."

"Three ladies, Mary Jane," said Aunt Kate.

The two young gentlemen asked the ladies if they might have the pleasure, and Mary Jane turned to Miss Daly.

"O, Miss Daly, you're really awfully good, after playing for the last two dances, but really we're so short of ladies to-night."

"I don't mind in the least, Miss Morkan."

"But I've a nice partner for you, Mr. Bartell D'Arcy, the tenor. I'll get him to sing later on. All Dublin is raving about him."

"Lovely voice, lovely voice!" said Aunt Kate.

As the piano had twice begun the prelude to the first figure Mary Jane led her recruits quickly from the room. They had hardly gone when Aunt Julia wandered slowly into the room, looking behind her at something.

"What is the matter, Julia?" asked Aunt Kate anxiously. "Who is it?"

Julia, who was carrying in a column of table-napkins, turned to her sister and said, simply, as if the question had surprised her:

"It's only Freddy, Kate, and Gabriel with him."

In fact right behind her Gabriel could be seen piloting Freddy Malins across the landing. The latter, a young man of about forty, was of Gabriel's size and build, with very round shoulders. His face was fleshy and pallid, touched with colour only at the thick hanging lobes of his ears and at the wide wings of his nose. He had coarse features, a blunt nose, a convex and receding brow, tumid and protruded lips. His heavy-lidded eyes and the disorder of his scanty hair made him look sleepy. He was laughing heartily in a high key at a story which he had been telling Gabriel on the stairs and at the same time rubbing the knuckles of his left fist backwards and forwards into his left eye.

"Good-evening, Freddy," said Aunt Julia.

Freddy Malins bade the Misses Morkan good-evening in what seemed an offhand fashion by reason of the habitual catch in his voice and then, seeing that Mr. Browne was grinning at him from the sideboard, crossed the room on rather shaky legs and began to repeat in an undertone the story he had just told to Gabriel.

"He's not so bad, is he?" said Aunt Kate to Gabriel.

Gabriel's brows were dark but he raised them quickly and answered: "O, no, hardly noticeable."

"Now, isn't he a terrible fellow!" she said. "And his poor mother made him take the pledge on New Year's Eve. But come on, Gabriel, into the drawing-room."

Before leaving the room with Gabriel she signalled to Mr. Browne by frowning and shaking her forefinger in warning to and fro. Mr. Browne nodded in answer and, when she had gone, said to Freddy Malins:

"Now, then, Teddy, I'm going to fill you out a good glass of lemonade just to buck you up."

Freddy Malins, who was nearing the climax of his story, waved the offer aside impatiently but Mr. Browne, having first called Freddy Malins' attention to a disarray in his dress, filled out and handed him a full glass of lemonade. Freddy Malins' left hand accepted the glass mechanically, his right hand being engaged in the mechanical readjustment of his dress. Mr. Browne, whose face was once more wrinkling with mirth, poured out for himself a glass of whisky while Freddy Malins exploded, before he had well reached the climax of his story, in a kink of high-pitched bronchitic laughter and, setting down his untasted and overflowing glass, began to rub the knuckles of his left fist backwards and forwards into his left eye, repeating words of his last phrase as well as his fit of laughter would allow him.

. . . . .

Gabriel could not listen while Mary Jane was playing her Academy piece, full of runs and difficult passages, to the hushed drawing-room. He liked music but the piece she was playing had no melody for him and he doubted whether it had any melody for the other listeners, though they had begged Mary Jane to play something. Four young men, who had come from the refreshment-room to stand in the doorway at the sound of the piano, had gone away quietly in couples after a few minutes. The only persons who seemed to follow the music were Mary Jane herself, her hands racing along the key-board or lifted from it at the pauses like those of a priestess in momentary imprecation, and Aunt Kate standing at her elbow to turn the page.

Gabriel's eyes, irritated by the floor, which glittered with beeswax under the heavy chandelier, wandered to the wall above the piano. A picture of the balcony scene in *Romeo and Juliet* hung there and beside it was a picture of the two murdered princes in the Tower which Aunt Julia had worked in red, blue and brown wools when she was a girl. Probably in the school they had gone to as girls that kind of work had been taught for one year. His mother had worked for him as a birthday present a waistcoat of purple tabinet, with little foxes' heads upon it, lined with brown satin and having round mulberry buttons. It was strange that his mother had had no musical talent though Aunt Kate used to call her the brains carrier of the Morkan family. Both she and Julia had always seemed a little proud of their serious and matronly sister. Her photograph stood before the pierglass. She held an open book on her knees and was pointing out something in it to Constantine who, dressed in a man-o'-war suit, lay at her feet. It was she who had chosen the names of her sons for she was very sensible of the dignity of family life. Thanks to her, Constantine was now senior curate in Balbriggan and, thanks to her, Gabriel himself had taken his degree in the Royal University. A shadow passed over his face as he remembered her sullen opposition to his marriage. Some slighting phrases she had used still rankled in his memory; she had once spoken of Gretta as being country cute and that was not true of Gretta at all. It was Gretta who had nursed her during all her last long illness in their house at Monkstown.

He knew that Mary Jane must be near the end of her piece for she was playing again the opening melody with runs of scales after every bar and while he waited for the end the resentment died down in his heart. The piece ended with a trill of octaves in the treble and a final deep octave in the bass. Great applause greeted Mary Jane as, blushing and rolling up her music nervously, she escaped from the room. The most vigorous clapping came from the four young men in the doorway who had gone away to the refreshment-room at the beginning of the piece but had come back when the piano had stopped.

Lancers were arranged. Gabriel found himself partnered with Miss Ivors. She was a frank-mannered talkative young lady, with a freckled face and prominent brown eyes. She did not wear a low-cut bodice and the large brooch which was fixed in the front of her collar bore on it an Irish device and motto.

When they had taken their places she said abruptly:

"I have a crow to pluck with you."

"With me?" said Gabriel.

She nodded her head gravely.

"What is it?" asked Gabriel, smiling at her solemn manner.

"Who is G. C.?" answered Miss Ivors, turning her eyes upon him.

Gabriel coloured and was about to knit his brows, as if he did not understand, when she said bluntly:

"O, innocent Amy! I have found out that you write for *The Daily Express.* Now, aren't you ashamed of yourself?"

"Why should I be ashamed of myself?" asked Gabriel, blinking his eyes and trying to smile.

"Well, I'm ashamed of you," said Miss Ivors frankly. "To say you'd write for a paper like that. I didn't think you were a West Briton."

A look of perplexity appeared on Gabriel's face. It was true that he wrote a literary column every Wednesday in *The Daily Express*, for which he was paid fifteen shillings. But that did not make him a West Briton surely. The books he received for review were almost more welcome than the paltry cheque. He loved to feel the covers and turn over the pages of newly printed books. Nearly every day when his teaching in the college was ended he used to wander down the quays to the second-hand book-sellers, to Hickey's on Bachelor's Walk, to Webb's or Massey's on Aston's Quay, or to O'Clohissey's in the by-street. He did not know how to meet her charge. He wanted to say that literature was above politics. But they were friends of many years' standing and their careers had been parallel, first at the University and then as teachers: he could not risk a grandiose phrase with her. He continued blinking his eyes and trying to smile and murmured lamely that he saw nothing political in writing reviews of books.

When their turn to cross had come he was still perplexed and inattentive. Miss Ivors promptly took his hand in a warm grasp and said in a soft friendly tone:

"Of course, I was only joking. Come, we cross now."

When they were together again she spoke of the University question and Gabriel felt more at ease. A friend of hers had shown her his review of Browning's poems. That was how she had found out the secret: but she liked the review immensely. Then she said suddenly:

"O, Mr. Conroy, will you come for an excursion to the Aran Isles this summer? We're going to stay there a whole month. It will be splendid out in the Atlantic. You ought to come. Mr. Clancy is coming, and Mr. Kilkelly and Kathleen Kearney. It would be splendid for Gretta too if she'd come. She's from Connacht, isn't she?"

"Her people are," said Gabriel shortly.

"But you will come, won't you?" said Miss Ivors, laying her warm hand eagerly on his arm.

"The fact is," said Gabriel, "I have just arranged to go——"

"Go where?" asked Miss Ivors.

"Well, you know, every year I go for a cycling tour with some fellows and so——"

"But where?" asked Miss Ivors.

"Well, we usually go to France or Belgium or perhaps Germany," said Gabriel awkwardly.

"And why do you go to France and Belgium," said Miss Ivors, "instead of visiting your own land?"

"Well," said Gabriel, "it's partly to keep in touch with the languages and partly for a change."

"And haven't you your own language to keep in touch with—Irish?" asked Miss Ivors.

"Well," said Gabriel, "if it comes to that, you know, Irish is not my language."

Their neighbours had turned to listen to the cross-examination. Gabriel glanced right and left nervously and tried to keep his good humour under the ordeal which was making a blush invade his forehead.

"And haven't you your own land to visit," continued Miss Ivors, "that you know nothing of, your own people, and your own country?"

"O, to tell you the truth," retorted Gabriel suddenly, "I'm sick of my own country, sick of it!"

"Why?" asked Miss Ivors.

Gabriel did not answer for his retort had heated him.

"Why?" repeated Miss Ivors.

They had to go visiting together and, as he had not answered her, Miss Ivors said warmly:

"Of course, you've no answer."

Gabriel tried to cover his agitation by taking part in the dance with great energy. He avoided her eyes for he had seen a sour expression on her face. But when they met in the long chain he was surprised to feel his hand firmly pressed. She looked at him from under her brows for a moment quizzically until he smiled. Then, just as the chain was about to start again, she stood on tiptoe and whispered into his ear:

"West Briton!"

When the lancers were over Gabriel went away to a remote corner of the room where Freddy Malins' mother was sitting. She was a stout feeble old woman with white hair. Her voice had a catch in it like her son's and she stuttered slightly. She had been told that Freddy had come and that he was nearly all right. Gabriel asked her whether she had had a good crossing. She lived with her married daughter in Glasgow and came to Dublin on a visit once a year. She answered placidly that she had had a beautiful crossing and that the captain had been most attentive to her. She spoke also of the beautiful house her daughter kept in Glasgow, and of all the friends they had there. While her tongue rambled on Gabriel tried to banish from his mind all memory of the unpleasant incident with Miss Ivors. Of course the girl or woman, or whatever she was, was an enthusiast but there was a time for all things. Perhaps he ought not to have answered her like that. But she had no right to call him a West Briton before people, even in joke. She had tried to make him ridiculous before people, heckling him and staring at him with her rabbit's eyes.

He saw his wife making her way towards him through the waltzing couples. When she reached him she said into his ear:

"Gabriel, Aunt Kate wants to know won't you carve the goose as usual. Miss Daly will carve the ham and I'll do the pudding."

"All right," said Gabriel.

"She's sending in the younger ones first as soon as this waltz is over so that we'll have the table to ourselves."

"Were you dancing?" asked Gabriel.

"Of course I was. Didn't you see me? What row had you with Molly Ivors?"

"No row. Why? Did she say so?"

"Something like that. I'm trying to get that Mr. D'Arcy to sing. He's full of conceit, I think."

"There was no row," said Gabriel moodily, "only she wanted me to go for a trip to the west of Ireland and I said I wouldn't."

His wife clasped her hands excitedly and gave a little jump.

"O, do go, Gabriel," she cried. "I'd love to see Galway again."

"You can go if you like," said Gabriel coldly.

She looked at him for a moment, then turned to Mrs. Malins and said:

"There's a nice husband for you, Mrs. Malins."

While she was threading her way back across the room Mrs. Malins, without adverting to the interruption, went on to tell Gabriel what beautiful places there were in Scotland and beautiful scenery. Her son-in-law brought them every year to the lakes and they used to go fishing. Her son-in-law was a splendid fisher. One day he caught a beautiful big fish and the man in the hotel cooked it for their dinner.

Gabriel hardly heard what she said. Now that supper was coming near he began to think again about his speech and about the quotation. When he saw Freddy Malins coming across the room to visit his mother Gabriel left the chair free for him and retired into the embrasure of the window. The room had already cleared and from the back room came the clatter of plates and knives. Those who still remained in the drawing-room seemed tired of dancing and were conversing quietly in little groups. Gabriel's warm trembling fingers tapped the cold pane of the window. How cool it must be outside! How pleasant it would be to walk out alone, first along by the river and then through the park! The snow would be lying on the branches of the trees and forming a bright cap on the top of the Wellington Monument. How much more pleasant it would be there than at the supper-table!

He ran over the headings of his speech: Irish hospitality, sad memories, the Three Graces, Paris, the quotation from Browning. He repeated to himself a phrase he had written in his review: "One feels that one is listening to a thought-tormented music." Miss Ivors had praised the review. Was she sincere? Had she really any life of her own behind all her

propagandism? There had never been any ill-feeling between them until
that night. It unnerved him to think that she would be at the supper-table,
looking up at him while he spoke with her critical quizzing eyes. Perhaps
she would not be sorry to see him fail in his speech. An idea came into his
mind and gave him courage. He would say, alluding to Aunt Kate and Aunt
Julia: "Ladies and Gentlemen, the generation which is now on the wane
among us may have had its faults but for my part I think it had certain
qualities of hospitality, of humour, of humanity, which the new and very
serious and hypereducated generation that is growing up around us seems
to me to lack." Very good: that was one for Miss Ivors. What did he care
that his aunts were only two ignorant old women?

A murmur in the room attracted his attention. Mr. Browne was advancing from the door, gallantly escorting Aunt Julia, who leaned upon his
arm, smiling and hanging her head. An irregular musketry of applause
escorted her also as far as the piano and then, as Mary Jane seated herself
on the stool, and Aunt Julia, no longer smiling, half turned so as to pitch
her voice fairly into the room, gradually ceased. Gabriel recognised the
prelude. It was that of an old song of Aunt Julia's—*Arrayed for the Bridal*.
Her voice, strong and clear in tone, attacked with great spirit the runs
which embellish the air and though she sang very rapidly she did not miss
even the smallest of the grace notes. To follow the voice, without looking at
the singer's face, was to feel and share the excitement of swift and secure
flight. Gabriel applauded loudly with all the others at the close of the song
and loud applause was borne in from the invisible supper-table. It
sounded so genuine that a little colour struggled into Aunt Julia's face as
she bent to replace in the music-stand the old leather-bound song-book
that had her initials on the cover. Freddy Malins, who had listened with
his head perched sideways to hear her better, was still applauding when
everyone else had ceased and talking animatedly to his mother who
nodded her head gravely and slowly in acquiescence. At last, when he
could clap no more, he stood up suddenly and hurried across the room to
Aunt Julia whose hand he seized and held in both his hands, shaking it
when words failed him or the catch in his voice proved too much for him.

"I was just telling my mother," he said, "I never heard you sing so well,
never. No, I never heard your voice so good as it is to-night. Now! Would
you believe that now? That's the truth. Upon my word and honour that's the
truth. I never heard your voice sound so fresh and so . . . so clear and
fresh, never."

Aunt Julia smiled broadly and murmured something about compliments
as she released her hand from his grasp. Mr. Browne extended his open
hand towards her and said to those who were near him in the manner of a
showman introducing a prodigy to an audience:

"Miss Julia Morkan, my latest discovery!"

He was laughing very heartily at this himself when Freddy Malins turned to him and said:

"Well, Browne, if you're serious you might make a worse discovery. All I can say is I never heard her sing half so well as long as I am coming here. And that's the honest truth."

"Neither did I," said Mr. Browne. "I think her voice has greatly improved."

Aunt Julia shrugged her shoulders and said with meek pride:

"Thirty years ago I hadn't a bad voice as voices go."

"I often told Julia," said Aunt Kate emphatically, "that she was simply thrown away in that choir. But she never would be said by me."

She turned as if to appeal to the good sense of the others against a refractory child while Aunt Julia gazed in front of her, a vague smile of reminiscence playing on her face.

"No," continued Aunt Kate, "she wouldn't be said or led by anyone, slaving there in that choir night and day, night and day. Six o'clock on Christmas morning! And all for what?"

"Well, isn't it for the honour of God, Aunt Kate?" asked Mary Jane, twisting round on the piano-stool and smiling.

Aunt Kate turned fiercely on her niece and said:

"I know all about the honour of God, Mary Jane, but I think it's not at all honourable for the pope to turn out the women out of the choirs that have slaved there all their lives and put little whipper-snappers of boys over their heads. I suppose it is for the good of the Church if the pope does it. But it's not just, Mary Jane, and it's not right."

She had worked herself into a passion and would have continued in defence of her sister for it was a sore subject with her but Mary Jane, seeing that all the dancers had come back, intervened pacifically:

"Now, Aunt Kate, you're giving scandal to Mr. Browne who is of the other persuasion."

Aunt Kate turned to Mr. Browne, who was grinning at this allusion to his religion, and said hastily:

"O, I don't question the pope's being right. I'm only a stupid old woman and I wouldn't presume to do such a thing. But there's such a thing as common everyday politeness and gratitude. And if I were in Julia's place I'd tell that Father Healey straight up to his face . . ."

"And besides, Aunt Kate," said Mary Jane, "we really are all hungry and when we are hungry we are all very quarrelsome."

"And when we are thirsty we are also quarrelsome," added Mr. Browne.

"So that we had better go to supper," said Mary Jane, "and finish the discussion afterwards."

On the landing outside the drawing-room Gabriel found his wife and Mary Jane trying to persuade Miss Ivors to stay for supper. But Miss Ivors, who had put on her hat and was buttoning her cloak, would not stay. She did not feel in the least hungry and she had already overstayed her time.

"But only for ten minutes, Molly," said Mrs. Conroy. "That won't delay you."

"To take a pick itself," said Mary Jane, "after all your dancing."

"I really couldn't," said Miss Ivors.

"I am afraid you didn't enjoy yourself at all," said Mary Jane hopelessly.

"Ever so much, I assure you," said Miss Ivors, "but you really must let me run off now."

"But how can you get home?" asked Mrs. Conroy.

"O, it's only two steps up the quay."

Gabriel hesitated a moment and said:

"If you will allow me, Miss Ivors, I'll see you home if you are really obliged to go."

But Miss Ivors broke away from them.

"I won't hear of it," she cried. "For goodness' sake go in to your suppers and don't mind me. I'm quite well able to take care of myself."

"Well, you're the comical girl, Molly," said Mrs. Conroy frankly.

"*Beannacht libh*," cried Miss Ivors, with a laugh, as she ran down the staircase.

Mary Jane gazed after her, a moody puzzled expression on her face, while Mrs. Conroy leaned over the banisters to listen for the hall-door. Gabriel asked himself was he the cause of her abrupt departure. But she did not seem to be in ill humour: she had gone away laughing. He stared blankly down the staircase.

At the moment Aunt Kate came toddling out of the supper-room, almost wringing her hands in despair.

"Where is Gabriel?" she cried. "Where on earth is Gabriel? There's everyone waiting in there, stage to let, and nobody to carve the goose!"

"Here I am, Aunt Kate!" cried Gabriel, with sudden animation, "ready to carve a flock of geese, if necessary."

A fat brown goose lay at one end of the table and at the other end, on a bed of creased paper strewn with sprigs of parsley, lay a great ham, stripped of its outer skin and peppered over with crust crumbs, a neat paper frill round its shin and beside this was a round of spiced beef. Between these rival ends ran parallel lines of side-dishes: two little minsters of jelly, red and yellow; a shallow dish full of blocks of blancmange and red jam, a large green leaf-shaped dish with a stalk-shaped handle, on which lay bunches of purple raisins and peeled almonds, a companion dish on which lay a solid rectangle of Smyrna figs, a dish of custard topped with grated nutmeg, a small bowl full of chocolates and sweets wrapped in gold and silver papers and a glass vase in which stood some tall celery stalks. In the centre of the table there stood, as sentries to a fruit-stand which upheld a pyramid of oranges and American apples, two squat old-fashioned decanters of cut glass, one containing port and the other dark sherry. On the closed square piano a pudding in a huge yellow dish lay in waiting and behind it were three squads of bottles of stout and ale and minerals, drawn up according to the colours of their uniforms, the first two black, with brown and red labels, the third and smallest squad white, with transverse green sashes.

Gabriel took his seat boldly at the head of the table and, having looked to the edge of the carver, plunged his fork firmly into the goose. He felt quite at ease now for he was an expert carver and liked nothing better than to find himself at the head of a well-laden table.

"Miss Furlong, what shall I send you?" he asked. "A wing or a slice of the breast?"

"Just a small slice of the breast."

"Miss Higgins, what for you?"

"O, anything at all, Mr. Conroy."

While Gabriel and Miss Daly exchanged plates of goose and plates of ham and spiced beef Lily went from guest to guest with a dish of hot floury potatoes wrapped in a white napkin. This was Mary Jane's idea and she had also suggested apple sauce for the goose but Aunt Kate had said that plain roast goose without any apple sauce had always been good enough for her and she hoped she might never eat worse. Mary Jane waited on her pupils and saw that they got the best slices and Aunt Kate and Aunt Julia opened and carried across from the piano bottles of stout and ale for the gentlemen and bottles of minerals for the ladies. There was a great deal of confusion and laughter and noise, the noise of orders and counter-orders, of knives and forks, of corks and glass-stoppers. Gabriel began to carve second helpings as soon as he had finished the first round without serving himself. Everyone protested loudly so that he compromised by taking a long draught of stout for he had found the carving hot work. Mary Jane settled down quietly to her supper but Aunt Kate and Aunt Julia were still toddling round the table, walking on each other's heels, getting in each other's way and giving each other unheeded orders. Mr. Browne begged of them to sit down and eat their suppers and so did Gabriel but they said there was time enough, so that, at last, Freddy Malins stood up and, capturing Aunt Kate, plumped her down on her chair amid general laughter.

When everyone had been well served Gabriel said, smiling:

"Now, if anyone wants a little more of what vulgar people call stuffing let him or her speak."

A chorus of voices invited him to begin his own supper and Lily came forward with three potatoes which she had reserved for him.

"Very well," said Gabriel amiably, as he took another preparatory draught, "kindly forget my existence, ladies and gentlemen, for a few minutes."

He set to his supper and took no part in the conversation with which the table covered Lily's removal of the plates. The subject of talk was the opera company which was then at the Theatre Royal. Mr. Bartell D'Arcy, the tenor, a dark-complexioned young man with a smart moustache, praised very highly the leading contralto of the company but Miss Furlong thought she had a rather vulgar style of production. Freddy Malins said there was a negro chieftain singing in the second part of the Gaiety pantomime who had one of the finest tenor voices he had ever heard.

"Have you heard him?" he asked Mr. Bartell D'Arcy across the table.

"No," answered Mr. Bartell D'Arcy carelessly.

"Because," Freddy Malins explained, "now I'd be curious to hear your opinion of him. I think he has a grand voice."

"It takes Teddy to find out the really good things," said Mr. Browne familiarly to the table.

"And why couldn't he have a voice too?" asked Freddy Malins sharply. "Is it because he's only a black?"

Nobody answered this question and Mary Jane led the table back to the legitimate opera. One of her pupils had given her a pass for *Mignon*. Of course it was very fine, she said, but it made her think of poor Georgina Burns. Mr. Browne could go back farther still, to the old Italian companies that used to come to Dublin—Tietjens, Ilma de Murzka, Campanini, the great Trebelli Giuglini, Ravelli, Aramburo. Those were the days, he said, when there was something like singing to be heard in Dublin. He told too of how the top gallery of the old Royal used to be packed night after night, of how one night an Italian tenor had sung five encores to *Let me like a Soldier fall*, introducing a high C every time, and of how the gallery boys would sometimes in their enthusiasm unyoke the horses from the carriage of some great *prima donna* and pull her themselves through the streets to her hotel. Why did they never play the grand old operas now, he asked, *Dinorah, Lucrezia Borgia?* Because they could not get the voices to sing them: that was why."

"O, well," said Mr. Bartell D'Arcy, "I presume there are as good singers to-day as there were then."

"Where are they?" asked Mr. Browne defiantly.

"In London, Paris, Milan," said Mr. Bartell D'Arcy warmly. "I suppose Caruso, for example, is quite as good, if not better than any of the men you have mentioned."

"Maybe so," said Mr. Browne. "But I may tell you I doubt it strongly."

"O, I'd give anything to hear Caruso sing," said Mary Jane.

"For me," said Aunt Kate, who had been picking a bone, "there was only one tenor. To please me, I mean. But I suppose none of you ever heard of him."

"Who was he, Miss Morkan?" asked Mr. Bartell D'Arcy politely.

"His name," said Aunt Kate, "was Parkinson. I heard him when he was in his prime and I think he had then the purest tenor voice that was ever put into a man's throat."

"Strange," said Mr. Bartell D'Arcy. "I never even heard of him."

"Yes, yes, Miss Morkan is right," said Mr. Browne. "I remember hearing of old Parkinson but he's too far back for me."

"A beautiful, pure, sweet, mellow English tenor," said Aunt Kate with enthusiasm.

Gabriel having finished, the huge pudding was transferred to the table. The clatter of forks and spoons began again. Gabriel's wife served out spoonfuls of the pudding and passed the plates down the table. Midway down they were held up by Mary Jane, who replenished them with raspberry or orange jelly or with blancmange and jam. The pudding was of Aunt Julia's making and she received praises for it from all quarters. She herself said that it was not quite brown enough.

"Well, I hope, Miss Morkan," said Mr. Browne, "that I'm brown enough for you because, you know, I'm all brown."

All the gentlemen, except Gabriel, ate some of the pudding out of compliment to Aunt Julia. As Gabriel never ate sweets the celery had been left for him. Freddy Malins also took a stalk of celery and ate it with his pudding. He had been told that celery was a capital thing for the blood and he was just then under doctor's care. Mrs. Malins, who had been silent all through the supper, said that her son was going down to Mount Melleray in a week or so. The table then spoke of Mount Melleray, how bracing the air was down there, how hospitable the monks were and how they never asked for a penny-piece from their guests.

"And do you mean to say," asked Mr. Browne incredulously, "that a chap can go down there and put up there as if it were a hotel and live on the fat of the land and then come away without paying anything?"

"O, most people give some donation to the monastery when they leave," said Mary Jane.

"I wish we had an institution like that in our Church," said Mr. Browne candidly.

He was astonished to hear that the monks never spoke, got up at two in the morning and slept in their coffins. He asked what they did it for.

"That's the rule of the order," said Aunt Kate firmly.

"Yes, but why?" asked Mr. Browne.

Aunt Kate repeated that it was the rule, that was all. Mr. Browne still seemed not to understand. Freddy Malins explained to him, as best he could, that the monks were trying to make up for the sins committed by all the sinners in the outside world. The explanation was not very clear for Mr. Browne grinned and said:

"I like that idea very much but wouldn't a comfortable spring bed do them as well as a coffin?"

"The coffin," said Mary Jane, "is to remind them of their last end."

As the subject had grown lugubrious it was buried in a silence of the table during which Mrs. Malins could be heard saying to her neighbour in an indistinct undertone:

"They are very good men, the monks, very pious men."

The raisins and almonds and figs and apples and oranges and chocolates and sweets were now passed about the table and Aunt Julia invited all the guests to have either port or sherry. At first Mr. Bartell D'Arcy refused to take either but one of his neighbours nudged him and whispered something to him upon which he allowed his glass to be filled. Gradually as the last glasses were being filled the conversation ceased. A pause followed, broken only by the noise of the wine and by unsettlings of chairs. The Misses Morkan, all three, looked down at the tablecloth. Someone coughed once or twice and then a few gentlemen patted the table gently as a signal for silence. The silence came and Gabriel pushed back his chair and stood up.

The patting at once grew louder in encouragement and then ceased altogether. Gabriel leaned his ten trembling fingers on the tablecloth and smiled nervously at the company. Meeting a row of upturned faces he raised his eyes to the chandelier. The piano was playing a waltz tune and he could hear the skirts sweeping against the drawing-room door. People, perhaps, were standing in the snow on the quay outside, gazing up at the lighted windows and listening to the waltz music. The air was pure there. In the distance lay the park where the trees were weighted with snow. The Wellington Monument wore a gleaming cap of snow that flashed westward over the white field of Fifteen Acres.

He began:

"Ladies and Gentlemen,

"It has fallen to my lot this evening, as in years past, to perform a very pleasing task but a task for which I am afraid my poor powers as a speaker are all too inadequate."

"No, no!" said Mr. Browne.

"But, however that may be, I can only ask you to-night to take the will for the deed and to lend me your attention for a few moments while I endeavour to express to you in words what my feelings are on this occasion.

"Ladies and Gentlemen, it is not the first time that we have gathered together under this hospitable roof, around this hospitable board. It is not the first time that we have been the recipients—or perhaps, I had better say, the victims—of the hospitality of certain good ladies."

He made a circle in the air with his arm and paused. Everyone laughed or smiled at Aunt Kate and Aunt Julia and Mary Jane who all turned crimson with pleasure. Gabriel went on more boldly:

"I feel more strongly with every recurring year that our country has no tradition which does it so much honour and which it should guard so jealously as that of its hospitality. It is a tradition that is unique as far as my experience goes (and I have visited not a few places abroad) among the modern nations. Some would say, perhaps, that with us it is rather a failing than anything to be boasted of. But granted even that, it is, to my mind, a princely failing, and one that I trust will long be cultivated among us. Of one thing, at least, I am sure. As long as this one roof shelters the good ladies aforesaid—and I wish from my heart it may do so for many and many a long year to come—the tradition of genuine warmhearted courteous Irish hospitality, which our forefathers have handed down to us and which we in turn must hand down to our descendants, is still alive among us."

A hearty murmur of assent ran round the table. It shot through Gabriel's mind that Miss Ivors was not there and that she had gone away discourteously: and he said with confidence in himself:

"Ladies and Gentlemen,

"A new generation is growing up in our midst, a generation actuated by new ideas and new principles. It is serious and enthusiastic for these new ideas and its enthusiasm, even when it is misdirected, is, I believe, in the main sincere. But we are living in a sceptical and, if I may use the phrase, a thought-tormented age: and sometimes I fear that this new generation, educated or hypereducated as it is, will lack those qualities of humanity, of hospitality, of kindly humour which belonged to an older day. Listening tonight to the names of all those great singers of the past it seemed to me, I must confess, that we were living in a less spacious age. Those days might, without exaggeration, be called spacious days: and if they are gone beyond recall let us hope, at least, that in gatherings such as this we shall still speak of them with pride and affection, still cherish in our hearts the memory of those dead and gone great ones whose fame the world will not willingly let die."

"Hear, hear!" said Mr. Browne loudly.

"But yet," continued Gabriel, his voice falling into a softer inflection, "there are always in gatherings such as this sadder thoughts that will recur to our minds: thoughts of the past, of youth, of changes, of absent faces that we miss here to-night. Our path through life is strewn with many such sad memories: and were we to brood upon them always we could not find the heart to go on bravely with our work among the living. We have all of us living duties and living affections which claim, and rightly claim, our strenuous endeavours.

"Therefore, I will not linger on the past. I will not let any gloomy moralising intrude upon us here to-night. Here we are gathered together for a brief moment from the bustle and rush of our everyday routine. We are met here as friends, in the spirit of good-fellowship, as colleagues, also to a certain extent, in the true spirit of *camaraderie*, and as the guests of—what shall I call them?—the Three Graces of the Dublin musical world."

The table burst into applause and laughter at this allusion. Aunt Julia vainly asked each of her neighbours in turn to tell her what Gabriel had said.

"He says we are the Three Graces, Aunt Julia," said Mary Jane.

Aunt Julia did not understand but she looked up, smiling, at Gabriel, who continued in the same vein:

"Ladies and Gentlemen,

"I will not attempt to play to-night the part that Paris played on another occasion. I will not attempt to choose between them. The task would be an invidious one and one beyond my poor powers. For when I view them in turn, whether it be our chief hostess herself, whose good heart, whose too good heart, has become a byword with all who know her, or her sister, who seems to be gifted with perennial youth and whose singing must have been a surprise and a revelation to us all to-night, or, last but not least, when I consider our youngest hostess, talented, cheerful, hard-working and the best of nieces, I confess, Ladies and Gentlemen, that I do not know to which of them I should award the prize."

Gabriel glanced down at his aunts and, seeing the large smile on Aunt Julia's face and the tears which had risen to Aunt Kate's eyes, hastened to his close. He raised his glass of port gallantly, while every member of the company fingered a glass expectantly, and said loudly:

"Let us toast them all three together. Let us drink to their health, wealth, long life, happiness and prosperity and may they long continue to hold the proud and self-won position which they hold in their profession and the position of honour and affection which they hold in our hearts."

All the guests stood up, glass in hand, and turning towards the three seated ladies, sang in unison, with Mr. Browne as leader:

> "For they are jolly gay fellows,
> For they are jolly gay fellows,
> For they are jolly gay fellows,
> Which nobody can deny."

Aunt Kate was making frank use of her handkerchief and even Aunt Julia seemed moved. Freddy Malins beat time with his pudding-fork and the singers turned towards one another, as if in melodious conference, while they sang with emphasis:

> "Unless he tells a lie,
> Unless he tells a lie,"

Then, turning once more towards their hostesses, they sang:

> "For they are jolly gay fellows,
> For they are jolly gay fellows,
> For they are jolly gay fellows,
> Which nobody can deny."

The acclamation which followed was taken up beyond the door of the supper-room by many of the other guests and renewed time after time, Freddy Malins acting as officer with his fork on high.

.   .   .   .

The piercing morning air came into the hall where they were standing so that Aunt Kate said:

"Close the door, somebody. Mrs. Malins will get her death of cold."

"Browne is out there, Aunt Kate," said Mary Jane.

"Browne is everywhere," said Aunt Kate, lowering her voice.

Mary Jane laughed at her tone.

"Really," she said archly, "he is very attentive."

"He has been laid on here like the gas," said Aunt Kate in the same tone, "all during the Christmas."

She laughed herself this time good-humouredly and then added quickly:

"But tell him to come in, Mary Jane, and close the door. I hope to goodness he didn't hear me."

At that moment the hall-door was opened and Mr. Browne came in from the doorstep, laughing as if his heart would break. He was dressed in a long green overcoat with mock astrakhan cuffs and collar and wore on his head an oval fur cap. He pointed down the snow-covered quay from where the sound of shrill prolonged whistling was borne in.

"Teddy will have all the cabs in Dublin out," he said.

Gabriel advanced from the little pantry behind the office, struggling into his overcoat and, looking round the hall, said:

"Gretta not down yet?"

"She's getting on her things, Gabriel," said Aunt Kate.

"Who's playing up there?" asked Gabriel.

"Nobody. They're all gone."

"O no, Aunt Kate," said Mary Jane. "Bartell D'Arcy and Miss O'Callaghan aren't gone yet."

"Someone is fooling at the piano anyhow," said Gabriel.

Mary Jane glanced at Gabriel and Mr. Browne and said with a shiver:

"It makes me feel cold to look at you two gentlemen muffled up like that. I wouldn't like to face your journey home at this hour."

"I'd like nothing better this minute," said Mr. Browne stoutly, "than a rattling fine walk in the country or a fast drive with a good spanking goer between the shafts."

"We used to have a very good horse and trap at home," said Aunt Julia sadly.

"The never-to-be-forgotten Johnny," said Mary Jane, laughing.

Aunt Kate and Gabriel laughed too.

"Why, what was wonderful about Johnny?" asked Mr. Browne.

"The late lamented Patrick Morkan, our grandfather, that is," explained Gabriel, "commonly known in his later years as the old gentleman, was a glue-boiler."

"O, now, Gabriel," said Aunt Kate, laughing, "he had a starch mill."

"Well, glue or starch," said Gabriel, "the old gentleman had a horse by the name of Johnny. And Johnny used to work in the old gentleman's mill, walking round and round in order to drive the mill. That was all very well; but now comes the tragic part about Johnny. One fine day the old gentleman thought he'd like to drive out with the quality to a military review in the park."

"The Lord have mercy on his soul," said Aunt Kate compassionately.

"Amen," said Gabriel. "So the old gentleman, as I said, harnessed Johnny and put on his very best tall hat and his very best stock collar and drove out in grand style from his ancestral mansion somewhere near Back Lane, I think."

Everyone laughed, even Mrs. Malins, at Gabriel's manner and Aunt Kate said:

"O, now, Gabriel, he didn't live in Back Lane, really. Only the mill was there."

"Out from the mansion of his forefathers," continued Gabriel, "he drove with Johnny. And everything went on beautifully until Johnny came in sight of King Billy's statue: and whether he fell in love with the horse King

Billy sits on or whether he thought he was back again in the mill, anyhow he began to walk round the statue."

Gabriel paced in a circle round the hall in his goloshes amid the laughter of the others.

"Round and round he went," said Gabriel, "and the old gentleman, who was a very pompous old gentleman, was highly indignant. 'Go on, sir! What do you mean, sir? Johnny! Johnny! Most extraordinary conduct! Can't understand the horse!'"

The peals of laughter which followed Gabriel's imitation of the incident was interrupted by a resounding knock at the hall-door. Mary Jane ran to open it and let in Freddy Malins. Freddy Malins, with his hat well back on his head and his shoulders humped with cold, was puffing and steaming after his exertions.

"I could only get one cab," he said.

"O, we'll find another along the quay," said Gabriel.

"Yes," said Aunt Kate. "Better not keep Mrs. Malins standing in the draught."

Mrs. Malins was helped down the front steps by her son and Mr. Browne and, after many manoeuvres, hoisted into the cab. Freddy Malins clambered in after her and spent a long time settling her on the seat, Mr. Browne helping him with advice. At last she was settled comfortably and Freddy Malins invited Mr. Browne into the cab. There was a good deal of confused talk, and then Mr. Browne got into the cab. The cabman settled his rug over his knees, and bent down for the address. The confusion grew greater and the cabman was directed differently by Freddy Malins and Mr. Browne, each of whom had his head out through a window of the cab. The difficulty was to know where to drop Mr. Browne along the route, and Aunt Kate, Aunt Julia and Mary Jane helped the discussion from the doorstep with cross-directions and contradictions and abundance of laughter. As for Freddy Malins he was speechless with laughter. He popped his head in and out of the window every moment to the great danger of his hat, and told his mother how the discussion was progressing, till at last Mr. Browne shouted to the bewildered cabman above the din of everybody's laughter:

"Do you know Trinity College?"

"Yes, sir," said the cabman.

"Well, drive bang up against Trinity College gates," said Mr. Browne, "and then we'll tell you where to go. You understand now?"

"Yes, sir," said the cabman.

"Make like a bird for Trinity College."

"Right, sir," said the cabman.

The horse was whipped up and the cab rattled off along the quay amid a chorus of laughter and adieus.

Gabriel had not gone to the door with the others. He was in a dark part of the hall gazing up the staircase. A woman was standing near the top of the first flight, in the shadow also. He could not see her face but he could see the terra-cotta and salmon-pink panels of her skirt which the shadow made appear black and white. It was his wife. She was leaning on the banisters, listening to something. Gabriel was surprised at her stillness and strained his ear to listen also. But he could hear little save the noise of laughter and dispute on the front steps, a few chords struck on the piano and a few notes of a man's voice singing.

He stood still in the gloom of the hall, trying to catch the air that the voice was singing and gazing up at his wife. There was grace and mystery in her attitude as if she were a symbol of something. He asked himself what is a woman standing on the stairs in the shadow, listening to distant music, a symbol of. If he were a painter he would paint her in that attitude. Her blue felt hat would show off the bronze of her hair against the darkness and the dark panels of her skirt would show off the light ones. *Distant Music* he would call the picture if he were a painter.

The hall-door was closed; and Aunt Kate, Aunt Julia and Mary Jane came down the hall, still laughing.

"Well, isn't Freddy terrible?" said Mary Jane. "He's really terrible."

Gabriel said nothing but pointed up the stairs towards where his wife was standing. Now that the hall-door was closed the voice and the piano could be heard more clearly. Gabriel held up his hand for them to be silent. The song seemed to be in the old Irish tonality and the singer seemed uncertain both of his words and of his voice. The voice, made plaintive by distance and by the singer's hoarseness, faintly illuminated the cadence of the air with words expressing grief:

> "O, the rain falls on my heavy locks
> And the dew wets my skin,
> My babe lies cold . . ."

"O," exclaimed Mary Jane. "It's Bartell D'Arcy singing and he wouldn't sing all the night. O, I'll get him to sing a song before he goes."

"O, do, Mary Jane," said Aunt Kate.

Mary Jane brushed past the others and ran to the staircase, but before she reached it the singing stopped and the piano was closed abruptly.

"O, what a pity!" she cried. "Is he coming down, Gretta?"

Gabriel heard his wife answer yes and saw her come down towards them. A few steps behind her were Mr. Bartell D'Arcy and Miss O'Callaghan.

"O, Mr. D'Arcy," cried Mary Jane, "it's downright mean of you to break off like that when we were all in raptures listening to you."

"I have been at him all the evening," said Miss O'Callaghan, "and Mrs. Conroy, too, and he told us he had a dreadful cold and couldn't sing."

"O, Mr. D'Arcy," said Aunt Kate, "now that was a great fib to tell."

"Can't you see that I'm as hoarse as a crow?" said Mr. D'Arcy roughly.

He went into the pantry hastily and put on his overcoat. The others, taken aback by his rude speech, could find nothing to say. Aunt Kate wrinkled her brows and made signs to the others to drop the subject. Mr. D'Arcy stood swathing his neck carefully and frowning.

"It's the weather," said Aunt Julia, after a pause.

"Yes, everybody has colds," said Aunt Kate readily, "everybody."

"They say," said Mary Jane, "we haven't had snow like it for thirty years; and I read this morning in the newspapers that the snow is general all over Ireland."

"I love the look of snow," said Aunt Julia sadly.

"So do I," said Miss O'Callaghan. "I think Christmas is never really Christmas unless we have the snow on the ground."

"But poor Mr. D'Arcy doesn't like the snow," said Aunt Kate, smiling.

Mr. D'Arcy came from the pantry, fully swathed and buttoned, and in a repentant tone told them the history of his cold. Everyone gave him advice and said it was a great pity and urged him to be very careful of his throat in the night air. Gabriel watched his wife, who did not join in the conversation. She was standing right under the dusty fanlight and the flame of the gas lit up the rich bronze of her hair, which he had seen her drying at the fire a few days before. She was in the same attitude and seemed unaware of the talk about her. At last she turned towards them and Gabriel saw that there was colour on her cheeks and that her eyes were shining. A sudden tide of joy went leaping out of his heart.

"Mr. D'Arcy," she said, "what is the name of that song you were singing?"

"It's called *The Lass of Aughrim*," said Mr. D'Arcy, "but I couldn't remember it properly. Why? Do you know it?"

"*The Lass of Aughrim*," she repeated. "I couldn't think of the name."

"It's a very nice air," said Mary Jane. "I'm sorry you were not in voice to-night."

"Now, Mary Jane," said Aunt Kate, "don't annoy Mr. D'Arcy. I won't have him annoyed."

Seeing that all were ready to start she shepherded them to the door, where good-night was said:

"Well, good-night, Aunt Kate, and thanks for the pleasant evening."

"Good-night, Gabriel. Good-night, Gretta!"

"Good-night, Aunt Kate, and thanks ever so much. Good-night, Aunt Julia."

"O, good-night, Gretta, I didn't see you."

"Good-night, Mr. D'Arcy. Good-night, Miss O'Callaghan."

"Good-night, Miss Morkan."

"Good-night, again."

"Good-night, all. Safe home."

"Good-night. Good-night."

The morning was still dark. A dull, yellow light brooded over the houses and the river; and the sky seemed to be descending. It was slushy underfoot; and only streaks and patches of snow lay on the roofs, on the parapets of the quay and on the area railings. The lamps were still burning redly in the murky air and, across the river, the palace of the Four Courts stood out menacingly against the heavy sky.

She was walking on before him with Mr. Bartell D'Arcy, her shoes in a brown parcel tucked under one arm and her hands holding her skirt up from the slush. She had no longer any grace of attitude, but Gabriel's eyes were still bright with happiness. The blood went bounding along his veins; and the thoughts went rioting through his brain, proud, joyful, tender, valorous.

She was walking on before him so lightly and so erect that he longed to run after her noiselessly, catch her by the shoulders and say something foolish and affectionate into her ear. She seemed to him so frail that he longed to defend her against something and then to be alone with her. Moments of their secret life together burst like stars upon his memory. A heliotrope envelope was lying beside his breakfast-cup and he was caressing it with his hand. Birds were twittering in the ivy and the sunny web of the curtain was shimmering along the floor: he could not eat for happiness. They were standing on the crowded platform and he was placing a ticket inside the warm palm of her glove. He was standing with her in the cold, looking in through a grated window at a man making bottles in a roaring furnace. It was very cold. Her face, fragrant in the cold air, was quite close to his; and suddenly he called out to the man at the furnace:

"Is the fire hot, sir?"

But the man could not hear with the noise of the furnace. It was just as well. He might have answered rudely.

A wave of yet more tender joy escaped from his heart and went coursing in warm flood along his arteries. Like the tender fire of stars moments of their life together, that no one knew of or would ever know of, broke upon and illumined his memory. He longed to recall to her those moments, to make her forget the years of their dull existence together and remember only their moments of ecstasy. For the years, he felt, had not quenched his soul or hers. Their children, his writing, her household cares had not quenched all their souls' tender fire. In one letter that he had written to her then he had said: "Why is it that words like these seem to me so dull and cold? Is it because there is no word tender enough to be your name?"

Like distant music these words that he had written years before were borne towards him from the past. He longed to be alone with her. When the others had gone away, when he and she were in the room in the hotel, then they would be alone together. He would call her softly:

"Gretta!"

Perhaps she would not hear at once: she would be undressing. Then something in his voice would strike her. She would turn and look at him. . . .

At the corner of Winetavern Street they met a cab. He was glad of its rattling noise as it saved him from conversation. She was looking out of the window and seemed tired. The others spoke only a few words, pointing out some building or street. The horse galloped along wearily under the murky morning sky, dragging his old rattling box after his heels, and Gabriel was again in a cab with her, galloping to catch the boat, galloping to their honeymoon.

As the cab drove across O'Connell Bridge Miss O'Callaghan said:

"They say you never cross O'Connell Bridge without seeing a white horse."

"I see a white man this time," said Gabriel.

"Where?" asked Mr. Bartell D'Arcy.

Gabriel pointed to the statue, on which lay patches of snow. Then he nodded familiarly to it and waved his hand.

"Good-night, Dan," he said gaily.

When the cab drew up before the hotel, Gabriel jumped out and, in spite of Mr. Bartell D'Arcy's protest, paid the driver. He gave the man a shilling over his fare. The man saluted and said:

"A prosperous New Year to you, sir."

"The same to you," said Gabriel cordially.

She leaned for a moment on his arm in getting out of the cab and while standing at the curbstone, bidding the others good-night. She leaned lightly on his arm, as lightly as when she had danced with him a few hours before. He had felt proud and happy then, happy that she was his, proud of her grace and wifely carriage. But now, after the kindling again of so many memories, the first touch of her body, musical and strange and perfumed, sent through him a keen pang of lust. Under cover of her silence he pressed her arm closely to his side; and, as they stood at the hotel door, he felt that they had escaped from their lives and duties, escaped from home and friends and run away together with wild and radiant hearts to a new adventure.

An old man was dozing in a great hooded chair in the hall. He lit a candle in the office and went before them to the stairs. They followed him in silence, their feet falling in soft thuds on the thickly carpeted stairs. She mounted the stairs behind the porter, her head bowed in the ascent, her frail shoulders curved as with a burden, her skirt girt tightly about her. He could have flung his arms about her hips and held her still, for his arms were trembling with desire to seize her and only the stress of his nails against the palms of his hands held the wild impulse of his body in check. The porter halted on the stairs to settle his guttering candle. They halted, too, on the steps below him. In the silence Gabriel could hear the falling of the molten wax into the tray and the thumping of his own heart against his ribs.

The porter led them along a corridor and opened a door. Then he set his unstable candle down on a toilet-table and asked at what hour they were to be called in the morning.

"Eight," said Gabriel.

The porter pointed to the tap of the electric-light and began a muttered apology, but Gabriel cut him short.

"We don't want any light. We have light enough from the street. And I say," he added, pointing to the candle, "you might remove that handsome article, like a good man."

The porter took up his candle again, but slowly, for he was surprised by such a novel idea. Then he mumbled good-night and went out. Gabriel shot the lock to.

A ghastly light from the street lamp lay in a long shaft from one window to the door. Gabriel threw his overcoat and hat on a couch and crossed the room towards the window. He looked down into the street in order that his emotion might calm a little. Then he turned and leaned against a chest of drawers with his back to the light. She had taken off her hat and cloak and was standing before a large swinging mirror, unhooking her waist. Gabriel paused for a few moments, watching her, and then said:

"Gretta!"

She turned away from the mirror slowly and walked along the shaft of light towards him. Her face looked so serious and weary that the words would not pass Gabriel's lips. No, it was not the moment yet.

"You looked tired," he said.

"I am a little," she answered.

"You don't feel ill or weak?"

"No, tired: that's all."

She went on to the window and stood there, looking out. Gabriel waited again and then, fearing that diffidence was about to conquer him, he said abruptly:

"By the way, Gretta!"

"What is it?"

"You know that poor fellow Malins?" he said quickly.

"Yes. What about him?"

"Well, poor fellow, he's a decent sort of chap, after all," continued Gabriel in a false voice. "He gave me back that sovereign I lent him, and I didn't expect it, really. It's a pity he wouldn't keep away from that Browne, because he's not a bad fellow, really."

He was trembling now with annoyance. Why did she seem so abstracted? He did not know how he could begin. Was she annoyed, too, about something? If she would only turn to him or come to him of her own accord! To take her as she was would be brutal. No, he must see some ardour in her eyes first. He longed to be master of her strange mood.

"When did you lend him the pound?" she asked, after a pause.

Gabriel strove to restrain himself from breaking out into brutal language about the sottish Malins and his pound. He longed to cry to her from his soul, to crush her body against his, to overmaster her. But he said:

"O, at Christmas, when he opened that little Christmas-card shop in Henry Street."

He was in such a fever of rage and desire that he did not hear her come from the window. She stood before him for an instant, looking at him strangely. Then, suddenly raising herself on tiptoe and resting her hands lightly on his shoulders, she kissed him.

"You are a very generous person, Gabriel," she said.

Gabriel, trembling with delight at her sudden kiss and at the quaintness of her phrase, put his hands on her hair and began smoothing it back, scarcely touching it with his fingers. The washing had made it fine and brilliant. His heart was brimming over with happiness. Just when he was wishing for it she had come to him of her own accord. Perhaps her thoughts had been running with his. Perhaps she had felt the impetuous desire that was in him, and then the yielding mood had come upon her. Now that she had fallen to him so easily, he wondered why he had been so diffident.

He stood, holding her head between his hands. Then, slipping one arm swiftly about her body and drawing her towards him, he said softly:

"Gretta, dear, what are you thinking about?"

She did not answer nor yield wholly to his arm. He said again, softly:

"Tell me what it is, Gretta. I think I know what is the matter. Do I know?"

She did not answer at once. Then she said in an outburst of tears:

"O, I am thinking about that song, *The Lass of Aughrim.*"

She broke loose from him and ran to the bed and, throwing her arms across the bed-rail, hid her face. Gabriel stood stock-still for a moment in astonishment and then followed her. As he passed in the way of the cheval-glass he caught sight of himself in full length, his broad, well-filled shirt-front, the face whose expression always puzzled him when he saw it in a mirror, and his glimmering gilt-rimmed eyeglasses. He halted a few paces from her and said:

"What about the song? Why does that make you cry?"

She raised her head from her arms and dried her eyes with the back of her hand like a child. A kinder note than he had intended went into his voice.

"Why, Gretta?" he asked.

"I am thinking about a person long ago who used to sing that song."

"And who was the person long ago?" asked Gabriel, smiling.

"It was a person I used to know in Galway when I was living with my grandmother," she said.

The smile passed away from Gabriel's face. A dull anger began to gather again at the back of his mind and the dull fires of his lust began to glow angrily in his veins.

"Someone you were in love with?" he asked ironically.

"It was a young boy I used to know," she answered, "named Michael Furey. He used to sing that song, *The Lass of Aughrim*. He was very delicate."

Gabriel was silent. He did not wish her to think that he was interested in this delicate boy.

"I can see him so plainly," she said, after a moment. "Such eyes as he had: big, dark eyes! And such an expression in them—an expression!"

"O, then, you are in love with him?" said Gabriel.

"I used to go out walking with him," she said, "when I was in Galway."

A thought flew across Gabriel's mind.

"Perhaps that was why you wanted to go to Galway with that Ivors girl?" he said coldly.

She looked at him and asked in surprise:

"What for?"

Her eyes made Gabriel feel awkward. He shrugged his shoulders and said:

"How do I know? To see him, perhaps."

She looked away from him along the shaft of light towards the window in silence.

"He is dead," she said at length. "He died when he was only seventeen. Isn't it a terrible thing to die so young as that?"

"What was he?" asked Gabriel, still ironically.

"He was in the gasworks," she said.

Gabriel felt humiliated by the failure of his irony and by the evocation of this figure from the dead, a boy in the gasworks. While he had been full of memories of their secret life together, full of tenderness and joy and desire, she had been comparing him in her mind with another. A shameful consciousness of his own person assailed him. He saw himself as a ludicrous figure, acting as a pennyboy for his aunts, a nervous, well-meaning sentimentalist, orating to vulgarians and idealising his own clownish lusts, the pitiable fatuous fellow he had caught a glimpse of in the mirror. Instinctively he turned his back more to the light lest she might see the shame that burned upon his forehead.

He tried to keep up his tone of cold interrogation, but his voice when he spoke was humble and indifferent.

"I suppose you were in love with this Michael Furey, Gretta," he said.

"I was great with him at that time," she said.

Her voice was veiled and sad. Gabriel, feeling now how vain it would be to try to lead her whither he had purposed, caressed one of her hands and said, also sadly:

"And what did he die of so young, Gretta? Consumption, was it?"

"I think he died for me," she answered.

A vague terror seized Gabriel at this answer, as if, at that hour when he had hoped to triumph, some impalpable and vindictive being was coming against him, gathering forces against him in its vague world. But he shook himself free of it with an effort of reason and continued to caress her hand. He did not question her again, for he felt that she would tell him of herself. Her hand was warm and moist: it did not respond to his touch, but he continued to caress it just as he had caressed her first letter to him that spring morning.

"It was in the winter," she said, "about the beginning of the winter when I was going to leave my grandmother's and come up here to the convent. And he was ill at the time in his lodgings in Galway and wouldn't be let out, and his people in Oughterard were written to. He was in decline, they said, or something like that. I never knew rightly."

She paused for a moment and sighed.

"Poor fellow," she said. "He was very fond of me and he was such a gentle boy. We used to go out together, walking, you know, Gabriel, like the way they do in the country. He was going to study singing only for his health. He had a very good voice, poor Michael Furey."

"Well; and then?" asked Gabriel.

"And then when it came to the time for me to leave Galway and come up to the convent he was much worse and I wouldn't be let see him so I wrote him a letter saying I was going up to Dublin and would be back in the summer, and hoping he would be better then."

She paused for a moment to get her voice under control, and then went on:

"Then the night before I left, I was in my grandmother's house in Nuns' Island, packing up, and I heard gravel thrown up against the window. The window was so wet I couldn't see, so I ran downstairs as I was and slipped out the back into the garden and there was the poor fellow at the end of the garden, shivering."

"And did you not tell him to go back?" asked Gabriel.

"I implored of him to go home at once and told him he would get his death in the rain. But he said he did not want to live. I can see his eyes as well as well! He was standing at the end of the wall where there was a tree."

"And did he go home?" asked Gabriel.

"Yes, he went home. And when I was only a week in the convent he died and he was buried in Oughterard, where his people came from. O, the day I heard that, that he was dead!"

She stopped, choking with sobs, and, overcome by emotion, flung herself face downward on the bed, sobbing in the quilt. Gabriel held her hand for a moment longer, irresolutely, and then, shy of intruding on her grief, let it fall gently and walked quietly to the window.

She was fast asleep.

Gabriel, leaning on his elbow, looked for a few moments unresentfully on her tangled hair and half-open mouth, listening to her deep-drawn breath. So she had had that romance in her life: a man had died for her sake. It hardly pained him now to think how poor a part he, her husband, had played in her life. He watched her while she slept, as though he and she had never lived together as man and wife. His curious eyes rested long upon her face and on her hair: and, as he thought of what she must have been then, in that time of her first girlish beauty, a strange, friendly pity for her entered his soul. He did not like to say even to himself that her face was no longer beautiful, but he knew that it was no longer the face for which Michael Furey had braved death.

Perhaps she had not told him all the story. His eyes moved to the chair over which she had thrown some of her clothes. A petticoat string dangled to the floor. One boot stood upright, its limp upper fallen down: the fellow of it lay upon its side. He wondered at his riot of emotions of an hour before. From what had it proceeded? From his aunt's supper, from his own foolish speech, from the wine and dancing, the merry-making when saying good-night in the hall, the pleasure of the walk along the river in the snow. Poor Aunt Julia! She, too, would soon be a shade with the shade of Patrick Morkan and his horse. He had caught that haggard look upon her face for a moment when she was singing *Arrayed for the Bridal*. Soon, perhaps, he would be sitting in that same drawing-room, dressed in black, his silk hat on his knees. The blinds would be drawn down and Aunt Kate would be sitting beside him, crying and blowing her nose and telling him how Julia had died. He would cast about in his mind for some words that might console her, and would find only lame and useless ones. Yes, yes: that would happen very soon.

The air of the room chilled his shoulders. He stretched himself cautiously along under the sheets and lay down beside his wife. One by one, they were all becoming shades. Better pass boldly into that other world, in the full glory of some passion, than fade and wither dismally with age. He thought of how she who lay beside him had locked in her heart for so many years that image of her lover's eyes when he had told her that he did not wish to live.

Generous tears filled Gabriel's eyes. He had never felt like that himself towards any woman, but he knew that such a feeling must be love. The tears gathered more thickly in his eyes and in the partial darkness he imagined he saw the form of a young man standing under a dripping tree. Other forms were near. His soul had approached that region where dwell the vast hosts of the dead. He was conscious of, but could not apprehend, their wayward and flickering existence. His own identity was fading out into a grey impalpable world: the solid world itself, which these dead had one time reared and lived in, was dissolving and dwindling.

A few light taps upon the pane made him turn to the window. It had begun to snow again. He watched sleepily the flakes, silver and dark, falling obliquely against the lamplight. The time had come for him to set out on his journey westward. Yes, the newspapers were right: snow was general all over Ireland. It was falling on every part of the dark central plain, on the treeless hills, falling softly upon the Bog of Allen and, farther westward, softly falling into the dark mutinous Shannon waves. It was falling, too, upon every part of the lonely churchyard on the hill where Michael Furey lay buried. It lay thickly drifted on the crooked crosses and headstones, on the spears of the little gate, on the barren thorns. His soul swooned slowly as he heard the snow falling faintly through the universe and faintly falling, like the descent of their last end, upon all the living and the dead.

Study Guide

Text by

Gina Taglieri

(M.A. Columbia University)

English Department
Fashion Institute of Technology
State University of New York
New York, New York

Contents

> **Each story includes List of Characters,**
> **Summary, Analysis, Study Questions and**
> **Answers, and Suggested Essay Topics.**

SECTION ONE

Introduction

The Life and Work of James Joyce

James Joyce was born in 1882 in a suburb of Dublin, Ireland in a large, Catholic family, and received a private education in Jesuit schools; thereafter, he attended University College, Dublin, on scholarship. His family life, though warm, was immersed in the turbulent Irish politics of the time and the early arguments Joyce overheard about various Irish leaders filtered their way into Joyce's fiction.

When Joyce was nine, the family's finances began to dwindle when his father was forced into early retirement (never finding steady work again). The family moved several times, each resulting in a less respectable address. With poverty looming, however, Joyce's father arranged for the boys to attend a prestigious Jesuit prep school on scholarship. Despite the boys' promising education, the Joyce's family life was fractious because of financial worries and the father's drinking; James was the only son to have a close relationship with the elder Joyce.

Entering University College, Dublin, on scholarship in 1898, Joyce studied English literature and foreign languages. At university, Joyce began to formulate his feelings towards family, church, and homeland that would be played and replayed in his fiction. Like his hero Stephen Dedalus (who appears in *A Portrait of the Artist as a Young Man and Ulysses*), Joyce chose not to remain a member of the Catholic church; nevertheless, he disapproved of religious hypocrisy and retained the benefits of his liberal and intellectual Jesuit training. Unlike Stephen, Joyce had a terrific sense of humor, as much of his fiction and many of his letters make clear. Even as a youth, he loved puns, word games, titillating malapropisms, etc. This fascination makes itself evident in *Portrait, Ulysses* and especially *Finnegans Wake*.

Another strong influence on Joyce's work was his love for and ability in music. He studied voice and piano, briefly considering a career as an Irish tenor (he befriended the great John McCormack) as a young man. His earliest collection of poems, *Chamber Music* (1907), is based mostly on ballad form, and music's importance is stressed throughout his work. However, Joyce's increasingly deteriorating eyesight forced him to rely more on hearing music than seeing it. As a result, accurate representations of sounds, accents, voices, street noises, folksongs, etc., bring color and naturalism to his writing.

In college, Joyce was drawn to study drama, particularly Henrik Ibsen, who was a lifelong influence. After publishing an early article on Ibsen in a drama journal in 1900, the 18 year-old critic received a (translated) note of thanks from the Norwegian dramatist. Recognition from a famous founder of the modern dramatic movement enabled Joyce to view himself as a budding European intellectual/writer rather than a mere Irish college boy. In effect, it was a turning point in his early artistic life.

Joyce toyed with medical school after college, while simultaneously trying to establish himself in Dublin literary circles. Moving to Paris in 1902, ostensibly to study medicine, Joyce found there a liberated society completely opposite that of his native city. Joyce felt he could be intellectually freer as an exile in Paris. In fact, the theme of the *exile* appears throughout his fiction and is the title of his play. As Ellmann states, Joyce realized that the trip to Paris transcended a faint desire to study medicine or escape from his family's financial misery. "To measure himself and his country," Ellmann states, "he needed to take the measure of a more alien world." (Ellman, *James Joyce*, 110)

For the rest of his life, with the exception of a few intermittent stays in Dublin, Joyce made Trieste, Paris, and Zurich his most frequent homes, although his writing always focussed on the Irish capital.

Having moved back to Dublin from Paris in 1903 to comfort

his dying mother, Joyce felt stultified in his native city but lacked the means to travel. Occasionally, he worked with ambition, beginning preliminary work that would evolve into *Portrait* in a single day. In 1904, he met his future wife, Nora Barnacle, an unsophisticated country girl from the west coast of Ireland, and was almost instantaneously smitten with her. Though not nearly his equal intellectually, Nora provided the source and inspiration for much of Joyce's ground-breaking portrayals of women in his fiction, most notably for *Ulysses'* Molly Bloom. That same year, the unmarried couple departed for Paris together (a scandalous act at the time) and remained together—despite Joyce's temperament, his extreme jealousy, and numerous financial troubles—for the rest of their lives.

In 1914, the year *Dubliners* finally reached publication, *A Portrait of the Artist as a Young Man* was also published in magazine installments, and published as a novel in 1916. *Portrait is* mainly, though not entirely, autobiographical, taking place (like all of Joyce's work) in Dublin. Using the technique of stream-of-consciousness narration, Joyce attempts to show the evolution of a young artist as he frees himself from the restrictions of religious parochialism and a clinging, suffering family. His hero, Stephen Dedalus, the renegade ex-Catholic, reflects Joyce's own early conflicts between his devotion to art and traditional spiritual duty. Like Stephen, Joyce believed that art was his religion and literature the definitive affirmation of the human spirit.

Stephen Dedalus appears again in Joyce's most famous work, *Ulysses*, the chronicling of the events of a single summer's day in Dublin, 1904. Using the Greek Ulysses myth as a basis for its structure, the novel studies the experience of moment-to-moment events through the eyes of several key characters. Heavily reliant on the stream-of-consciousness method, *Ulysses* also employs the technique of free indirect discourse, in which the author's narrative style mimics the tone and language use of the character perceiving the events described.

Serialized in a Paris journal, *Ulysses*, like *Dubliners*, faced obstacles in publishing because of its sexual content, its publication temporarily halted in France due to obscenity charges.

Published finally in French in 1922, the novel was smuggled out of Paris by curious readers and intellectuals for several years before the English edition was finally cleared of obscenity charges in the United States in 1934.

Visiting a family friend in the midst of the obscenity hearings, Joyce was told by his mother that the novel "was not fit to read." If such was the case, Joyce responded, "life isn't fit to live." (Ellmann, *James Joyce*, 537). This clarifies Joyce's stance (shared by D. H. Lawrence, Jean Rhys, Gertrude Stein, Djuna Barnes, among others) that literature was an appropriate arena for discussions about and explorations of sexual issues. Joyce believed that *Ulysses* reflected real life among working-class Dubliners; all aspects of such life were worthy of examination.

Over the course of many years and despite many costly operations, Joyce's eyesight, always weak, grew increasingly worse. The editing process of *Ulysses* (first in French, then in English) was grueling for him, and as he began writing his last major work, *Finnegans Wake*, his eyesight was almost completely lost. The prose poem, begun in 1923, has been described as a "labyrinth" of literary devices and complex, sometimes arcane, references. Though Joyce considered it his masterwork and its difficulty has made it a challenge to Joyce scholars, it remains less accessible to most readers, who are only somewhat familiar with it.

While Joyce's literary achievements and obsessive devotion to his art have made him a pillar of Modernist literature, they also made life difficult for himself and his family. He secured a loyal English patron to subsidize his writing, but—in light of his lifelong inability to manage money—his wife and two children rarely enjoyed the material comforts of his success. Although his work earned him admirers throughout the world, Joyce's sense of suspicion and imperious ego often alienated supporters when he needed them most. In addition, his terrible eyesight made writing and editing, the mainstays of his life, agony.

When *Finnegan's Wake* was finally published in 1939, Joyce's health was failing and his daughter, having suffered a severe nervous breakdown, was confined to a Swiss institution. While *Finnegan's Wake* failed to receive the reception that Joyce felt it deserved, his reputation among the writers of the period was certain. When France fell to the Nazis in 1940, James and Nora left Paris for neutral Switzerland, where Joyce died in 1941.

Historical Background

As he portrays it in his work, Joyce's Dublin was composed mostly of lower-to middle-class residents oppressed by financial hardships, foreign political dominance, fractiousness among rival Irish nationalist groups, and the overwhelming influence of the Irish Catholic Church. Combined, in Joyce's eyes, these forces and travails left the ordinary Dubliner with few options for self-expression or freedom of the soul; hence, Joyce's theme of "paralysis" was established.

In the late 1800s, Ireland was still reeling from the agricultural disasters of mid-century and the massive Irish immigration (mainly to the United States) that followed. Several references in the stories suggest that well-paying employment was scarce and that even working class Dubliners struggled under subsistence wages. Consistently throughout the stories, characters agonize over a crown or even a shilling; this underscores the prevailing financial difficulties among most citizens.

Politically, Ireland was ruled by the British monarchy, and the attitude among the Irish towards the occupying British ranged from one of skepticism and distrust to open hostility. In addition to its aversion to Catholicism, the British government disdained the Irish for their general lack of education (especially in the countryside), their superstitious ways, and the often squalid living conditions necessitated by the country's weak economy. That the British profited from its presence in Ireland—even while regarding its people with contempt—only served to further infuriate the Irish at the British presence.

During the 1880s, the possibility for Ireland's sovereignty was strengthened by the efforts of political leader Charles Stewart Parnell. Owing to his influence, political savvy and uncompromising support of home rule, Ireland's independence seemed more viable under Parnell's leadership than ever before. However, the disclosure of a romantic scandal in 1889 sullied Parnell's reputation, allowing his opponents and groups of zealous Catholics (Parnell was Protestant), working in concert, to discredit him and weaken his power base. This turnaround in fate and the betrayal of even his closest allies broke Parnell, leading to his political defeat and—ultimately—his death in 1891.

Turn-of-the-century Dublin, as portrayed in Joyce's collection, is still haunted by Parnell's ghost and the promise of Irish independence that died with him. Gradually, many Irish realized they had themselves to blame for allowing Parnell's dream of independence to vanish, and the themes of failed promise and betrayal are common in the works of many Irish writers of the period, Joyce's especially.

Finally, an overwhelming force in the Ireland of Joyce's period was that of the Irish Catholic Church, since a vast majority of the Irish were Catholics. According to his biographer, Richard Ellmann, Joyce believed that the "real sovereign of Ireland [was] the Pope" (Ellmann, *James Joyce*, 256). Although Joyce left the Church, Ellmann adds, he "continued to denounce all his life the deviousness of Papal policy," finding the Church and the papacy "deaf" to Irish cries for help (Ellmann, *James Joyce*, 257). Clearly, Joyce believed the Church reacted inadequately in failing to help unburden the Irish of the hostile British presence, nor did it sufficiently attempt to lift Ireland out of its literal and figurative poverty. He believed Church doctrine encouraged docility and subservience on the part of the Irish, this attitude only further enhancing Ireland's political exploitation and lack of independence.

In preparation for *Dubliners*, Joyce kept a notebook of revelations, or "epiphanies," which are central to understanding the stories. While the word most commonly describes a religious revelation, Joyce's understanding of the epiphany is the recognition of the essential essence of a moment, an exchange, an experience. It is the sudden "revelation of the whatness of a thing," Joyce maintained, and in Dubliners, the epiphany marks a character's realization about him or herself—even if the psychic realization is a painful one. (Ellmann, *James Joyce*, 83).

Joyce composed the *Dubliners* stories with great ease, basing groups of stories on his experiences in childhood, adolescence, and mature life. In a letter to his brother Stanislaus in 1905, Joyce stated

Dublin's importance as a world capital and indicated his desire to present it to the world (Ellmann, *James Joyce*, 208). Though he lived abroad while writing about his homeland, Joyce did not allow his portrayal of Dublin to be cosmetized by a sense of homesickness. In a speech he characterized Ireland as a country "weakened by centuries of useless struggle and broken treaties," where "individual initiative is paralyzed[.]" (Ellmann, *James Joyce*, 258).

Not surprisingly, publishers backed away from his unblinking portrait of Dublin's citizenry; it took Joyce an exhausting nine years to see *Dubliners* published. "I seriously believe," Joyce wrote to would-be publisher Grant Richards in 1905, "that you will retard the course of civilisation in Ireland by preventing the Irish people from having one good look at themselves in my nicely polished looking glass" (Ellmann, *Selected Letters*, 90). Although Richards appreciated the collection and even signed a contract, his printer objected to the profanity and tawdry scenes included in therein. When these were brought to Richards' attention, he asked Joyce to remove them, but the stubborn Joyce refused and Richards cancelled his commitment. *Dubliners* travelled from publisher to publisher, each one disturbed at the stories' pessimism, sordid scenes, profanity and sexual subtleties. The image Joyce reflected was far from complimentary, but he remained convinced that it was accurate and therapeutic. *Dubliners* portrays the soul of that city, chronicling the decay of its morals and the weakening of its spiritual life by focussing on the psychic and emotional paralysis of its inhabitants.

When finally published in 1914, sales of *Dubliners* were disappointing. While intellectuals such as W. B. Yeats and Ezra Pound appreciated *Dubliners*, most critics' objections were similar to those of the many unwilling publishers: they found the stories depressing, showing only an unseemly side of Dublin. Further, they had difficulty finding the "point" in the collection, failing to realize that to read *Dubliners* (indeed, all of Joyce's work) one must read for symbolical meaning.

As Joyce's subsequent literary works became more well-known, critics began to develop the skills of symbolic reading required to appreciate the *Dubliners* stories.

Master List of Characters

The Sisters

Narrator—*Boy, 8–9 years old.*

Father Flynn (dead)—*Boy's mentor.*

Narrator's Aunt and Uncle

Nannie and Eliza—*Priest's elderly sisters.*

Old Cotter—*Family friend.*

An Encounter

Narrator—*Boy, 8–9 years old.*

Mahoney—*School friend of the Narrator.*

Leo Dillon—*School firend of the Narrator.*

Joe Dillon—*Leo's brother.*

Older Man in Field—*Quite likely a sexual pervert.*

Araby

Narrator—*Boy, 9–12 years old.*

Mangan's sister—*Sister of narrator's friend with whom the boy is in love.*

Narrator's Aunt and Uncle

Eveline

Eveline Hill—*Young woman, 18–20 years old.*

Eveline's Alcoholic Father

Eveline's Mother—*Who died and Eveline loved.*

Frank—*Eveline's betrothed.*

After the Race

Jimmy Doyle—*Wealthy 20–21 year-old Irishman.*

Charles Segouin—*Owner of a French race car, his friend.*

Andre Riviere—*Friend of Segouin.*

Villona—*Hungarian friend of Segouin.*

Routh—*English friend of Segouin.*

Farley—*American friend of Riviere.*

Two Gallants

Corley—*A womanizer about 25 years old.*

Lenehan—*His buddy, approximately the same age.*

Servant Girl ("Slavey")—*Whom Corley is dating.*

The Boarding House

Mrs. Mooney—*Owner of the boarding house.*

Polly Mooney—*Her 19-year-old daughter.*

Bob Doran—*Boarder with whom Polly has become romantically involved.*

A Little Cloud

Little Chandler—*Thirty-ish clerk and amateur poet.*

Ignatius Gallaher—*Little Chandler's school friend, now a journalist living in London.*

Little's Wife (Annie) and Baby Son

Counterparts

Farrington—*Forty-ish clerk and alcoholic.*

Mr. Alleyne—*Farrington's boss.*

Weathers—*An English entertainer whom Farrington meets in a pub.*

Several of Farrington's Drinking Companions

Clay

Maria—*Middle-aged worker in an Irish charitable laundry.*

Joe Donnelly—*Her nephew.*

Joe's Family

A Painful Case

James Duffy—*Middle-aged ascetic and scholar.*

Emily Sinico—*Middle-aged married woman who becomes attached to Duffy intellectually and personally.*

Ivy Day in the Committee Room

Old Jack—*Caretaker of headquarters.*

O'Connor—*Young political canvasser.*

Hynes—*Canvasser whom others suspect of working for the rival side.*

Henchy—*A canvasser.*

Crofton—*A canvasser.*

Lyons—*A canvasser.*

Richard Tierney (not present)—*Politician running for office in the Royal Exchange Ward and for whom the canvassers are working.*

Father Keon—*De-frocked priest and friend of Tierney.*

Charles Stewart Parnell—*(dead) Irish Revolutionary in whose honor ivy is worn on the lapel to commemorate anniversary of his death.*

A Mother

Mrs. Kearney—*Overbearing mother and socially ambitious member of Dublin middle class.*

Mr. Kearney—*Her quiet, ineffectual husband.*

Kathleen Kearney—*Her teenage daughter.*

Mr. Holohan—*Assistant secretary to the Eire Abu Society.*

Mr. Fitzpatrick—*Secretary to the Eire Abu Society.*

Grace

Tom Kernan—*A tea merchant and alcoholic.*

Messrs. Power, Cunningham, M'Coy and Fogarty—*Tom Kernan's friends.*

Mrs. Kernan—*His wife.*

Father Purdon—*Priest running the "businessman's retreat" at the local church.*

The Dead

Gabriel Conroy—*Teacher and amateur writer.*

Gretta Conroy—*His wife.*

Julia and Kate Morkan—*Gabriel's aging aunts, piano and voice teachers in Dublin.*

Mary Jane—*Gabriel's cousin, an unmarried piano teacher who lives with the aunts.*

Molly Ivors—*Gabriel's colleague and passionate Irish nationalist various party guests of the Morkans.*

Michael Furey—*(dead) Adolescent love of Gretta Conroy.*

Summary of the Short Stories

In turn-of-the-century Dublin, the lives of several lower and middle-class Irishmen are described by the author. The first of these stories, "The Sisters," portrays a boy of 8-9 years whose friend and mentor, Father Flynn, has just died. The boy and his aunt pay their respects to Flynn and his sisters at the sisters' house.

In "An Encounter," the narrator and his school-boy friend, Mahoney, cut a day's school to have an adventure in Dublin. Just when it seems that nothing exciting will happen to them, they meet an elderly eccentric in a park. As it turns out, the older man is a sexual pervert and describes to the narrator his fantasies, which frightens the boy.

In "Araby," the narrator describes in retrospect an intense crush he had on a friend's sister when he was about 12-13 years old. At the time, he promised the sister that he'd go to a local fair and bring her back a gift (perhaps making her his girlfriend), but the mission ended with disappointment when he found nothing suitable for her.

"Eveline" finds a 19-year-old girl about to leave her father's home in Dublin to elope to South America with her beau. However, she is too afraid of change and believes she owes her loyalty to her father; at the story's end, she won't join her pleading boyfriend on the trans-atlantic steamer.

Jimmy Doyle, in "After the Race," is one of the collection's few well-to-do characters. Having invested a large sum of money in a French racecar, he joins his French friends in a cross-Dublin auto race and meets with them later in the evening for dinner and gambling. However, he plays poorly and loses an untold (but considerable) amount of money at cards.

Corley and Lenehan in "Two Gallants" discuss Corley's latest female conquest and the lengths she'll go to please her boyfriend. By the end of the story, we see that she will even steal money from her employer for Corley, a fact that Lenehan regards with admiration and awe.

Polly Mooney, in "The Boarding House," has ensnared Bob Doran into becoming engaged to her through her seductive behavior and the actions of her calculating and manipulative mother. Doran is helpless against these two conniving women and agrees under force to the marriage although he doesn't feel love for Polly.

"A Little Cloud" describes the fading literary desires of Little Chandler who meets a much more successful friend (a journalist) in a bar after work. At first Little hopes his friend can help his career, but he soon realizes that the man would never help him. Returning home from the pub, Little is extremely discouraged with his life's circumstances.

In "Counterparts," the alcoholic clerk, Farrington, has an argument with his boss and recovers from the fight by getting drunk in a bar after work. At the bar, surrounded by his cronies, he's humiliated by a fellow patron and returns home so angry and frustrated that he beats his young son.

Maria, in "Clay," visits her brother and his family on Hallowe'en, bringing them cakes and goodies. Although they're happy to see her, a series of minor upsets discompose Maria, and it's difficult for her to enjoy herself at this much-anticipated party.

James Duffy, in "A Painful Case," meets a woman at a concert with whom he becomes close friends. When their relationship becomes too intense for him, he breaks it off, only to discover several years later that the woman has committed suicide on a railway in the city. Though he initially blames the woman's unbalanced mental state for this occurrence, he comes to realize the part he's played in her death.

A group of political workers in "Ivy Day in the Committee Room" gather together at party headquarters to drink stout, complain about corrupt Dublin politics and reminisce about the happier times when Charles Stewart Parnell was still active in Irish politics. One member of the group recites a poem he wrote to commemorate the death of Parnell.

Mrs. Kearney in "A Mother" is an overbearing stage parent who wants her daughter Kathleen to play the piano at an Irish concert and be paid the contracted fee for the performance. When the directors of the pageant try to unfairly nullify Kathleen's contract, Mrs. Kearney becomes furious, barring her daughter from performing further and threatening the management of the concert. Neither side can compromise enough to reach an agreement.

In "Grace," three of Tom Kernan's friends and drinking buddies convince him to attend a religious retreat with them in order to clean up their lives and atone for their sins. Although it's unlikely that any of them understand the significance of their actions, they attend the retreat together, convinced that this experience will help save their souls.

Finally, Gabriel Conroy and his wife Gretta, in "The Dead," attend the Christmas party of Gabriel's aging aunts. Throughout the evening Gabriel constantly second-guesses his actions and never truly relaxes or enjoys himself. After the party, as he's about to approach his wife romantically, Gabriel learns from her that, as a teenager, she was deeply in love with a country boy who died of heartbreak over her. This news so upsets the unsuspecting Gabriel that it shatters his picture of his life, forcing him to reconsider everything he's previously taken for granted.

Estimated Reading Time

Although all are fairly short, most of the stories in *Dubliners* are deep, and some of the vocabulary is complex. Therefore, set aside at least a week (ideally, two weeks), with several sittings, to read *Dubliners*. It is suggested that each story be read through once, while underlining unfamiliar words and marking items of importance. After looking up the vocabulary in a dictionary, and reviewing the commentary and notes, re-read the story; many more things will be noticed the second time and the reading will be even more enjoyable.

Notice, too, that these stories are meant to fit together: the theme in one often relates to that in several others, and many characters have similar (although never identical) circumstances. Consider the people of *Dubliners* as a group and try to understand their struggles and disappointments. Joyce intended to show his city to itself and the world, and these stories will recreate the atmosphere of that period in Dublin if they are read attentively.

Dubliners

The Sisters (pages 1–7)

New Characters:

Narrator: *boy, 8–9 years old*

Father Flynn (dead): *boy's mentor*

Narrator's Aunt and Uncle

Nannie and Eliza: *priest's elderly sisters*

Old Cotter: *family friend*

Summary

This story is narrated by a young boy, probably about eight or nine, discussing the imminent death of Father Flynn, an older priest whom he has befriended. After three strokes, the priest is paralyzed, but the boy hesitates to ask for certain if he has died. His aunt, uncle, and a family friend discuss the priest's odd habits, the friend adding that the priest might not be a good influence on a younger person. The boy takes offense at what he believes is a patronizing statement, but says nothing.

After having a nightmare about Fr. Flynn, the boy discovers a notice at the priest's sisters' home that Flynn has died. Rather than feeling mournful, however, the boy feels an inexplicable freedom. He recollects the details about Catholicism that he learned from Flynn, but he still cannot interpret his giddiness.

Going to pay his respects with his aunt later in the evening, the boy is distracted, cannot pray, and cannot make smalltalk

with Eliza (one of Fr. Flynn's sisters) as his aunt can. Instead he
listens to the sisters and his aunt discuss the priest's disappointing career and life in the clergy, which was muddled by his dropping a chalice during a mass earlier in his career. Eliza claims that
this error—coupled with the heavy demands of the priesthood—
began to wear down his peace of mind, even implying that Fr.
Flynn had begun to lose his mind. The boy, still contemplating the
priest and their relationship, says nothing.

Analysis

Father Flynn, the dying priest in "The Sisters," has suffered
three strokes and now lies paralyzed on the brink of death. This
paralysis is the watchword for Joyce's entire collection of stories,
as virtually all the significant characters in *Dubliners* are psychi-
cally paralyzed by their life circumstances. Young and old, they
are inert or helpless in the face of their own suffering and indecision. The narrator of this story, a young boy who has befriended
Flynn, recognizes the fearsome quality of the paralysis and also
longs to understand it, "to be nearer to it and to look upon its
deadly work."

Although the boy is seen by his aunt as having a "great"
friendship with the priest, his family's friend, Old Cotter, per-
ceives something unseemly, believing that Flynn's attention has
somehow suffocated—perhaps even corrupted—the boy. The
narrator bristles at Cotter's patronizing observations, but the relationship is not, in fact, a healthy one. The boy dreams of Flynn's
"grey face," imagining "that it desired to confess something." Both
the boy and the face smile "feebly" at each other in the dream,
demonstrating an uncertain understanding, even a forgiveness,
of the other.

That the priest should show a desire to confess to the boy
demonstrates for the reader the perversity of their relationship,
as it controverts the priest's main spiritual role. Studying their
friendship, we see that the priest "amused himself" during the
boy's visits "by putting difficult questions" to him. Flynn forced
the narrator into interrogation sessions about minutiae involving
church doctrine, requiring him to strain for an answer about spiritual issues which the boy had "always regarded as the simplest

acts." In turning the simple and spiritual into the tortuous and strained, Flynn acts as a sadist, with the boy as his compliant victim.

His perversity is further underscored by Joyce's revolting visual description of him: inert and grey, covered with snuff stains and trembling. The narrator's recollection of the priest's smile—his tongue lasciviously lying along his lower lip—"made me feel uneasy in the beginning." It makes the reader uneasy as well, since the sexual image is completely inappropriate. The allusion to sexual impropriety is enhanced slightly further in the boy's dream, which takes place "in some land where the customs were strange—in Persia, I thought ..." Though Joyce doesn't complete the dream, the strangeness of the priest's behavior, combined with Old Cotter's admonitions, suggest to the reader the unhealthiness of the bond.

When the narrator learns of Flynn's death, he feels at odds with himself. Knowing he should feel grief, he instead discovers in himself "a sense of freedom as if I had been freed from something by his death." Indeed, the boy has been freed from the priest's oppressive emotional lock on him. Clearly, Flynn represents, as Edward Brandabur has pointed out, "the corrupt features of Irish Catholicism," turning spirituality into a burden and torture. In Joyce's mind, Irish Catholicism had leeched life out of the population as the priest had leeched it from the boy. The Irish, Joyce felt, were paralyzed by the trivialities and rules of the Catholic church, as the narrator felt his own coming paralysis in a relationship with the priest.

When he and his aunt visit the dead priest's home to pay their respects, the boy cannot pray beside the coffin as the others do, distracted by thoughts of Flynn and feeling—with his passing— the loss of his own spirituality, albeit a somewhat confused one. Significantly, Flynn holds a chalice (the holy cup used to hold the eucharist) loosely in his hands, symbolizing his insecure grasp on spirituality and his failure as a priest.

Eliza offers the visitors sherry and crackers, symbolic of the wine and wafer during the mass, but the boy refuses them. Partly, this shows his awkwardness with the traditions of the church, though it's not clear that he's abandoned the church altogether.

Brandabur suggests that it represents his unwillingness to accept secular substitutes for the sacraments from the secular bearer, Eliza, as opposed to receiving them from a priest. In effect, the boy's refusal is a last vestige of allegiance to the dead priest, regardless of Flynn's suitability for his role.

As Eliza and his aunt discuss Flynn's troubles in the priest-hood, it becomes clear that he never thoroughly embraced the spiritual nature of his calling, that he was, in fact, doomed to failure early on. His sister believes his life was "crossed," Joyce's play on words to connect the ill-fated priest to the holy crucifix. The chalice he broke, she adds, "contained nothing," but this too emphasizes Flynn's empty spirituality and the emptiness of Irish Catholicism as a whole. When Flynn was discovered alone and laughing in his confessional, it symbolizes not only his incompetency as a priest but the absurdity he sensed in his inability to function as one. Eliza's comment that there was "something gone wrong" with her brother can include the lives of many Dubliners in the book that this story introduces. In each, the reader finds characters whose souls are paralyzed and who live a contorted and frustrated life similar to that of Father Flynn's.

Study Questions

1. Interpret the significance of the first sentence.

2. When the boy dreams of Fr. Flynn, why does he "try to think of Christmas"?

3. The boy, considering the intricacies of Church doctrine, thinks: "I wondered how anybody had ever found the courage to undertake [learning] them." Explain the irony in this.

4. When viewing the body, the boy says that the candles looked like "pale thin flames." What is the symbolism of this?

5. When Flynn was paralyzed, he dropped his breviary to the floor. Can you interpret this?

6. When Eliza reminisces about her brother, she says that when he was ill, "You wouldn't hear him in the house any more than now." Why is this ironic?

7. Eliza blames the Flynn's dropping of the chalice on the [altar] boy. How does this relate to the narrator?

8. According to his sister, Flynn had dreamed of renting "one of them new-fangled carriages" and riding around for the day, but never did. Is there significance in this?

9. What is the significance of the "idle chalice" on the priest's chest?

10. After viewing the body, the boy doesn't take any refreshment, nor does he talk about the priest. What does this signify?

Answers

1. "No hope" is the theme of the Dubliners' lives. The "third" stroke indicates both the holy trinity and the three times that Christ was betrayed by Peter.

2. He thinks of Christmas because it has an overtly Christian message which he can grasp, unlike the enigmatic approach to the Church that Fr. Flynn represents.

3. Father Flynn never had courage and was actually spiritually bankrupt. The boy admires him for something he doesn't have.

4. Fr. Flynn was a degenerate priest; the flames are an allusion to hellfire.

5. Once Flynn became emotionally paralyzed, he lost his spiritual belief. Therefore, the dropping of the prayer book is a metaphor for the dropping of religion from his life.

6. The irony is this: he was no more alive before his death than he is now that he's passed away.

7. If Flynn blames his failure on the priesthood on this initial incident, he may associate the narrator with the altar boy who allegedly failed him long ago.

8. Evidently, Flynn longed for movement or development, as opposed to the literal and figurative paralysis he had to endure.

9. The chalice (the holy cup) the priest holds is idle; it does nothing and fulfills nothing, just like Fr. Flynn himself.

10. The priest is associated with spiritual as well as physical paralysis. The boy, influenced by having viewed the dead priest, is unable to respond, just as he was.

Suggested Essay Topics

1. Discuss the concept of paralysis as it relates to as many characters in the story as applicable.

2. The boy says that the word "paralysis" ... "filled me with fear, and yet I longed to be nearer to it and to look upon its deadly work." If the boy fears the concept of paralysis, how do you interpret his fascination with it?

An Encounter (pages 8–14)

New Characters:

Narrator: *boy, 8–9 years old*

Mahoney: *school friend of the narrator*

Leo Dillon: *school friend of the narrator*

Joe Dillon: *Leo's brother*

Older Man in Field: *quite likely a sexual pervert*

Summary

The narrator of this story is once again a boy around eight or nine years old (possibly the same boy as in the previous story, but not specified), who loves reading stories of the Wild West and American detective tales. Although he acts out some of these western adventures with his friends, he feels stifled by both these childish games and school. With his two friends, Leo Dillon and Mahoney, the narrator plans to skip school for one day and have a real adventure in Dublin. Each puts in a sixpence to fund the adventure and they agree to meet in the morning.

When Leo Dillon fails to show up (presumably out of

cowardice), Mahoney decides that he has forfeited his sixpence and the two split the extra money. They wander the quays and buy snacks, but the boys feel vaguely dissatisfied with their escapade. As the time for their return home draws nearer, they sit aimlessly in a field while Mahoney tries to slingshot a cat.

An older, dishevelled-looking man approaches them and begins to make conversation, asking them about school, books, and girlfriends. Though bored, they respond politely, but the narrator is made uneasy by the man, while Mahoney more or less disregards him. After the conversation turns back to school children, the older man excuses himself and retreats to the edge of the field where Mahoney spots him either urinating or masturbating (written in 1905, the story would not have been published if the act had been more carefully described). Mahoney sees him in the act, but the narrator doesn't look up, even when Mahoney speaks out in alarm. The narrator then suggests that if the older man asks their names, they give him aliases.

After he returns to the narrator, the older man speaks even more animatedly about boys and their proper punishments, and the narrator makes up his mind to leave. Calling out to his friend (using the alias), the narrator is greatly relieved when the friend responds, even though he admits to the reader that he's never liked Mahoney very much.

Analysis

The narrator of this story, possibly the same narrator as in the previous story, seeks a life of adventure and fulfillment; he looks westward, at the Wild West, realizing that "real adventures do not happen to those who remain at home." James Joyce realized this in his own life and fled Ireland, but the narrator—too young to flee—seeks adventure through the imagination and through literature, which "opened doors of escape" from his dreary schoolboy life. Still, detective stories and westerns can't sate his desire for experience, and he longs for an event that goes beyond playacting and stories.

Stanislaus Joyce writes in his memoir that his brother based this story loosely on a day in their youth when the boys skipped school and met an elderly eccentric in their wanderings. However, the story resonates far beyond a day's "miching." The suggestion of perversion, following on the previous story, darkens the theme of "The Sisters" and augments the vulnerability of this story's narrator.

The other key theme in "An Encounter" is that of deception and betrayal, which pervades virtually every element in the story and many others throughout *Dubliners*.

In order to experience "real adventure," the narrator, Leo Dillon, and Mahoney must deceive the school as well as their families. To secure the plot, the boys each pledge a sixpence; Leo Dillon, however, is too nervous to follow through with the plot and therefore forfeits his money. The narrator sees the forfeiture as somehow unfair to their friend, but Mahoney justifies it without troubling his conscience. Earlier, the narrator comments that "the confused puffy face awakened one of my consciences." Again, the specter of Leo Dillon troubles the narrator—he knows the act is unfair—but he's persuaded to overlook his own instinct by his more ruthless companion.

Most of the boys' actions in the story are predictable: a visit to the quays to look at ships signifies their desire to see the world, to escape. They buy a snack and wander, but the narrator comments twice on how tired they are; the two are worn out by the futility of their quest for adventure. It's obvious to them (and the reader) that their goals were unrealistic, and Mahoney looks ruefully at his slingshot (the closest thing to conquest that either of them can muster).

Ironically, just as they abandon the likelihood for excitement, something unusual does happen to them when approached by the elderly gentleman. At first, his conversation seems banal; Mahoney is more interested in his slingshot than wary of the man. The narrator examines him more closely, though, noticing the "great gaps in his mouth between his yellow teeth." This may remind the reader of Joyce's description of Father Flynn, or just indicate that the man has an unsavory element to him. The narrator also feels an unease with "the words in his mouth," though most of his conversation seems harmless, even meaningless.

Like his demeanor, the man's conversation is also innocuous at first, discussing happy school days. His comments on Edward

Bulwer-Lytton, a nineteenth century romantic writer, causes the narrator to scrutinize him further, since some of the author's writings were considered risque in Victorian society. Once again, however, Mahoney fails to see the signs and the narrator doesn't communicate his thoughts to him.

As the older man's conversation progresses, the intensity of his thoughts about school children increases, discussing the soft skin and hair of young girls, repeating his phrases over and over, "surrounding them with his monotonous voice." The narrator hears something alarming in the man's tone, noticing that he spoke "mysteriously as if he were telling us something secret which he did not wish others to overhear." As in the first story, the man makes a confession to the boy, almost seeking approval for his words. This, too, is a perversion, since children customarily seek approval from adults.

When Mahoney notices the man after he briefly excuses himself, it's unclear whether the latter is urinating or masturbating. In 1905, Joyce could never have indicated or specified either act, but Mahoney labels him correctly: "He's a queer old josser!"

The extent of the older man's perversions becomes most clear immediately after this act, when he speaks heatedly about the "nice warm whipping" that some boys deserve, indicating that "there was nothing in the world he would like so well" as to administer such a punishment. In listening, the narrator acts as a kind of collaborator and confessor, since his willingness to listen makes the speaker believe that he might gain understanding from him. In this, the narrator betrays not only his instincts—which tell him to flee—but the man as well, since the boy cannot and does not understand the man's depraved need.

Sensing danger, the boy rises, feigning politeness, and with embarrassment calls out to Mahoney with the alias he'd previously arranged for this situation. Although he feels silly for this "paltry stratagem," the boy is enormously relieved when Mahoney runs toward him, as if to his rescue. To the reader, though, the narrator admits his feelings of guilt, since he actually despises Mahoney for his rude and somewhat violent behavior. This represents the story's final act of betrayal as their adventure draws to a close.

Study Questions

1. Why is it surprising that Joe Dillon chooses the priesthood for a vocation?

2. What is the overall significance of the statement: "Real adventures, I reflected, do not happen to people who remain at home: they must be sought abroad"?

3. Explain how Leo Dillon represents the narrator's conscience.

4. What is the symbolism of the color green in the story?

5. Why does Mahoney brag about having "totties"?

6. Why is Mahoney unconcerned about the bizarre qualities of the man, while the narrator notices them?

7. Why does the old man "seem to plead" with the boy "that [he] should understand him"?

8. What is the significance of Mahoney chasing the cat with a slingshot, and his focus on this?

9. Why does the narrator believe that the older man is repeating his statements about girls as if "he had learned them by heart"?

10. Why does the narrator listen to the older man's warped dialog for so long before leaving?

Answers

1. Because he "played too fiercely" for the other children and is the most violent of the narrator's acquaintances.

2. This concept permeates the lives of many of the Dubliners in this collection: Eveline, Little Chandler, Jimmy Doyle.

3. His "confused puffy face" awakens the narrator's conscience at school; also, Leo chooses not to skip school because he's afraid of the consequences.

4. The boy looks for a green-eyed sailor because green eyes traditionally indicated gullibility. The old gentleman has green eyes but, ironically, it's the boy who seems gullible.

5. He wants to appear grown up. Also, Mahoney is considerably coarser than the narrator, and this off-hand remark indicates this.

6. The narrator is much more observant and deeper than Mahoney.

7. The older man realizes that he's perverted and is hoping for the boy to somehow forgive him in a quasi-religious sense.

8. Mahoney, also, is sadistic, in that he wants to torture/punish a (harmless) cat.

9. The older man seems much more interested in boys than in girls, but it's socially more acceptable for a man to praise the softness of girls' hands, etc. Therefore, he's repeating what's generally accepted.

10. He waits, partly, because he's afraid. Also, he's playing the role of the masochist to the man's sadistic stance, much like the boy and the priest in the previous story.

Suggested Essay Topics

1. The narrator says that Leo Dillon's pudgy face "awakened one of my consciences." How do you interpret the fact that he has more than one conscience?

2. In what ways are the situations of this narrator and the narrator in "The Sisters" similar? In what ways are they different?

Araby (pages 15–19)

New Characters:

Narrator: *boy, 9–12 years old*

Mangan's sister: *sister of narrator's friend with whom the boy is in love*

Narrator's Aunt and Uncle

Summary

"Araby" is a puzzling story upon first reading because very little happens in terms of plot. The narrator, looking back upon his youth (he is approximately 12 years old), recalls a time when he was deeply in love with his neighbor, Mangan's sister. Although we never learn the narrator's or the sister's name, we understand that the boy has a vivid imagination and is desperate to prove his devotion to the object of his affection.

When he hears of an exotic neighborhood fair called Araby, the boy asks the sister if she plans to attend. She tells him she must attend a religious retreat instead, and he promises to bring her something as a memento. After he promises her this, the boy is simultaneously excited and terrified at having made this vow, and what his commitment implies.

On the day of Araby, the boy is extremely anxious and cannot concentrate; he fears that his uncle will forget to give him pocket money, and his fears are justified. When the uncle returns home late in the evening, there is a danger that the boy won't be allowed to attend, but his aunt intervenes for him, and he takes a late train to the fair site.

Entering Araby, the boy feels unsettled because it is nearly empty and quite dark. Momentarily, he is so confused that he forgets his mission entirely and must re-focus upon his quest. Upon finding a gift counter with presents suitable for Mangan's sister, the boy loses interest in the knickknacks and declines help from an English shopgirl who offers to serve him. After she looks over at him a few more times (presumably to keep him from stealing), the boy, completely disappointed, walks out, having abandoned his quest and regretting the plans and promise he made.

Analysis

The narrator of "Araby" is obviously telling us a story of his youth from the perspective of adulthood; the sophistication of his language indicates this. Because the boy in the story is still young enough to depend on his aunt and uncle for money, but old enough to fall in love, it's safe to judge his age at about 12–13.

North Richmond Street, where the boy lives (and where the

Joyce family also lived) is described as being "blind," or a dead end, but this is only one of the many metaphors and similes which Joyce has worked into his story. The street—like the narrator—is blind to its own limitations, the houses gazing out with "brown imperturbable faces."

The boy's environment tells us much about him. He lives in the former home of a dead priest; in other words, where religion once was, it is no longer. The priest's belongings, especially his books, are further symbols. Scott's *The Abbot* is a romantic novel about Mary I, a Catholic queen of Scotland, while *The Devout Communicant* is, surprisingly, a Protestant book of religious devotion. Finally, *The Memoirs of Vidocq* (the boy's favorite) is a lurid, tell-all confessional by a notorious detective and arch-criminal. That these books are the boy's connection to the priest is ironic and revealing.

When the narrator widens the scene to describe his neighborhood, it is "sombre," with "feeble lanterns," "dark muddy lanes" and "odorous" stables and ashpits. The environment is gloomy and oppressive; the only source of light—or uplift—is the object of the boy's love, Mangan's sister. (Note that none of the story's key characters is given a name.)

The sister, described in detail twice in the story, is a figure of light: she stands "defined by the light" of her front door, the lamp light falling on her hair, on "the white curve of her neck," on her hand and petticoat. Like an angel or the Virgin Mary in a vision, the sister appears in an aura of light, complete with a halo. Although the boy behaves toward her as would any adolescent, she is clearly a figure of fervent, almost religious, devotion, and her effect on him is intense: "her name was like a summons to all my foolish blood."

All connections the boy makes to the sister have religious associations. In the noisy and vibrating marketplace, the narrator imagines he carries a "chalice" (the holy cup used during Catholic mass) of love, and her name calls to mind "prayers and praises." His is a "confused adoration" because he has replaced religious love (taught at home and in school) with the earthly love for the young girl. ("Adoration" is a word usually used to describe a love of Christ; clearly, he is confused!) Mangan's sister is the boy's secular angel; thoughts of her lift him out of his bleak and uninspiring existence to an other-worldly consciousness. Like an angel, she plays the "harp" of his body with her "words and gestures" (another religious metaphor).

Like all boys in his position, the narrator desires to speak to his beloved. He contemplates this by entering the room where the priest died and praying—not to God, as might be expected— but to (earthly) love itself: "I pressed the palms of my hands together until they trembled, murmuring: O love! O love! many times."

His prayers are answered in the very next line: "At last she spoke to me." When they speak, they discuss the Oriental fair, Araby, which the girl cannot attend because her school's religious retreat prevents her.

When the narrator promises to bring Mangan's sister a present, he is instantly overwhelmed by the importance of this task, since he hopes a gift will validate his love for her. The quest for the gift is also important symbolically. Araby is a festival with a vaguely Oriental-Middle Eastern ambience. As any Christian at Joyce's time would know, believers in the Middle Ages sometimes made pilgrimages to the holy land, usually bringing back a token or relic as a symbol of religious devotion. Joyce creates a parallel here between the narrator and the early Christian pilgrims—both seeking to bring back a relic to symbolize their devotion, the latter a love for Christ, the former a love for the girl. This replacement of the girl for God clarifies for the reader that the boy has abandoned Christianity in hopes of substituting it with earthly love.

As the day of the fete draws nearer and the commitment becomes more real, however, the reader notices a foreshadowing of negative events. The boy, worried that his uncle will forget, cannot wait to see the sister at the parlour window. Though this might seem trivial, he interprets it pessimistically: "The air was pitilessly raw and already my heart misgave me."

By evening, when the uncle tarries before coming home, the aunt suggests he forget about the fair, "for this night of Our Lord." Although it is Saturday, the evening of the Sabbath, the boy will certainly not substitute religious piety for this extremely important journey to Araby. His boring religious schooling, an uncle who returns home late (and drunk), and his aunt's irritating and pious visitor all highlight the lack of importance religion plays in this boy's life.

The train to Araby is deserted, and the gloomy ride foreshadows the negative aspect of the boy's mission. Once there, the narrator sees that the fair is dark and empty, with an atmosphere "like that of a church after a service." Like the dead priest, the empty church further symbolizes the emptiness of religion in the boy's life. The analogy to an empty church after mass is underscored by the counting of coins, which also takes place after a mass, except that this hall represents an ordinary commercial event, not the site of spiritual fulfillment. Therefore, the narrator has "difficulty remembering why [he] had come."

After examining the insignificant little gifts at the counter, the boy notices the English accents of two men and a woman flirting and speaking shallowly about the woman's "fib." This word, a euphemism for "lying," emphasizes the lie the boy suddenly understands he is living. He experiences an epiphany when he realizes that no gift will allow him to substitute the love of a common girl for the lost love of a God in which he no longer believes. Although he lingers, "to make [his] interest in her wares seem more real," he recognizes that his pilgrimage to Araby for love and fulfillment is "useless," that he has—in fact—been deceiving himself.

When he hears a voice calling that the "light was out," the boy is indeed in the dark about the meaning of spirituality, having failed to find it both in heaven and on earth. This recognition of his own vain and pretentious notions allows him to see himself as he really is: deluded, with little hope of saving himself. Though the epiphany is a painful and lasting one (remember that the narrator still recalls it as an adult), the boy *has* learned something about his own nature and the danger of attempting to fool oneself with false hopes. His "anguish and anger" are directed toward himself.

Study Questions

1. Knowing how important religious symbols are in "Araby," what do you make of the "wild garden" in the boy's backyard, with its "central apple-tree"?

2. The first sentence of "Araby" describes the Christian Brothers' School "set[ting] the boys free" at the day's end. How is this wording significant?

3. Although the narrator is madly in love with Mangan's sister, he reveals this to no one. What does this imply?

4. The narrator says that her name "sprang to his lips [...] in strange prayers and praises which I myself did not understand." Why isn't he able to understand or interpret them?

5. What is the significance of the fact that Mangan's sister cannot attend Araby because of a retreat?

6. After making his promise, the boy loses all interest in learning, stating that he began to "chafe against the work of school." Why does he have this reaction?

7. When the uncle returns home late and is talking to himself, the boy states: "I could interpret these signs." Can you?

8. Although the boy rides in a "special train for the bazaar," its atmosphere doesn't seem very special at all. What is the significance of this?

9. How does the salesgirl treat the narrator?

10. Why doesn't the boy buy anything at the bazaar?

Answers

1. The "wild garden" reminds us of Adam and Eve's sin in the Garden of Eden and the fact that the boy lives in a falsely pious environment. The apple tree, of course, is another symbol of the Garden of Eden.

2. The school releases them at the day's end, but the word "free" reminds us how oppressive Joyce felt a religious education could be.

3. He tells no one because in his emotions he is extremely isolated from everyone.

4. The boy has not understood for himself his attempt to substitute the young girl's love for the love of God. Therefore, he doesn't understand why her name is mingled with prayers.

5. Formal religion interferes with the narrator's pursuit of her, isolating him further. Again, it recalls the oppressiveness Joyce saw in the Catholic church.

6. He reacts this way because he considers school "child's play" and the love he feels for Mangan's sister is an intense adult love.

7. The uncle is drunk.

8. The train's empty and tawdry atmosphere shows us how isolated the boy is in his quest, and also how unlikely it is that he'll find spiritual fulfillment at the fair.

9. She treats him with disdain and looks over her shoulder at him because she suspects he might steal something. This symbolizes the British and Irish dislike and distrust for each other.

10. He buys nothing because he realizes suddenly how futile his quest is, how impossible it would be to find cosmic fulfillment in the love of an ordinary teenage girl.

Suggested Essay Topics

1. The narrator is bitterly disappointed at the end of the story. Do you believe he has "set himself up" for this disappointment, or did external events cause this to happen? Explain.

2. Bearing in mind the narrator's disappointment at the story's end, might anything positive arise from this painful revelation? Elaborate on what you feel might be the consequences.

Eveline (pages 20–23)

New Characters:

Eveline Hill: *young woman, 18–20 years old*

Eveline's Father: *an alcoholic*

Eveline's Mother: *who died and Eveline loved*

Frank: *Eveline's betrothed*

Summary

Nearly all the events in this story take place in Eveline Hill's mind as she prepares to run away from her father's home and elope with a sailor. About 18–20 years old, Eveline has supported and cared for her alcoholic father for an unspecified number of years after her mother's death. Although her existence is described in her thoughts as extremely empty, she has profound misgivings about leaving: her duty to her father, her promise to her dying mother that she would look after the home, and the fear of making such a significant change in her life all appear to immobilize her.

Finally, when Eveline reaches the port where her fiance is waiting and where their ship will depart, she's overcome by inertia and can't leave with him, although he begs her.

Analysis

The protagonist and namesake of this story is not named by the author until the last few lines of the story. This should indicate to the reader that Eveline Hill does not possess a fully-developed sense of self; she exists for other people, and this is the crux of her dilemma.

Eveline sits at the window, tired, inert, and considering the "rather happy" times of her youth, although she is still only a young woman. Many of the most important or uplifting people in her life are dead: her brother, her friends, and most significantly her mother, whose spirit and memory keep Eveline where she is. Having promised her mother that she would "keep the home together as long as she could," Eveline is torn between enduring the misery of her father's alcoholism and escaping to a life with her betrothed. Regardless of the fact that she has tried as hard as she could, Eveline still feels indebted to her mother's memory and cannot move herself out of the paralysis that keeps her tied to this pathetic existence.

Looking around the room at familiar objects, she cannot conceive "where on earth all the dust came from." This allusion is Biblical, reminding us that we begin from and return to dust after our deaths. The image of death—spiritual and physical—pervades Eveline's consciousness as the dust pervades her household.

The parlour of their house is dreary, decorated by a few meaningless objects and the print of Blessed Margaret Mary Alacoque. This seventeenth-century saint epitomized suffering for the love of Christ, inflicting wounds upon herself and taking it upon herself to endure great trials, for she believed that the holy father wished her to assume the burden of others' misery. That Eveline looks and prays to Saint Margaret Mary indicates the degree of suffering which she feels she must endure in order to be a good Christian and dutiful daughter. Joyce obviously does not condone her feelings, since Eveline suffers abuse from her father and degradation at work—both with little rewards.

The parallels and contrasts between Eveline's father and her intended warn the reader that no route Eveline takes is a guarantee to happiness. She considers her father, though abusive, to be nice "sometimes," having to reach far back in her memory to an event at which he behaved even remotely lovingly. While Frank obviously feels more tender about her, Eveline's feelings are not as clear: when he sings to her, she feels "pleasantly confused," and this feeling she confuses with affection. Indeed, love between them never crosses her mind, for the relationship evolved first as "an excitement for her to have a fellow and then she had begun to like him." Her inability to respond to Frank's kindness indicates that her sacrifices have robbed her of life-giving emotions, and that—without change—her existence will be devoid of any meaning whatsoever.

The only love Eveline can clearly recognize is that for her dead mother, but this is suffused with guilt, which Eveline assuages by sacrificing her own happiness. Although the mother is no longer alive, she ironically exhibits the greatest force in the story; her daughter is so passive that she seems on the point of (spiritual) death. Indeed, as the time draws near for her to meet Frank, she recognizes that "[h]er time was running out." Significantly, Eveline can identify the futility of her mother's life as "commonplace sacrifices closing in final craziness," but is unable to see the sacrifices that this life is currently causing for her.

When Eveline goes to the quay with Frank, the ship's portholes are illuminated as if to cast a bright light on her escape route. Nevertheless, Eveline feels numb, in "a maze of distress" over her departure from this life, and prays to God for direction. Understanding that she worships Saint Margaret Mary, the reader knows that Eveline believes all sacrifice is holy; her mother martyred herself for the family as the saint sacrificed herself for her religion. Therefore, Eveline determines that her own salvation and happiness mean nothing in light of her mother's dreadful pull upon her and her obligation toward suffering. Significantly and for the first time, Frank calls out Eveline's name in the story, since he is the only one in her life to value her for herself, but she cannot respond. Terrified at the prospect of actually deciding her own destiny, Eveline stands "passive, like a helpless animal" and does not return his affection or even his appeals. Importantly, when Frank is drawn into the crowd, Eveline looks at him with neither affection, farewell, nor even recognition, since she is—in effect—spiritually dead and completely unable to generate emotion.

Study Questions

1. What is the overwhelming characteristic of Eveline's youthful memories?

2. Explain the significance of the nameless priest whose photo hangs on the wall.

3. Frank's background is given, but he's not physically described. Why not?

4. How can we tell that Eveline is not in love?

5. What is the significance of all the "dust" in the house?

6. Why is Eveline's job at the Stores mentioned?

7. Why does Eveline find her life not "undesirable" at the moment she's about to leave it?

8. Explain the significance of the Italian organ player's music when Eveline is getting ready to leave.

9. Eveline is afraid both to go with Frank and to turn him away, especially "after all he had done for her." What does this imply?

10. At the end of the story, Eveline clings to the gate and won't follow Frank. Interpret this.

Answers

1. Everyone Eveline truly cared about is dead.

2. The father cares so little about his religion that he doesn't even bother to remember the priest's name. It is an empty symbol to him.

3. Eveline is so numb to the concept of love that Frank is hardly a reality to her. He's a means of escape, but not one of which she avails herself.

4. Eveline believes "she had begun to like" Frank, but this is the only emotion mentioned regarding him. She also doesn't think of him in physical terms.

5. According to the Bible, we are made from dust and to dust we return. The dust in the home represents death.

6. In her position at the Stores, she's treated like a servant, just as she is at home. There is no outlet for her, and no place where she feels her own significance.

7. She so fears change that her subconsciousness is attempting to convince her that her life isn't that bad. In reality, of course, it's unbearable.

8. The foreign music indicates a foreign influence and Eveline's potential escape from her life and Dublin with Frank.

9. Eveline bases her responses on obligations to other people: her father, her (dead) mother, her (dead) brother, etc. Frank has come to symbolize just another obligation, but not romantic love.

10. She is literally and figuratively paralyzed; fear of change has frozen her in her current life.

Suggested Essay Topics

1. Discuss the parallels and differences between Frank's role in Eveline's life and her father's role.

2. Joyce juxtaposes an image of the mother's final delirium and Eveline's concept of "escape." Discuss why these two images are next to one another in the story.

After the Race (pages 24–28)

New Characters:

Jimmy Doyle: *wealthy 20–21 year-old Irishman*

Charles Segouin: *owner of a French race car, his friend*

Andre Riviere: *friend of Segouin*

Villona: *Hungarian friend of Segouin*

Routh: *English friend of Segouin*

Farley: *American friend of Riviere*

Summary

The story begins with a young, wealthy Dublin college gradu-ate, Jimmy Doyle, engaging in a motor car race through Dublin with three Europeans from the continent: two Frenchmen and a Hungarian. Although Jimmy's family is known in Dublin for its wealth, among the sophisticated Europeans, he is more in awe of them than their equal, and he is thrilled at being seen in their company by his Irish friends.

After the race, Jimmy attends a dinner at the home of Seg-ouin, the owner of the race car, where he meets an English friend of Segouin and talks about Irish politics. But before the conversation can become serious, the host interrupts and the group goes for a walk in the streets. Meeting an American friend of Riviere, the men drink, carouse and return to Segouin's to play cards. Playing far into the night, Jimmy loses a considerable, but unspecified, amount of money due to his drinking and lack of gambling skill. Nevertheless, he continues to be dazzled by the international suavity of the group until daybreak comes and the debts are calculated.

Analysis

Of all the stories in his collection, Joyce felt that "After the Race" was among the least successful. The story of Jimmy Doyle and his careless wealth is a bit cliched; his international playboy friends are also somewhat predictable. At the heart of the story, though, is Dublin within an international arena, aching to be recognized on its own, even if the price of that recognition is exploitation. Jimmy's story is Dublin's (and Ireland's) in microcosm, although Jimmy is substantially wealthier than the other Dubliners in this collection. When the reader learns more about him, we discover that Jimmy's father was "an advanced [Irish] nationalist" but moderated his views early, only then gaining his wealth. Significantly, that wealth allowed Jimmy an upbringing far removed from native Irish traditions: he attended school in England, studied at Dublin University (the prestigious Protestant college in Dublin with close British ties), and then returned to Cambridge (England) to "see a little life." Thus, the life to which Jimmy is exposed is hardly an Irish one, despite his father's early nationalist leanings.

Consequently, Jimmy's acquaintances (whom he considers friends) in the race car are an international group, for he finds great pleasure in those who have "seen so much of the world." Indeed, everything about the race through Dublin, described as a "channel of poverty and inaction" along the racing route, exhilarates Jimmy. Not once does he realize that the cheering crowds of the "gratefully oppressed" represent his kinship with the city; he much more willingly identifies with Segouin and his *bon vivant* crowd. Having been seen in this company, Jimmy enjoys his condescending return to the "profane world of spectators" and basks in their admiration of his status, wealth, and worldliness.

Yet amid the worldliness, Jimmy is still a Dubliner hoping for recognition from the outside world. He and his parents feel "pride" and "eagerness" as Jimmy anticipates the sophisticated dinner at Segouin's home. Once there, he's dazzled by the company and conversation, although the description of the latter is hardly harmonious. When the British Routh's comments awaken the "buried" nationalist zeal of Jimmy's father in the younger Doyle, the reader imagines that Jimmy might identify with the Irish at last. Rather, Segouin proposes an ironic toast to "Humanity" and Jimmy's momentary flash of nationalism disappears.

As the night continues and more friends are encountered, Jimmy finds himself awash in an international sea of cosmopolitan debauchery. To his naive mind, the silly dancing and drinking songs are tantamount to "seeing life," yet the author adds the additional thought "at least." With this, Joyce indicates Jimmy's vague doubts about the value of the "merriment," but he suppresses these doubts as he did his earlier feelings of nationalism.

Feelings of doubt also infiltrate Jimmy's thoughts regarding his business venture in Segouin's motor car, a deal which translated into "days' work that lordly car in which he sat" earlier in the afternoon. He and his father both support the deal, but the author shrewdly keeps the extent of Jimmy's financial involvement ambiguous; the reader is made to feel uneasy about the investment's security. If Jimmy's ego were not so easily flattered by Segouin's attentions, Joyce intimates, Jimmy might feel more alert—and more uneasy as well.

The insecurity of the investment is re-figured at the end of the story in the group's night of card playing. Reckless and unskilled, Jimmy knows he's outmatched by the experienced Europeans but is "glad of the dark stupor that would cover up his folly." Apparently, the privilege of being swindled by sophisticated continentals more than makes up for his crushing losses. Significantly, Routh—the British guest—wins the game, symbolizing Britain's exploitation of Ireland in international affairs. The "Daybreak!" call at the story's end indicates that Jimmy must now face the unpleasant consequences of having been defrauded by his "friends," just as Ireland, Joyce suggests, must awaken to the realities of its own exploitation by foreign powers.

Study Questions

1. Interpret the significance of Jimmy's inconsistent education.

2. Why is it meaningful that Jimmy's father becomes wealthy only after he abandons his patriotic beliefs?

3. Jimmy's investment in Segouin's racecar is ambiguously described. Why has the author failed to provide further details?

4. Interpret the sentence: "Rapid motion through space elates one; so does notoriety; so does the possession of money."

5. What's ironic about Seguouin's toast to "Humanity"?

6. The story describes the circuitous route taken by the "friends" as they wander around after the race. What is the symbolism implied in their wandering?

7. While they celebrate, the author writes that Dublin harbor "lay like a darkened mirror at their feet." Is there significance in this?

8. Why does Jimmy's father, a shrewd businessman, not question Jimmy's investment more carefully?

9. Why is Jimmy unconcerned about his heavy losses at cards?

10. Why is it Villona who shouts, "Daybreak, gentlemen!"

Answers

1. The inconsistency signifies that Jimmy lacks focus; the overwhelmingly British influence of his education shows us that Jimmy's family doesn't value Irish culture.

2. This symbolizes the impoverished Irish nationalist movement.

3. The investment is obviously risky; it's likely that its details are also ambiguous to Jimmy himself.

4. With his "rapid motion," Jimmy is staving off paralysis; his fame and wealth also help him escape the fate of the other Dubliners in this book.

5. He interrupts with the toast so that Routh and Jimmy will not argue about Irish independence.

6. The group—like Jimmy himself—lacks direction.

7. One cannot see anything in a "darkened mirror." Jimmy can't discern the true nature of these "friends," who are about to swindle him in cards.

8. He's so eager for his son to be a social success that he's willing to risk a poor investment.

9. Like his father, Jimmy is so eager to enter into a cosmopolitan European world that he's willing to let himself be exploited.

10. Villona, who has no money, doesn't gamble. He's the only one to see the light of day, but now it's time for Jimmy to recognize the reality of things as well.

Suggested Essay Topics

1. Explain the parallel relationship(s) between Jimmy's heavy gambling losses, his ambiguous investment, and his father's support of that investment.

2. Interpret the line during the young men's "merriment" when the author tells us: "Jimmy took his part with a will; this was seeing life, at least!"

Two Gallants (pages 29–37)

New Characters:

Corley: *a womanizer about 25 years old*

Lenehan: *his buddy, approximately the same age*

Servant Girl ("Slavey"): *whom Corley is dating*

Summary

The story commences as Corley and Lenehan are walking through Dublin at the end of the workday, discussing Corley's exploits with women and passing time before Corley's date. Currently, he is involved with a servant girl (a "slavey") whom he uses and has sex with but has no intention of marrying. Lenehan enjoys listening but offers little judgment and no stories of his own.

As they pass a club, they hear a harpist on the street playing an Irish folksong to a crowd. Soon thereafter, Corley spots the servant girl, whom Lenehan looks over in appraisal. After the two leave on their date, Lenehan walks aimlessly through the city, eats dinner at a cheap shop, and continues to think about Corley's exploits and audaciousness with the girl.

Finally, after the time at which they'd agreed to meet, Lenehan spots Corley as he walks the girl home. He sees her enter the house, come out cautiously for a moment, and then return.

Lenehan is so overwhelmed with curiosity that he calls out to the now-solitary Corley, who at first doesn't answer him. Ultimately, Corley smiles and shows Lenehan the gold coin in his hand, which the servant has given to him.

Analysis

The late addition of this story to *Dubliners* caused delays in the book's publication, for Corley's casual attitude toward sex and the men's use of profanity (which Joyce agreed to omit) disquieted both the book's printer and publisher. Joyce remained adamant, however, and the story was included.

The ironic nature of this story is immediately obvious in the title; Corley and Lenehan are not "gallants" but coarse, manipulative figures. Both men are grotesque. Corley is obnoxious and self-centered, staring "as if he were on parade," concerned only with his ego and physical gratification. Lenehan is a talker but not a doer; his "tongue was tired for he had been talking all afternoon," but he has no similar stories of womanizing to share with Corley. Rather, he looks up to Corley with wonder throughout the story and in the end is described as Corley's "disciple." Whereas Corley is brutish and aggressive in an exaggeratedly macho sense, Lenehan suggests the same extreme in opposite form. His "air of gentility" and ineffectual bearing suggest his emasculated character. His need to follow Corley like a puppy shows us his lack of initiative or ability for independent thought.

Corley delights in the attention of his follower, drawing out for Lenehan tales of his exploits with women, all of which highlight Corley's lack of humanism (not to mention manners!) and kindness. When he discusses his current prospect, a servant girl whom he terms a "slavey," he boasts of all he has gotten from her: cigarettes, cigars, and sex. He fears temporarily that she'll become pregnant, but protects himself by concealing his true identity, which also protects his power in their relationship.

When he later discusses a former girlfriend who is presently "on the turf" (a prostitute), Lenehan suggests that Corley is responsible for the woman's downfall. Corley—predictably—abdicates responsibility. The juxtaposed images of the prostitute and the current "slavey," as well as Lenehan's description of his friend as a "base betrayer," indicate to the reader the servant girl's probable fate should she remain loyal to Corley. His power over her is further evidenced by the fact that he always "lets her wait a bit" for their rendezvous.

While still anticipating meeting the slavey, the two men stop before the club on Kildare Street (known in Joyce's time as an exclusive Anglo-Irish club) to listen to a harpist playing "Silent, O Moyle." The harp traditionally symbolizes Ireland and the ballad is a folksong about Fionnuala, the Irish daughter of the sea. It is an ironic paradox that these two powerful Irish symbols are employed to solicit spare change on a street corner in front of an Anglo-Irish club. Significant too is the author's description and personification of the harp itself: "[h]eedless that her coverings had fallen about her knees" and "weary of the eyes of stranger." The harp, like the servant girl friend of Corley, are both being prostituted for insignificant reward; both are "weary" and accustomed to careless treatment. As A. Walton Litz points out, the slavey and the harp "represent Ireland's contemporary subjugation," the former by Corley, the latter by England.

This point is furthered when Lenehan later looks over the slavey just as the passersby glance heedlessly at the harpist on the corner. The girl, dressed in "Sunday finery" of blue and white, wears the traditional colors of the Virgin Mary, but the "contented leer" of her smile and Corley's graphic assessment of her guarantee to the reader that she does not represent Catholic Ireland's purity.

After Corley departs, Lenehan's energy leaves him; his face looks older and his spirits darken. More thoughtful than Corley, Lenehan senses that the aimless wandering through Dublin streets and meaningless exchanges with women won't fulfill him. His vision of Corley seducing the slavey makes Lenehan "feel keenly his own poverty of purse and spirit," but he does not understand that following Corley is an unsuitable—ultimately unsatisfying—preoccupation for him.

Lenehan is obsessed over Corley's success with the girl, so much so that the reader believes Lenehan to be gaining vicarious pleasure (perhaps even erotic pleasure) from his imaginings. Repeatedly, he wonders "had Corley managed it successfully," experiencing "all the pangs and thrills of his friend's situation." The reader undoubtedly believes that Corley is attempting to have sex with the slavey, yet his earlier concern with her potential pregnancy leads us to believe that they have already consummated the affair.

Lenehan is so excited to see Corley at the evening's end that he can hardly contain himself—so anxious is he to know the outcome. The reader, too, wants to know the extent of Corley's success. Like the arrogant brute he is, though, Corley keeps Lenehan and the reader waiting for his answer, and at the very last minute pompously shows his "disciple" (and us) the gold coin that the slavey has stolen for him.

That the girl debases herself both in stealing and in paying for Corley's affection brings the theme back to Ireland's degradation, for the slavey represents the Irish peasant who is exploited in her attempt to eke out a satisfactory life for herself. Corley profits from her weakness and needs; Lenehan—weaker and less cunning than Corley—looks on admiringly.

Study Questions

1. What is the symbolism of the "veiled moon" in this story?

2. Is there religious significance in Lenehan's repeated statement that Corley's exploits "take the biscuit"?

3. What effect can we draw from Corley's always walking "as if he were on parade"?

4. Corley used to date a higher class of girls before he started dating a "slavey." Why has he "traded down"?

5. The slavey is wearing blue and white for their date, the traditional colors of the Virgin Mary. What is the meaning of this?

6. After Corley leaves him, Lenehan is famished. What's the significance of this?

7. Rather than just having encounters, Lenehan would like to "settle down" and "live happily." What's the importance of this?

8. Joyce goes to great lengths to represent Lenehan's wandering route through the Dublin streets. Why?

9. Beyond the fact that the slavey's stealing money for him is immoral, how does it connect to the fact that Corley's former girlfriend is now "on the turf"?

10. Lenehan imagines "Corley's voice in deep energetic gallantries." What's the irony in this?

Answers

1. The moon is traditionally a romantic image, but Corley's treatment is abusive and contemptible; it's hardly romantic.

2. Lenehan is Corley's disciple in the underhanded treatment of women. Therefore, the "biscuit" referred to represents the Holy Eucharist.

3. He is very conceited and self-absorbed.

4. Women with less money and no education are easier for Corley to manipulate and less demanding.

5. The symbolism is ironic; the slavey is not pure and probably not a virgin if she's involved with Corley.

6. Corley's exploits are titillating but not emotionally satisfying for Lenehan because they are empty. He longs for something more meaningful.

7. Although he admires Corley in a perverse way, Lenehan is a very different person, as is evidenced by Lenehan's mild criticism of Corley's "adventures."

8. Torn between Corley's way of life and his own desires, Lenehan leads a directionless and "wandering" existence."

9. Both women have been lead to commit crimes through Corley's negative influence.

10. Corley is no gallant; Lenehan only imagines that he has that potential.

TWO GALLANTS

Suggested Essay Topics

1. Joyce's description of Corley is overly male or macho, while Lenehan seems more effeminate. What is the meaning of this polarity among the two friends?

2. What attitude does Lenehan demonstrate throughout the story regarding Corley's abuses of women? Does he approve, disapprove, or is he torn? Explain his emotional stance.

The Boarding House (pages 38–43)

New Characters:

Mrs. Mooney: *owner of the boarding house*

Polly Mooney: *her 19-year-old daughter*

Bob Doran: *boarder with whom Polly has become romantically involved*

Summary

Polly Mooney, 19, lives in her mother's boarding house with her brother and the young male boarders and tourists who make up its inhabitants. Polly is pretty, and she receives flirtatious advances from many of the boarders and reciprocates, but Mrs. Mooney is frustrated by her daughter's lack of progress in finding a husband. When Polly begins to have a not-too-subtle affair with one of the boarders, Bob Doran, Mrs. Mooney stays surprisingly quiet and her daughter wonders if she's acquiescent. In fact, Mrs. Mooney waits until the relationship between them is quite advanced before she decides to talk—first to Polly and then to the young man.

When Polly turns to Bob, she confesses that she's frightened of her mother's suspicions and the consequences of their situation; Bob reassures her limply. Soon thereafter, Mrs. Mooney asks to speak with Bob in private. Although he understands the content of their meeting and feels full of dread, he complies.

Meanwhile, Polly composes herself in her room and relaxes

as she thinks of her liaisons with Bob. When her mother calls her from below, she tells Polly to come downstairs because Bob wants to speak with her. The reader never learns the exact content of either of the two conversations.

Analysis

The overt theme of prostitution in "The Two Gallants" is played out more subtly in Mrs. Mooney's boarding house. Joyce begins the story with a synopsis of Mrs. Mooney's dreadful marriage: struggling to succeed as a woman in a patriarchal society, she married Mr. Mooney and suffered through his alcoholism and ruinous business practices. Owing to Mrs. Mooney's common sense and ferocious determination, she succeeds in spite of her husband, running a boarding house and supporting her family. Thus, it's highly ironic that Mrs. Mooney—having been almost destroyed in a wretched marriage—is so eager to enter her daughter, Polly, into a union that is flawed at best and disastrous at worst.

Having looked over the many boarders with whom Polly has flirted, her mother decides that Bob Doran is the most likely marital prospect among them. Therefore, even when Polly and Bob's liaison becomes obvious in the house, Mrs. Mooney pretends not to notice. If she noticed, her obligation as a Christian and mother would force her to demand its end. If she doesn't recognize the affair, she can let it progress so far that Doran will have no option but to marry Polly when confronted. In effect, Mrs. Mooney allows Polly to sell herself to Doran in exchange for the marital obligation he will ultimately owe her. The arrangement is a manipulative and exploitive one, highlighting Mrs. Mooney's nickname among the boarders as "The Madam," since she's prostituting her daughter.

As far as Polly's culpability in the arrangement is concerned, she senses her mother's plan and cooperates tacitly with it. The song she sings ("I'm a naughty girl.../You know I am") indicates her character, and her brazen seduction of the meek Bob Doran shows the reader that Polly has inherited her mother's determination. With Bob, however, Polly behaves timidly and remorsefully; she leans on him to assume the burden of guilt and fear, and

Bob ambivalently complies. The reader should rightfully suspect Polly's meekness, since she has already identified herself as a "naughty girl," and the author describes her as resembling "a little perverse madonna." This contrasts ludicrously with the hapless and limp image she presents to Doran; the reader can easily see the disingenuousness of this guise. Further, the description of Polly at the story's end shows a fully composed woman reliving the "secret amiable memories" of her tryst with Doran. Far from penitent, Polly is portrayed as a sensual woman relaxing at the very scene of her seduction.

Polly's melodramatic reaction over the situation only heightens Doran's guilt and recognition that "reparation must be made for such a sin." The term reparation means financial repayment, but it also bears a religious meaning: the amendment(s) made to God for sinful acts. Doran thinks of this affair as a sin, and his career with a Catholic employer demands that he maintain a spotless record. He has discussed penance with a priest in terms of seeking "a loophole of reparation" but realizes that under the circumstances, the church allows him no option besides marriage.

It is significant that Doran wants to amend the sin only to secure his position and not for the sake of his soul. Likewise, Mrs. Mooney and her daughter see amendment for the "sin" in financial terms, since Bob has a "good screw" (job) and "a bit of stuff" (savings) as well. Considering the situation, Mrs. Mooney's thoughts are appropriate for a deal-maker or gambler rather than a mother concerned with her child's honor: "[s]he felt sure she would win" and deals with moral problems "as a cleaver deals with meat."

Doran's situation is hopeless, since Mrs. Mooney knows she has Catholic tradition and Irish societal values on her side. In this, Joyce condemns the parochial Irish beliefs that would force a marriage between so unlikely a pair. Polly, for her part, leaves the direct confrontation to her capable mother and manipulates Bob in more beguiling and subtle ways. Because of this tradition and its flaws, the author tells us, both Polly and Bob are doomed to unhappiness, as was Polly's mother when she married out of financial necessity years before.

Study Questions

1. What is implied in the fact that Polly couldn't continue to work in the corn-factor's office?

2. Why is Mrs. Mooney so intent on her daughter marrying practically anyone?

3. How innocent was Polly's initial approach to Bob Doran?

4. Interpret the statement: "She was an outraged mother."

5. The "short twelve" Mrs. Mooney hopes to catch after her conversation is the abbreviated noon-time mass. What's the symbolism implied in this?

6. Bob seeks religious counsel after the affair has become serious. What is the irony in this?

7. Why is Polly's brother physically described before Bob talks to Mrs. Mooney?

8. Why does Joyce continually refer to Bob's glasses becoming dim with moisture?

9. Why is the maid's name Mary?

10. Why does Polly forget "what she had been waiting for"?

Answers

1. Due to her loose morals, she probably began a liaison with the "disreputable sheriff's man."

2. Without a husband, a young woman had absolutely no value and no rights at this time in society. In Mrs. Mooney's eyes, a poor match was better than no husband at all.

3. Not very innocent at all. The clothing she wore (combined with her history as a flirt) leads us to believe it was calculated.

4. If Mrs. Mooney were outraged, she would have acted sooner and prevented the affair. She is merely using her mock outrage as leverage against Bob.

5. The spiritual content of the mass means nothing to her, which is why she hopes to catch the shortened version of

it. There's further irony in her hoping to attend mass after she's prostituted her daughter.

6. Bob doesn't care about the state of his soul so much as he does about his status at work.

7. Jack is physically threatening and Bob fears him; this is another reason why he'll acquiesce to Mrs. Mooney's demand.

8. Bob so fears the consequences of his discussion with Mrs. Mooney that he is close to tears.

9. In this house of mock prostitution, it's ironic that the maid shares the same name as the Blessed Virgin.

10. Like Bob, Polly has no free will; she isn't waiting for anything because the decision is completely in her mother's hands.

Suggested Essay Topics

1. Discuss the ironic parallels between Mrs. Mooney's marital situation (as a young woman) and her daughter's current situation.

2. Waiting for Mrs. Mooney's demand, Bob thinks to himself: "Perhaps they could be happy together...." Considering the situation, prognosticate the likelihood of a successful marriage between Polly and Bob Doran.

A Little Cloud (pages 44–54)

New Characters:

Little Chandler: *Thirty-ish clerk and amateur poet*

Ignatius Gallaher: *Little Chandler's school friend, now a journalist living in London*

Little's Wife (Annie) and Baby Son

Summary

Little Chandler, a 30-year-old legal clerk, is anticipating his evening meeting with Ignatius Gallaher, a friend from his youth. In the eight years since they've seen each other, Gallaher has moved to London to become a journalist, a situation which both impresses Little and makes him envious. He covets Gallaher's freedom to travel as well as his career as a writer. As he prepares for their meeting, Little allows himself to hope that Gallaher might be able to help him launch a literary career as a poet, perhaps even outside of Dublin.

Gallaher, however, talks mostly about himself—not about Little's literary ambitions—and Chandler finds his manner slightly vulgar, especially when discussing the immorality that abounds abroad. After several more drinks than Little's customary number, they discuss Little's wife and baby son. Although Gallaher congratulates him he swears that he would never marry and, at the end of their last drink, patronizes the entire notion of marriage.

When Chandler returns home he argues with his wife about a petty complaint and she leaves him with the baby to run an errand. Alone with his son, Chandler begins to resent and regret the different elements of his life that he believes are holding him back. As Little reads poetry and considers the likelihood of a career as a writer, his child wakes up screaming and cannot be comforted. His wife returns, furious that Little has disturbed the child. As she comforts the baby, Little's own eyes begin to fill with tears.

Analysis

Joyce drew the title for this story from I Kings 18:44. The prophet Elijah, having defeated false prophets and returned his people to the Lord, announces that the end of a long drought is at hand: "there ariseth a little cloud out of the sea, like a man's hand." The long drought of Little Chandler's life and career, however, shows no sign of ending in the story.

Throughout the story, Thomas Chandler is described in infantile terms, highlighting for the reader his ineffectual presence. He is "fragile," his voice "quiet," and he has "childish white teeth." His nickname, of course, articulates his overly-boyish qualities, as do the author's descriptions of his "infant hope" and adolescent shyness both with Gallaher and his wife.

Little dreams of being a poet, but even his dreams are unassuming: "If he could give expression to it in a book of poems perhaps men would listen," he thinks, and longs to establish a "little circle of kindred minds." (emphasis added) It's clear to the reader that Little has dim hopes of taking the literary world by storm; the author tells us that "he was not sure what idea he wished to express" with his writing, and his career as a poet (and the poems themselves) are sketchily conceived. His reading of Byron at the story's end and his longing to "write like that" are absurd given his nature; Byron's romantic and daring persona represent the complete antithesis of Little's juvenile character and bearing.

When we meet at last the highly-anticipated Ignatius Gallaher, we can see immediately that he offers no hope in amending Little's dilemma. Crude, unhealthy-looking, and boorish, Gallaher seems to have returned to "dear dirty Dublin" merely to patronize the city and brag to his awestruck friends. Gallaher is portrayed as a non-believer and drunkard. When Little questions him timidly about the immoral nature of Paris, Gallaher makes a "catholic gesture with his right arm," as if blessing the tawdriness found on the continent. Gallaher also encourages Little to "liquor up" beyond his ability, and Little—in an attempt to impress Gallaher with his manliness—drinks beyond his measure. For his part, Gallaher is described by Joyce as "emerging from clouds of smoke." His discussion of his journalist's life in Europe is full of allusions to alcohol: "it's a rum world," he tells Little. "Talk of immorality! I've heard of cases—what am I saying?—I've known them: cases of…immorality." (emphasis added)

While at first Little is overwhelmed by Gallaher's experience, he finds himself justifiably "disillusioned" with his friend and finds in his manner "something vulgar [...] which he had not observed before." He also finally sees—long after the reader has noticed it—that Gallaher is "patronizing [Little] by his friendliness just as he was patronizing Ireland by his visit." Gallaher obviously visits Dublin to crow among his friends and feel superior, but Gallaher's unbridled bitterness towards life and his drinking indicate his own dissatisfaction with himself. Although Gallaher boasts of financial opportunities with women and attempts to glamorize the sinfulness of the continent, the reader—and even Little himself—sees through this pretense.

When Gallaher denigrates the idea of marriage, Little initially defends the practice, but later has no response, as he begins to agree with Gallaher's crude that it "must get a bit stale" over time. Having had too many drinks, Little worries that he has "betrayed himself" regarding his own unhappiness, yet threatens Gallaher by telling him: "You'll put your head in the sack…like everyone else."

Returning home to his wife, Annie, Little cannot stop re-playing his meeting with his former friend and the bitterness it inspired within him. Considering the differences between their temperaments, Little questions why Gallaher has received the lucky breaks and not he. "What is it that stood in his way?" he asks himself, answering immediately and correctly: "His unfortunate timidity!" Diagnosing that the problem lies within himself, Little grows even more frustrated with his life, since he recognizes that he has trapped himself with his "pretty" wife and furniture—neither of which continue to satisfy. When he considers escaping to London, he immediately becomes bogged down by obligations and worries about bill payments for the furniture, demonstrating his inability to imagine himself in a more fulfilling life. As he attempts unsuccessfully to read and calm the child simultaneously, Little's thoughts sum up his futility: "He couldn't read. He couldn't do anything….He was a prisoner for life."

Little's baby boy is an ironic comment on his own lack of maturity. Since Little has been described throughout the story as infantile, it seems almost impossible that he can adequately fulfill a father's role. Indeed, Little has obvious trouble in this capacity, since he cannot comfort his child and fears that his own incompetency may bring about its death.

When Annie rushes in, she shrieks at Little for his paltry skills, and he responds by stammering excuses like a terrified schoolboy. He can control neither the child's sobbing, nor his wife's temper, nor his own life.

Annie soothes her son, calling him a "little man" and speaking babytalk. Ironically, her husband is a little man whose marriage to an emasculating woman has even further diminished his ability and confidence. The author hints that Annie's suffocating love for the boy may turn him into a grown-up child like his father. Finally, at the story's end, we see how Annie's love has quieted the baby, but her resentment of Little—and his overwhelming despair at his situation—brings child-like tears to his own eyes, and the two males in the narrative have ironically reversed situations.

Study Questions

1. Why is Little made to appear so juvenile in the story?
2. What is the significance of Gallaher's working for the London press?
3. Interpret the line about Little: "At times he repeated the lines [of poetry] to himself and this consoled him."
4. Thinking of his meeting with Gallaher, Little feels "superior" to others "for the first time in his life." Why and what does this represent?
5. The restaurant where Gallaher is to meet Little is a swanky spot, where the waiters "spoke French and German." What's the significance of this?
6. Why is Gallaher described as possessing an "unhealthy pallor"?
7. What does Gallaher's heavy drinking symbolize?
8. Why does Little "allow his whiskey to be very much diluted"?
9. Explain the ironic significance of the two men's very different physical descriptions.
10. What is the irony of Little's tears at the story's end?

Answers

1. This description heightens our sense of his helplessness.
2. Britain ruled Ireland by a hostile and colonial mandate. Most Irish hated England's presence, and allusions to Britain are almost always negative and corrupt symbols in Joyce.
3. Little is content to repeat meaningless motions rather than move forward, the idea of which frightens him.

4. Little feels the reflected glory of his friend. He cannot feel superior because of his own accomplishments.

5. Little assumes that things influenced by continental Europe are naturally superior; he is biased against Dublin and Irish influence.

6. Gallaher's attitude toward life is corrupt and unhealthy.

7. It symbolizes the degree of his dissolution and also his personal dissatisfaction, in spite of all his bragging.

8. Literally, he is not a heavy drinker. Symbolically, Chandler feels an aversion to the Irish influence.

9. Although they are close in age, Gallaher is described as much older-looking. This emphasizes his debauched life, whereas Little's adolescent appearance emphasizes his innocence and naivete.

10. It is an ironic allusion to Little's helplessness and exaggerated innocence.

Suggested Essay Topics

1. How is Little's situation similar to that experienced by the narrator in "Araby"?

2. Explain the significance of Little's relationship to his wife as portrayed at the end of the story. What is the meaning of the episode with her blouse, and what does it say about Little's relationship to her? To women in general?

Counterparts (pages 55–63)

New Characters:

Farrington: *Forty-ish clerk and alcoholic*

Mr. Alleyne: *Farrington's boss*

Weathers: *an English entertainer whom Farrington meets in a pub*

Several of Farrington's Drinking Companions

Summary

When the story begins, Farrington, an alcoholic administrator in a law office, is enduring the chastisement of his boss, Mr. Alleyne, for his shabby work. Diving into a pub for a drink to calm his anger, Farrington returns to the office even more muddled than before and makes several more errors in his work. When Alleyne rebukes him, this time in front of a client, Farrington responds insultingly, and the boss nearly goes wild with anger.

Later, Farrington retreats to a bar with his friends. When he retells the scene during which he insulted his boss, Farrington grows obviously more proud of his wit, and the small party of men drinks in celebration. Weathers, a British performer, joins their crowd and allows several of the men to buy him a round of drinks without offering to buy one himself. This annoys Farrington, as money is tight and the Londoner orders expensive drinks. Later, when his friends suggest he arm wrestle with Weathers, Farrington is further annoyed when the performer beats him twice.

Furious that he's out of money and liquor and has been humiliated by a stranger, Farrington returns home in a foul mood. After his young son tells him that his mother has left to attend an evening mass, Farrington unleashes all of his anger on the child and beats him violently.

Analysis

The counterparts in this story are many and transcend the borders of the story itself. Farrington, like Little Chandler, is frustrated in his job and embittered in his marriage. Like Little, Farrington is condescended to (by his boss) and feels trapped by his life circumstances. Little's wife demoralizes him, whereas in "Counterparts" Farrington's boss treats him like an ineffectual non-entity. The endings of the two stories present unsettling parallels as well. Both show us fathers whose family life is out of control, and both end with a child (the son) in tears. However, in "Counterparts," Farrington has actively brought about his son's tears by beating him, and this represents an essential difference between Farrington and Little Chandler.

Unlike Little, Farrington is loathsome, not pathetic: an irresponsible alcoholic whose work and family suffer because of his volcanic temper and self-abuse. In his dealings with the egg-headed Mr. Alleyne, Farrington's self-respect is so diminished that his anger wells up at the very sound of Alleyne's voice. Significantly, Alleyne possesses a "Piercing North of Ireland accent" (suggesting he is Protestant and a British sympathizer). This polarity between the Catholic Farrington and his Protestant boss heightens their animosity. It also sets up the most important counterpart relationship in the story: that between (Protestant) Britain and (Catholic) Ireland.

Having scurried out of his office for a furtive drink, Farrington cannot concentrate on his work, makes even more mistakes, and brings Alleyne's growing wrath down upon him once again. When Alleyne insults and yells at him, Farrington—his tongue loosened by alcohol—responds with an insulting and surprisingly witty remark. Farrington feels emboldened by this "victory" over the boss, but cannot grasp that angering Alleyne will only engender more troubles for him. This, too, resembles Ireland's situation with the British: minor, trivial victories against the Empire would not gain meaningful freedom, just more abuse.

Reliving the incident with his friends in a pub makes Farrington feel like a man—not a groveling office boy—for the first time in the narrative, but only temporarily and only when he's drinking. This signifies to us the meager sense of self that Farrington actually possesses. When the British artiste Weathers joins the drinking men, Farrington is obliged to buy a round of drinks, but does so grudgingly; he feels immediate antipathy toward Weathers. This dislike is heightened by Weathers' ordering of expensive drinks (whiskey mixed with Appolinaris water) and by the entertainer's annoying refusal to reciprocate and buy drinks for the group of Irish men. It's important to remember that Farrington had to pawn his watch to pay for his desired alcohol; Weathers now takes advantage of him financially, only irritating him further.

This exchange also has political resonance, as once again the English element, represented by Weathers, exploits the poorer nation of Ireland, represented by Farrington, who can ill-afford such treatment. Indeed, when Weathers complains that their "hospitality was too Irish," he does so unconvincingly, since he willingly partakes of this generosity.

Finally, Farrington's drunken friends call upon him to "uphold the national honor" and arm wrestle with Weathers. The contest is seen jokingly as England versus Ireland, but once again, the political symbolism is profound. Weathers—thin and pallid—beats Farrington by cheating and Farrington feels humiliated at losing to "such a stripling." Time and again, the Irish of Joyce's time were defeated and humiliated by the British, often—Joyce believed—unfairly. Like the Irish, Farrington has no recourse and must suffer the sting of defeat, even though he has gone broke buying drinks for the man.

"Full of smoldering anger and revengefulness," Farrington returns home, still wanting to drink himself into a stupor to forget the two humiliations of his day. Even his wife, Joyce tells us, bullies—her husband whether he is drunk or sober. Like little Chandler, Farrington is trapped in an untenable life. When his son tells him Ada is at church, Farrington feels even more bereft of support and angry at his circumstances. Thus it shouldn't surprise the reader that Farrington lashes out at the only character in the story more helpless than he: his little boy.

As Farrington beats the child without reason, the boy falls to his knees in a manner of supplication and prayer, but even this won't deter his father from unleashing a full day's worth of anger upon him. The frightened boy begs him to stop, attempting to assuage his fury by offering to pray for him, but this appeal is meaningless to Farrington. In the face of degradation such as that which Farrington has endured, Joyce tells us, the contrivances of Irish Catholicism are useless, as ineffectual as the boy's helpless pleas for mercy.

Study Questions

1. What tone does Alleyne take when reprimanding Farrington?

2. Why does Joyce describe Alleyne as small and egg-shaped in appearance?

3. Where does Farrington imply that he's been going all afternoon?

4. What is suggested by the fact that Farrington holds out for an extra shilling (a small amount) at the pawnbroker's?

5. What is the symbolism implied in Farrington's pawning of his watch?

6. The bartender is referred to as a "curate." What's the irony in this?

7. What is the significance of the alluring woman at the bar?

8. Farrington's wife is at the chapel when he returns. What is the irony in this?

9. Why is Farrington so often referred to as "the man" instead of by name?

10. Why can't Farrington recognize which of his children approaches him at the end of the story?

Answers

1. He condescends to Farrington as if the latter were a child, implying Farrington's absolute powerlessness.

2. Alleyne is childlike in appearance, indicating that he, too, is powerless among his own level. None of these characters has meaningful control over his destiny.

3. He implies that he's been visiting the men's room, but it isn't believed.

4. It indicates how broke Farrington actually is.

5. The watch represents time and the future. However, he doesn't care about his future since he needs a drink so badly.

6. A "curate" is also a name for a priest. Farrington needs alcohol like others need religion.

7. She represents another element that Farrington can't have (like money or power). It's a further frustration for him.

8. Although she's religious, this can't salvage her terrible life with her husband.

9. He has no individual identity; he's just another unimportant clerk.

10. His children mean nothing to him. They, too, lack individual identities for him.

Suggested Essay Topics

1. Discuss the ultimate cost of Farrington's witty retort to his boss.

2. Draw the parallels between Little Chandler's circumstances and Farrington's. Why has Joyce juxtaposed their stories?

Clay (pages 64–69)

New Characters:

Maria: *middle-aged worker in an Irish charitable laundry*

Joe Donnelly: *her nephew*

Joe's Family

Summary

Maria, the protagonist in this story, works in a charitable laundry service in Dublin. This evening, Halloween, she has the night off after serving the laundresses their holiday cakes. On her way to visit her nephew Joe and his family, Maria carefully calculates how much she can spend on treats and picks up special desserts for Joe's family.

Once she arrives at their home, Maria discovers that she's left one of the costly treats in the tram and becomes upset at her absent-mindedness, but the family comforts her. Thereafter, the children play a holiday game in which the player is blindfolded and chooses between a number of objects laid out on a table. When Maria plays, she puts her hand in a mound of clay, which unsettles the family and upsets Joe's wife. The children re-arrange the objects and Maria chooses a prayer book on her second try.

Finally, Maria is asked to sing; she chooses an Irish ballad but mistakenly sings the first verse of the song twice. No one points out her error and her nephew's eyes fill with tears at the close of the ballad.

Analysis

Maria is a female celibate, a virgin, and her name calls to mind the Virgin Mary. Like a nun or a saint, Maria is a "veritable peace-maker," and her life revolves around the Dublin by Lamplight laundry. The laundry, according to Joyce's notes, was set up by a committee of Protestant society women to keep lower class girls and women off the streets of Dublin after dark. This presumably prevented them from theft or prostitution and engaged them in a useful chore instead. Maria functions as an ironic presence among these bawdy women and brings cheer but is saintly rather than sinful, or even potentially sinful. Additionally, Maria is at peace with her Protestant employers; even though some of their traditions are strange to her, she finds them "very nice people." Her understanding, forgiveness, and kindness extend even to the drunk gentleman on the tram with whom Maria carries on a polite, restrained conversation.

Her life, however, is only half a life, Joyce indicates, because she has no intimate relationship, no sense of her physical self, and none of the longings of a mature adult. Playing the game of the barmbrack cakes on Halloween, Maria scoffs at the notion of finding the hidden ring (symbolizing love and marriage), telling Lizzie Flemming that "she didn't want any ring or man either." She finds her diminutive body "quaint" and "tidy," but Joyce never suggests Maria's womanliness; although she's clearly mature, it's unlikely that she's aware of this aspect of herself.

Buying cakes for her nephew, Maria blushes when asked (probably in jest) if she would like to buy a wedding cake, for the notion of an intimate union is completely foreign to her. This concept is furthered during the tram ride when, the author tells us, "none of the young men seemed to notice her" because her sexuality has been sublimated to the point of non-existence.

Joe's family delights in seeing Maria and receiving her gifts, but the first misstep of the evening is Maria's missing plum cake. Asking the children if they'd eaten it only annoys them, making the evening uncomfortable, and Maria feels disproportionately out of sorts by the loss, especially in light of its cost and the failure of her surprise.

The next embarrassment is the children's Halloween game of the saucers, wherein different items represent various life experiences: ring (romance, marriage); water (travel, adventure); prayer book (faith); clay (fear, death). Because of Maria's good works and faithful nature, the reader assumes she will choose the prayer book, but the children place the clay before her, to Maria's bewilderment and Mrs. Donnelly's vexation. It's clear, however, that Maria is afraid of life and is emotionally dead in her inability to form a close attachment. In this, she's similar to Eveline in the earlier story, though Maria's age and her lack of self-awareness lead us to believe that she will never even consider a change in her life. On her second try, Maria does indeed get the book, but the clay's negative implication colors the evening.

Finally, at her family's request, Maria sings "I Dreamt I Dwelt," an Irish song about love from the opera *The Bohemian Girl*. Her choice of song is ironic because Maria doesn't even dream about love (much less consider it a possibility). Furthermore, the "mistake" that her family doesn't point out is Maria's omission of the important second verse of the song which concerns being courted and loved by many suitors. Her omission symbolizes that Maria's consciousness cannot even contemplate a circumstance such as courtship, that she has obliterated this from her mind.

Maria believes her life full, but the minor upsets in the story become major losses to her because her life lacks any significant human (com)passion. She loves her nephew, but he cannot return the affection when drunk, as he often is, and his children seem alienated from her. Indeed, Maria seems alienated from the world due to her inability to see the emptiness in her life.

Study Questions

1. Joyce had originally intended to title this story "Hallowe'en." Why was the title changed to "Clay"?

2. To what degree is Maria able to develop a relationship at her job?

3. How does Maria's early relationship with her nephews compare to her present one?

4. What is the irony of Maria's description as a "peace-maker"?

5. Why is Joyce's description of Maria so grotesque?

6. Why, ironically, is Maria able to converse with the man on the train?

7. What is the significance of Joe's drinking problem?

8. How can we tell that Maria is alienated from Joe's children?

9. What is the ironic parallel between Maria visiting on Halloween and her description?

10. What is the significance of Maria's "mistake" in the song?

Answers

1. Clay is lifeless, like the meaningless relationships represented in this story.

2. She can develop no close relationships, since she works among Protestants (who do not share her religion) and lower class women (who do not share her lifestyle).

3. Although able to love them as children, Maria is too self-conscious to feel at ease with Joe now, and Alphy is far away.

4. The irony is that her two nephews no longer speak to one another, and it's impossible for Maria to make peace between them.

5. The degree to which she has lost her sexuality and sense of herself is so exaggerated that Maria is a grotesque (highly exaggerated and unrealistic) figure.

6. He's drunk, and therefore no meaningful conversation can take place.

7. Although Maria looks forward to a pleasant evening, she's obviously deluded about how enjoyable the experience actually is, since Joe needs to get drunk to enjoy it.

8. They immediately take offense when she asks them where the plumcake is.

9. Her witch-like physical appearance makes her an unwelcome visitor on Halloween, even though she's a deeply religious person.

10. It signifies her inability to conceptualize the idea of love—either romantic love or a non-romantic, but deep, connection to another person.

Suggested Essay Topics

1. How does Maria's attitude compare with Eveline's? Does either of the characters stand a chance at happiness?

2. Maria is a good person but not a balanced one. How (if at all) do her good intentions mitigate the degree to which her life is distorted?

A Painful Case (pages 70–77)

New Characters:

James Duffy: *middle-aged ascetic and scholar*

Emily Sinico: *middle-aged married woman who becomes attached to Duffy intellectually and personally*

Summary

James Duffy is a middle-aged ascetic who lives an isolated and intellectual life. He writes and reads philosophy, attends concerts, but lives far removed from human companionship.

At a concert, he meets Mrs. Emily Sinico, who attends the concert with her daughter. After she makes a comment, Duffy speaks to her. At their next chance meeting at another concert, he speaks more personally, finding out that her husband, a sea captain, often travels for long periods.

After their third accidental meeting, Duffy makes an appointment to see Mrs. Sinico, which then becomes routine. Fearing that he'll appear under-handed, he asks to be invited to Mrs. Sinico's home. Her husband encourages Duffy's visits for he thinks Duffy intends to ask for his daughter's hand in marriage.

In Emily, Duffy finds an intellectual companion with whom he can share books, discuss music and politics. Over time, the pair become more intimate until one evening, when Emily becomes so caught up in his conversation that she seizes Duffy's hand and presses it to her cheek. Duffy is repelled by her response and almost immediately breaks off his friendship with her.

Four years later, Duffy notices a news item in the paper stating that Mrs. Sinico was killed along a rail track in Dublin. Further in the article, Duffy notes comments from Emily's family that she had been acting strangely in recent years and also had begun drinking. Duffy is horrified that he had ever spoken to a person of Emily's temperament about his most intimate thoughts. Later, wandering around Dublin and considering her case, Duffy begins to second-guess himself about having broken off their relationship. Finally, he realizes that his withholding of a human connection with Emily had deprived him of companionship as well.

Analysis

In his memoir about his brother, Stanislaus Joyce states that this story was inspired by his own relationship with an older woman whom he met at a concert. The relationship ended without the bombast in this story, but James Duffy does share aspects of Stanislaus' character (the collecting of little quotations) as well of those of the author (the penchant for Nietzsche and the distrust of middle-class intellectuals).

Like Maria in "Clay," Duffy is a celibate leading an ascetic's life, and living "at a little distance from his body." Unlike her, Duffy enjoys no human intercourse. In fact, he avoids it; "visiting his relatives at Christmas and escorting them to the cemetery when they died" are his only obligations to others. Joyce is sarcastic in his description of Duffy's "spiritual" life, which has "neither companions nor friends, church nor creed," and no human communion whatsoever. One might well ask on what Duffy bases such "spirituality," but his own pompousness and condescension toward everyone else indicate that he worships only his own thoughts. That he composes short sentences about himself in the third person (i.e., "he") and in the past tense shows us even more strongly his alienation from his physical self.

Into his hermit's life wanders Emily Sinico, a lively, thoughtful woman whose husband "had dismissed his wife so sincerely from his gallery of pleasures that he did not suspect that anyone else would take an interest in her." Emily willingly, hungrily, shares Duffy's books, ideas, and intellectual life. Joyce tells us: "She listened to all." She becomes his spiritual sounding board, his "confessor," and Duffy revels in the audience she provides.

In Emily, Duffy senses someone who can reflect back to him his own glory. "He thought," Joyce tells us, "that in her eyes he would ascend to an angelical stature." Emily admires Duffy and attempts, futilely, to being him out of himself, to encourage him to enter the world. When she suggests that he publish his thoughts, he responds, "For what[?]" since he has no notion of what one gains from interaction with others. Nevertheless, their union wears away his resistance to another person, and he does begin to open emotionally to the woman. However, when Emily reaches out to him physically, Duffy is repulsed by the (presumed) intensity of her gesture and afraid of the burden of her emotional needs. Almost immediately, he breaks off their friendship and returns to his former habits.

One evening, years later, he reads in shock that Mrs. Sinico has thrown herself before a moving train. His shock, however, isn't sadness but revulsion that he allowed himself to share his "sacred" thoughts with a woman he believes so obviously unbalanced. Duffy is so self-involved that he fails to grasp the woman's sense of loss and sadness, feeling instead that she had "deceived" him from seeing her true nature. Initially, he unquestioningly agrees with the paper's statement that attached "no blame" to anyone for the incident.

Wandering through the city streets and, ironically, ordering a "hot punch," Duffy begins to feel both his loss and his culpability. Emily was his confessor; he now has none. Moreover, he never sought out her feelings, never troubled himself to understand her obviously intense needs. Only her suicide awakens him to her life and its loneliness, but—he recognizes—this realization comes too late.

Similar to Henry James' John Marcher in "The Beast in the

Jungle," Duffy recognizes he "withheld life" from the person most receptive to him and that he was now "an outcast from life's feast." At the story's end, he thinks he hears the sound of her name in the droning train engine, signifying his hope for some still-remote connection to her. However, this sound is illusory and, Joyce writes with finality, Duffy "felt that he was alone."

Study Questions

1. Mr. Duffy lives in Chapelizod, in legend associated with the great romance of Tristan and Isolde. Comment on the irony of this.

2. The reader is surprised to find a copy of Wordsworth's poetry on Duffy's shelf. Why?

3. Why is his liking for Mozart described as a dissipation?

4. Duffy collects quotations and communicates with Emily through them. What's the significance of this?

5. Why does Duffy insist that they meet at her house?

6. Why has it never occurred to Duffy to publish his ideas?

7. When he first learns of Emily's death, Duffy feels no responsibility. Why not?

8. Where does Duffy go to think about Emily, and why is this ironic?

9. Why does Joyce describe Duffy's reading of the obituary as in Secreto, like a priest?

10. Explain the significance of the very last word of the story.

Answers

1. It's ironic because Duffy is incapable of any love, let alone one as intense as that between Tristan and Isolde.

2. Wordsworth, probably one of the greatest Romantic poets of all time, expressed a desire to become more attuned to one's emotions through an understanding of one's environment and the natural world. Duffy is completely out of touch with his environment.

3. It is a dissipation in Duffy's eyes, not Joyce's. Duffy sees any enjoyment as somehow base.

4. It means he's unable to speak directly and honestly to her or express his own emotions.

5. He wants to meet there to avoid even the hint of under-handed behavior.

6. Publication implies a dialog with others, which involves a recognition of others. Duffy's has been previously inca-pable of this.

7. It's inconceivable to Duffy that he is responsible for the well-being of another human. This emphasizes how detached his life is.

8. He visits a secluded spot in Dublin called Magazine Hill. It's ironic because this is where lovers go to be alone with each other.

9. Duffy's celibate life has resembled a priest, but it's ironic because he has no spirituality.

10. Duffy is doomed to spend the rest of his life alone. It's too late for him to have "learned his lesson" and move on.

Suggested Essay Topics

1. Compare and contrast the life Maria is living (in "Clay") to that of James Duffy's.

2. After he learns of Emily's death, Duffy goes out and orders a "hot punch" (an alcoholic drink). Do you interpret this as a positive or negative sign about his ability to improve and change his life?

Ivy Day in the Committee Room (pages 78–90)

New Characters:

Old Jack: *caretaker of headquarters*

O'Connor: *young political canvasser*

Hynes: *canvasser whom others suspect of working for the rival side*

Henchy: *a canvasser*

Crofton: *a canvasser*

Lyons: *a canvasser*

Richard Tierney: *politician running for office in the Royal Exchange Ward and for whom the canvassers are working*

Father Keon: *de-frocked priest and friend of Tierney*

Charles Stewart Parnell: *(dead) Irish Revolutionary in whose honor ivy is worn on the lapel to commemorate anniversary of his death*

Summary

On the anniversary of the death of Irish political leader Charles Stewart Parnell, several political canvassers meet at headquarters to compare progress and discuss an upcoming campaign. Although they all believe they're skilled pollsters and persuasive political manueverers, they are very cynical about their candidate, Richard Tierney, and the Dublin political process in general. They also fear that they might not be paid by Tierney; furthermore, he's even failed to deliver a complimentary case of Irish stout as promised.

As the canvassers converse with the caretaker of headquarters, other canvassers come and go, several checking to see if the money—or the stout—has been delivered. A de-frocked priest and friend of Tierney's, Father Keon, also appears but leaves almost immediately.

Finally, a boy delivers the stout to headquarters, and all of the canvassers partake of the alcohol, including the boy, whom they invite to drink before he departs. Suddenly, the canvassers are considerably more generous about Tierney than they first appeared, but another member discloses that he suspects one of the canvassers (Hynes) of betraying their campaign and working with a rival politician. They further question whether Edward VII is any more suitable a political leader than was Parnell during his lifetime, and the conversation switches to Parnell.

The group of canvassers becomes nostalgic for Parnell and prevails upon Hynes to recite a poem he had written on the death of the leader. After his reading, the group applauds.

Analysis

James Joyce was highly politicized as a child by his father, a fierce supporter of Irish nationalism and Charles Stewart Parnell, the leader of its cause at the time. When a love affair scandalized Parnell's name, he was ostracized by the very Irish masses who worshipped him and—in 1891—died after having been betrayed by many of his supporters. The concept of betrayal and Ireland's parochial and unforgiving stance toward Parnell, left a profound effect on the nine year-old James. These themes are a constant in his writing and very strong in this story, which takes place on the anniversary of Parnell's passing. To commemorate Parnell, the canvassers wear a sprig of ivy on their lapels.

Contradictions in this story abound, from the small and subtle to the large scale. O'Connor is described as a "grey-haired young man" with a "husky falsetto" voice. Although all the men are canvassing votes for Richard Tierney, none likes him and all distrust him, calling him "Tricky Dicky" and referring to his "little pig's eyes" and unscrupulous character. In light of their distrust, it's ironic that the men willingly campaign for him, promising one voter that "He's a respectable man."

Ironies include their reversal of opinion about Tierney after the politician sends the promised case of free alcohol to their headquarters. Before Tierney sends the complimentary stout, all the men accuse him of miserly and unfair practices; everyone anticipates being cheated of wages. After the delivery, they decide that Tierney is "not so bad after all. He's as good as his word, at least." Clearly, a case of alcohol goes a long way in redeeming the sender's character. This, too, gives evidence of the men's weak political commitment, their mercurial judge of character.

They delight in having the stout and drink it eagerly, offering a bottle to the delivery boy as a tip. After he's gone, however, they condemn the boy for under-age drinking, stating, "That's the way it begins" in reference to alcoholism. Ironically, they notice the boy's imagined problem but fail to scrutinize themselves.

Further hypocrisy is evidenced by the men's distrust of each other in spite of the forced air of camaraderie. Henchy suspects Hynes of double-crossing them with another candidate; Crofton believes his colleagues are beneath him. Although they all wear ivy to commemorate Parnell, several men strongly support King Edward VII's visit to Ireland, a trip that Parnell himself protested in 1885. Finally, many of them are willing to overlook King Edward's moral transgressions although Parnell, a hero, was shunned from Irish politics for his. When Henchy asks, "Can't we Irish play fair?" the answer, apparently, is no.

Given their confused morals and uncertain stance on politics, fairness, and the betterment of Ireland, it's not surprising that the caretaker, Old Jack, cannot keep a successful fire burning at headquarters. The fire—or passion—for a free and just Ireland has obviously gone out among these men. Twice O'Connor is asked by another: "What are you doing in the dark?" The dark is literal and figurative because all the men lack light and direction in their political consciences.

Despite the political atmosphere at headquarters, the one vibrant and respectable politician is, ironically, Parnell himself, whom Joyce believed could actually have saved Ireland. When Parnell's name arises, O'Connor vows "we all respect him now that he's dead and gone." Ironically, of course, their respect, the sprigs of ivy, and their false sentiment are meaningless to Parnell and Ireland "now that he's dead and gone." During the discussion of Parnell, the reader notices the corks flying out of the bottles of stout, which have been placed by the fire. Although the men are merely uncorking their alcohol, the repeated "Pok! Pok! Pok!" of the flying corks sarcastically resembles the military salute a fallen leader receives at a funeral. In Parnell's case, the pathetic uncorking of Irish stout is the best he receives from this gang of questionable campaigners, just as the shabby treatment of his political supporters was the best he received in his lifetime.

When the group becomes nostalgic for Parnell's day, when there was—Jack says—"some life in it then," they call upon Hynes to recite the poem he wrote to honor Parnell's passing. The poem praises Parnell as one of "Erin's heroes" and condemns the many who turned against him and tried to "smear the exalted name" of the politician. Ironically, the poet is the same man whom Henchy suspects of current political treachery, and many in the room—Joyce suggests—did nothing to save Parnell except make empty gestures. Hynes' poem closes by providing a hope that Parnell's political spirit may once more inspire Ireland to "rise like the Phoenix" to freedom. However, considering the ignoble and hypocritical state of Irish politics, this—Joyce believes—is an unlikely dream.

Study Questions

1. The men wear their collars turned up due to the weather. What is the irony in this?

2. Jack longs for the good old times of Ireland and Irish politics, but the younger men don't. What does this imply?

3. Before he was a politician, what was Richard Tierney's profession?

4. The men are extremely focused upon the arrival of the stout. What does this imply?

5. There's irony in their distrust of Tierney in light of question #4. What is it?

6. Why is Fr. Keon described as looking like "a poor clergyman or a poor actor"?

7. What does Tierney's connection with Keon imply?

8. What does O'Connor's unwillingness to discuss Parnell's history tell us?

9. What is the significance of all the contradictory elements in the story's narrative?

10. Comment on Crofton's response to Hyne's poem at the very end of the story.

Answers

1. The irony is that the ivy (which they wear in Parnell's honor) cannot be seen.

2. Jack, because he's older, has a greater sense of Parnell's significance, but the younger generation of Dublin politicians can't recognize this.

3. He ran a used clothing store, taking advantage of people and over-charging them.

4. It implies that they're alcoholics.

5. As soon as the stout arrives, their opinion of Tierney improves remarkably.

6. Keon is probably a de-frocked priest and not good at acting like one.

7. It implies that Tierney's background is questionable, like his friend Keon's.

8. It signifies a guilty conscience and an unwillingness to be honest about the past.

9. The men say they support what's best for Ireland, but they are—in fact—corrupt. They have no political consciences.

10. Crofton says "It's a fine piece of writing," but doesn't comment on the sentiment, which is its most important characteristic.

Suggested Essay Topics

1. What is ironic in Hyne's poem about the line: "For he lies dead whom the fell gang/Of modern hypocrites laid low"?

2. Comment on the last line of Hynes' poem in which he refers to the "One grief—the memory of Parnell." How does this relate to the characters in the story and their attitude(s)?

A Mother (pages 91–100)

New Characters:

Mrs. Kearney: *overbearing mother and socially ambitious member of Dublin middle class*

Mr. Kearney: *her quiet, ineffectual husband*

Kathleen Kearney: *her teenage daughter*

Mr. Holohan: *assistant secretary to the Eire Abu Society*

Mr. Fitzpatrick: *secretary to the Eire Abu Society*

Summary

Mrs. Kearney, a socially ambitious middle-class mother, arranges for her daughter Kathleen to play the piano at a fairly prestigious Celtic revival festival in Dublin. In order for the several performances to turn out splendidly, Mrs. Kearney spends extra money on the daughter's clothes, arranges the program, and orders several tickets for acquaintances. The arranger of the festival and assistant secretary to the society, Mr. Holohan, is so hapless in this planning stage that he accepts Mrs. Kearney's help gladly.

When the first two concerts arrive, Mrs. Kearney nervously observes that the house is nearly empty and the program poorly run. When told that the third and penultimate concert will be cancelled to guarantee a fuller house on the last night, Mrs. Kearney underscores to the society's secretary, Mr. Fitzpatrick, that this should not alter her daughter's contracted fee. Fitzpatrick is non-committal.

On the evening of the final night, Mrs. Kearney once again attempts to confirm that Kathleen will receive her promised sum. When Fitzpatrick pays her four shillings short and doesn't discuss the remainder, Mrs. Kearney informs him that Kathleen will not play—even though the program has already commenced and the performers need an accompanist. Furious that her daughter's contract is of so little importance, Mrs. Kearney stubbornly insists, refusing to compromise, although such behavior attributed to the girl could ruin her future in Dublin music circles. Ultimately, Fitzpatrick, Holohan and Mrs. Kearney part, both sides furious with the other, and Kathleen having had no say in her own participation in the event.

Analysis

The surface incidents in "A Mother" portray Mrs. Kearney as an overbearing stage mother, and, to a degree, she certainly is.

However, like the previous story, "A Mother" has political meaning which transcends this plot.

Because her daughter's name is Kathleen (the traditional name and personification of Ireland), Mrs. Kearney "takes advantage of her daughter's name" and involves her in the Gaelic revival movement popular among the Dublin middle class at the time. According to the author, this consists merely of learning Gaelic phrases and sending "Irish picture postcards" back and forth to friends; neither Kathleen nor her mother is genuinely politicized. Thus, Mrs. Kearney sees the invitation from the *Eire Abu* society (a patriotic society whose Gaelic name means "Ireland to victory!") as the perfect opportunity to showcase Kathleen's talents and culture. That the society hopes to generate support for and interest in native Irish culture doesn't seem significant to Mrs. Kearney, but she throws herself into its planning to guarantee a good audience for her daughter's debut. Taking over almost completely for Mr. Holohan, Mrs. Kearney arranges the program, buys tickets in advance, and provides for Kathleen's expensive gown.

Therefore, it stuns her to see the near-empty house on the festival's first night, a clear indicator of Dublin's lack of interest in things Gaelic. Further, Mrs. Kearney feels a growing frustration with Messrs. Fitzpatrick and Holohan (the secretary and assistant secretary of the society) who laconically accept the poor planning, bad attendance, and mediocre artistic performances.

Mrs. Kearney's annoyance and the men's inertia exemplify Joyce's impression of the Irish political movement: troubled from within by divergent goals and personalities, thwarted from success by inept management. Although there's obviously a problem in the concert's planning, only Mrs. Kearney notices it; the others are too involved in the importance of their own roles to focus on the larger good. Additionally, Mrs. Kearney is not a director although she at times behaves like one; as a woman, she has no power to command attention or run the operation. Ironically, her husband, by virtue of his "abstract value as a man" could exercise some authority but is too weak and passive to do so. As a result, the concert, like the Irish political movement itself, is a chaotic mess.

When the society secretaries intimate that Kathleen Kearney's contract won't be honored in full, Mrs. Kearney justifiably feels her efforts taken for granted and her daughter exploited. The society, however, fails to grasp the injustice, simply seeing it as a result of the concert's poor attendance. This also symbolizes Ireland's dilemma, as the failure of the cause punishes members who have expended a great deal in return for its failure. "We did our best," shrugs a woman backstage, but this doesn't comfort Mrs. Kearney who feels bitter about the failure and subsequent deception.

Stubbornly, she insists upon the contract, even when the management offers a lukewarm compromise. Other performers choose sides between the two groups, and the scene backstage resembles a battlefield—or a boxing match—with each warring faction and its supporters in a separate corner.

Due to the conflict, a character remarks, "Kathleen Kearney's musical career was ended in Dublin." As an additional affront, Miss Healy, a great friend of Kathleen, agrees to substitute for her, effectively wiping Kathleen's musical future away. Mrs. Kearney takes no heed of the controversy's deleterious effects on Kathleen or her future. The society, itself dedicated to Ireland's victory, feels no unease about swindling a young member. Because of the warring from within, Gaelic culture isn't celebrated successfully and the union breaks down completely. This poorly managed and bitter experience, Joyce implies, is the future of Irish nationalism, washed up by mutual stubbornness, pettiness, and self-absorption.

Study Questions

1. What is the significance of Mr. Holohan's limp?

2. Why is Mrs. Kearney so overbearing and eager to showcase her daughter at any cost?

3. Explain the similarity between Mr. Holohan and Mr. Kearney.

4. The story's controversy centers around Kathleen Kearney's playing, but she never speaks. What the implication of this?

5. Madam Glynn, the English soprano, is described as "startled" and "meagre." What does she represent?

6. What is ironic about the *Eire Abu* society?

7. What is Joyce's implication in the poor quality of the performances artistes?

8. The name Healy was notorious in Joyce's day because it was the name of one of Charles Parnell's most famous political betrayers. What is the significance of Miss Healy's name in this story?

9. What is the significance of the two groups of Irish fighting at a festival for Irish culture?

10. What is the significance of the "threats" at the story's end?

Answers

1. It implies his ineffectiveness and incapacity; he symbolizes the Irish independence movement's impotency.

2. She hopes to make her daughter a star in society.

3. They are both ineffective and weak men; therefore, Mrs. Kearney can manipulate them.

4. It implies that she's as domineered by her mother as her father is; she's merely a pawn or instrument or her mother's ambition.

5. She represents the negative influence British culture has on Ireland's culture. Her presence adds nothing to the event.

6. Their name means "Ireland to Victory," so it's ironic that they can't even successfully put on a talent show. This is Joyce's sarcastic comment about ineffectual organizations that can't approach Irish nationalism meaningfully.

7. He implies that their talents in the performing arts are akin to their "talents" as participants in Ireland's independence.

8. When Kathleen refuses to perform out of principle, Miss Healy takes her place. Healy's playing is a betrayal of her "great friend," as was the case with Parnell.

9. It symbolizes the Irish conflict between Protestants (in the north) and Catholics (primarily in the south).

10. The threats are ambiguous and imply an unresolved conflict, just as the tension between the Irish (and with Britain) remained unresolved and bitter.

Suggested Essay Topics

1. Compare and contrast Mrs. Kearney and her situation to Mrs. Mooney ("The Boarding House") and hers.

2. Comment on the role Irish culture does (or does not) play in this story.

Grace (pages 101–118)

New Characters:

Tom Kernan: *a tea merchant and alcoholic*

Messrs. Power, Cunningham, M'Coy and Fogarty—*Tom Kernan's friends*

Mrs. Kernan—*his wife*

Father Purdon—*priest running the "businessman's retreat" at the local church*

Summary

The beginning of "Grace" finds Tom Kernan, a tea merchant, lying face-down and drunk on the lavatory floor of a Dublin pub. Helpless and incoherent, Kernan is saved from further embarrassment by his friend, Mr. Power, who delivers him home to his wife.

Two days later, Kernan receives three visitors: Messrs. Power, Cunningham, and M'Coy. Unbeknownst to Kernan, Power has informed Mrs. Kernan that the three friends intend to bring Tom to a church retreat that will help him mend his ways. The three shrewdly suggest that Kernan join and he agrees, believing it was his idea—and not theirs—that he come along.

The retreat has been specifically designed for businessmen,

and the four friends are joined by a fifth, the grocer Fogarty, and many other merchants whom they know from the community. The priest, Father Purdon, delivers a sermon on a passage from the Gospel of Luke (16:8-9), which he tells them is designed for men who live "in the world and, to a certain extent, for the world." The men listen attentively.

Analysis

Stanislaus Joyce tells us that his brother patterned Tom Kernan's progress in this story after Dante's *Divine Comedy*: the "fall down the steps of the lavatory is his descent into hell, the sickroom is purgatory, and the Church [...] is paradise at last" (228). Of course, a close reading shows us that Kernan and his friends will never reach paradise, as they really have no clear concept of the soul, penance, or the divine act of Grace itself. This sarcastic comparison to Dante is the basis for Joyce's story: he felt too many Irish Catholics believed in a lazy, spiritually devoid religion that Kernan's group represents. According to his brother, Joyce attended a sermon on Grace at the same Gardiner Street church referred to in the story, and returned "angry and disgusted" at the distorted exposition he heard. Because it so infuriated him that "such shoddy stuff should pass for spiritual guidance," Stanislaus writes, the concept behind the story was born.

Ironically, Tom Kernan is a tea-taster by profession, but it is whiskey—not tea—that has caused him to career down the stairs of a men's room in a drunken stupor. Having bitten off the end of his tongue as well, Kernan can't even express himself until the young cyclist and Kernan's friend, Power, rescue him.

As he recuperates, Kernan is visited by three of his friends: Power Cunningham, and M'Coy. Joyce intentionally assembles three visitors to construct a mock trinity, not the holy trinity in the Christian sense. In fact, the friends, representing (with their allegorical names) power and cunning, have come to make Kernan "the victim of a plot" intended, ironically, to save his soul.

As the men speak of the Church and Catholicism, the substance of their discussion tells us a great deal about their potential for Grace and salvation. For example, although he provides them with a seemingly endless supply of information about Christianity, the Pope and Church doctrine, Martin Cunningham's recollection of "facts" and "history" is completely erroneous. Joyce tells us his words "built up the vast image of the Church in the minds of his hearers"; however, virtually all of Cunningham's statements are a mixture of mistakes, lies, and general misinformation. Since his friends are equally ignorant about the Church, they accept his statements unquestioningly and even admiringly.

In the matter of faith and redemption, the men are equally inadequate, seeing Tom's salvation as "a little…spiritual matter" and comparing his participation at the retreat to "a four-handed reel." (emphasis added) The characters' use of slang to discuss spiritual issues, such as Cunningham's suggestion that they "wash the pot" together, further indicates their inability to recognize the act of contrition as a serious matter. Indeed, the retreat itself—traditionally a time of contemplation and atonement—is described by Cunningham as "just a kind of friendly talk, you know, in a common-sense way." Joyce knew from his Jesuit training that spiritual Grace and redemption were profound and mysterious, not to be approached through "common sense" with a priest who "won't be too hard" on his listeners.

As the men drink whiskey to celebrate their renewed vow of piety, Cunningham inadvertently pronounces Joyce's judgment of such Catholics: "we may as well admit we're a nice collection of scoundrels."

Inside the Gardiner Street church where the retreat is set, Joyce describes the men, joined by Mr. Fogarty, as "well dressed and orderly" with their hats carefully resting upon their knees. Although they look respectable, the assembled group is indeed a "collection of scoundrels": a money-lender, a political dealer and "mayor-maker," a pawnshop owner, and others with similarly questionable backgrounds. Among this group, the alcoholic Kernan "began to feel more at home" since he's surrounded by unrepentant sinners like himself.

Father Purdon (whose name reminds us of "pardon") preaches on the parable of the unjust steward from Luke, but his reading of this excerpt contorts its biblical meaning for the convenience and complacency of his listeners. Contrary to Purdon's statement, it's unlikely that the parable was specifically designed to guide "business men and professional men" in their worldly affairs. Because Purdon is also "a man of the world" and not a man of God, he simplifies the complex workings of Grace and faith, telling the men misleadingly that "Jesus Christ was not a hard task master." The goals of their retreat, he adds, are neither "terrifying" nor "extravagant." The irony, of course, is this: were the men actually able to discern the degenerate state of their souls (as the readers are), they would be terrified to grasp the extent of their corruption.

As the deluded men and the unscrupulous priest approach the mystery of Grace "in a businesslike way," we understand that their redemption is impossible, for spirituality is *not* business. The laziness and misguidedness of this self-deceiving group will forever prevent them from adequately examining the state of their consciences. In effect, Joyce hopes that his story acts as a parable to shake the reader out of a similar complacency.

Study Questions

1. Considering the title, why is Kernan's fall ironic?

2. Comment on the meaning of grace in the following quote: "[Kernan] had never been seen in the city without a silk hat of some decency and a pair of gaiters. By grace of these two articles of clothing, he said, a man could always pass muster."

3. Why is it ironic that Mrs. Kernan celebrated her anniversary by waltzing with her husband "to Mr. Power's accompaniment"?

4. What is significant about Mr. M'Coy's comment that the Jesuits are "the boyos [that] have influence"?

5. When Kernan recollects hearing Fr. Tom Burke preach, he recalls that he sat in "back near the door." What does this symbolize?

6. Mr. Kernan refers to the lighting of a sacramental candle as "the magic-lantern business." What does his attitude tell us about his belief?

7. What is the symbolism of the "distant speck of red light" in the Gardiner Street church?

8. Why does Purdon appear to be "struggling up" to the pulpit for his sermon?

9. Why does Joyce tell us the priest covers his face with hands when he prays towards the light?

10. What is ironic about the concept of a priest acing as a "spiritual accountant" for these men?

Answers

1. In the sense that grace connotes "graceful," Kernan stumbles because he's drunk. He lacks grace of the spiritual or physical kind.

2. For Kernan, his friends, and even Fr. Purdon, grace is seen as something superficial. Kernan believes that if he looks presentable on the surface, he can "pass muster."

3. Even though Kernan has not been a good husband, Power is determined to keep the couple together; he acts as their bond.

4. All of the men consider spirituality a "business" matter, so it's ironic and humorous that M'Coy would talk about priests as having "influence" with God!

5. Kernan was unable to actually approach the idea of salvation; his sitting near the door implies his figurative and literal distance from God.

6. Jesus said that he was the light of the world, but Kernan does not want to partake of the lighting ritual. This indicates his lack of commitment to the matter of salvation.

7. The red light in a church indicates the presence of the Blessed Sacrament. In this church, with these listeners, the sacrament is very "distant."

8. He struggles because he is a corrupt priest who doesn't belong in the pulpit.

THE DEAD

9. His covering his face indicates his unworthiness to preach and lead a congregation. He's unable to face the light of the Sacrament.

10. These men are so materialistic and unspiritual that they can only think in terms of money and accounts. It's ironic and pathetic that they even think in terms of their souls as account ledgers.

Suggested Essay Topics

1. Compare and contrast the figure of the priest in "The Sisters" and in "Grace."

2. Discuss the use of irony as it applies to all the men in this story. (Kernan's friends, the priest, and Kernan himself)

The Dead (pages 119–152)

New Characters:

Gabriel Conroy: *teacher and amateur writer*

Gretta Conroy: *his wife*

Julia and Kate Morkan: *Gabriel's aging aunts, piano and voice teachers in Dublin*

Mary Jane: *Gabriel's cousin, an unmarried piano teacher who lives with the aunts*

Molly Ivors: *Gabriel's colleague and passionate Irish nationalist various party guests of the Morkans*

Michael Furey: *(dead) adolescent love of Gretta Conroy*

Summary

At the opening of "The Dead," Gabriel Conroy, a teacher and amateur writer, arrives with his wife, Gretta, at a Christmas party given by his aunts, Julia and Kate Morkan. Though the mood of the annual affair is festive, Gabriel is unnerved by a series of misunderstandings and uncomfortable events during the evening. In chatting with the maid, Gabriel makes a slight *faux pas*

THE DEAD

to which she answers bitterly. Later, dancing with a colleague from school, Gabriel argues with her about Irish nationalism and her response offends him. Finally, in making a toast to the evening's hostesses, Gabriel agonizes over what to say—and second-guesses himself for the rest of the evening about whether his choice was appropriate.

When the time comes to leave for the hotel at which they're staying, Gabriel finds his wife listening to a tenor singing an Irish ballad in the music room, and his thoughts about Gretta turn amorous. On the way home in the cab, Gabriel anticipates a night of passion but waits until the moment they're alone to approach her. Gretta, on the other hand, seems distracted and tired, which annoys him. When he finally does approach her, Gretta stuns her husband by telling him about a country boy, Michael Furey, whom she loved years ago and who died at 17.

After Gretta cries herself to sleep, Gabriel considers this new knowledge about his wife, pondering what it says about his life and his identity. As snow begins to fall, Gabriel imagines he sees Michael Furey outside the window, and then considers his own mortality and the irrevocability of death that awaits everyone.

Analysis

According to a letter Joyce sent to his brother in 1905, he had crafted the *Dubliners* stories into groups representing childhood, adolescence, maturity, and Dublin's private life (Ellmann, *James Joyce*, 208). "The Dead" could easily be placed in either of the last two categories. However, this story was added later, in 1907, after Joyce had seen—and become disillusioned with—other cities in Europe. Therefore, his original intention to paint a gritty and unflattering portrait of his native city in *Dubliners* was somewhat mellowed by the time he approached this narrative. As a result, while the story contains similar themes of paralysis and spiritual moribundity that the other stories share, Joyce's treatment of the characters and issues is slightly less caustic and more merciful than in the previous pieces.

Gabriel Conroy, the story's protagonist, bears the name of the archangel Gabriel who brought news of the births of both John the Baptist and the Messiah to the world. However, each message that Gabriel conveys and encounters in this story has a disappointing and sometimes unsettling result for him. His small talk with Lily the maid brings up the subject of young suitors and annoys her thoroughly. While recovering from her bitter retort, Gabriel begins to agonize over the toast he'll give later to his aging aunts, Julia and Kate Morkan. Though the party and hostesses are full of warmth and good cheer, Gabriel is distracted by the inadequacy and inappropriateness of the message, since the partygoers' "grade of culture differed from his." Intellectually, Gabriel is a snob who consciously detaches himself from his acquaintances and friends. Yet his self-confidence is as low as his anxiety is high, and he worries that his toast "would fail with them just as he had failed with the girl in the pantry."

Although named after a celestial messenger, Gabriel cannot express himself clearly and honestly; part of his frustration comes from an inability (seen so often in *Dubliners*) to understand and express his emotions, to reach out to another in genuine communion.

While dancing with Molly Ivors, Gabriel is interrogated about the extent of his patriotic feelings, since Molly is an ardent nationalist. Progressively, Molly's questions become more accusatory, demanding to know why he doesn't embrace his native country and native language (Gaelic). Gabriel can neither defuse the conversation nor provide a suitable response, exploding suddenly: "I'm sick of my own country, sick of it!" As a final launch against his beliefs (or lack thereof), Molly whispers in Gabriel's ear "West Briton!" implying that he is an Anglicized Irishman, and effectively destroying his mood for the rest of the evening.

Hoping for succor from his wife, Gabriel tells Gretta about Molly's plan to visit western Ireland, but—rather than support Gabriel's decision—Gretta jumps for joy at the thought of re-visiting her childhood home and is summarily denied. For Gabriel, the tension between the western and eastern sections of the country represents his discomfort with his Irishness and his own personality. Investigating the western part of Ireland or Irish traditions, Joyce suggests, would force Gabriel to confront a different side of himself, a more emotional side. Allusions to the west, which abound here and towards the end of the story, are potentially threatening to him. For example, Gabriel shows offense when Molly reminds him that his wife is from Connacht (in the west) and still resents his dead mother for once deeming Gretta too countrified.

Joyce implies that the rural, western section of the country (his own wife's birthplace) was emotionally freer, more authentic, less repressed and distorted by its proximity to England and the continent whose influences bastardized Irish culture. Gabriel, however, feels uncomfortable with the openness of feeling this implies, just as he's uncomfortable with Molly's blunt questioning and his wife's rural background. Indeed, Gabriel feels much more at home with English and European influences rather than those of Ireland. For example, he considers quoting Browning (an English poet) in his toast, prefers vacations in France, Belgium, or Germany, and even introduces his family to the habit of wearing galoshes, telling Aunt Julia "everyone wears them on the continent."

The toast Gabriel strains over, however, does genuinely praise the Irish tradition of hospitality which Joyce felt was unmatched throughout Europe. The carefully described dinner scene—with its table-load of delicacies—emphasizes this tradition that the Morkans represent—traditions that, unfortunately, may die out with their generation. Ironically, Gabriel praises these traditional Irish qualities and recognizes them even while regarding his aunts as "two ignorant old women." A further irony is Gabriel's criticism of the "new generation" of "hyper-educated," "thought-tormented" intellectuals, since Gabriel considers himself an intellectual, and overly-educated for his milieu. This comment in the toast could also reflect Joyce's feelings about himself and fellow intellectuals, whose detached view of the world might have sometimes compromised their emotional vibrancy.

The dinner conversation about the late-great opera singers further illustrates Joyce's theme that the magnificence of the past is fading, if not gone completely. It also reflects Dublin's glorious past but now uncertain future, because many of the "good singers" no longer choose to perform there, preferring instead the cities on the continent. Finally, the story of the dead opera heroes, the monks who sleep in their coffins, and Patrick Morkan's deceased horse all highlight the topic of death, returning us to the title and theme of the story. The greatness they admire (be it in opera singers or Ireland's cultural past) lies in the past with the dead. The living, the author suggests, are doomed to remember and long for it, but they cannot rekindle it, as many of these scenes reflect.

The most stunning recollection of the past is Gretta's admission that she was passionately loved by a teenager, Michael Furey, when she was a girl in western Ireland. Listening to the simple Irish ballad "The Lass of Aughrim" reminds Gretta of his profound love, and Michael suddenly becomes more vivid an experience for her than those in her present life. Ironically, Michael (whose last name reminds us of "fury" or "passion") brings about a more impassioned reaction in her than her own husband does, even though Gabriel had deeply passionate fantasies about Gretta as they rode to the hotel.

Although this discovery makes him jealous and irritable at first, Gabriel dwells on thoughts of Michael Furey long into the night, after Gretta has fallen asleep. For the first time in the story, Gabriel abandons his own self-consciousness and narcissism to sympathize with Gretta and empathize with Michael, as "[g]enerous tears fill his eyes." Confronting Gretta's private emotions for the first time, Gabriel is able to understand the quality of her earlier love; though he doesn't possess the capacity for such passion, he recognizes its importance. In a delusionary vision, Gabriel imagines that he sees the figure of Michael Furey standing under a tree outside his window. This signifies the degree to which Gabriel is able to share his wife's emotion (and loss), as his soul "approache[s]" that region where dwell the vast hosts of the dead."

Gabriel is devastated by Gretta's disclosure, but the emotional epiphany it inspires allows him to reach a more profound understanding of his world than he has yet evidenced in the story. His empathy for Gretta, his elderly aunts, and even Michael Furey suggests that he may have broken through his previous emotional paralysis.

The snow falling "all over Ireland" is a double signifier at the end of Gabriel's reverie. Snow, obviously, is frozen and connotes things "frozen in place"; this indicates that Gabriel's awakening and the state of his marriage may not develop a great deal more than they have already. Likewise, the people in his world long for earlier times and repeat the same customs and traditions, regardless of their intrinsic value; there is little forward movement or evolution. On the other hand, the snow is "general," falling, Joyce tells us, "upon all the living and the dead" and suggesting a kind of commonality or kinship between past and present. As Richard Ellmann suggests, the snow implies "mutuality" among men, "a sense of their connection with each other, a sense that none has his being alone" ("Backgrounds of 'The Dead'"). If Gabriel senses this even unconsciously, he can at least begin to recognize his emotional isolation, and this—Joyce suggests—is the key to remediating the spiritual and emotional paralysis that plagues his Dubliners.

Study Questions

1. What function does the "fringe of snow" on Gabriel's coat play at the story's beginning?

2. When Mary Jane plays the piano, "the only persons who seemed to follow the music was Mary Jane herself." What does this signify?

3. Why is it ironic that Molly Ivors and Gabriel dance to an Irish tune during their argument?

4. During the argument, Gabriel "wanted to say that literature was above politics," but he doesn't. What is Joyce's opinion about that belief?

5. What is signified by the fact that Gabriel—standing in the party—longs to "walk out alone, first along the river and then through the park"?

6. What is ironic about Aunt Julia's choice of song for the guests: "Arrayed for the Bridal"?

7. Why does Gabriel's mood suddenly lift right before dinner?

8. Gabriel's toast to "the past, of youth, [...] of absent faces" is ironic in light of Gretta's later revelation, why?

9. Gabriel gazes at his wife who stands in "a dark part of the hall." What does this tell us about his relationship to her?

10. What is the "impalpable and vindictive being" that over-takes Gabriel when he learns that Michael Furey may have died for love of Gretta?

Answers

1. It foreshadows the importance of the snow imagery at the end of the story.

2. It signifies the sterile and emotionless quality that complex art has for its viewers and listeners. Joyce wants us to compare this to the moving performances of the Irish folk ballads further on in the story.

3. It's ironic because they are arguing about the value of Irish culture while dancing to an Irish song.

4. Joyce believed that politics and literature were intimately and indelibly linked.

5. It speaks of Gabriel's emotional isolation.

6. Wearing dark clothes, with her sunken grey face and distracted air, Aunt Julia is the antithesis of a bridal image and more closely represents death in her appearance and manner.

7. He discovers that Molly Ivors has left and blames her for his foul mood.

8. Because Gretta will soon be distracted by thoughts of her past youth and the absent, haunting face of Michael Furey.

9. Gabriel is "in the dark" about his wife's emotional life, although later he longs to "be the master of her strange mood."

10. It is the force of the dead.

Suggested Essay Topics

1. How does Gabriel's inadequacy and discomfort with his surroundings compare and contrast with that of James Duffy's ("A Painful Case")?

2. Gabriel longs to write, think, and even paint expressively, reminding us of Little Chandler ("A Little Cloud"). How are the two similar? Different?

3. Discuss the many ironies presented in Gabriel's toast to his two aunts and cousin.

4. Compare the circumstances of Gabriel's life and aspirations to those of Little Chandler in "A Little Cloud."

SECTION THREE

Bibliography

Quotations from *Dubliners* are taken from the following edition:

Joyce, James. *Dubliners*. (1916) Eds. Robert Scholes and A. Walton Litz. New York: The Viking Press, 1982.

Other Sources:

Brandabur, Edward. "The Sisters." *Dubliners*. eds. Robert Scholes and A. Walton Litz. New York: The Viking Press, 1982. 333–343.

Ellmann, Richard. "The Backgrounds of 'The Dead.'" Dubliners. eds. Robert Scholes and A. Walton Litz. New York: The Viking Press, 1982. 388–403.

_____. *James Joyce*. New York: The Viking Press, 1975.

_____. ed. *Selected Letters of James Joyce*. New York: The Viking Press, 1975.

Joyce, Stanislaus. *My Brother's Keeper: James Joyce's Early Years*. New York: The Viking Press, 1958.

Litz, A. Walton. "Two Gallants." *Dubliners*. eds. Robert Scholes and A. Walton Litz. New York: The Viking Press, 1982. 368–387.

Stone, Harry. "'Araby' and the Writings of James Joyce." *Dubliners*. eds. Robert Scholes and A. Walton Litz. New York: The Viking Press, 1982. 344–367.